a reginald p. gawker mystery

DEADLY RAMPAGE

a reginald p. gawker mystery

DEADLY RAMPAGE

donald e. clem

T<small>ATE</small> P<small>UBLISHING</small> *& Enterprises*

TATE PUBLISHING
& Enterprises

Tate Publishing is committed to excellence in the publishing industry. Our staff of highly trained professionals, including editors, graphic designers, and marketing personnel, work together to produce the very finest books available. The company reflects the philosophy established by the founders, based on Psalms 68:11,

"THE LORD GAVE THE WORD AND GREAT WAS THE COMPANY OF THOSE WHO PUBLISHED IT."

If you would like further information, please contact us:

1.888.361.9473 | www.tatepublishing.com

TATE PUBLISHING & Enterprises, LLC | 127 E. Trade Center Terrace

Mustang, Oklahoma 73064 USA

Published in the United States of America

ISBN: 978-1-6024725-3-2

07.09.06

Dedication

This book is dedicated to all the police officers, mental health workers, and others for their work with those people who have mental and behavioral problems that endanger all who come in contact with them.

Acknowledgement

If not for the support of my wife, family, and friends, and the able help of my proofreader, Johanna Rose Ferguson, and my editor, both of whom labored mightily in correcting all the goofs, fluffs, and general errors, this book would not have been possible. Thanks to my college professors and the psychologists and psychiatrists, whom I have known over the years, for giving me insight into the minds of those who engage in dangerous and destructive behavior.

A fine line separates sanity and insanity.

Prologue

The quiet Ozark Mountain town of Mountain View, Arkansas, is the idyllic home to permanent residents and several thousand visitors during the summer. Crime is practically non-existent except for some occasional drunks, car thefts, and drug violations. The atmosphere is one of innocence and idyllic living 365 days a year, so when the unexpected happened one evening in April, the town's innocence was shattered and not even the most imaginative of the residents could have predicted the events that would soon unfold in their peaceful community.

Terrible things don't happen there like the ones that caused mayhem to snowball in the quiet town. They only occur in the large cities far removed from the Ozarks. Yet, as much as the residents wished the trouble would go away, it created the beginning of a more sinister plot that would endanger Reginald, Sherry, and the good people of the county. A diabolical criminal came prowling in their midst, and he meant to kill selected residents for reasons they didn't know. Fear filled the town instead of tranquility.

Chapter

ONE

Tuesday, April 9, 1996, time, 9:30 a.m., and a nice day to be alive to enjoy the fine spring morning. The temperature neared seventy degrees. Officer Durward McGee, assigned to the patrol division of the Little Rock, Arkansas, Police Department, sat in his patrol car with both front windows fully open so he could enjoy the morning breeze. He idly watched the shabbily dressed man drop a package into the corner mailbox at Markham and Rodney Parham. Officer McGee thought it odd that the man had mailed it there instead of at the post office, but then again, he knew that people did odd things and that probably wasn't a bit odder than most of what he had observed in his twelve years of patrolling the streets in his town. He had a degree in abnormal psychology and enjoyed watching humans behave in odd ways as long as the abnormal behavior wasn't violent. He tried to give it no more thought as the man disappeared around the corner.

Still, there was something in the bum's manner that made Officer McGee suspicious. He started the engine of his patrol car and turned north on Rodney Parham. He saw the man walking slowly along the side walk looking around quickly, but he didn't seem to be looking at anything in particular. Just to satisfy his curiosity, McGee decided to stop and question the man to make sure everything was okay. More than once a hunch had paid off for him in similar situations. More than likely everything was all right, but a nagging familiarity about the man wouldn't go away and it pointed to a suspicion he couldn't place.

The patrol car rolled to a stop next to the curb and Officer McGee hollered at the man walking along next to the open right side window. "Mister, come over here a minute. I want to talk to you." The man looked at him and continued walking past the police car. He began muttering and gesturing, swiveling his head wildly from side to side, ignoring the officer. McGee picked up his radio mike.

"Car 234 to West Division radio."

"Radio, car 234."

"Send a back up to Rodney Parham just north of the Markham intersection. I'm going to question a suspicious acting subject. Hold on. He's walking back to me, approaching on my side of the car."

When the back up arrived three minutes later, the man had vanished and Officer McGee was dead with a gunshot wound over his left ear. The headlines in the *Arkansas Democrat-Gazette* the next day read, "Little Rock Policeman Killed." The news story related that the only suspect was the unknown subject that Officer McGee had mentioned to West Division Dispatch and that his identity remained unknown. The article contained a request to the public asking for anyone who might have seen the unknown subject to contact the police department.

•

Sgt. of Detectives Reginald P. Gawker, a detective in the Mountain View Police Department, read the news account as did the other residents of the town. Those who read the paper that morning breathed a sigh of relief that those kinds of things didn't happen in their town. Small towns had their problems but none like the big cities, or so the readers thought, and Reginald was one of them.

At 3:30 p.m. Thursday, April 11, 1996, the telephone rang in the dispatch room of the Mountain View Police Department. The radio operator, Mazy Sink, rang the intercom line in Reginald's office. Reginald picked up and answered. Mazy said, "I've got a call for you. Subject reported a burglary."

"Okay. Where is it?" Pause. "The Happy Camper Motor Home Park lot 23?" Pause. "Got it."

Ten minutes later, Reginald arrived at the Happy Camper Motor Home Park on Sylamore Avenue. He found lot 23 vacant. He walked over to the next lot and knocked on the door of a big motor home. A man came to the door and Reginald identified himself. The man said that 23 had been vacant for two days and he had no idea who might have called. As he started to leave, a man came running up out of breath.

"Are you Sgt. Gawker? I've seen you around, so I took a chance it was you."

"I am, and who are you?" Reginald asked.

"I'm L. Jason Callman. Call me L. J. for short. I need to talk to you. I'm scared."

"What about and why are you scared?"

"My motor home is over on number 34. Come over and I'll tell you." They entered the detective's car and drove over to Callman's space. Reginald couldn't help but notice that Callman acted nervous and looked scared. They stopped at the motorized castle and went inside. Callman asked if Reginald wanted something to drink and he said no.

"Are you the one that called me to come over to investigate a burglary and told the operator lot 23?"

Callman looked bewildered. "I didn't call you. I was ready to call when I saw you over there at that other motor home. I had it parked on 23 when I left town, but parked it here on 34 when I returned two weeks ago. Who said I called?" L. Jason Callman stopped talking, obviously totally confused. His eyes darted nervously around the living room and then he spoke. "I didn't call and there isn't a burglary. I mean … uh … You won't tell anyone about what I want to tell you, will you? I mean, I'm scared." The man's whole body began shaking; his eyes showing extreme fear.

"Whatever you tell me will only be in a report and the only ones that will know are other policemen who might be part of any investigation should it be necessary for others to assist," Reginald said, offering assurance to Mr. Callman.

"What do you mean by, 'should it be necessary to assist?' Are you tryin' to jerk me around? Man, this is serious." L. Jason Callman looked ready to explode.

"I won't know until you tell me. Fair enough? Now tell me what's wrong. And why are you scared?" Reginald said, trying to stop Callman's fuse from burning any shorter.

After calming down Callman said, "I got a letter yesterday. I don't know who sent it or why." He handed it to Reginald who instructed him to lay it on the small table in front of him. Reginald took a pair of latex gloves from his pocket and pulled them on before picking it up by the corners. Callman watched him intently as he began to read. *Hey Lavon, you are being watched. You know what you did and you will pay when I am ready for you to pay. Just like Candid Camera, it will happen when you least expect it. I am your Executioner.*

Reginald sat for a moment looking at the letter and at Callman, then went to the car, and returned with some plastic evidence bags. He inserted the page into a bag, sealed it, recorded the time and the date, and marked the bag with his initials. "Where is the envelope the letter was in?"

"Oh, right here. I nearly forgot it." He handed the envelope to Reginald who placed it in a separate bag.

"When did you get it?"

"It was in the mail when I picked it up at the post office awhile ago. I rented a box when I came here near the end of winter."

"Who would know you're here?" Reginald asked.

"I suppose most anyone who knows me and knows where I used to live would know that I've been coming here for several years each summer.

"I noticed the coach has Indiana plates. Is that where you used to live?"

"Near Stanford, Indiana, a small town on Indiana 45 west of Bloomington. Actually, it's just a wide spot in the road with a grocery store, lawnmower shop, and a garage, and not much else unless you count the chickens, hogs, and an occasional speeder. Speeders are the only excitement they have there as far as I know. But I haven't been there for almost two years."

Reginald examined the envelope and saw that it had a Little Rock post mark of April 9, two days before. He asked Callman, "Do you know anyone in Little Rock?"

"Not a soul unless it is someone I used to work with or met at a convention. I was a salesman for Jaxco Chemical Company located in Cleveland, Ohio, and traveled all over the central United States. I never put any roots down until I retired in 1991 and moved to Stanford. I lived there maybe three years and then moved on. A cousin lived there, but he's dead now. He died in the fall of 1994 and I had no reason to stay after he was gone. He gave me his little patch of land and his shack on Breeden Road, so I guess that's where I live. I keep a post office box in Bloomington and claim Indiana as my residence for tax and plate purposes since I own that land and have the post office address. Seldom get any mail there though. I go through and check the box every five or six months or so. Sometimes there's something worthwhile but most of the time only ads." Callman looked blankly at Reginald, having run out of something to say.

Reginald started to speak, and Callman interrupted. "I'm sorry for rattling on like that. I'm really scared and it's just … just … " He became quiet and resumed the blank look.

"What was your cousin's name?"

"Why is that important? It doesn't have anything to do with this, does it? I don't see how it does," Callman barked, his temper flaring again. The shaking resumed.

"Just covering all bases and collecting information for now; trying to learn as much as possible that might help identify the sender of the letter," Reginald said calmly. "Now, what's your cousin's name?"

"Buford H. Callman. He was my father's brother's son; my uncle's only child. We were somewhat close as kids, and when I retired, I went to see him. He had no immediate family left and I was his only relative. Neither of us ever married." A faraway sad look settled in Callman's eyes.

As Reginald made his notes, he glanced at Callman, all the while trying to digest what he had heard before asking more questions. "Since you have a box in Bloomington, why do you have one here in Mountain View? Do you have your mail forwarded to you?"

"I have a few friends here and there that I keep in touch with and notify from time to time where I'll be if I am going to stay in one spot awhile," Callman said hurriedly, showing his nervousness.

Reginald nodded his head. "Now back to the letter. You have no idea who might have sent it?"

"I have no idea who would do that and it really has me scared. Whoever it is used my first name and must know I hate it. I didn't think I had any enemies ... guess I do." The shaking continued as fear etched itself into Callman's face.

Reginald remained silent for a few minutes, pretending to be deep in thought as he studied the letter, but he was actually watching Callman who continued to show increasing nervousness. "I'll check all this out and get back to you. I know things like this can be very upsetting."

Callman bristled and said, "How would you know that things like this are upsetting? You have never been threatened."

"Mr. Callman, I have been threatened in ways that you will never know. I understand how it is when these types of things occur. As I said, I'll let you know what I find out."

Reginald left the coach and went to his car. He glanced over his shoulder as he drove away and saw Callman watching him intently from the doorway of the motor coach. Reginald was mystified by the burglary call for an empty lot—a burglary call that wasn't a burglary—and a call Callman claimed he didn't make. He drove back to his office with the strange events running through his mind. Very strange; all very strange indeed was all he could think of at the moment. He made a mental note to check with the dispatcher about the burglary call that wasn't.

Chapter

TWO

Reginald laid the evidence bags on his desk and called the department secretary for a case number. He turned on his computer and opened a report cover sheet, filled in the vitals, and wrote a brief description of the case. Opening a supplemental page, he began to type the narrative of the interview with Callman when the light blinked on his private line. "Hello, Sgt. Gawker."

"My, aren't we formal today?" Sherry said, her voice filling the room.

Reginald laughed and said, "I never take chances on the phone with unidentified callers. It might be the boss."

"And am I not the boss?" Sherry asked, trying to keep from laughing.

Reginald realizing the phone speaker was on quickly turned it off. "Well, yes you are, come to think of it," he said, chuckling into the phone. He listened for a moment. "What time?" Pause. "I'll be there." He hung up with a smile on his face. Fried chicken and all the trimmings were only part of the reason for the smile. He had an invite to see Sherry, which explained the rest of the reason for the glow spreading across his face. He turned back to the case reports.

Finishing the reports, he checked out for the day and went home. He showered and went out to his *new baby,* as he called his pickup, a 1949 Ford flat head V-8. The twin pipes were the only modification he had made to the truck. Since Darcy's 1953 Mercury had left town, he put glass pack mufflers on the truck because he missed the sound on the Mercury's flat head V-8 so much. The older men in the town liked the sound of his Ford, too; it brought back memories of days gone by when they harassed the local cops with the window rattling noise of the V-8's mufflers sounding off. Reginald didn't do that now, but he did gently rack the pipes at times to enjoy the smiles it brought to the faces of those who liked to reminisce about times past.

The truck arrived at Sherry's house and when he stepped from the cab onto the driveway, one of Sherry's neighbors, Madeline Crompton, who lived across the street hollered at him. "Reginald, you got a minute?" she asked, hurrying to meet him.

"Sure. Mrs. Crompton. Good to see you."

Madeline was so excited she didn't bother to say hello. "Can I tell you something? It's the strangest thing. You won't think it is spying or gossip, will you?"

"I won't know until you tell me. But I bet it is important or you wouldn't have hailed me out here. Go ahead."

Mrs. Crompton glanced around as if spies were hiding in the bushes. She got up close to Reginald and said in a whisper, "The last two nights I have seen a dark blue Ford, a late model—don't know the year—parked down the street with a man in it. I turned out the lights so he couldn't see me and watched him through a crack in the blinds. The first time he got out of the car he walked up and looked at Sherry's house, and then got back in the car and left. She was gone at the time. The second time she came home while he was parked there. He left as soon as her garage door closed. Probably nothing, but I thought you ought to know. She's such a sweet young woman, and I don't want anything to happen to her and I know you don't either."

Reginald smiled at Mrs. Crompton and thanked her for the information. He wrote his home phone number on the back of a card and told her to call him at the police department in the daytime and at his house at night, no matter the time, if she saw the car again or any car of suspicious nature. She said that she would and he entered Sherry's house.

Sherry kissed him and said, "What did Mrs. Crompton want? Did she have some juicy gossip I don't know about and should know?"

"No, she wanted to know when I was going to ask her for a date. She's jealous." He ducked the swing of Sherry's right hand, and they both laughed.

"Seriously, what did she want? It looked conspiratorial."

"The other evening when you came home, did you see a blue late model Ford with a man in it parked up the street?"

"Not that I remember. Why?"

"Mrs. Crompton said that twice she has seen a blue Ford parked up the street from your house. It was there once when you were gone and the second time when you came home. The first time he got out of the car and walked up to the house and looked around and then left. The second time he left after you closed the garage door. At the moment, we don't know who he is or what he's doing, so be careful. Not all the nuts in the world are in bags at the grocery store."

A far away look filled Sherry's eyes for an instant. She looked at Reginald and said, "That's odd. I got the strangest feeling the other day I was being followed. I'm sure now that there was a man across the street watching me through the bank window. I left for a few minutes and when I came back, he was gone. It's probably just my imagination, but I will be careful."

"If you're being watched then I best try to find out who it is and why. I'll pass the word to all shifts for everyone to be watching for that car." Silent for a few seconds, he said, "This is as odd as what happened today." After telling her about the event, she was as puzzled as Reginald that the complaint wasn't a burglary and that the call wasn't made by Callman.

After the dishes were in the washer, they went to the Yellow Bee Drive-In for banana splits. They went inside and were finishing their dessert when a patrol unit pulled into the drive and skidded to a halt. Officer Nance Porter burst through the door and said excitedly, "Sarg, there's been a shooting downtown. Some guy on the square got shot in the back. The ambulance is on the way, and we need you there."

"Nance, can you take Sherry home?"

Nance started to answer when Sherry interrupted. "No way will I go home, I'm going with you. Remember, I'm an unpaid county deputy. Let's go."

Before Reginald could protest, she went out the door and climbed into the truck. They headed for the square with Nance giving a *Code 3* escort.

By the time Reginald, Sherry, and Nance arrived at the scene a large crowd had gathered. The ambulance with its lights on and the siren going full volume sped away from the scene. George Dugan had strung yellow crime scene tape and county deputies began arriving to help keep the crowd back. Reginald radioed dispatch and requested that George Mansard, of Mansard Construction, be called to see if he could bring his portable lights and generator to the scene since it was getting dark. He sent word back that in half an hour he would have five high powered lights there for them. Twenty-five minutes later with the County Sheriff, Thomas Dawson, providing the escort, the lights arrived at the town square. Fifteen minutes later the south side of the courthouse looked like a bright day at high noon.

Reginald divided the nine officers on the Scene Into groups of three. He and Sherry co-coordinated the search effort, telling two of the teams how they wanted evidence collected and preserved. Sheriff Thomas Dawson, an expert in crime scene photography, stood ready with his camera to make shots of evidence where it lay when and if any was found. The other team began to look for and interview witnesses among the several hundred by-standers.

Three witnesses were located. One saw the victim fall. Another heard a small pop, and the third saw a man walk away, but he couldn't give any description other than 5'10" and 180 to 200 pounds. The suspect wore dark clothing and had dark hair. There weren't any additional witnesses or a better description available. The officers informed Reginald who recognized that the assailant's description fit a large number of people in the crowd, which made finding the right one impossible. No one knew the victim's identity.

The officers searching for physical evidence didn't fare any better. Reginald had told them to pick up anything that looked out of place or that didn't look like the normal debris that would be found in the area. They found three items that were photographed and triangulated to pinpoint the exact place they rested; then they bagged and tagged the items with the chain of custody noted. The items were a broken flat toothpick, a blue button, and a small silk handkerchief. Not much to work with, but it was better than nothing considering that the area was covered with leaves, twigs, rocks, and the normal trash deposited by the crowd that day. Reginald made a note in his crime scene book that no shell casing was found. Likely that meant the shot came from a revolver, not an automatic, since an automatic would eject the spent shell. The pop one witness heard indicated a small caliber or a firearm with a cheap silencer or both.

Close to midnight, all but two officers cleared the scene. The lights were left in place and left on. The two remaining officers received instructions from Reginald to guard the area until it could be searched again in the daylight. Maybe something more could be found, but it wasn't likely, and they still didn't know the identity of the man who was shot. He had been flown by Med Flight from Stone County Medical to Little Rock Baptist. He was in critical condition but expected to live.

At 3:00 a.m., a torrential rain began, and driven by the wind, it destroyed in a few minutes any evidence that might have been missed. Reginald, called back to the square by the two officers, watched rivers of water rush across the crime scene. Feeling defeated, he sent the officers home and turned off the floodlights. Alone in his truck, he didn't know what to make of the evil that had arrived in his quiet town. *Maybe the three pieces of evidence will tell us something,* he said silently. He would take them to the State Police Crime lab early that morning, along with the letter and envelope, in the hope that the lab could reveal the unknown.

Just as he was leaving the square, a patrol car arrived. Bob Fairway, who had gone on duty at 10:00 p.m., ran up to Reginald and said,

"We just got a call from Baptist Medical. The victim is going to be okay. He lost a lot of blood and thankfully, he had no serious damage to any organs from the gunshot. He came to and told the nurses his name. The vic is L. Jason Callman." Reginald sat stunned when he heard the man's name. What did all this mean? He was at a total loss to explain anything that he knew, which was mostly nothing when he ran what he did know through his mind.

Chapter

THREE

ix o'clock came too early. Reginald didn't get into bed the second time until well past three and didn't go to sleep until nearly 4:00 a.m. He dreaded the long drive to Little Rock, but he knew that it had to be done. The phone rang before he could leave the house. He listened for a few seconds. "I'll be careful and I love you too," he stammered. His face colored as usual when he answered. Reginald could mentally see her delight through the phone when she heard the words. Before hanging up, he told her the new information gained since he last saw her.

Arriving at the police department, he asked Mazy Sink, the dispatcher, about the burglary call of the previous day. "There were two calls and I assumed that they were both made by the same caller. But now that I think back on it, it could have been two different voices." She stared back at Reginald. "Now on second thought, I don't think so." Giving Reginald an exasperated look, Mazy continued. "Frankly Sarg, I don't know whether it was one or two." Reginald nodded, deciding silence was the best course of action.

The phone log showed that the second call came two minutes after the first one. The first caller said lot 23 and reported a burglary, and the second caller, sounding very excited, plainly indicated lot 34, but he didn't mention any burglary. Neither Mazy nor Reginald knew what to make of the second call, except that maybe the caller was worried no one would show up. She had told the caller that an officer was on the way, believing the second caller was the same as the first one.

"Don't let it worry you, Mazy," Reginald said. "We'll figure it out, and if we don't, it may not make any difference anyway. Don't feel like you're by yourself. I'm confused by it too and right now I think confusion is my middle name."

"Okay Sarg, since you say so, I won't worry about it," Mazy said, sounding relieved.

After collecting the evidence, Reginald headed for Little Rock. It was over a two hour drive to State Police Headquarters and it gave him plenty of time to think. He needed to visit Little Rock P.D. to see Major L.P. Wellman, the Chief of Detectives. It being Friday, he hoped Wellman would be in his office.

•

Entering state headquarters, the first person he saw was Darcy Broadway, a state police undercover officer. At the same instant, they both exclaimed, "What are you doing here?"

A voice behind them said, "If you two are going to sing duets, don't give up your day jobs."

They turned around and stared open mouthed at William Broadway, Chief of Police in Newport, Arkansas. Now a trio, the three exclaimed simultaneously, "What are you doing here?"

They began laughing when another voice said, "You would have to pay me to hear you three perform. From what I heard for free, it would have to be high dollar to get me there." The head of the State Police, Col. B. Truman Cordly, appeared in the doorway of his office. The four of them guffawed loudly, exchanging pleasantries. Reginald thought, not for the first time, that Truman was a peculiar name for a Republican and chuckled to himself.

William Broadway asked Reginald about Sherry Westermann, his daughter, and with the fun and games over, each went onto the other business that they had to conduct. Reginald went to the document section to have the letter and envelope examined. Lt. Boyce Waldron took the items and told Reginald it would be at least one week before the results were known. Since L. Jason Callman was in the hospital's intensive care unit, a finger print card couldn't be made any time soon. Reginald said he would try to get a set of prints as soon as the doctor would permit it.

Next, he went to the lab and spoke to the technicians who would do a DNA analysis of the toothpick and the handkerchief, and a search for possible trace elements on the items. They would also try to determine the type of button, manufacturer, and the type clothing it came from, which would be a real long shot and nothing more.

Reginald went to L.R.P.D. headquarters to find L.P. Wellman. Wellman, a native of Stone County, had graduated from high school six years ahead of Reginald. Their parents had known each other well, but Reginald and L.P. knew each other only slightly due to the age difference. He spoke to Wellman's secretary who called on the intercom. She hung up and said, "Go on in, he's sounds excited to see you."

Wellman jumped up from his desk and stuck out his hand. "Reginald P. Gawker, haven't seen you since your father's funeral some years ago. How have you been? I understand you're now a detective. Congratulations."

They exchanged some other pleasantries and then Wellman asked Reginald what he was doing in town. Reginald related information on the case he was working and asked, "How is the investigation of the shooting of Officer McGee coming along?"

Wellman said, "Unfortunately, it's nowhere at the moment since we have very little to go on. We found two witnesses that think they saw the bum McGee wanted to question, but they never saw him after he walked up Rodney Parham; nor did they see Officer McGee stop to talk to him.

"Do you think he's the one who killed Officer McGee?"

"I do, but that's only because we don't have anyone else to look for at this time."

"What did the witnesses say?"

"They said that while in a place of business on the corner of

Markham and Rodney Parham, they saw Officer McGee parked in the corner of the service station lot. His sergeant had sent him to that intersection to ticket drivers going north on Rodney Parham who persist in running the stop light. There have been several accidents there because of that and the traffic units have been cracking down on red light violations there, and all over the city. It's a real problem. Now, where was I? Oh, the bum. Apparently, the suspect attracted McGee's attention for some reason that he never relayed to the dispatcher."

"And no one saw what happened after McGee stopped the man?"

"Not that we can find. The two witnesses said they saw the man near the mail box but thought nothing of it. One said the guy dropped a package of some sort into it and the other said she didn't see anything. Something made McGee suspicious and we don't know what it was.

"What do the postal people say?"

"They don't know either and by the time we knew about it, the mail had been picked up, taken in for sorting, and had then gone out to who knows where. We struck out all around. And the regular on that box pickup route had left for the day." Reginald could see frustration written all over Wellman's face.

Wellman spoke into Reginald's tomb of silence, breaking in on his thoughts. "What makes you interested in this case?"

"I don't know right now. I just have a nagging pain in the back of my head that I can't explain and I guess I am looking for something to make it go away. I tried aspirin but that didn't help, so it must not be my brain that's the problem. Though some in Mountain View might disagree," he said ending with a chuckle.

"Don't let it get to you. Every town has those types," Wellman said laughing.

"L.P., I do want to keep up on this case. That nagging and the hunch will keep bothering me. You've been there. You know what I mean," Reginald said.

"I sure do. If it weren't for hunches and pains in the back of the head, some crimes would never be solved. I'll keep you posted on anything that turns up."

"Thanks. I appreciate it." They shook hands and said good bye. Reginald left more perplexed than ever about what he knew, which he realized made a mountain of what he didn't know.

·

Arriving back in Mountain View, he found a note on his desk to call Sherry at the bank. He dialed and she told him she needed to see him immediately. He hurried out the door and headed for the bank.

At the bank, he accompanied Sherry to the back room to talk in private with Merton Houston, the bank president, and Sherry's great-uncle. Sherry said, "Something strange happened this morning in bookkeeping. A stop payment came in for a check on an account we don't have. The twenty five dollar stop fee was attached to the request. The name on the account is J. Daniel Bushman and the account number is 0042 7989. We don't have any accounts with double zero forty two and the other banks in town don't have those numbers in that exact order either."

"Did the request indicate who the check was written to?" Reginald asked.

"It was written to Sprinkle's Hardware Store, wherever that is. I have no idea."

"Why was a stop payment put on the check?"

"The request said that the check was never cashed."

What's the date it was written?"

"February 1, 1996. Sure took a long time to get here. It wasn't deposited until a few days ago. That is really odd."

"Was there a return address on the envelope?" Reginald asked.

Sherry produced the envelope. "Yes, in Searcy, Arkansas, but there isn't any such street or address as 5605 North Winding Way in that town; nor do any of the banks there have that account number. I called the post office and the banks there to check on both. I have a bad feeling that this is connected with that shooting on the square, but I don't know what it could be. It may be my imagination and a total coincidence."

Reginald looked at her and said, "I don't think it's your imagination or a coincidence. I agree with you that there is a connection, but we don't have enough information yet to know what makes it connected."

Sherry, her great-uncle, and Reginald looked at each other in silence for a long time. Merton Houston, who had been listening intently, broke the silence. "Sherry, I don't know what is taking place, but what I do know is that Reginald is going to need some help, so you take whatever time you need to help solve whatever it is that has payed us a most unwelcome visit; and if anyone complains, then they can talk to me. I own the bank and can assign the employees as I please to where I want them to work. If the board complains, I'll handle it. We received that stop payment for some reason, so it looks like we're involved in some way with whatever is going on, whether we like it or not."

"Thanks, Uncle Merton. I appreciate it and I know Reginald does too." Reginald nodded his head in agreement. She continued, "I have checked and found seven other towns named Mountain View; they're scattered from Hawaii to Georgia with California, Colorado, Wyoming, Oklahoma, Arkansas, and Missouri, in between. None of those towns have a street or road named North Winding Way that I could find, so we know that address is fictitious, at least for those cities. Unless someone is really being cute, we have to assume that the account number is legitimate. Too bad whoever it is didn't put the bank routing number on the form." She paused to reflect a moment on what she said. "But now that I think about it, a hunch makes me think that we got the contents of an envelope that was meant for someone else."

Reginald looked at her a long minute and said, "If that's true, then someone else received whatever was going to be sent here. Now I wonder what that is and where it did go."

"There's only one way to find out," Sherry said. "I'll begin a search for banks in each of the towns and their phone numbers. I'll start with the closest one and work my way out. We also have to consider that the bank that received whatever was meant for here isn't in any town named Mountain View."

"Well, it's worth a try. It probably won't turn up anything, but strange things do happen by chance. And it looks like chance is all you have at this point. I'm not even sure it's fifty-fifty. The horses at Oak Lawn in Hot Springs would be a better bet than this one," Merton said.

Sherry began to work the computer. Merton returned to his office and Reginald went back to the police department. There was a note on his desk to call both the state police lab and Lt. Waldron. Urgent in red block letters jumped out at him. He began to dial the number hoping for some good news for a change.

Chapter

FOUR

The phone rang in the police lab. Reginald identified himself and asked the tech what he had found.

"Really, not much, but it may be interesting to you."

"I hope it's good."

"I don't know how good it is, but here is what we found. But first, what we didn't find. We didn't find out anything of help on the button. The button was just ordinary and could have come from anywhere. From the marks, it looks like it might have been lying awhile where it was found, since it was scuffed like it had been stepped on several times. The handkerchief did tell us something though." He paused for effect. "We found powder residue and lead on the material in a pattern that suggests a revolver."

"How do you know that?" Reginald inquired. He perked up at what he hoped would be good news.

"A revolver has a slight gap for clearance between the cylinder and the breech as you know. A small amount of the hot gas, a powder flash, will escape from that small space when the round is fired. If something is laid over the cylinder, it will collect the residue from each side of the opening, but not the top where the strap shields it. The cylinder is probably out of alignment with the barrel because there were minute amounts of lead in the cloth indicating it is out of alignment to the left. The lead on the left side of the cloth indicates it had a draped position over the gun cylinder and frame. In other words, it shaved lead and the cloth caught it. We found a similar silk handkerchief and tested it with a .38, a .357, and a .22. Each piece left a pattern similar to the one we found on the silk you brought in, but not the shaving effect. We can't tell the caliber from the test, but my guess it is a .22 due to the small amount of residue present. The two larger calibers left more residue than the .22."

Reginald went silent for a few seconds as he ran through his mind what he had just heard. "That's real interesting because one of the witnesses standing close by said he heard a small pop like a silencer or a small caliber weapon. I'm going to call the hospital and see if they recovered the bullet. I left instructions for them on what to do if they found it. Hang onto that handkerchief and button. This sure helps. Thanks a lot."

Before Reginald could hang up, the tech said, "We sent some pieces of the handkerchief over to the serology section before the powder tests. It might show some DNA, but it'll be a long shot."

"Any DNA results on the toothpick yet?"

"That will take several days. We'll let you know."

"Thanks again. I need to talk Lt. Waldron. Can you transfer me?"

"Sure thing, hold on."

The line clicked, and Lt. Waldron said, "Hello, Reginald?"

"It's me. What do you have? Good news I hope?"

"That depends, but I will say it isn't bad. There are some latent prints on the letter that can be identified and some smudges that are useless. I sent a tech over to the hospital on the off chance that Callman could be printed. The doctor reluctantly agreed and we got a full ten set. All of the readable latents on the letter belong to Callman. Based on the latent print pattern, it indicates that he opened the envelope and pulled the letter out with his thumb and index and middle fingers of his right hand. The rest of the patterns show that he held it with both hands, though the prints on the back aren't all that clear."

"You didn't find any others?"

"Only the unreadable smudges on the letter. Callman's prints were on top of the smudges so I would guess that whoever made the smudges typed the letter."

"Did you find anything on the envelope?"

"Callman's prints were on the envelope as you would expect. A couple of prints are clear but nothing to compare them to unless you print everyone that works at the post office. Probably the letter sorters and whoever else touched the envelope while it was in the mail."

"That's it?"

"Not entirely. I checked the type and believe it was typed on a manual typewriter, but I don't know what kind. Some of the letters are filled with dried ink and trash so they don't impression clearly. If you find the machine, a match will be easy to make. I have sent the envelope and letter to the chem testing section to see if they can identify what made the smudges. I'll give you a call when we find anything."

"Thanks. I'll be waiting to hear from you."

"Glad to help." The phone clicked and left Reginald with more puzzle pieces to add to the box filling with mystery parts he couldn't explain. *Somewhere is an answer to all of this, but I don't know where to find it,* he agonized. He knew that somehow they would have to find a way to shake up the puzzle box and find the way that the pieces were supposed to fit together.

He dialed Baptist Hospital and told the person that answered who he was and what he wanted. He was transferred to a lady that didn't want to give out any information due to the privacy concerns. He explained the reason for the call, that it was a criminal investigation, but she still wouldn't tell him anything. He then asked if Doctor Benjamin Shelbourne was in the hospital. She paged him and after a few minutes, Shelbourne came on the line.

"Doctor Shelbourne. How may I help you?"

"This is Sgt. Reginald P. Gawker of the Mountain View, Arkansas, Police Department. I talked to you late Wednesday night about L. Jason Callman, the gunshot victim."

"Oh yes, I remember now. You want to know about a bullet recovery. Is that right?"

"You're right. What can you tell me?"

"We recovered the bullet and did as you asked to preserve it. It's locked in my office safe in a box for which I have the only key."

"Do you know what caliber it is?"

The doctor, silent for a few seconds, said, "I don't know much about guns and bullets, but I think it is a .22 short. I have seen pictures of bullets that look like it. And it is ... on the end ... uh ... what do you call it ... uh ... "

"Pointed or slightly rounded, perhaps jacketed," Reginald volunteered.

"Yeah, that's it. It has a ... I guess the copper piece on the front you mentioned would be the jacket. The guy got lucky when he was hit by that thing. It didn't hit any bone or vitals. We found it in the right side front abdominal area in layman's terms. Yes, very fortunate man."

"Is the bullet damaged?"

"No. It's in good shape I would say, though I don't know much about bullets and guns, as I said."

"Thank you, Doctor. Keep the bullet, and I'll pick it up in a few days. I have to come to Little Rock again, and I'll get it then. Is your office in the medical building?"

"Yes, it is. In the Doctor's Building to the north of the main building, on the sixth floor, A-632, Suite B, Room 1."

"I'll call before I drive down. Thank you again."

"It's my pleasure, Sgt. Gawker ... anytime." The line clicked and Reginald P. Gawker had to admit he liked the sound of that title in front of his name.

Reginald sat at his desk and smiled. He now had some facts that corresponded to the witness statements. But what did he know for sure? It was now time to put some puzzle pieces in place. He made careful entries in his notebook in a column for the known facts and another column of entries for the facts that had no answers. Facts and no answers:

(1) Someone had mailed a letter to Callman, careful not to leave any prints. Maybe Callman mailed it to himself but for what reason?

(2) If he mailed it to himself, what is he doing that he wants hidden? Maybe it's a cover for something else.

(3) If he didn't mail the letter to himself, then who did and why?

(4) Callman was shot with a .22. Why was he shot?

(5) Does the broken toothpick mean anything?

(6) The silk handkerchief was used by the shooter to conceal the gun. Who is the shooter and why Callman? What is the connection?

(7) Where does the stop payment request fit, if it does?

Known:

(1) A man was shot on the square. The pop heard was the .22 and the cloth covered the gun.

(2) The bullet has a copper jacket.

Reginald looked at the list and tried to make sense of what he knew. *A few of these things I know for sure and that is all I know. The rest is a mystery.* A weary Reginald leaned back in his chair and when the phone rang on his private line, it startled him. He fumbled for the receiver and dropped it. He picked it up and groggily said, "Hello."

"Are you going to spend the night there? Do you know what time it is?"

Foggy minded, Reginald said, "Huh?"

"Do you know the time?"

"No. Uh ... who wants to know the time? Oh, it's you Sherry. I guess I fell asleep. What time is it anyway?"

"It's seven o'clock. I got worried when no one answered at your house so I called the P.D. They thought you had gone for the day since your office door was locked. So I tried your private line there before I sent out the Saint Bernard with the keg under his chin. Can you come over?"

"I'll be there in ten minutes." He left for Sherry's house, but he didn't see the blue 1989 Ford following a half a block back.

When Reginald parked in the driveway the car went on past, turned around and parked a block away. The driver didn't know it, but Mrs. Crompton saw him go by and park up the street, headed out toward Main. She debated with herself and decided against calling Sherry. After thinking about it, she decided to get a license number when the car went past. "The neighbors can call me nosy if they want, but there's a lot of suspicious activity going on and I might be onto something," she said to the empty room. She found a paper and pencil and settled in by the window.

Reginald went into the house and ate supper with Sherry. She told him that she had located the banks in the small towns but hadn't had a chance to make any phone calls. Reginald related the facts he knew and what he didn't know. After some more talk and being tired, he told her he needed to go home and get some rest. He kissed Sherry good-bye and went out the door. He looked toward the blue Ford, but he didn't really notice it. He backed out of driveway and the blue Ford followed. Mrs. Crompton watched. Her pencil and paper were held at ready to record the license number when the car went by. But there was a problem. The car didn't have a license plate.

Mrs. Crompton started to call Sherry then noticed the light was out in the living room and decided not to disturb her. She knew she should call Reginald, but she decided it was too late. She didn't want him or Sherry to think she was nosy and spying on them. She would figure something out so they wouldn't think she was a prying busybody. Turning out the light, Madeline crawled into bed. Right before she fell asleep, she decided she would call him in the next day or two.

FIVE

The private line ringing broke the stillness in Reginald's office. He picked up the phone and said, "Sgt. Gawker, how may I help you?"

"As fast as you can come to the bank and as soon as possible. I can't talk right now. Get here quickly." Sherry hung up before Reginald could collect his thoughts enough to say anything in reply. Reginald hurried out of his office and as he passed the door to dispatch, he told Mazy Sink where he was going.

In her usual funny way she said, "10–4, Sarg. No Code 3 allowed for doughnuts. Tell Sherry hi for me."

The worried look on Sherry's face told Reginald that things weren't good. She and Merton motioned for him to go into the conference room. They followed him in and closed the door. The Mountain View Police Chief, Darrell Cumberland, and Stone County Sheriff, Thomas Dawson, were in the room. They had worried looks on their faces too. Reginald said, "What's this about? The crazy case we're working on, I suppose."

Darrell Cumberland spoke first. "Reginald, this case began with craziness and now has turned worse. And the searches we did for another Mountain View were wild goose chases. Then we received a call from the First Bank Savings and Loan, Mountain Home, Arkansas. The bank received an envelope with a return address of 5605 North Winding Way, Searcy, Arkansas. It had a note in it to Sherry. I told a bank employee about the stop payment we received for a check. She said that the checking account is in their bank, but she doesn't know the physical identity of the customer. All she knows is the account holder's name."

"What's Sherry got to do with this anyway?" Reginald asked.

"Unfortunately, we don't know," Merton Houston said. "Darrell was in here when they called and he talked to the bank president, Sam Hazelton. They have sent the letter down here by a state policeman. He'll be here in two hours. According to Darrell, any prints are probably worthless since several at that bank handled it."

"Reginald, when it gets here you can take it to Little Rock and have it examined," Darrell said, "but in the mean time, we need to be real careful. Tell him Thomas, what happened this morning north of here up by Allison."

"A man by the name of Robert H. Blandford is having a big house built on the mountain off Highway 9 northeast of Allison. It's just barely in Stone County. Some of the property is in Izzard County, but the house lot is in Stone. The view is spectacular to use a word from an ad in the *Ozark Times* describing the area. It sits up on the side of the mountain overlooking Sylamore Creek. Great view from there, especially in the fall with all the leaves changing color."

Reginald asked, "Who is this Blandford?"

"He's the president of an industrial equipment manufacturing company, Amalgamated Incorporated, in Dayton, Ohio. He has been coming to these parts for several years, ever since a relative left him the property. He has been staying at the Robin's Nest Motel. I've been here for two weeks looking after the house construction."

"What happened this morning?" Sherry asked.

"He went out to the building site early, around 5:30 or 6 o'clock. He walked to the house and when he came out at 7:00 a.m. all the tires on his car were flat. They had been punctured with something. He tried to use a compressor at the building site to inflate them, but they wouldn't hold air. He's having the car towed into Sharp's Service."

"Did he see anyone around?" Darrell asked.

"No, the driveway isn't finished enough to get his car close to the house. The road is only good enough for the construction trucks to get up there. The house is 300 yards or so from the highway and where he parked the car is only half way to the site. He walked the rest of the way to the house. It would have been easy for anyone to slip up there from the highway without being seen. The question is why?"

The room grew silent except for their breathing. What seemed like minutes passed before Sherry broke the silence. "Sounds like he's being watched or someone just doesn't like foreigners in these parts building houses."

"Could be either," Thomas said, "but there was a typewritten note on the windshield. He read the note to them. *I can get you anytime I want. Payback will be my pleasure and your pain. It will be the pain you caused me. Expect it.*"

Reginald asked, "Does he have any idea what this is about?"

"He says he doesn't and I believe him," Dawson said.

"He did say that when he inherited the land a dispute began with a man who lives a mile up the road in Izzard County. The man claimed that he had been promised the land and could make trouble if he was of a mind to do it. The properties join each other and make close to 300 acres total. Each property is about 150 acres."

"Does Blandford think that's who flattened the tires?" Sherry asked.

"He knows that it wasn't him. He moved away and is now in a nursing home somewhere, or at least that is what he heard from the son awhile back."

"Could it have been the son?" Reginald wanted to know.

"I doubt that it's him. They have formed a friendship, though in the beginning the kid was pretty bent out of shape because his dad didn't get the land so he and his dad could hunt on it. Everything seems to be okay between them now, but in these parts grudges often hang on and die hard, so you never know for sure when someone isn't playing straight on these things. But I don't think the son is the culprit. It's someone else. I'll check on his whereabouts for early this morning just to tie it up."

The phone intercom rang in the conference room interrupting the conversation. Merton picked it up and said, "Put him on." He listened for a moment and said, "Just a minute." He put his hand over the receiver and said to no one in particular, "It's the bank in Mountain Home. That check to the hardware store just came in. I told them this morning to hang onto it if it showed up. We are in luck, too. The address of the store is on the back." He went back to the phone and listened again. "That's right. Don't handle it more than needed to get it into a plastic bag. I am going to put the Chief of Police on and then I want to talk to you again."

Darrell took the phone and said, "Sgt. Gawker will be up there this afternoon to pick up the check. We'll appreciate your assistance in whatever way you can help. Here is Merton again." He handed the phone to the bank president.

"Sam, pay that check and see what happens. Since the guy sent the stop payment here, you have an excuse to go ahead and honor it. Might be interesting what he will do when he sees that it cleared. He may come in and then we can find out who he is." Pause. "Okay. We'll be in touch. Thanks." He hung up and looked at the phone and then at everyone in the room. He said, "Stuff like this only happens in big cities, not in a small town." The silence in the air hung like dense fog on a sunless day.

Before Reginald left, he asked Sheriff Dawson to have Joe at Sharp's Service hang onto the tires so they could be examined for whatever punctured them. He hoped that an examination of the tires would help reveal more evidence in the most perplexing case they had to date.

Reginald arrived early in the afternoon at the First Bank Savings and Loan and was shown into the bank president's office. Introductions were made and Sam Hazelton, the president said, "Heard some good things concerning you Sgt. Gawker. I knew your daddy when you were still a pup. My father and yours fished together up at Norfork Lake. He was a nice man as I remember. My dad really liked him."

"Thank you Mr. Hazelton, my dad was okay. I know many people liked him. I ... "

"Just call me Sam, if you don't mind."

"Okay. Just call me Reginald."

"Let's see. You came to look at that check. Here it is."

He handed a clear plastic envelope to Reginald. The check inside was handwritten and made to Sprinkles Hardware Store, signed by J. Daniel Bushman. On the "*For*" line were the words, Special Hardware. On the reverse side, the endorsement stamp showed the depositor: Sprinkles Hardware Store, 1221 South Highway 57 Petersburg Indiana 47567.

"Where's Petersburg, Indiana?" Sam asked. "I saw that when the check came in."

"I don't know, but we might find out on the Internet."

Sam turned to his computer and in a few seconds had a map of Indiana on his screen. They looked and saw that it was in the southwestern part of the state on Highway 57.

Reginald looked at the screen and said, "Can you pull up Stanford, Indiana? It's located west of Bloomington on State Road 45 according to what I was told. I am curious where it is relative to Petersburg."

The map appeared and they located the wide spot in the road. They saw its location northeast of Petersburg and from Bloomington, the most direct route to Petersburg indicated 45 to 54 through Bloomfield. Then west of Bloomfield, a left turn onto 57 for the drive to Petersburg would take the travelers through some of the best farm land in the world. *Very interesting*, Reginald thought to himself as he looked at the map. He recalled what Callman had said about living in Stanford. *The hardware store is on the route that could be taken to and from Arkansas. Callman had been a salesman and would know the area well, or he supposed he would know it well. Better not be too hasty with conclusions*, he warned himself. *But if this isn't a coincidence, I might be onto something important.*

Sam Hazelton jarred him out of his trance. "Is everything all right, Reginald?"

"Oh. Right, I'm okay. I was thinking about some of the things in the investigation. I may be stumbling onto something, but I really don't know what it means at this point or even whether it will be important when I do find out. If you learn anything, especially if the account holder contacts you because you payed the check, give me a call if you would. Also, it would be nice if you could monitor that account and keep us informed."

Sam Hazelton thought a moment and said, "If you can get a court order we'll be happy to comply with it since this involves what looks to be criminal activity. I've already contacted the Postal Inspector and made a copy for him, but I haven't heard anything back from him. If I do, I'll let you know."

"Okay. I'll get the court order request rolling as soon as I get back to Mountain View."

Sam said, "I'll call the judge and tell him what we need and why. I think he'll issue it without you coming back here if all the paper work is in order."

"I'll have Chief Cumberland start the process and then we'll go from there. Maybe we can learn something from watching the account activity. Now I need to be going."

"Wait a minute. Before you leave, I'll give you the address where we send the statements on that account. Be right back." Sam left and returned in five minutes with a puzzled look on his face. "That account has been open since July 1995 and every statement, but July and August of '95, has been returned marked *Addressee Unknown* for reasons we don't know."

Sam called the postmaster. He hung up and looked at Reginald. "He told me that the box number was vacated in September of 1995 after a change of address was made to send all mail bearing that post office box address to what is now a vacant lot where the house that was there burned. What's odd is that house address is listed on the account records and only the box number is on the checks where the statements are being sent. According to the postmaster, the change of address was made by the box holder Bushman a few days before the fire in September of 1995. I remember that two people died there, but the coroner thinks they were dead before the fire. They were burned so badly that the state lab pathologist couldn't tell the cause of death. Other than what I have told you, I don't know any other details."

"For reasons we don't know, the forwarding address was deliberately changed to what is now a vacant lot and your bookkeeping department wasn't told of the change," Reginald said, making sure he understood the information.

"That's correct. It may be that in the excitement of the house burning a couple of days after the box was terminated, Mr. Bushman forgot to notify us of a new address. But since there isn't any problem with the account and everything appears legal, except for suspected criminal activity, we can't do anything to change the mailing address until he tells us to change it. I suspect that he was going to move there and the house burned before he could move in."

"It could be the reason I suppose. Anything's possible. I'll check all the angles and let you know if I find anything on it," Reginald said. He thanked Sam Hazelton and left, more confused than ever with questions that he couldn't answer. It was too late to inquire into the house fire and any connection was doubtful at this point. Nonetheless, just to tie up loose ends, it needed to be investigated, but it would have to be done later. Too bad the note was already on its way to Mountain View. He could have had it too if the check had come in earlier.

It was 4:00 p.m. when Reginald walked by the dispatch office. The second shift operator, Randy Flockman, got his attention and handed him an urgent message to call Sherry. He unlocked his office door and saw the private line light blinking. "Hi, Sherry," he said cheerfully, "I got your message. What is so urgent?"

"How did you know it was me?" Sherry asked.

"I'm psychic or didn't you know?" He heard subdued laughter on the other end.

"Reg, this is serious. Come to the bank as quickly as you can get here. Whatever is taking place is worse than we have thought. Bye."

Reginald quickly finished the paper work on a burglary case he had ready to send to the prosecutor. "At least that case was simple to solve," he said, "and thank you, God, for simple things." He left in a hurry for the bank.

Merton Houston met Reginald at the bank door. They went into his office where Sherry waited. Houston twirled the combination knob on the documents safe and took out the note and envelope that were inside sealed plastic covers. Merton said, "The state policeman arrived a half an hour after you left. He had to answer a call or he would have been here earlier."

He handed the paper to Reginald who read the type written note aloud. "*You will suffer pain for the loss that I have suffered. You helped create my terrible hurt. I can get you anytime I decide. Neither you nor that detective boyfriend of yours can stop me. He is on the list for pain too.*" All three sat and stared at each other and at the note in Reginald's hand. Sherry was stunned by what she had just heard and the look of fear crept into her pretty features and eyes. She couldn't speak. Her mouth opened and closed silently. Reginald could only look at her, unable to speak due to a total loss of words.

Merton broke the uneasy silence. "I have talked to Darrell and Thomas and they both are more than a little concerned with all of this. They are very worried that something big is going to happen, so all of us are going to have a meeting tomorrow in Clinton at the Van Buren County Sheriff's Department."

"Why there?" Reginald asked.

"Darrell and Thomas think we're being watched. There are so many tourists in town it's impossible to know who it could be and they don't want to take any chances."

"What time is the meeting?" Reginald asked.

"It's set up for 11:00 a.m. and Sherry is going with me. We're going to leave at 8:45 and take Highway 5 to 25, then 25 to Drasco, 92 to Greers Ferry, and then 16 to Clinton. Thomas is going to go through Shirley and Darrell is going to drive out to Leslie at 9:30 a.m., then go south on 65 to Clinton. Reginald, Darrell wants you to leave early enough so that you can work your way to Clinton by going through Quitman. He wants you to cut across to 65 on 124 and arrive in Clinton from the south."

Reginald began to grin. "Did Darrell think this up?"

"He did after we saw that note addressed to me," Sherry said.

Reginald thought for a moment. "Now I know why he's the Chief of Police. He's too smart to be a detective." Sherry and Merton laughed and then became quiet. Reginald continued. "If we are being watched and followed, whoever it is will have a tough time with this plan. It will look like business as usual."

"From now on we can't be too careful. A perp is running loose here and we have unfortunately become the targets," Sherry said.

Reginald had been studying the note as Sherry spoke. "I just remembered something. Lt. Waldron said he was sure that the letter to Callman had been typed on an old manual typewriter because the letter impressions weren't clear. The type was filled with dried ink and trash. The note on Blandford's car looked the same way and this note to Sherry has bad letters too. I'll bet that all three notes were written on the same machine. We definitely need to find that typewriter." He was silent for a moment and then added, "Might as well look for a needle in a haystack."

"We have to find the haystack and the needle both," Sherry said. "The trouble is we don't know what the haystack looks like and we have no idea who is holding the needle, whatever it is besides the typewriter."

"Those notes create a link that hopefully will give us more to work with than we've had before now. It suggests one perp, but who is he and why has he chosen to pick on the people of this town? Maybe we are dealing with a psycho of some kind. It looks like a nut has escaped the bag. There are enough of them out there now on a normal day and we don't need a dangerous one hanging around to plague us," Reginald said.

"True, but we never think that there are psychos in Mountain View. There may be some odd folks and square pegs in round holes living here, but they aren't like this one seems to be," Sherry said.

Merton Houston picked up a note from his desk and handed it to Sherry and said, "Right after Reginald left the Mountain Home Bank, Sam called."

Sherry looked at the note. "Whoever has that account made a cash deposit? Was he in the bank?" she asked wide eyed.

"No, he mailed it in and it has the same return address that is on the other two envelopes and from the way it looks, he intends to remain invisible. The deposit was five one hundred dollar bills and post marked April 22 in Little Rock. No note. No nothing, except the deposit slip and the money wrapped in two sheets of blank paper. Sam is sending the slip, the paper, and the envelope to me."

They left the bank and Reginald followed Sherry home. They stood outside a few minutes and talked and then kissed good night.

Reginald didn't notice the tan 1995 Ford parked down the street. The driver of the Ford was sitting in the car when Reginald turned west on Main Street. He waited until Reginald was a block away and then he pulled out and began to follow. Reginald soon realized he had a tail so he sped up to make the stoplight at Sycamore Avenue and Main. He made a quick turn into the car wash west of Best Burgers and got out of his truck, inserted coins, and started the water in the washer wand. He saw that the Ford had stopped at the light. He watched for the car and when it eased by, he pretended not to look but was able to see the front plate number, AMK 043, Missouri. The driver glanced at Reginald, but it was too dark to get a description of the man. The car disappeared from sight.

Reginald washed the truck and went home. He didn't know where the tan Ford had picked him up, but he knew from experience that it was possible the car had followed him to Sherry's house. The more he mulled over the case, the more he knew he didn't know; but yet he knew some things, and by experience and bird dog persistence, he knew the solution to the puzzle would be found.

When he opened the door to the house, his phone was ringing. He picked it up and said, "Hello ... Hello ... " He heard nothing but breathing in response.

Disgusted and ready to hang up, a smoker's raspy voice said, "Thought you were real smart pulling into that car wash didn't you? Sleep tight." The line went dead. He looked at his caller ID and saw that the number had been blocked.

Reginald's brain was in a whirl when he went to bed. The whole case seemed to be a maniacal twister, slowly turning into a living nightmare that they couldn't escape. Sleep didn't come easy.

SEVEN

The next morning, at the agreed upon intervals, several vehicles left Mountain View by the prescribed routes. Merton Houston and Sherry saw nothing unusual as they left the bank and headed east on Main Street and Highway 5. When Merton made the right turn onto Highway 5, he glanced in his rear view mirror and saw a blue Ford Crown Victoria also turn right, following them a few car lengths back. He said to Sherry, "Don't look now, but I think we have company. We are being followed by a blue Ford."

Sherry took a comb and a tube of lipstick from her purse. She pulled the visor down and adjusted it so that the visor mirror allowed her to see the car behind them. She applied lipstick and combed her hair, moving her head as she combed so she could see the tail. She said, "Uncle Merton, if he turns when you turn right onto 25, then we'll have a good idea that he's following us. We have to lose him somehow if he is a tail. We sure don't need him tagging along."

Merton was quiet and watched the Ford in the rear view mirror as the rolling hills, the view of distant mountains, trees, cows, and the countryside, silently glided past. When he made the turn south onto 25 to go toward Drasco, the blue Ford pulled into the vacant lot on the corner. It didn't reappear before they were around the next curve. The road dropped into a small valley and exited in a curve on a narrow ridge. The curves and hills helped hide them from any vehicle that might be following. Thankfully, no blue Ford appeared in the mirror. He began to think it was his imagination and felt a measure of relief.

As they approached Drasco, Merton checked the mirror again and saw the car 200 yards back. He sighed and said, "That car is back there again. I thought it might be gone. Now we can't turn on 92 and take the chance we can lose him. If we go on down the highway, maybe we can ditch him by turning onto a side road. You got any suggestions? I'm not any good at the cops and robbers stuff like you are."

Sherry didn't say anything until they were past the Highway 92 intersection with 25 at Drasco. She looked at her uncle and said. "I have an idea, but it's a long shot. Let's stop and see your brother at the First Citizen Bank."

"Why go see him? How's that going to help?"

"I am thinking on a plan. You two look enough alike to be twins, even though he's four years younger than you are. We might be able to pull a switch long enough to fool the tail."

"How are we going to do that?"

"I don't know yet, but if whatever I can devise works, we might even be able to keep him from knowing we're onto him."

"I don't see how," Merton said with his voice full of anguish.

"Leave the cops and robbers stuff to me. As you said, you aren't good at it." Merton looked at Sherry and laughed.

When Merton and Sherry arrived at the bank, the blue Ford went on by, turned around quickly, and came back. The driver parked between two cars in the lot across the street. Just by chance, as they were entering the bank, a friend of Sherry's was coming out. She introduced her uncle and the brief conversation gave Sherry the opportunity for a few seconds to discreetly watch the driver of the Ford. They entered the building and went into Mervin Houston's office.

Surprised at seeing his brother and great niece, Mervin said, "What brings you two by? It's been a spell since we have visited. How are your folks, Sherry? How's Nadine doing, Merton?"

"Daddy and mother are fine or at least they were when I saw them three weeks ago." Sherry looked at Merton waiting on his answer.

"Nadine is as fine as a well tuned fiddle. When are you and Bessie coming over again? Let us know and she will cook something up."

"I'll do that. Now is this a social call or business?"

"A bit of both," Sherry said, and briefly explained the problem and what she wanted.

Mervin began to laugh. "I told your mother one time that it's a good thing you are on our side. How do you come up with these things?"

"She's devious," Merton said. They all laughed.

Mervin punched his intercom line button and then spoke. "Are you three ready to go?" He hung up and after a few words to explain the plan to everyone, they left the bank.

The man in the blue Ford had grown restless and was ready to leave, when a white 1996 Cadillac exited the bank parking lot. Mervin Houston, who Sherry hoped looked enough like his brother Merton to fool Mr. Tail, was at the wheel of Merton's Cadillac. Melody Mason, Mervin's great niece, head of customer relations, who from a distance was the look alike of her cousin Sherry, was in the back seat with the wife of the bank vice-president, who sat in front. The man saw them exit the bank, enter the Cadillac, and leave. He watched the car turn south on Business Route 25. He took the bait and followed the decoy. Merton and Sherry waited for a few minutes before leaving in Mervin's Lincoln. Slightly more than one hour later, Merton and Sherry arrived at the sheriff's office in Clinton a couple of minutes before the scheduled meeting.

When they walked into the meeting room, they were surprised to see Darcy Broadway. He had the full image of a mountain man, sporting a bushy beard, overalls, blue short sleeve denim shirt, boots, and a floppy felt hat. He sat at a table munching doughnuts and drinking coffee, not that he was the only one eating the goodies. He said, "Hi, Sherry. You look surprised at seeing me here. You must know that the only reason I came was because of the doughnuts." The room roared with laughter.

Merton and Sherry were introduced to Jake Winthrop, the Van Buren County Sheriff, and after some small talk, Sherry asked Darcy, "What are you doing here besides scarfing up the free doughnuts?"

"I got a call from your daddy last night. Darrell and Thomas talked it over with Merton and decided that since you were involved in something that none of them can figure out, they needed the state police in on it. Captain Brady told me to come up here and do whatever you need done. So here I am." Darcy grabbed another chocolate covered doughnut and took a huge bite from it. "Just gettin' in practice for my new image," he said, and took another big bite.

"If you keep chomping on doughnuts everyone will know for sure you are a cop," Sherry needled. Everyone had a good laugh, and then she noticed Reginald looking at her intently. She decided to tease him a little bit. "Hi, I'm Sherry. I think we've met before. Don't you recognize me?"

"Huh? Oh, right. Oh for Pete's sake, of course I know who you are. You just look different." He paused and then said, "It's that dress. Is that yours? I've not seen it before," Reginald said, finally gaining his senses. "Where did you get it?"

"It belongs to my cousin over in Heber Springs."

"It's your cousin's? Why are you wearing her dress? You run out of clothes?" Reginald asked rapidly.

"My cousin Melody is Uncle Merton's and Uncle Mervin's great niece. I guess I had better tell you what happened to get me into this dress. And no, I haven't run out of clothes." She related the story of the blue Ford and the switch at the bank. "We were never able to see the back of the tail car, so we couldn't get the license number before we arrived at the bank. Merton said he would pull off to the side so the car would have to go on by, but we didn't want to tip the driver that we were suspicious of him, so I hatched the diversion. I wore a pale blue dress today and Melody had this one on. It's a bit darker blue than my dress, but it's similar in style. We swapped clothes and the man in the blue Ford was far enough away that he never caught on. Merton and Mervin both wore dark blue suits today and the tail didn't spot the difference in their looks and age. I hope it takes him awhile to figure out his mistake. At least until we get back to Mountain View. And unfortunately, we weren't able to see the plate clearly from the bank when the car left the parking lot across the street, so we still don't have any identification for the driver."

The meeting turned to the problem they were facing. After what seemed like hours of discussion, it was decided that Thomas would ask the Circuit Judge for an order to put a line tap and recorder on the home phone lines of Reginald, Sherry, Darrell, Thomas, and Merton. All phones would be equipped with caller ID in each of their houses if they didn't already have one. The sheriff's radio and the P.D. had recording capability, so that was covered. All work would be coordinated through Darrell and Thomas.

"All the city policemen and deputies will be alerted and updated with regular meetings. They will be cautioned not to talk to civilians except when needed to investigate possible events. We have four immediate problems facing us. One is trying to learn his identity. The second is to find out what is taking place and thereby prevent more events; three, finding evidence so we can arrest him; and four, we want to prevent as much as possible any wild rumors. Public information might scare the perp away before we find out who he is or what he's planning," Darrell said. All nodded their heads in agreement.

Darrell turned to Jake Winthrop and the others assembled and said, "We are dealing with someone and something that appears to be capable of becoming deadly. Whoever it is, is stalking Sherry and Reginald and a fellow by the name of Robert H. Blandford. He also may be the one who shot L. Jason Callman the other night on the square. Why we don't know. And there may be others in danger too." He turned to Darcy and said, "You bring in another undercover man if you want and drift around the town. See if you can get a handle on something useful. Keep a watch on Sherry and Reginald the best you can. As I said, we have no idea why he is singling them out.

"I know just the man, Darrell. He will blend in with everyone." Reginald laughed inwardly when he heard the familiar words, blend in. They brought back memories.

"Get him," Darrell replied and turned to Reginald. "Have you learned anything more?"

"I ran a 10-28 and 29 on that Missouri plate this morning before leaving. It came back registered to a blue 1989 Ford owned by Henry Bottoms of Ava, Missouri, a little town north of Mountain Home. Ava is forty-five miles above the Missouri state line on Missouri 14. The car that plate is on now is a 1995 tan Ford Crown Vic. When I get back, I'll make some calls to try to find his identity and what he does for a living. If I can't learn anything, I'll need to go interview him to find out why that plate is on a different car and why he's following us around," Reginald replied.

Sherry looked at her watch and said, "Uncle Merton, my watch says 12:30 and we need to be back in Heber by 3:00 p.m. That bank meeting will be over by then and they'll be back at the bank by 4:00 p.m. We need to be inside the building before it's locked in case our friend decides to follow them home, and we need to have Uncle Mervin's Lincoln back in its parking space so the suspect won't know it left. Besides, I need to get my dress back."

After a bit more discussion, they left for the day. All the dough-nut munchers, except Merton and Sherry who left for Heber Springs, went to lunch. Darcy said doughnuts could only last so long.

The drive back on the mountain plateaus, hills, and valleys was uneventful and pleasant. The spring scenery along the route from Clinton through Quitman contained a blend of shades of green and early flowers. When they arrived at the bank parking lot, the blue Ford was nowhere in sight. They had been inside less than ten min-utes when Mervin returned and the blue Ford took up a spot across the street between two cars. Sherry swapped her dress and when they left the lot, the faithful blue Ford tagged along at a distance. Sherry noticed a front fender. "I don't think that car had any damage when we first saw it this morning and now the right front fender is crum-pled. But it does look like we fooled him." They both laughed but the tension remained. She made some notes and told herself to remember to tell Reginald the blue Ford had a smashed right front fender when it returned from Searcy.

By the time Merton and Sherry arrived in Mountain View at the bank, the tail had disappeared. They went inside for a few minutes and then left for their respective homes. Neither saw the man watching them through the window of the Home Cookin' Cafe across the street. His face turned to stone as he watched Sherry drive away.

The lady at the next table shivered when she saw him turn and look at her. His pie and coffee order arrived. While he ate, he appeared to her to be deep in thought; then a cold smile appeared and his fierce eyes appeared to burn through her when he looked at her again. She called the waitress over to her table, received her dinner check, paid her bill, and hurriedly left. The man left part of his pie and coffee. He left a two dollar tip, quickly paid his bill, and opened the door to leave. The waitress saw the money and said thank you before the door closed. He turned and looked at her with cold steel grey eyes filled with hatred.

EIGHT

When Reginald walked into his office late in the afternoon, he stared his desk. It had suffered a Post-It-Notes blizzard. The yellow notes were everywhere, covering all the bare spots he knew were there when he left. He waded through the usual calls from the usual people, but the one that interested him the most was from L. Jason Callman, who was still in the Baptist Hospital. He was ready to go home and would be released on Monday. He wanted Reginald to get him since he had no other way to return to Mountain View. Then Reginald found the notes to call the state police lab and Chief of Detectives Wellman at the Little Rock P.D. He called the lab and learned there wasn't any DNA on the handkerchief pieces examined. The results weren't ready on the toothpick. The smudges on the letter paper were made by 3-In-One Oil. He then called the L.R.P.D. and asked for Major Wellman.

L.P. Wellman picked up the phone and said without any formalities, "Reginald, I hope you are ready for what I am going to tell you."

Reginald hesitated and then said, "Go ahead, I won't be surprised by anything at this point."

"The .22 caliber rounds taken from the Officer McGee and your victim up there match. The same gun fired both bullets, copper jacket shorts."

Reginald was more silent than a neglected haunted house until he let out a loud exhale and said, "Are you sure ... er ... I mean ... how ... ?" and then he fell silent again.

Wellman heard Reginald's mental stumbling around and said, "I reacted the same way when the lab boys told me."

"Why did they decide to run a comparison on the bullets?"

"I remembered what you said about having a headache that you couldn't explain, so on a hunch, I called the state lab and asked the tech to take a look. I figured we had nothing to lose, so I took our bullet over to the ballistics lab. A long shot that paid off."

"A long shot that hit the bull's eye to be exact; so what are we dealing with now?"

"I don't know now, but it looks like we have a connection of some kind in the two cases."

"Right, and that headache is getting stronger now and a Bufferin won't help this one. I have that odd feeling that there's a lot more we're going to find out that isn't going to make anyone happy. I'm going to Baptist Monday morning to pick up Callman and I'll try to get some more out of him. I think he might have the key to this mess and doesn't know it yet."

"Okay, Reginald. Keep me posted."

"Thanks L.P. I don't know what all this means except that my headache just got bigger. I'll let you know whatever I find out."

"Oh Reginald, tell Sherry hello for me." Wellman could almost see through the phone the surprised smile run across Reginald's face.

"I will and one more thing. Can we keep this out of the paper? I have a hunch the perp thinks we'll never make a connection. The less he knows what we know the better off we are. To date, all the public knows is that a police officer was killed and a man was shot in my town. They have no reason to make a connection at this point and you can be sure I'm not going to tip them off."

"Me either. That will be handled and my detectives will keep it quiet too. No one will tell the newspaper hounds until we're ready."

"Good. Will keep you posted." They hung up, each with more questions than answers again.

L.P. Wellman sat back in his chair after cradling the phone and smiled; then the troubled look returned. They had a real problem and not much to go on. He said, "I wonder if the postal boys can tell us anything more. I need to call them Monday morning." He left his office for home with his mind spinning like a carnival tilt-a-whirl. He also knew that the press would scream to high heaven when the story was finally released. He thought, *so what, let them complain.*

Reginald called Darrell Cumberland at home and filled him in on the events of the day. He discussed some ideas with the Chief and then hung up. Next, he called Sherry and when she answered he said, "What's cooking? I can smell it clear over here," and chuckled into the phone.

"Is that a hint that I should invite you over to eat, buster?"

"Well, how do you like that? Buster, is it? Only gone for part of one day and you have forgotten my name already."

Sherry laughed and said, "Come on over. At least with the invitation you won't be barging in unexpectedly. And I do have some things to tell you that happened today. How does scrambled eggs and sausage with all the trimmings sound?"

"I can taste it already. I'll be there as soon as I wrap up some stuff here. It'll be in thirty minutes or less." She said good bye with a kiss noise. His face changed color and he hung up.

Sherry greeted Reginald at the door. "Hi, Reg," she said. A quick kiss brought a flash of red to his cheeks. She smiled at him and he had the awe shucks look as he contemplated the toes of his shoes. He stammered, "You sure know how to make me happy. An invitation to eat always does it."

She said, "The kiss didn't make you happy?" His face turned an even deeper shade of red.

Sherry grabbed his hand and led him to the kitchen. They ate and discussed the case. Sherry told him the blue '89 Ford had a damaged right front fender and that it followed them to Heber Springs and back.

"Was the fender damaged before he returned to Heber from following the decoys?"

"I didn't notice it before we arrived at the bank. It must have hap-

pened after he left Heber to follow Uncle Mervin to Searcy. Maybe
we can find out who he is now."

"I have to go to Little Rock Monday ... uh ... " He stopped and
gave Sherry a peculiar look.

"What's wrong?"

"You don't know do you?"

"What don't I know, Reg?"

"You don't know about the gun."

"Which gun?"

"The one used to kill the officer in Little Rock. The bullet taken
from his head and the one that hit Callman were both fired from the
same .22."

Sherry's jaw dropped in amazement.

"Matched?"

"Both rounds are .22 shorts with copper jackets and were fired
from the same gun."

They both sat silently looking at each other and then Sherry said,
"Does that mean that whoever it was that shot them is more than
likely the same one that sent me the note and the bank the stop payment? If it is though, where is the connection?"

"It would seem that way. I have been thinking, trying to make
a connection with that bank account in Mountain Home and the
address being a vacant lot. It was valid until that fire. Something tells
me this is all connected, but I don't know how or why."

"Is there a link between Mr. Callman and the slain officer?"

"There's none that I know of at the moment, but we just learned
of the match on the bullets today. My hunch is that the officer saw
something that made the shooter nervous. But we have no way of
knowing what it was. All we know from the witnesses is that the suspected perp dropped something into the mailbox. But why would the
same gun be used on Callman and what does he have to do with it?
None of it makes sense."

Sherry looked at him for a second and then said, "Why don't
I check with the state police and the Searcy Police Department on

Monday morning to see if an accident was reported today involving a blue '89 Ford?"

"Do that while I go to Little Rock to pick up L. Jason Callman. I'll also contact the P.D. in Mountain Home and arrange to go up there next week since the phone calls didn't turn up anything. There are other elements in this case that don't seem connected, but if we keep digging, some of them might link up."

NINE

Reginald was ready to go home after a great evening, looking forward to the weekend, when the phone rang. Sherry answered and said, "He's here," and handed the phone to Reginald.

Reginald took the phone and said, "What you got?" he paused and then his face changed color. "They reported what?" Pause. "Who is it?" More silence as he listened. "Okay. Tell whoever is working to get the yellow tape up. Notify the Coroner, the Chief, and Sheriff Dawson. Sherry and I will be right there." He hung up and said to Sherry, "Come on, Matilda Herrington has been found dead in her house. It looks like she was murdered."

When Reginald's truck made the turn south off Gaylor onto Vine, he and Sherry saw police cars clustered at Oak Street with the red and blue roof lights piercing the night, casting eerie forms on the trees and nearby houses. Spotlights illuminated the front porch and side yard next to Oak. The house, situated on the Southeast corner facing Vine Street on the west, was surrounded by a crowd of silent gawkers who stood outside the yellow crime scene tape strung on all four sides of the property. The Mountain View Police, Stone County Deputies, and two state policemen were keeping the crowd from entering the scene. A few of the onlookers were murmuring, "Nothing like this ever happens in this town." Reginald heard the talk as he made his way through the lookers and thought to himself, *it has now.*

The officers guarding the scene moved aside as Reginald and Sherry stepped onto the porch. A quick examination by the first officers on the scene, Nance Porter and Allen Handley, found that the perpetrator had arrived and left by the back door. Two sets of large muddy footprints pointed to and away from the house. Footprints leading into the house were found on the back porch. Muddy tracks were also found on the kitchen floor and in the hallway. There were signs of a struggle near the back door that continued across the kitchen and down the hall toward the living room.

Since Matilda was an elderly small woman, the resistance against a larger assailant or assailants wouldn't have amounted to much. Throw rugs were scattered and there were scuff marks on the wall where her shoes might have made contact. The officers told Reginald and Sherry that a neighbor, Mary Sheldon, had found the victim face down in her bed at 9:15 p.m. She had gone over to Mrs. Herrington's house with a hot apple pie she had just made. She and Matilda were going to have some pie and ice cream. Reginald asked the whereabouts of Mrs. Sheldon and Nance said she had been taken back home after they got there. Ginger Rifling, a nurse who worked at the Stone County Medical Center, was with her.

Reginald and Sherry slipped on plastic shoe covers and went inside. They began looking at the scene, being careful not to disturb anything. A couple of minutes later Sherry stepped outside and asked one of the state police officers to send for a crime scene unit. The officer said it would take three hours or more for the unit to arrive from Little Rock, but maybe he could get a police chopper to fly a couple of techs up to save time. A few minutes later, the trooper said that two techs would be at the airport in an hour and a half to two hours. He said he would pick them up when they arrived.

The coroner examined Mrs. Herrington and placed the time of death tentatively from 8:50 to 9:00 p.m., fifteen to twenty-five minutes before Mrs. Sheldon found her neighbor dead, based on the initial information Mrs. Sheldon had furnished. He said he couldn't be sure until an autopsy was performed, but he believed the marks on her face and nose indicated that someone tried to silence her with tape across her mouth. There was some sticky residue clinging to the lips and skin around her nose that might have come off the tape. But he didn't think the tape was the cause of death. There was a large swelling on the right side of her head above the ear, but no blood associated with it. The State crime lab pathologist in Little Rock would look for other injuries and issue the official cause of death. Before the coroner left, he bagged the victim's hands to preserve evidence.

At 11:15 p.m., the crime scene techs arrived and at 12:10 a.m., the lab truck drove up with two more men aboard. While they processed the scene, Reginald and Sherry went next door to interview Mary Sheldon, Mrs. Herrington's neighbor to the south. They introduced themselves and seeing that Mrs. Sheldon was distraught, Reginald suggested that they might wait until the next day, but Mary said she wanted to tell her story while it was fresh in her mind. He asked Mrs. Rifling to step outside but to remain on the scene so he could ask her some questions. Reginald began the interview by asking her if she heard any noise.

Mary Sheldon collected her thoughts and replied, "No, I didn't hear a sound. I had the TV on and at 8:30 p.m. or a bit after, the phone rang. It was Matilda calling to tell me to knock when I came with the pie since the front door would be locked." She smiled slightly as if remembering something pleasant when she mentioned locked. She continued. "We have pie, ice cream, and coffee every Friday night at either her house or mine. It was my turn to bake the pie and go over there. We eat and watch a show and the 10 o'clock news and then go home." She began crying again and let out big sobs. Reginald and Sherry remained silent. She dried her eyes and looked at Reginald.

"Are you okay?" Sherry asked. She nodded her head that she was.

"Do you still want to talk or would you rather do it tomorrow?" Reginald inquired.

"No. I want to tell you. I'll be all right."

"What time was it when you went over to her house?"

"It was 9:15. I always go before 9:30 ... but no later than 9:20, because there's a show we like to watch together. It was right before the news. That gives us time to get the pie cut and the ice cream ready so we don't miss the show." Tears slowly leaked from her sad looking eyes. Small sobs came from her throat.

Reginald waited while she dabbed away the tears and composed herself. He asked, "When you went over to the house, did you knock?"

"Yes. I held the pie on my left hand and I knocked with my right hand made into a fist." She demonstrated how she held the pie and had knocked.

"How many times did you knock?"

"Oh, three or four times with three or four knocks each time, I guess."

"How did you get in if the door was locked?"

"It wasn't locked."

"Not locked?"

"No, it was unlocked. I grabbed the knob and turned it and the door opened. I thought that was strange since she told me that the door would be locked."

"Maybe she forgot," Sherry said. A chilling silence filled the air.

"I don't think she forgot," Mrs. Sheldon said as tears ran down her cheeks.

"What makes you say that?"

"It's always locked when I go over on Friday night," Mary Sheldon said, again dabbing the tears from her eyes.

"You sure she always locks it?" Reginald asked.

"Sgt. Gawker, we have been sharing pie and ice cream on Friday night for over twenty-five years. There hasn't been a time that the door wasn't locked and Matilda always told me to knock because the door would be locked." Reginald saw Mrs. Sheldon smile. "When I told you that the door is always locked, I had to smile. She has done that for all these years. She locked it at 9:00 p.m. each night. You could almost set your watch by her locking that door."

Sherry, who had been making notes of her own, spoke up. "I

noticed the smile when you said locked and I had no idea what you were thinking."

"Matilda had her ways and that was one of them," Mrs. Sheldon said. "She was my dearest friend. She has lived in this town all her life. I don't think she had been more than fifty miles from here but once or twice, since she was born. She and her husband owned the local drive-in for years. She had no enemies. Who would want to kill her?" Tears ran down her face again.

Reginald waited for a few seconds and asked, "What did you do after you found the door unlocked?"

Tears continued to slide down her cheeks and when she was again composed, she said, "I opened the door and didn't hear or see anything. I called, 'Matilda, I'm here.' She didn't answer, and I began looking for her. I found her on the ... " Once again, tears filled Mrs. Sheldon's eyes and slid silently down her cheeks. She dabbed them away with a soggy tissue and began speaking rapidly. "I'm sorry. I can't help it. She was my best friend. I don't know any thing else." Sadness beyond description filled the face of the distraught woman.

Reginald said with as much gentleness as he could muster, "I need to ask a few more questions, and then we'll go." Mrs. Sheldon nodded her head in assent.

"Did Mrs. Herrington have any brothers or sisters?"

Mrs. Sheldon brightened for a moment and said, "Oh my yes, she had a twin sister, Helen, but no brothers."

"Where did the sister live?"

"I'm not sure. She lived in Little Rock at one time, but she moved and I don't know where she went. Her first husband died and she remarried some years later. I think that is when she moved. Matilda said something to me one time."

"Do you remember her married name?"

"Let me think, her first husband was Galen Magerson. But I don't know who she married the second time. Matilda told me once, but it has been so long I have forgotten."

Reginald could see that Mrs. Sheldon wouldn't be able to hold out much longer. "One more question," he said gently. "Did Mrs. Magerson work anywhere that you know of?"

"She did, but I don't know where. I don't think Matilda ever told me. Even though they were twins, they didn't see each other very often. I never met her." Mrs. Sheldon was the perfect picture of sadness, if such a picture can be perfect.

Sherry got up and whispered to Reginald. He nodded his head and stepped outside to speak to the nurse who left quickly. In thirty minutes, Mrs. Sheldon's doctor arrived and he and the nurse went into Mrs. Sheldon's house. Sherry left and joined Reginald outside. They looked at each other and said nothing. They both knew that evil had come to visit their peaceful town. Reginald said to no one in particular, "What is going to happen next? I have a bad feeling."

•

The sun peeking over the mountain ridge to the east had set the trees ablaze with pink light when the crime scene techs left for Little Rock. Matilda Herrington's body had been taken to the lab by chopper before midnight. Her next of kin, a son and daughter, both of whom lived in Illinois, had been notified. They said they would be in Mountain View the following afternoon to make funeral arrangements. Reginald and Sherry left the victim's house determined to find the answer as to why anyone would want to kill such a kind lady.

Reginald had dropped Sherry off at her house and had gone home to grab a couple of hours of sleep and rest. Sleep proved to be elusive. He got out of bed and prowled around the house while trying to get his mind off the homicide. Weary from lack of rest, he sat down to watch the early news on TV. He gave up on the news, showered, and left for a quick breakfast at Fanny's Fast Food. He arrived early at the P.D. to pick up his car, said a few words to Mazy, and then went to Sharp's Service to look at the punctured tires taken off Blandford's Chrysler. He got out of the car and saw Joe Sharp through the window drinking from a big coffee cup. He entered the office and said, "Drinking real heavy this early in the morning I see," and laughed.

Joe laughed and said, "Tell me you didn't have a big cup already and some doughnuts. I know what you guys eat. I've seen those empty doughnut boxes." He laughed at his own joke and then said, "I heard you keep late hours now. What's going on in this town anyways?"

"Joe, if I knew that I wouldn't be here to look at those tires. It would be over and done with." Realizing that he sounded like he was irritated, he quickly said, "I didn't mean to sound cross with you. It's just that … well … I don't know and wish I did. Let's go look at the tires. And being bone weary isn't helping. Not enough time to eat doughnuts, I guess." They both laughed.

Joe unlocked a big locker type cabinet where the tires were stored. He checked the serial numbers and knew they were the same ones that had been on Blandford's car. He looked at Joe and said, "You know more about tires than I do. What do you think caused them to go flat? I don't see any cuts like a knife would make."

"I know for sure it wasn't a knife."

"What do you think it was?"

"My best guess is an ice pick. Look here." He pointed to several puncture type marks on the sidewall of a tire. Reginald examined the marks and looked up at Joe who said, "I counted eight stabs on each tire. Looks to me like a madman did it."

"It isn't the usual type vandalism with so many punctures on each tire. You could be right and it does appear that the act may be more than just trying to flatten the tires." Reginald made a note of the number of holes in each of the tires and then told Joe to keep the tires locked up.

Joe took the tires back to the locker, put the padlock in place, and handed Reginald the key. "Here, now some smart aleck lawyer can't claim the tires you saw today aren't the ones I took off the car. You have the only key to the locker. I've been watching some of the cop shows and know how to protect evidence."

Reginald suppressed a smile and said, "Okay," and slipped the key on his key ring, laughing to himself at Joe and the cop shows. But he also knew that Joe did the right thing when he locked up the tires and gave him the key.

Chapter

TEN

Saturday was supposed to be Reginald's day off, but he knew that he couldn't rest with all the craziness taking place. He made a call to the state lab and talked to the supervisor. The supervisor said they would have a report ready for him on Wednesday since it was a murder case and that they had received notice to work it out quickly. The supervisor said he would call when the report was ready.

Reginald called L.P. Wellman at home, told him the facts of the murder, and asked if he had heard anything else. Wellman said he hadn't. The news reporters had been snooping around and fortunately, they hadn't gotten any scent and he hoped they didn't. Reginald thanked him and went out to do interviews on the Herrington homicide.

Not wanting to bother Mrs. Sheldon, Reginald went to the house across the street from Mrs. Herrington. The house was not well kept and looked tired, which was the way he felt. It needed a coat of paint and the roof fixed. Ivy haphazardly covered the clapboard siding. Big flat weeds kept the yard from being bare of growth. He knocked several times and finally Walter Munsford peeked out and opened the door. Reginald said, "I'm Sgt. Reginald P. Gawker of the Mountain View Police Department. I want to ask you some questions concerning what you saw last night."

Munsford looked at him. "I know who you are. Why didn't you question me last night? I was here," he said sourly. Reginald thought Munsford looked like he wanted to whip the world.

"Mr. Munsford, I was busy last night and didn't have the time. Besides, I assumed you were in bed and I didn't want to bother you. I'm working on my day off and I would appreciate your co-operation."

"Gawker, you listen to me. Day off or not, I didn't see anything or hear anything. I want nothing to do with this. Had you asked me last night I would have told you the same. Now go away." He slammed the door and left Reginald standing there wondering what had put the bee in his bonnet. As he looked at the shut door, he knew that Munsford would call Chief Cumberland again. He had called at one time or another about every policeman on the force. Now it was his turn to be in Munsford's sights. He laughed silently.

Reginald went to the next house south of Munsford. A kindly lady answered the door and asked him to come in, calling him by name. He recognized her as a friend of his mother from years ago.

Hazel Hancock, surprised and pleased at seeing Reginald at her door, said, "My word, I haven't seen you in many years, not since your momma died. Oh, I mean I have seen you, but this is the first time I have had a chance to talk to you. I am so happy that you are with the police department. And I know why your here."

Reginald smiled at Mrs. Hancock and said, "I assume you knew Mrs. Herrington, and I do want to ask you some questions that involve her."

"Oh my, I sure did know her. One of my best friends, and she was Mary's friend too. They always had pie and coffee every Friday before they went to bed."

"Did you ever go over?"

"A few times, but I don't get around too well so I stay close to home. That was their time and I didn't interfere. Once in a while, they both would come over here. But I don't know anything that will help."

Reginald looked around the neat little living room. The furnishings were what would be expected; old, worn from years of use, but well cared for. It made him feel comfortable and reminded him of his parent's house when he was growing up.

He broke the silence. "Mrs. Hancock, I need to know anything you can tell me. I will decide whether it will help or not. Did you talk to your friend yesterday?"

"Now that you mention it, I did. My memory isn't as good as it used to be, but yes, I did talk to her on the phone before four o'clock. She invited me to go out and eat with her and I couldn't go. My daughter was coming over and I had to stay home. Otherwise, I would have gone with her."

"Do you know where she went to eat?"

"Why yes, she went to that nice place on Main Street across from the bank. She eats there all the time. Mary and I go … well we did go with her sometimes and we always had a good time." Tears appeared and Reginald remained quiet while Mrs. Hancock left the room and composed herself. When she returned she said, "I'm sorry. Now where were we?"

"Maybe I should come back," Reginald said.

Hazel Hancock looked at him with sad eyes and said, "No, I want to help you catch whoever it is that … I'll be okay. Ask your questions."

"Thank you. I appreciate your help. Now, do you know what time she left for the restaurant?"

"I think it was a little before 4:30. I was watching a TV show that goes off at that time. I got up to get a drink of water and saw her car turn the corner off Oak onto Vine here. She parks in the garage behind her house. The drive is reached from Oak."

"You didn't see anyone or a car you didn't recognize did you?"

She hesitated for a moment and then said, "You know, after Matilda came home I saw a strange car go up the street."

"What time was that?"

"I think it was 5:30 to 5:45. My daughter was just leaving and I saw the lights on in Matilda's house. I'm pretty sure she had returned from eating a few minutes before. That was when I saw the car. The man driving looked at her house. The car went by real slow."

Reginald studied her and then made some notes. He said, "Mrs. Hancock, do you know what kind of car it was?"

"Oh, I don't know cars. All I know is that it was a big dark colored car. A four door, I think. But as I said, I don't know cars so I can't do any better than that. I mind my own business, and I just didn't see anything else. I was tired so went to bed at 8:30 p.m. or a few minutes before."

"Did you notice whether it had a damaged right front fender?"

"Now that you mention it, there was something different about that car. Maybe it was the fender. But I don't really know what it was."

Reginald tried to conceal the new worry that the information brought to his mind, but Mrs. Hancock picked up on it. "Is there something wrong with what I said?" she asked. "You look worried."

The answer came quickly. "No, you have been a big help. But I need to ask you another question and then I'll go. Have you told anyone else?"

"Oh no, I have kept quiet. I thought it best to do so. I don't gossip."

"Mrs. Hancock, that's good. I want you to stay quiet and do one more thing for me and ... well ... actually for yourself. Call your daughter and ask her to come and get you. Go stay with her until this is finished, whatever it is."

She didn't hesitate. "I can do that right now and you can talk to her." Mrs. Hancock looked relieved and Reginald knew she was scared, though she didn't say it.

Mrs. Hancock made the call and Reginald talked to Helen Ferver, the daughter. She said she would be there within the hour and wanted Reginald to stay with her mother. Less than one and a half hours later, Hazel Hancock was on her way to Leslie to stay with her family. Reginald hoped he had headed off another event as he preferred to call it.

It was 10:00 a.m. and the day wasn't getting a bit shorter. He went back to the P.D. and called Sherry and told her he would pick her up in ten minutes. When she got in the car, he outlined to her what he wanted and took her to the station. He also told her about the big car Mrs. Hancock saw and the possibility of it having a damaged fender. He left for the restaurant to see if the waitress that had worked the evening before was working the Saturday shift.

Reginald entered the restaurant just as a customer was leaving. He noticed the man walked with a slight limp in the right leg and was heavy for his approximate 5'10" height. The man avoided looking at Reginald directly in the eyes. He had never seen him before, but there were all kinds of people he had never seen before. After all, Mountain View was a tourist town and many strangers appeared there every day and every week, so he gave it no more thought and walked to the counter. The waitress he wanted to see wasn't working and was told she would be back on Monday morning. He went back to the police station and found Sherry in his office.

Sherry immediately asked when he walked in, "Did you find her?"

"No, she won't be in until Monday. How did you do?"

"I got a hold of Daddy and he and mother will be here before one o'clock. I called Mrs. Sheldon and she will be ready to go when they get here. They will pick her up and take her to Newport to stay with her daughter until we solve this. The daughter has wanted her mother to come and live with her and now maybe she will.

"Who's her daughter?"

"She's a school teacher whose husband is a sheriff's deputy in Jackson County. He's working so he can't come over to get her, and I told the daughter that it would be best if she didn't either. Since we don't know who we're looking for, I didn't want to chance it. Is she safe until they get here?"

"I think so. I don't think he'll try anything in the daylight. And the nurse and a close friend from Calico are there right now, so I think she's okay," Reginald said.

"Reg, is last night's homicide part of the Callman shooting?"

"I don't know, but I don't want to take any chances. I don't see how it could be though. What connection would there be?"

"I don't know a bit more than you do. I called Mrs. Sheldon and made some other calls and no one I talked to could offer anything that connected to Callman. They said they didn't know him and neither does Mrs. Sheldon from all the indications I could find. And you say those tires were probably poked with an ice pick?"

"They were. Did Mrs. Sheldon know Blandford?"

"She said she had no idea who he is. She never heard the name before I mentioned it." Sherry became silent as she looked through the window into the cloudy distance. "Looks like rain again," she said idly with other things on her mind.

The time dragged along slowly with the coffee tasting worse with each cup. The rain began, driven by the wind that threw it against the window. A typical May in Stone County was all Reginald's mind could muster. He was tired and wanted to go home.

At 12:45 p.m., the phone rang. Reginald answered and handed it to Sherry. She said, "Hi, Daddy. How was the trip over?" She listened and then filled him in on the particulars of the case. She listened for a few more moments. "I would like to see you too, but since we don't know who we are looking for or why, Reginald and I don't want to take the chance that the perp might make a connection with us." Again, she listened, and then said, "We'll let you know whatever we learn." Pause. "Okay, tell mother not to worry and I love you both." She listened some more. "I'll tell Reg."

Reginald looked at Sherry and said, "Tell me what?"

"Daddy said hello and for you to watch out for me. He didn't say it, but he thinks you are a good cop. I can tell by the way he talks about you when I see him."

Reginald grinned at her and said, "That's the best recommendation anyone could give me. It sure is different than it was the first time we met." They both laughed and left to get something to eat. Reginald dropped Sherry off after eating, went home, and climbed into bed. He didn't awaken until the phone jarred him awake early the following morning.

Reginald shook the sleep out of his brain and looked at the clock. The red display glowed 1:48 a.m. He picked up the phone and said, "Hello, what do you want?" expecting it to be the dispatcher.

"You really think you are smart don't you? You got those two women out of town before they could be hurt. I should say before I could hurt them permanently. Now I will have to find someone else to hurt the way I have been hurt." The voice was gravelly and strained.

Reginald wanted to keep the caller on the line. He asked, "What did you have against the lady you killed?"

"You're dumber than I thought. I didn't say I killed anyone. I just hurt people permanently."

"Okay, have it your way. Why did you hurt her?"

"That is my business, so knock it off. I know that you have never been hurt the way I have, and soon you are going to find out the meaning of my type of hurt. Some people need lessons. I am going to give you one and soon." The line went dead. The caller ID listed a local number. He wrote it down and before he could even think to go back to sleep, the phone rang again. The clock showed it was 1:50 a.m. It was the dispatcher, Billy Able.

Reginald said, "Not again," after he listened for a few seconds. "Okay, I'll go over there. Glad it's only a burglary." He dressed and drove the few blocks to Vine Street, reminding himself to check the line tap as soon as possible.

Chapter

ELEVEN

When Reginald arrived at the Vine Street scene, the red and blue lights of two patrol units were again casting eerie shadow formations on the trees and houses. The shadows made by the lights danced from the trees and bushes in some resemblance of a ghostly hide and seek; hiding and then reappearing, daring to be caught. Nance Porter was in front of Mrs. Sheldon's house looking at the porch and Allen Handley was standing in front of the Hancock house. As the bar lights made their sweep across the landscape, Reginald caught a glimpse of Walter Munsford peeking through the faded water stained curtains on the living room window. He suspected Munsford had seen something and hoped that when he questioned him, he wouldn't be as crotchety as he had been before.

Nance Porter hailed Reginald as he exited his truck. "Hey, Sarg, come over here. I want to show you what I found on the porch." Shining his flashlight on the object, Reginald saw a piece of wood that had fresh blood on it lying next to the door. They bent down to get a closer look. Nance was the first to speak. "What do you make of it?"

Reginald studied the object for a few minutes and said, "I think it's a broken handle from an ice pick." He looked up at the edge of the door and continued. "Look at the jab and gouge marks next to where the latch is located. Looks like whoever was here trying to jimmy the door broke the tool and somehow was injured. And from the looks of it, he didn't get in. When did you get the call, Nance?"

"Allen and I got the call at 1:48 a.m. I was nearby and got here in less than two minutes. Allen arrived a minute later. Dispatch said the caller wouldn't give his name."

Reginald thought for a few moments and said, "That's okay, I think I know who called. The perp called me at 1:48 and you were getting the call to come over here at the same time he called me. Did you call dispatch to notify me before or after you got here?"

"It was before we arrived. I remembered what you said could happen and told them to call you. The dispatcher said the line was busy. You must have been on the line with the perp when Billy tried to call you."

"It must have been. The perp's call didn't last long and as soon as I hung up, Billy called."

Reginald looked at Nance and then walked across the street to speak with Officer Handley. As he entered the yard, he again saw Walter Munsford peeking around the curtain. "What did you find if anything?"

"The back door has been jimmied with some kind of tool that splintered the wood away. The front is okay." They went to the back door and Allen shined his flashlight on the lock edge of the door. Jab and gouge marks had damaged the door jam strip and the door. The door was slightly ajar. Allen nudged the door open with the flashlight and they looked in. They couldn't see much and not wanting to disturb any evidence, they decided to wait until daylight to enter. Reginald closed the door carefully in order to not destroy any prints that might be on the knob or glass panes. They both thought the evidence at each house indicated that the intruder had entered the Hancock house first; had then gone to Mrs. Sheldon's house, hurt himself, and failed to gain entry.

Reginald said, "Allen, you put up crime scene tape here. After we get photos of the evidence where it's lying at Mrs. Sheldon's house, Nance will bag it and mark it. I want to go talk to our unidentified caller. I think he'll co-operate this time." Officer Handley laughed softly and left for the tape.

When he returned, Reginald headed next door to see Walter

Munsford and to have a talk with him. As he walked away he said, "I'll get Thomas Dawson to do the crime scene search. He knows the photography stuff and knows how to search the scene. We need to get a couple of you men trained and certified to do this too."

That was music to Allen Handley's ears. He said, "Thanks, Sarg. Nance and I want to be considered for that."

Reginald replied, "I'll talk to the Chief," and made a bee line for Munsford's house.

After repeated knocking, the door opened to reveal a sour looking Walter Munsford. He said, "I knew you would be nosing around here again bothering decent folks," and set his jaw in defiance.

Reginald looked at the crusty old codger for a few seconds and decided to push aside his natural inclination to be easy going and to approach Munsford with a bit more force. "Okay, here is the way we're going to play it. The last time I was here, you wouldn't answer any questions, and I knew then and I still know that you have some useful answers. I know you made the call this morning and I can prove it. You have called so many times complaining that the dispatchers know your voice. We also record all calls and have caller ID on every line. So now knock off the defiant attitude and answer my questions."

Munsford, surprised at Reginald's change of attitude, stepped back from the open door and motioned him into the living room. The room was disorderly and dirty looking. The furniture was old and worn. An ancient black and white console TV set, angled toward a well used overstuffed chair, clung to the north wall next to the bedroom door. Mr. Munsford motioned to Reginald to sit on the couch. Munsford took the overstuffed chair in the corner across the room from the TV. Reginald said after sitting down, "Now tell me what you saw the night Mrs. Herrington was killed and what you saw and heard tonight."

"Just because I let you in doesn't mean I'll tell you anything. I only let you in because I didn't want the neighbors to see you standing out there. It might give me a bad reputation."

Reginald let the last remark slide. "Mr. Munsford, I don't know whether you're afraid to talk or are just being cussedly stubborn, but I do know that you could be in danger too, since you live next to the crime scenes. You can do one of two things." Reginald paused for effect. "You can tell me what you know and call your son to take you to live with him, or I will call a judge and ask him to issue a court order to put you in protective custody somewhere. Now which will it be?"

Walter looked at Reginald with a mixture of fright and defiance and said, "You know I don't have much truck with the law ever since that deputy shot and killed my nephew." Reginald started to say something and then Munsford continued, "Yeah, I know he was shot during that hold up at Fifty-Six, but his gun wasn't loaded and that is the same as shooting an unarmed man in my book."

Reginald had all he could take and said, "Do you know why his gun wasn't loaded? It was because he had emptied it in the store at the clerk. Fortunately, she survived with only a bullet in the arm. Now I have heard enough," and started to get up to leave.

Alarmed by Reginald's behavior, Munsford asked, "Where're you going?"

"I am going to go wake up the judge and get a protective order and take you into custody. I will get it because for one thing, the judge won't like it that I have awakened him, and two, you are refusing to co-operate in an investigation of crimes about which you have knowledge. Now what is it going to be? Talk to me or I talk to the judge?"

Walter's face changed from defiance to fright. He said, "Okay, I know you well enough to know you will do it. And you think I'm cussedly stubborn." Resigned to the situation, Munsford's reluctance to talk disappeared. "It's just that I'm … I guess, scared. What do you want to know?"

Reginald nodded his head and asked him to begin with the night Mrs. Herrington was killed.

"It was maybe two or three minutes after 8:00 p.m. when I saw headlights on Oak, west of Rock. I was in the bedroom getting ready for bed. I had turned out the lights and could see the lights through the curtains. The car moved slow up to Vine and turned right. I thought no more of it and crawled into bed. Then five minutes later, I heard a muffled sound and got up to look. I didn't see anything at first. Then I saw a man walk across the street and stand there for a few seconds. He came back across Vine Street. A minute or two later, I heard a car start up and go east on Oak and saw it turn left on Rock. I went back to bed and didn't see anything else until your cops showed up."

"Do you know what made the sound?"

"No. I just heard the noise is all."

"What kind of a car was it?"

"I don't know. All I could see was that it was a big dark colored car. Come to think of it, the car didn't have any lights on when it went east on Oak."

"Could you see if the right front fender was damaged?"

"I never noticed. It was too dark," Munsford snapped. He looked at the ceiling and then at Reginald. "Now that I think about it, the fender wasn't damaged. It looked normal."

"Can you tell me what the man you saw looked like?"

Walter Munsford squinted up his eyes as if he was trying to squeeze something out and looked at the ceiling. Silence hung heavy in the air for what seemed like minutes. Then his shaky voice interrupted the quietness of the room. "All I know is that he was a medium built man. He had on dark clothes and walked with a limp."

Reginald looked up from his note taking when he heard him say limp. "Did you say limp?"

"That's what I said. His right leg it looked like near as I could tell."

"You are sure it was his right leg?"

"Yes, I'm sure. I know a limp when I see one," he said with irritation rising again. He calmed and sat quietly watching Reginald.

Reginald waited and then asked, "And you can't tell me anything else?"

"What do you mean?"

"Did you see lights or a hear noise?"

"Come to think of it, the street lights were out, still are, and the security light behind Matilda's house has been out for several weeks. I reckon that is why no one saw anything. It was too dark."

"And you didn't hear anything?"

"I told you I didn't until your boys began making noise out there."

After some more questions, Reginald was satisfied he had gotten all he could from him about the night of the homicide and turned to the burglaries.

"Now let's discuss tonight. What did you first see or hear?"

Walter Munsford had begun to shake and could barely talk. He looked at Reginald with quivering lips and said, "I didn't see anything but heard a noise like some chipping or hacking on wood." He stopped and his lips quivered again.

"Where were you when you heard the noise?"

Through quivering lips he said, "I was in the kitchen getting a drink of water. I don't sleep well sometimes and getting up to get a drink and walking around for a few minutes helps. But I didn't see anything. I just heard it."

"How long did the noise last?"

Walter thought for a few moments and then said, "Maybe two minutes." He hesitated and then, "Oh, I don't know. I didn't look at the clock. It quit and when I didn't hear it again, I went back into the living room."

"Where do you think the noise was coming from?"

"I guess it was next door at Mrs. Hancock's house. I knew she was gone, and I knew whatever it was making the noise wasn't good."

"And you didn't go out to look around?"

"No, I'm an old man and I don't take chances. What luck would I have with someone? I mind my own business."

Reginald almost laughed at that one since he knew Munsford minded everyone's business as well as his own, and he just barely managed to keep a straight face. "You said you went to the living room." Walter nodded his head in agreement. "Then what did you do?"

"I looked out the window and saw a man walk across the street.

He went through the shadows and kept behind the bushes. He went up on Mrs. Sheldon's porch and began monkeying around with the door. I couldn't see what he was doing. It was too dark." He became silent again.

Reginald could hear his ragged breathing and then asked, "What did you see next?"

"Well ... all of a sudden the man acted like something happened."

"What do you mean?"

"He moved back a couple of steps and shook his left hand. He bent down; must have picked something up and then walked across Vine here, and that's last I saw or heard. Never did see or hear a car like the last time."

"What do you think happened to make him move back away from the door?"

"It looked like he hurt himself."

"What makes you say that?"

"That's what I saw and that's the way it looked to me."

"Did you see what he picked up?"

"No, it was too dark. I did well to see what I saw. My eyes ain't spotlights."

"Can you describe him?"

"I would say it was the same man I saw the night of the murder, limp, and all. That's all I know, and now are you done?"

"Now, a couple more things about what you saw. What time did you see the man at Mrs. Sheldon's house?"

"I don't know. Twenty-five minutes or so until two I guess. I didn't think much about the time."

What time did you call the police department?"

"I guess maybe twenty minutes or more later."

"What time did you see the man on the porch across the street leave?"

"Close to quarter till two, I guess. Probably it was before that."

"So you waited all that time to call after you first heard the noises and saw him across the street. Can you explain that to me?"

"I figured it was none of my business and then later decided you should know. I ain't the nosy type."

Reginald dwelled on Munsford's last words for a few seconds while he worked to suppress a laugh and said, "Now you need to call your son and go stay with him until I call you that it's okay to come home. Get your bags packed with whatever you need for a few days, such as medicine and other things. You're going with me to the station and you can call him from there." Munsford tried to protest and Reginald said, "Look, your neighbor is dead, two houses had attempted forced entry, and if those two ladies had been there, one of them would be dead, maybe both. Now do you want to be the third victim on this block?"

"No," Walter said quietly.

The son picked up his father at 9:00 a.m. and left for Batesville by going to Shirley first, left to Greers Ferry, and then left again to Drasco. It was the long way around, but Reginald wanted him to take no chances that the perp would find out where Mr. Munsford was going, if the perp was watching for an opening to kill again.

•

Thomas Dawson was notified and did the searches on the two crime scenes. Reginald went home, showered, and called Sherry. He picked her up and they went to church and then out to eat. They discussed parts of the case and what Sherry could do to help the investigation. He dropped her off and went home. He hoped that the rest of the day would be quiet so he could relax knowing that the following week was going to be hectic. Whoever was prowling the town had to be caught and it would take all the effort they could give. He fell asleep with that thought on his mind.

When the alarm clock sounded, Reginald looked at the time. It was 5:30 a.m. He yawned. He scratched and yawned some more. His feet hit the floor as he tried to stretch the weariness from his body. He had to be in Little Rock to pick up Callman at 11:00 a.m., but before that, he needed to see L.P. Wellman. The headache had returned and Wellman might be able to help it go away. He just thought that Wellman had some more answers, but Wellman didn't know it yet.

Reginald drove to the station to pick up his detective car, told Mazy Sink where he was going, and that he needed to have a meeting with the Chief, Sheriff Dawson, and Sherry when he returned. Mazy told him Bert had checked the line trace. It showed the perp's call at 1:48 a.m. had been made from a pay phone on East Main, which didn't surprise Reginald. He told Mazy he would phone ahead when he was an hour out. He hoped to have some answers to many questions when he returned.

Chapter

TWELVE

Sherry arrived at the bank on Monday morning at nine o'clock. She had been promoted to the commercial loan and real estate section so that she could have more time for police work. She now had the freedom to show up for work late when necessary, and the work outside with loans and real estate gave her the opportunity for investigations when needed. For all intents and purposes and as far as the public knew, she no longer worked for the state police and was simply a reserve part time county deputy. Through some account manipulations, her pay came from the state, but she was always paid with a check from the bank. She was a banker and county deputy and that was all anyone really needed to know.

Before leaving home to go to the bank, Sherry called Mountain Home P.D. to make an appointment to see the officer that had worked the fire at the address that was on the checking account of J. Daniel Bushman. He was on duty and would be expecting her around 10:30 a.m. Next, she called the Searcy, Arkansas, Police Department, to ask if there were any accidents between 10:00 a.m. and 3:00 p.m. on the previous Friday involving a blue 1989 Ford. She was put on hold and when the clerk came back, she said that there had been an accident that day at 11:00 a.m. involving a blue Ford sedan and a pickup on the northeast corner of the town square. Sherry told the clerk that she would be there Tuesday morning to get a copy of the report and that she wanted to talk to the officer that worked the accident. As she hung up she said, "Bingo," to herself. She knew the perp was making mistakes now and she hoped that he had made a big one last Friday.

Sherry drove over to the bank and parked in her reserved space near the back door. She reached over and picked up her briefcase and walked toward the employee entrance. A motion in the corner of her right eye caught her attention. She instinctively wanted to look but fought off the urge. Instead, she set her briefcase down and began fumbling in her purse for the key to the door. She stood and acted like she was stumped, but she didn't look at the car where she had seen the movement. She returned to her car to make it look like she was looking for the keys. When she exited the car with keys in her hand, she peeked in the direction of the car that had caught her attention. As she closed the car door, she made sure that the man who was watching saw the keys when she walked back to the door. She hoped his seeing the keys would make him believe that she had forgotten them. The car backed out and left the lot. It was a tan 1995 Ford Crown Victoria. The front plate was covered with mud. She had wanted to confront the man, but she knew it could be a foolish move at this point. Besides, he hadn't done anything illegal that she could determine, and further more a hunch told her that the subject wasn't the one they wanted for the homicides.

She entered the bank and nearly ran into a man crossing the lobby while hurrying to her Uncle Merton's office to talk to him. She told him that she was sure the driver of the car had taken her picture. To make it worse, Reginald, Darrell, and Thomas were out of town and couldn't help if she needed them. In the privacy of her office, she removed her .38 Chiefs Special from her purse, checked it out of habit to make sure it was fully loaded, and left for Mountain Home with the wariness of a hunted lioness.

The detective who handled the fire deaths was Dawson Langley. After the usual greetings, he told Sherry that the two men who died in the fire were business partners who had owned Sky High Scaffold Company in Little Rock.

Sherry listened intently to Detective Langley as he thumbed

through the case file folder. When she began asking questions, Langley thumbed some more pages and said, "What else do you want to know?"

"Who owned the company?"

"The owners were Bud Borders and Carl Alstrom."

"What were the two men doing in the house that day and who owned it?"

"They owned the house. A church here in town built a new building, and Sky High furnished the scaffolding. The congregation had a split and that left the contractor and his suppliers in a tight spot financially. Borders and Alstrom, as I understand it, agreed to take the house as payment for the rent on the scaffolding and the other services they supplied.

"So it appears they were inspecting their property that day."

"That's what it looks like. I think they were getting ready to sell it."

"What caused the fire?"

Langley looked through the file again and after a brief silence he said, "Cause is undetermined. A neighbor heard an explosion and the next thing he knew the house was engulfed in flames. They were found by the water heater. The fire department thinks that from what little evidence could be gathered that the water heater malfunctioned and the gas ignited. We know they were in the utility room and might have been checking the heater when it went off. I tell you, there was nothing left of that house. It was old, dry, and rotted, and it went up like kindling in a wood stove."

"Was there anyone else there that day and or anyone else around that could have seen it?"

"A couple of neighbors who heard the explosion, one now dead and the other in a nursing home with Alzheimer's disease, said that there were three, maybe four men there before the fire, not counting the two that died, but they figured that they were buyers since they all walked around outside looking at the house. The file notes indicate that two of the men climbed up onto the roof, so that was probably the case. We asked through the radio and newspapers for information and three men who were there contacted us as soon as they heard our request for information. One was a local contractor and the other two were from Midway looking for investment property. The three thought there was one more with the two that died, but they couldn't be sure since a few people from the neighborhood stopped by to talk and a couple of them went into the house. Four of those who stopped by responded to our request, but they didn't know or remember anything about the men and couldn't tell us how many were there. One even admitted to being nosy. No one could remember definitely how many might have been there and the neighbors said they might have mistakenly counted one man twice before the onlookers showed up. That's really all we know and as for the fourth man, if he exists, I don't know who he could have been." Langley looked out the window of his office.

Sherry reviewed her notes and considered the implications of the possible fourth man before speaking. "You say they wanted to sell the house?"

"That's correct. During the investigation, I learned that they were in a financial bind. They had been sued for several million dollars after a scaffold collapsed at a job in Little Rock. Several workers were hurt and three people killed. The insurance didn't cover all the damages and they were trying to scrape up some money. We at first thought the house was an insurance burn that went bad for them, but it wasn't insured. After they took possession they never put insurance on it, so that angle washed out."

"What happened to the company after they died?"

"It went belly up and disappeared with mountains of debt left behind. With nothing else to go on, we closed the case."

"Detective Langley, are you sure it was Borders and Alstrom who died?"

"We are as sure as we can be. Their truck was there after the fire and they were never seen again by anyone. We didn't have any reason to think differently." Langley looked at Sherry, obviously puzzled by the question. "What makes you doubt their identity?"

Sherry looked out the window for a minute or two and then said, "It's not that I doubt their identity, but there are some peculiar events connected to that fire that have taken place, and one that gnaws at me is why a customer at the Mountain Home Bank would keep a vacant lot for an address after the house burned."

Detective Langley looked up startled. "He did what? Kept that lot for an address on a bank account with no house there?"

"That's what Sam Hazelton, the bank president, told Sgt. Gawker when he was up here a few days ago."

After Sherry told Langley the other particulars of the case, he began shuffling through the case file, looking at the notes and the interviews. He started to close the file when suddenly he said, "Wait a minute." He read from a page of notes and then turned to Sherry, "I knew there was something else. The lady who heard the explosion said there were two trucks that looked alike. One she knew was the scaffold company truck that we found at the scene as I said, and the other she saw only briefly and never got a good look at it. And she didn't know when it left or how long before the fire, that she saw it. We know it didn't belong to the three men that were there that day. Again, we don't know anything else. But maybe there were four men there after all, but we never found the truck or anyone else who saw it."

Sherry thanked the detective for his help and the copies of the case file. There wasn't much to go on, but it would help, maybe. She went to the bank and didn't learn anything more from the account, except that deposits by mail with the false Searcy return address had been arriving regularly. The postmaster wasn't of any further help either due to the postal laws. She would have to contact the postal inspector if she needed anything more. It was late when she drove into Mountain View. She wondered when Reginald would get back and if he had learned anything from Callman. She showered and fixed an early supper. She was eating when the phone rang.

When she answered, Darrell Cumberland said over the speaker phone, "Sherry, we have a big problem."

Taken by surprise at his words she said somewhat startled, "Problem?"

"Yes, a problem. The newspaper wants the full story and the town is in an uproar. The *Democrat-Gazette* reporters have been snooping around. All the TV channels from Little Rock have satellite trucks and other equipment here. The media are all we need to make a mess of the investigation. But the one thing they don't know is that link up. You know which one I mean."

"I know, and as long as we can keep them from finding out we have a good chance of finding the killer. If they find out then the perp will know he messed up. Has Reg gotten back?"

"He got back a little while ago, but he's gone now."

"Gone?"

"Gone as in went to a safe place with Callman. When I told him the mess the news nosy types can make, we decided that the last thing we needed was for them to try to question Callman. When Reginald told Callman what we found out, Reginald said Callman started shaking. He didn't want to talk to anyone and couldn't get to a hiding place fast enough."

"Where did he take him?"

"I'll tell where when I see you. Right now I don't even trust the phone company."

"Gotcha," she said, and they both laughed to break the tension.

"Did Reg find out anything?"

"I don't know at this point since he left before we could talk."

"Did you find out anything?"

"Yes, a few things and all of us need to meet as soon as possible. I'll arrange it with Thomas and let you and Reginald know the date and time." They hung up.

THIRTEEN

That morning, an hour after Sherry had left town for Mountain Home, a hippie looking type drove into town in an old Chevy pickup and slowly made his way along Brewer Street going toward Main. The truck was rusty and banged up, badly in need of body work and paint redo. On second thought, paint couldn't hold that rust bucket together. The license plate was dangling down from one corner, fastened with a piece of baling wire to a badly bent bracket. The bed was filled with what looked like a tent and camping supplies. The driver had a beard and wore a floppy felt hat pulled low over his eyes. He wore dirty bib overalls and a short sleeved denim shirt; both he and the clothes looked as if they needed to be run through the local car wash. The whole rig, including the operator, appeared like an environmental disaster looking for a place to happen.

At the same time, a scruffy looking biker on an old Harley chopper moved slowly past the square going west on Main. The rider was lean, middle age, and wore heavy black motorcycle boots. The studded denim shirt had no sleeves. The edges of the shirt were ragged where the sleeves had been ripped off. A big tattoo of a rose was on the left forearm of the rider. His long hair and matted looking beard were dirty. A good scrubbing in the car wash would have helped his appearance as well.

No one was paying any attention to the biker except Officer Jack Pearson who was observing traffic from his partially hidden vantage point at the intersection of Franklin and Main. Suddenly the biker revved his engine and took off with an ear shattering roar of the exhaust pipes. As the bike sped west with Officer Pearson in pursuit, the old Chevy pickup driven by the hippie ran the stop sign at Brewer and Main and turned right. Officer Larry Phillips, who was headed east on Main, flipped on the reds and blues and curbed the truck. Officer Pearson pulled the biker over at the west edge of town. Soon the biker was in handcuffs, seated in the back seat of the police car. The hippie driver of the Chevy truck faired no better. He too was handcuffed after some words with Officer Phillips and a brief scuffle. Both were transported to the county jail and taken to the interrogation room and released from the handcuffs.

Sheriff Thomas Dawson entered the room. He looked at the two men and said, "You boys are in a fix now." All three of them laughed and then shook hands. He turned to Darcy Broadway, the hippie looking subject and said, "If you smell the way you look, I'm not keeping you in here very long. My budget won't allow me to buy that much air freshener." The deputies in the office could hear the laughter coming through the door. He turned to the biker, Martin Perkins, and said, "Martin, where did you get that Harley? That is one real slick bike. It sure is good to see both of you get into town. We have a real problem, and we need your help. Here's what we are going to do now to cover all this. I hope it works."

The sheriff discussed the murder of Mrs. Herrington with them and the attempted break-ins. They also discussed the plan that would be set in motion to keep the town under surveillance. Martin Perkins, aka Bad Biker, and Darcy, now known as Hippie Dude posted bail. A request was entered in the court plea book for a preliminary hearing some day distant. That was done in the unlikely event that someone would become nosy and make an inquiry. Dawson said the town was slowly becoming a multi-ring media circus, which wasn't going to help anything. News people were beginning to crawl around town like the uninvited ants that invade a picnic. "One job for the both of you is avoiding the newspaper and other media people. One whiff of your real identity and all is down the tubes," Thomas told them before they left the lock up.

Bad Biker and Hippie Dude were set free and began to move around the town together acting angry. They talked loudly and let anyone in ear shot know how badly the town clown cops had treated them. No one was remotely interested, but a few older citizens did tell them they should leave and stay gone. They would give them their best ruffian stare and move on. They listened and watched while mingling with the crowd, but soon they split up and tried not to arouse suspicion and attract attention. They were drifting around town pretending to see the sights, but they were looking for two different Fords, a blue 1989 and a tan 1995, both driven by subjects unknown. They both thought that the subjects they were looking for might be driving the cars. It was important to find them with nothing else much to go on at the moment. Also, they wanted to find the man with a limp who Mr. Munsford had seen.

The news reporters and TV people were growing more numerous and were sticking their microphones into the face of any individual who would talk. They found plenty of people who wanted to be in the news and on TV, but they didn't have much to offer except rumor. Hippie Dude and Bad Biker tried to stay away from the TV cameras on the off chance that someone somewhere, when they least expected it, would recognize them. Darcy was aware that a resident might recognize him from his time in the town with the car shop, but the ones he recognized didn't seem to know who he was so he grew less leery of being identified.

Bad Biker wasn't that well known, so if anyone made the connection of his being a former policeman, probably nothing would be thought of it. After all, even cops have a right to look bad, ride choppers, and avoid bathing when they retire.

Darcy was standing on the south side of the square when he heard a voice say, "How did you get out?"

He turned around and saw a nicely dressed lady in faux western style clothes. "Huh, you talkin' to me?" he asked with a slow drawl.

"You heard me. How did you get out? You're the one that the law took in this morning aren't you?"

"Lady, what business is it of yourn'?"

"I saw you try to fight that cop. I'm a witness, and I'm going to tell him what I know."

Darcy tried to walk off, but she grabbed his arm. "Now you listen to me, you smart aleck. If I had my way, you would still be in jail. Don't need your kind in this town." She was talking so loudly that she was attracting attention.

Darcy saw a camera coming and shook his arm loose. He quickly moved into the crowd and headed for Martin. As he walked by he said, "Get out of here. We have a problem." Martin made his way to the edge of the crowd and disappeared west on Washington. Darcy and Martin had been told where the truck and chopper had gone before they left the jail. Darcy worked his way to a parking lot one block south of the square where Henry Porter, Officer Nance Porter's grandfather, had parked the truck. That was where he saw the tan 1995 Ford with Missouri plates, AMK 043, parked nearby. He had the distinct feeling he was being watched and after looking under the tarp covering the bed, he decided to get in his truck and leave, acting as if he had nothing else to do. He heard Martin's chopper over on Brewer going south. He got in his truck and slowly headed east on Main. He drove slowly and as he expected, he saw the tan Ford in the rear view mirror. He went on east and turned right on Highway 5. The Ford continued down Highway 14 and out of town. Through prearrangement, they planned to meet at a spot south of town off Highway 9, and whichever one of them didn't show after thirty minutes, the one waiting would go back into town and hang out at The Burger Joint.

Three miles out of town, Darcy pulled off the highway into a secluded spot and waited. In less than fifteen minutes the tan Ford went past, headed east at a high rate of speed. When the car disappeared over the crest of a hill, Darcy drove back into town and hid his truck in Darrell Cumberland's garage. An old Plymouth two door was waiting for him, and he left with a big grin showing his doughnut chompers. The Plymouth was good cover. Some of the people who lived in Mountain View still drove the 50s, 60s, and 70s cars. They wouldn't take a second look at a nondescript two tone black and rust 1950 Plymouth. He headed for The Burger Joint and took a table where he could watch the street and be partially hidden at the same time.

The tan Ford rolled slowly through the parking lot of the restaurant located on the northwest corner of Main and Sycamore Avenue. The driver circled the building and went west on Main. Darcy was ready to leave when a man who appeared to be a bit older than thirty walked to his table, wearing a Burger Joint shirt with a name tag, Brad Sheldon, Mgr., on it, and said, "Say aren't you D ... "

Darcy cut him off and said, "You're right, Danny Turner."

Sheldon looked confused. "But I thought ... "

"Let's say there have been some changes." Sheldon looked even more confused. The diners at the next table kept looking and one lady frowned, exhibiting obvious displeasure. Maybe Darcy's loud talking or appearance or both irritated her. At this point, he wasn't in the mood to find out her problem and continued to ignore her. She continued to stare and when she left her table, she walked toward him. He suspected from the way she looked at him she was going to make an unwanted scene. Instead, she threw a sneer in his direction and left the store. He made small talk to keep Brad from talking until the diners left. Much to his relief, the room soon emptied of customers.

"Brad, I don't have a lot of time so you listen. First, you don't know me, haven't heard of me, and haven't ever seen me in case anyone asks you. Second, your mother is okay. She's with your sister and all is well. Don't tell anyone where she is no matter what. If anyone calls you and says anything, don't believe it. I'll be the one who calls and will tell you it is Lauren and you are the only one who knows the name Lauren. If your sister calls you, get in contact with us immediately because she isn't supposed to call you for any reason. If by some chance I am forced to call you, I'll tell you it is Danny instead of Lauren. That means that things aren't well. You got all of it?"

Brad shook his head that he did and said, "Do you know who it is yet?"

"No, but we have some clues. Now take off that badge and keep it off."

"D ... uh ... Danny, I can't. We have to wear it."

Darcy reached over and tugged on it and said, "Take it off. If the man we're looking for comes in here and sees that badge he might tumble to who you are ... "

"Do you think he's still in town?"

"Yes, we think he's still here, but we don't know his identity yet."

"But I can't work without the name badge," Brad protested again. "I'll get fired."

"Brad." Darcy said it with enough force Brad gulped. "Listen to me. I'll call your boss. I know him, and he will go along with it when I tell him the reason for it."

"What will I tell the employees when I show up without it?"

"Tell them you lost it."

"I can't lie," he protested.

"Brad, I am going to be blunt. You lie to them about the tag or maybe die, if that man finds you. Now make up your mind. Which will it be?"

Brad swallowed hard. He stammered and then looked around the store. He unpinned the badge, handed it to Darcy, got up and walked off. He grabbed his coat and left in a huff. Darcy hoped he would remember what he was told to do if or when push came to shove. None of it would probably be necessary, but it was better to be prepared than not, he reasoned.

•

Martin drove into and out of the lot. Darcy got up and went to the Plymouth. Twenty minutes later, they were sitting in Darrell Cumberland's living room. The motorcycle was hidden in the shed out back and the Plymouth was parked where Darcy had found it.

Darrell lived in a well kept house filled with antique furniture. Lacy curtains covered the windows and dark green floral design drapes hung in neatly arranged pleats on the sides of each window. A matching valance completed the look. Landscape paintings of familiar scenes around Stone County were on the walls. White glass lamps with brass trim adorned beautiful period end tables that matched the overstuffed claw foot divan and chairs. Elegant and comfortable were the words that ran through Martin's mind.

The phone rang and Darrell answered. It was Reginald back from taking Callman out of town. He was calling from Sherry's house. He said they would ride over with Thomas and would be there in thirty minutes.

As Darrell hung up the phone he said, "Darcy, look out front." Darcy looked and saw a tan 1995 Ford roll slowly past the house. It was the same one that had been seen the last few days driving around town. Darrell said, "This guy is really getting to me. We don't know who he is or what he's doing. The plate is registered to a blue 1989 Ford but it's on that '95. A blue Ford followed Sherry and Merton last Friday. If this is the guy we are looking for, then why is he advertising to us? It doesn't make sense. And there isn't enough evidence yet to bring him in."

Martin Perkins said, "Maybe he's a nut that has stripped threads."

"Could be," Darcy said, "but whoever he is, he's the same bird that followed me today and drove through The Burger Joint."

Darrell said, "I'll have another 10–28 run on that car tomorrow to make sure the plate belongs on another car. Sometimes DMV doesn't have the correct information."

Footsteps were heard on the porch and then a knock. "Come in with your hands up. Whoever has the pizza doesn't have to reach," Darrell said with mock seriousness.

Thomas Dawson entered carrying four large pizzas and a briefcase. Sherry and Reginald had their hands held high. Dawson looked at Darcy and Martin and said, "Hey, look at who's here. Our two jail birds. Hope you fellas enjoyed the hospitality. Sorry, you bailed out before we served supper. Now you have to eat this hot pizza."

Everyone groaned and dove for the pizza and drinks. Laughter and fun were the dessert. Then when the pizza had disappeared, the group grew somber as the reality of why they were meeting returned. The serious looks etched the worry lines deeper and magnified the strain showing on their faces. They were very concerned that another event would happen and drive the people of the town deeper into the type of fear that already gripped the town. There were enough problems with the unknown killer without having to deal with a town filled with fright.

FOURTEEN

Darrell turned to the Sheriff and asked, "How did you escape the news hounds when you drove over here, Thomas?"

"Sarah drove off and I slipped out the back door, went through the trees, and she picked me up on the other side of the woods. Four reporters are camped out in front of my house sitting in two TV vans thinking I'm still there, waiting to ambush me. She dropped me off at Sally's house, picked up Sherry and Reginald, returned with them to Sally's, and I drove Sally's old van over here. The news people don't know me in another car and out of uniform. The hounds haven't figured out Sherry's role and haven't noticed Reginald's truck yet. So far so good, but how long we can hold them off is anybody's guess."

"A lot of people from the bigger places think we're dumb. Matter of fact, a few of the people in this town thinks we are dumb. Whoever we're after also has us on the dumb list or at least, it appears that he does. You might say that at times dumb does have its reward, and I think we are on the right track to find who he is and why he's killing people," Reginald said.

"Reginald, what did you find out in Little Rock when you talked to Callman?" Darrell asked.

"First, I'll begin with L.P. After talking to him, I think we have a real squirrel on our hands. When I told him that we think an ice pick was used to puncture the tires on Mr. Blandford's car he nearly jumped out of his chair."

"Don't tell me there is a connection with the Little Rock slaying to Blandford and Mrs. Herrington," Thomas said.

"There seems to be, but what we don't know yet. And if that object that was found on Mrs. Sheldon's front porch is a broken ice pick handle then we have another connection, but why her is the question. I think we'll find the answer to that one too before we're finished."

"Maybe," Thomas said, "when the results on the stuff I found at her house come back from the lab. I had it carried down yesterday by a deputy. When he returned he said they promised some preliminary results by Friday."

"Why was Wellman interested in the ice pick angle?" Martin asked.

"L.P. called in the lead detective of the group that is working the McGee homicide. He told me that when they moved the patrol car that an ice pick was found lying in the street where the right rear wheel had been."

"You mean it was under the car?" Darcy exclaimed incredulously.

"That's where it was lying. They don't know how it got there or why, but they think whoever shot Officer McGee had it."

"Why would the guy have an ice pick?" Darcy asked.

"They aren't sure, but they think the perp walked up to the car and was going to stab Officer McGee with it for whatever reason best known to the attacker."

"What makes them think that?" Sherry asked.

Reginald opened the briefcase and took out some photos. He handed them to Sherry and said, "There are marks on the driver's door. You can see them in the photo where the dust on the lower part of the door is smudged. There is also a small dent that the photo doesn't show."

Sherry looked at them and handed the pictures to Darcy. "So would it be safe to say that McGee saw the ice pick, tried to open the door, and the perp dropped it? Then he shot McGee instead," she said.

Reginald grinned and said, "You would make a good detective," and everyone laughed. "That is precisely what they think."

"Why didn't McGee draw his weapon?" Darcy asked.

"They think because McGee was left handed and with the assailant against the door, he couldn't draw his firearm. That gave the shooter enough of an advantage to get his gun out and shoot the officer."

"How big was Officer McGee?" Darrell asked.

Reginald looked through the case file copies and said, "He was 5'11," 225 pounds according to his personnel file. If the perp was that size or bigger, it would have been a match. Bad position to be in for anyone."

"What caused the dent in the door? Maybe the dent was in it when he started his shift," Martin said.

"They don't think so for several reasons. The car is new. It went in service two days before and the dent wasn't seen at inspection that morning. But mainly, they said the dent corresponds to the smudged area."

"So they think it might have been caused by the door hitting the perp," Darrell concluded.

Reginald leafed through the notes and then looked up surprised. "One detective on the case thinks the dent was caused by the door hitting the perp's knee, possibly the right knee from the position of the dent on the door, right of the middle vertically, and knee high toward the right edge of the door."

Suddenly Sherry said, "Limper. The guy Walter Munsford saw the night Mrs. Herrington was killed."

"You may be right, and I may have seen him on Saturday coming out of the restaurant that morning."

Everyone looked at Reginald and said in unison, "You did?"

He continued. "I went into the cafe to question the waitress. She said Mrs. Herrington ate her evening meal there, and I wanted to find out if the waitress saw anyone in there that evening she considered suspicious looking. As I was going in right before noon, a man, 5' 10" to 5' 11" and maybe 250 pounds, came out. He had a neatly trimmed short beard and was wearing a green cap of some kind. I held the door for him and watched him walk away. He had a slight limp in his right leg."

Sherry said, "Maybe we are getting somewhere with who this guy is. He might be the one that the door could have hit." She twisted up her face, wrinkled her nose, and then said, "The guy that I am sure snapped my picture this morning had a beard and was wearing a green cap and was driving a tan 1995 Ford. Unfortunately, I couldn't see the front license number. Mud covered most of the plate, but what little color I could see makes me think the car has a Missouri license plate."

"That fits the description of the car that I saw go past the car wash and more than likely the same subject who called me and said that it wouldn't do any good to run the plate. I am going to check that plate again tomorrow," Reginald said. "Wish you could have seen a plate number."

"Is that all Wellman had to say?" Darrell asked.

"They know nothing else, but they're still working on some leads. They have to wait on the postal worker that picked up the mail in the box that morning to return to work. He's gone on extended time off and won't be back until next week. They want to see if he remembers anything unusual being in the drop box that day. It's a long shot, but you never know until you try all angles."

Thomas, who had been silent said, "This case has more twists and turns than a snake crawling through the rocks in my backyard. It's the worst one I have ever seen."

Reginald nodded his head in agreement with Thomas. "When you hear the rest of what I've learned, I think everyone will agree with you that it is the worst case we have ever had, and more than likely, the worst evil we have ever seen or ever will see." He hesitated and looked at Darrell and then said, "I just remembered. Where's Mattie?"

"Oh, she's next door with June Prather. They're working with other ladies on plans for a church party of some kind. She said she didn't want to be here with the jail birds." Darrel looked at Darcy and Martin when he said it. They laughed and hooted.

"Smart lady," Darcy said. "Never know what uncouth ruffians might do. They might try to heist a big box of doughnuts."

More laughter filled the room, and when it died down, they heard an engine noise outside. Darrell got up to look and saw a TV truck with a Little Rock channel number on it sitting in the street. "Trouble coming up the walk," he said. "Go into the dining room." There were footsteps on the porch and then a knock on the door. Fortunately, the blinds and drapes were closed and before Darrell answered the door, the others slipped quietly into the room, which couldn't be seen from the open front door. Darrell quickly picked up a book and used his left index finger for a place marker. He opened the door and stood face to face with a reporter and a camera man.

The reporter said, "Good evening sir, are you the Chief of Police?"

"Yes."

The reporter, not expecting such a short reply, was unsure about what to ask with such a big man silently staring down at him. He stammered and fumbled for words. "Well … I was wondering … if … uh … uh … who … " Intimidated by Darrell's size and cold gaze, he had trouble thinking of what to ask next. "I … what … who owns that Dodge van?" he finally asked, pointing to Sally's mini van. "I haven't seen it here before."

"Why do you want to know?"

"Well, we have been checking all over, town and I thought maybe you were having a meeting discussing the murder case and that you could give us something for the news," the reporter said breathlessly.

Darrell noticed that the camera hadn't been turned on and waved the book at the reporter. He said, "Does this look like I'm in a meeting?" and showed him the book, *The Firm*, by John Grisham.

"No sir, but I asked who owns the van," again pointing to Sally's vehicle.

"Mister, it really isn't any of your business, but to keep the record straight, it belongs to a friend of my wife. My wife is working on some business for the church. Now if you will excuse me, I have other things to do." Darrell began closing the door.

The reporter stuck out his arm and placed his hand on the door in an attempt to keep it from closing. "I just want to ask a few questions. There has been a murder, and I want answers from you."

"The answer is no. There will be a statement at noon tomorrow for the public. You can find out at the meeting whatever will be said. Now get your hand off the door. Good evening."

"Well, I think there is something going on here, and we will just stay until we find out," the reporter said belligerently. "I have my rights."

Darrell stepped out onto the porch, forcing the man to back away from the door. "Son, the only thing going on here at the moment is me talking to you. The next thing going on will be you going to jail if you don't get off my property. I have rights, too. Now get in that truck and leave."

The reporter bristled up to his full height, which still wasn't a match for Darrell Cumberland's stature, and said, "Well, I'm a reporter and as I just said, I have rights and I will stay parked in front of this house until we learn something. I don't guess you have heard of the First Amendment. It guarantees free speech and the press in case you need a refresher."

Darrell's patience had reached its limit. "I am very well aware of the First Amendment, free speech and the press, and I just exercised the first part of it when I told you to leave." He stepped back into the house and made a phone call. Five minutes later Nance Porter arrived in a patrol unit. He hurried to the porch and said, "Chief, what do you need?" The reporter and camera man eyed him warily as several neighbors stood back and watched.

"Officer Porter, this reporter was told to get off my property. He said he would sit out there in the truck until he found out what was going on here. If he doesn't get in that truck and drive off, you are to arrest him for trespassing, and have the truck towed for blocking the street."

The camera man retreated to the truck. The reporter stared at Darrell and said, "You can't get by with this. In Little Rock … " and with that Darrel cut him off.

"Officer Porter, call the tow truck and then place this gentleman under arrest when you finish the call. He needs to understand this isn't Little Rock, and he will obey the law here. This is Mountain View and not Little Rock in case you haven't noticed," Darrell said, addressing the reporter. "No one blocks the street, newsman, or no newsman. You show me the state law that gives you the right to block the street or disobey a direct and lawful order, and you can leave that truck there." The reporter only glared back.

Nance Porter returned to the patrol car and before he could open the door, the reporter went to the truck, slammed the door, and roared off. Nance came back and said, "Do you want me to hang around just in case one of them returns?"

"No, but keep your eye peeled in case one of them tries to sneak back. I sure am glad he didn't call the rest of those news hounds. I think he was a rookie the way he acted. All bark and no bite"

"Okay, I'll keep watch." Nance left and the neighbors disappeared.

Darrell went inside and said, "Y'all can come out of hiding now," and laughed. The fugitives from the news trooped back into the living room and sat down. "Where were we when that Farkleberry news hound arrived? As if we don't have enough problems, and now we have to put up with them. I hope that encounter doesn't make the news," Darrell said, exasperation evident in his voice.

"Reg, you were getting ready to tell us how your interview with Callman went. Reg, are you all right?" Sherry repeated.

"Oh, yeah right. I was thinking. Where was I? Oh yeah. I picked Callman up, and we started back. He said he had been in Little Rock a few times to make sales calls. The company he worked for, Jaxco, in Ohio, made and distributed cleaning chemicals of all kinds used in the process of manufacturing and the maintenance of industrial buildings. If it was a cleaner of some kind, they probably made it or sold it. I asked him where he sold his products in Little Rock. He named a few places, and I asked him what the companies did or made. They were mostly small companies and then he mentioned that his biggest customer in town went out of business near the time he retired. Became involved in a law suit and he had to testify about the chemicals he sold them."

"What was the nature of the suit filed?" Thomas asked.

"A scaffold collapsed that had been set up against the building so that the bricks could be replaced, cleaned, and sealed. Three people were killed, a mother and her two children. She and the kids were in a car waiting nearby for their daddy, Marion Easterly. It was crushed. They were killed instantly." Grimaces crossed all the faces.

"Sky High Scaffold Company," Sherry said.

Reginald yanked his head from his notes and said, "How do you know that?"

Sherry then related the facts as she knew them involving Sky High Scaffold and the deaths of the owners, Bud Borders and Carl Alstrom. "I wonder if any of this ties into this case. But what would be the connection if it does?"

"It sure sounds like too many ends to connect to make something work," Darcy said.

"Sounds like it," Martin chimed in. "It sure would be nice to know who we're looking for. Looking for him is like looking for a needle in a haystack. We just have to find him. But what is the connection? Did Callman ever work at the business that went under?"

Reginald looked in his notes. "No, but he did know the guy, Marion Easterly, whose family was killed. He first met him at an equipment convention and then talked to him a few times at the trial. Other than Easterly, he didn't really know the others except through brief sale calls when he talked with the purchasing agent and another employee when needed relative to the products he sold."

"Could the widower be the one we are after?" Darrel asked.

"I don't see how."

"Why do you say that?" Darcy asked.

"After Callman retired and the trial was over, the widower dropped by the house where Callman was living in Indiana with his cousin. He said he had gotten a good sized settlement from the insurance company and had left town after the company went broke. Then one day while roaming around the country in his motor home, after the cousin died, he went through Little Rock and stopped in to see a friend. He learned from the friend that Easterly had been found dead somewhere."

"Did he know where?" Sherry asked.

"He thinks somewhere in Illinois but doesn't know for sure. He said he would call his friend and maybe he could track it down."

"What caused his death?" Thomas asked.

"He thinks he burned up in his car, but he doesn't know the particulars. The friend told Callman that Easterly had taken to drinking pretty hard after his family was killed."

"When did the family get killed?" Martin asked.

"Sometime in 1990 before Callman retired in 1991. The trial was in 1992."

"When did Easterly visit Callman in Indiana?" Martin asked again.

Reginald looked in his notes and said, "October of 1994. He remembers that because as soon as the weather began to cool off, he left on a trip south in his motor home. He learned of Easterly's death, as I said previously, when he stopped in Little Rock last year on his way back north."

"Did he remember the year he died?" Thomas asked.

"He thinks it was the summer of '95, maybe June. Callman never saw him again after October of 1994."

"Borders and Alstrom died September 10, 1995. That eliminates Easterly as a suspect if he's dead. I was thinking it had to be him," Sherry said. "Still ... "

"You're not sure he's dead?" Reginald said.

"I can't say what I'm sure of at this point. Detective Langley is sure Alstrom and Borders died in that fire, but there were more people there that day than can be located.

Darcy looked at Reginald for a long instant and Reginald said, "What?"

"Reggie, what was the main business of the company Easterly worked for?"

"Callman said they made refrigeration equipment, and on the side they had a crushed ice delivery business for vending machines."

"What did Marion Easterly do there?" Darcy wanted to know.

"Callman wasn't sure, but said he could find out. While he's holed up he's going to make some calls to see what he can learn."

"After getting shot he no doubt wants this guy caught as much as we do," Darrel said.

"He said that but not in the same words. I won't repeat what he told me," Reginald said laughing.

"How did Easterly know Callman had the shack in Indiana?"

"Callman told him where it was and invited him to stop in if he was ever up that way. So he did."

It was well past 11:00 p.m. when the meeting was over. They laid out plans for the next few days, detailing who was going where to do what. No TV trucks were in sight so they scattered. Darcy and Martin stayed with Darrell for the night. They appreciated the Cumberlands' hospitality and enjoyed the great breakfast Mattie laid before them the next morning.

Early Tuesday morning Sherry left for Searcy to pick up a copy of the accident report for the blue 1989 Ford. She also planned to interview the officer that investigated the accident. She was glad to be gone since the news people had multiplied during the night. They were crawling around town like fleas on a homeless dog, but she had been able to avoid them. She wanted to keep it that way.

Reginald was headed to Ava, Missouri, to track down Henry Bottoms in an attempt to find out the circumstances of the plate on the 1995 Ford. He had run another check and the Missouri DMV again said it was supposed to be on a 1989 Ford. He hoped the trip would help clear up some of the loose ends. He also wanted to stop and see Sam Hazelton at the Mountain Home Bank. He had an idea that might work to identify the mystery account holder.

•

Both Darcy and Martin had special details and would carry them out as the circumstances during the day gave them opportunity. The thinking was that the perp, if he was still in town and saw them, wouldn't suspect that they were undercover cops. Everyone thought the two were low life thugs, so they cultivated that image wherever they went around town. They hoped they didn't run into the indignant lady again who told them to get out of town. And the news people were an ever present danger to them.

Darcy went to the Home Cookin Cafe for mid-morning coffee. He lumbered through the door and took a seat at a table near the back. He surveyed the room and smiled at what he saw. The walls of the room were covered with a floral design paper that showed its age. The lights were a mixture of fluorescent and incandescent, both struggling to ward off the gloom and darkness of the interior. He didn't know whether it was from dirt on the lamps or low wattage. Maybe both he decided. The counter top showed years of wear and some of the counter stool covers were ripped. Overall, he decided the best description of the place was dingy. He hoped the food and coffee were better than the place appeared. One other customer, a nondescript man sitting near the front windows, slowly sipped on a cup of coffee and took bites from a chocolate covered doughnut. He patted his lips with a napkin and watched Darcy.

Darcy knew that the waitress who had waited on Mrs. Herrington the Friday evening that she was killed was working now. The waitress, who he knew to be Mandy Gettner, came over and Darcy said, "Hi, Mandy," and gave her a big grin.

"How'd you know my name? Do I know you?" She was chomping on a wad of gum so hard Darcy thought his jaws would begin aching if she didn't stop. She didn't.

"Oh, I know lots of things."

"Well, do tell. What do you want?"

"Coffee, black," Darcy replied. She flounced off and came back with a cup but no pot.

"Where's my coffee?" Darcy asked as irritably as he could without sounding phony.

"You sure got an impatient attitude don't cha? It's makin. Now relax." She took off again, and he watched her pick up the pot and walk back to his table. She gave him a smirk and poured the coffee.

"Hey, you don't have to be that way. You're supposed to treat your customers nice," Darcy said.

"I treated you nice. I poured your coffee. What's your problem?"

Mandy studied Darcy for two beats, shaking her head in disapproval. "Man, your attitude is heading you for big trouble."

"I like my attitude just fine and if you don't sit down here and talk to me your attitude is heading you for real big trouble."

"Why would I want to sit with you? You don't look like anyone I want to talk to," she said, getting defensive and backing up from the table. She eyed Darcy warily. "I'll take my chances on my attitude causing me trouble too."

"Why? Because I told you to, that's why. Now come here before your attitude gets you in trouble," he demanded and reached for her arm. "Let's get acquainted."

"You're as acquainted with me as you're going to get. From the way you look, you probably stink."

Darcy glared at her and half-heartedly reached for her arm again when he saw Martin Perkins come through the door. "I said sit down," Darcy said forcefully. With long strides, Martin arrived at the table and said, "Miss, is this creep giving you a problem?"

"Nothing I can't handle," she said. "He can't make me sit down with him."

Darcy got to his feet and tried to grab her as Martin stepped between them. Darcy bristled up and said, "Mister, why don't you go mind your own business? I have business with this lady."

"I could say the same to you, loud mouth. The lady said she didn't want to sit down. Got that? Now leave," and shoved Darcy on the shoulder. The waitress backed up even more waving the coffee pot in the air like a club. Darcy hoped she didn't decide to hit him with it.

The customer near the window left. He went next door and immediately returned. He sat down near the windows again and settled in to watch the show. He ate the last of the doughnut. Darcy continued the shouting and shoving with Martin. The customer had a hard time stifling a laugh.

Three minutes later two patrol cars driven by Officers Larry Phillips and Jack Pearson slid to a stop in front. They burst though the door and Pearson shouted, "Okay, you two. That's enough," and moved toward Darcy and Martin quickly.

"Well would you lookee here? It's Bad Biker and Hippie Dude again. You two are under arrest for disorderly conduct, threatening, and disturbing the peace. Your kind never learns," Officer Phillips said forcefully.

The two officers spun Darcy and Martin around, and after a brief struggle, they were cuffed and lodged in the back seat of separate patrol cars by Officer Pearson. Officer Phillips said to Mandy, "Miss, you need to come to the station to give a statement." Mandy looked at him and started to shake her head no. "You can ride in my car, and I'll bring you back. It will only take thirty minutes, maybe less."

Mandy looked around not sure what to do when the owner, Joe Landers, came through the kitchen door. After he was told what was going on, he looked at Mandy and said, "Go on. I'll handle it until you get back. Are they the same two I saw yesterday walking around town?" Phillips nodded yes. The owner continued, "I knew they were trouble the first time I saw them. We don't need that kind around here. We are decent people. We don't like trash." Larry Phillips left with Mandy in tow.

The customer by the window, Darcy's uncle, Bob Jordan, a police officer in Bowling Green, Kentucky, in town on business and a short visit, got up and left. It all happened so quickly there weren't any other spectators, except those who came up outside to watch the police cars leave after it was over.

Mandy, sitting in the front seat of the patrol car, wasn't sure she needed to be in the police car going with them, but she was glad the two ruffians were under arrest. She was also relieved that she was in the car containing Bad Biker. She wanted nothing to do with Hippie Dude and said so. Bad Biker had a hard time keeping a straight face. Officer Phillips assured her all was under control and that when they arrived at the station she wouldn't see him. Good was all that she said.

Officer Phillips took a detailed statement from Mandy. Finished, he left and Darrell Cumberland came into the room. After he introduced himself Mandy said, "Well what do ya know, the Chief of Police, no less. What do you want? This must be pretty important stuff for the Chief to be here."

Darrell looked at her kindly and said softly, "Since you're here we want to ask you some questions hoping that you can help us with the investigation into the Herrington homicide. We are interested in your Friday evening activities at the restaurant before Mrs. Herrington was killed."

"Now wait a minute. You're not thinking I did it, are you?" Mandy exclaimed, her eyes as big as saucers with fear.

"No, Mandy we aren't. We want to know what you might have seen that evening in the restaurant."

"Like what? All I saw were customers, food, and dirty dishes. I hate dirty dishes. Boy, we get a lot of 'em. Wish I got as many tips as I get dirty dishes. I'd be rich. Now ask your questions. I need to go back to work. That crazy Joe will fire me if I don't. I need the money."

Darrell smiled and asked, "Do you remember Mrs. Herrington being in the restaurant last Friday evening?"

"Sure. She always came in on Friday. Last Friday was no different. She had fried chicken and a piece of banana cake for dessert. She always had that for desert. She left a nice tip as usual. Nice lady. I liked her."

"Yes, she was. Everyone liked her."

"You knew her?"

"I knew her for many years. She was a very fine lady." Darrell paused and looked at Mandy and saw the tears in her eyes. Her belligerent attitude was melting.

She looked at him sadly and said, "Okay, what else do you what to know?"

"What time did she arrive at the restaurant that evening?"

Mandy put her index finger against her cheek, rolled her eyes, pursed her lips, and said, "I'm not sure of the exact time but probably between 4:30 and 5:00. We were real busy as usual on Friday evening.

All Fridays are that way. She always came in early at that time to beat the crowd." Tears rolled down Mandy's cheeks. She dabbed them with a wadded up tissue that she poked back into a dress pocket.

"Mandy," Darrell said, a bit of strain showing in his tone, "did you see any strangers there that night?"

She looked at him wide eyed and said, "Chief, I see strangers all the time. Nearly everybody is a stranger in this town this time of year."

"Good point. Okay. Was there anyone that caught your attention?"

Mandy screwed up her face, blinked her eyes, and chomped on her gum. She said, "Yeah, now that I think back there was someone. There was a guy sitting at a table near the front window. He seemed to be watching something outside, but I don't know what."

"Did he say anything to you?"

"He ordered pie and coffee and that was it."

"Where was Mrs. Herrington?

"She was at a nearby table to his left and as I remember, it was where she always sits."

"Did the man say anything to her?"

"Not that I saw or heard. Of course, I was in the kitchen a lot getting orders. But I'll say he didn't." Mandy had a far away look in her eyes and then closed them and threw her head back. Her eyes opened, and she said, "Now I remember. Mrs. Herrington motioned me over and started to say something. That guy turned and looked at her and when I got to the table, I asked her what she wanted. She said, 'nothing now.' I gave her the check; she got up, went to the register, paid her bill, and left quickly."

"What did the man do?"

Mandy closed her eyes as if she was rewinding her memory. They opened, and she said, "He looked at me and then got up, paid his bill, and left. He left me a two dollar tip for serving him pie and coffee. He didn't finish it. He really gave me the creeps."

"Why did he give you the creeps?

"It was the way he looked. While he was looking through the window, his smile was so cold it would have frozen boiling water. I think he scared Mrs. Herrington."

"What makes you think that?"

"I don't know. That's just what I thought. I think about a lot of stuff. That was one my many thoughts that day." Mandy nervously tugged on the dangling ear ring in her right ear. She brushed her hair away from her eyes.

"Can you give me a description?"

Mandy went into rewind mode again and Darrell could almost see the counter rolling backward. "Yeah," she blurted, "he had a brown shirt, a blue cap, and jeans. His hair stuck out from under the cap. It really looked dorky." Darrell nearly laughed out loud but concealed it, or so he thought.

"I thought it was funny too, Chief," Mandy said. "Dorky is always funny."

Darrel recovered by running his big hand over his face and asked, "How big was he?"

"Oh, the size of that detective you got … uh … Sgt. Gawker. Is that his name?"

"That's his name. Anything else you noticed about the man? It's real important."

Rewind, click, fast forward, rewind, and then, "He limped when he left."

Darrell perked up and said, "Are you sure?"

"Yes. I'm sure. It was his right leg 'cause my granddaddy limps on his right leg."

"Anything else you can remember?"

Rewind, fast forward, click, and nothing registered. She said quietly, "No," and tears flowed again.

Darrell called his sister Sarah, Thomas Dawson's wife, and asked her to take Mandy back to the restaurant. He had checked the area near the restaurant before the sham arrests went down and didn't see anyone that he didn't know, but he didn't want to take any chances.

Sarah hauled people around all the time so he hoped one more trip wouldn't draw interest from anyone, especially whoever they were looking for. Even though the news people knew Sarah's car, he didn't think they would notice, and they hadn't learned of the "fight" at the restaurant. Before Sarah got there, he told Mandy to call immediately if that man came in the restaurant or if she saw him in town. She nodded her head. Sarah arrived, and Mandy left with her.

Darrel muttered to an empty room, "Now we are getting somewhere, but we have many miles to go. But why did he kill Mrs. Herrington?" He paused in his speech to no one and then said, "I'd bet a dozen of Sarah's doughnuts that he's the one."

Darrell, returning to his office, was greeted by blinking lights on the telephone. A press conference at noon was on his mind. That was one meeting he didn't want, but he knew there was no way to put it off. The news people were worse than hungry jackals looking for prey. He shuddered when he remembered he had once thought that he wanted to be a reporter. Then he laughed and prepared to meet the noisy hordes. Dread of the meeting continued to cloud his mind.

Chapter

SIXTEEN

The sign at the city limits read Ava, Missouri, population 2,938, 1990 Census. Reginald noticed the town also harbored more than a few dogs and assorted cats. A trotting horse association, Global Moving, and some other enterprises of note called the little town their home. Since the town was small, Reginald thought locating Henry Bottoms shouldn't be any problem, No address was listed for Bottoms so he would have to inquire. He stopped at a quick service store and asked if anyone knew Bottoms. No one did. He tried two more places and at the second, the woman standing outside puffing on a cigarette, said she knew where he could find Henry Bottoms. "You mean "Snoopy"?" The cigarette hanging from the corner of her mouth wagged up and down when she spoke. She squinted at Reginald through a cloud of smoke.

"Snoopy? Uh … who's Snoopy?" Reginald questioned.

She laughed, coughed, and replied, "Henry Bottoms. He's Snoopy. That's what everyone around here calls him, Old Snoopy. He lives on Washington Avenue. Hang a right on Washington," she said pointing north. "After you cross Third Street, it will be the red dump with white shutters on the left, three houses from the corner. You can't miss it. That place is so ugly a blind man would avoid it. Good luck with Snoopy. You'll need it." Smoke poured forth like a chimney when she laughed, which sent her into another hacking and coughing spell.

"Could you tell me where the police station is located?"

"Is Snoopy in trouble?" She watched Reginald suspiciously, her scrunched up eyes peering through the smoke dancing around on his face.

"I don't know of any at the moment." He looked at her intently and asked again. "Where's the police station?"

"It's at 208 South East Second Street, and the Sheriff is at 209 if you need him." She waited for him to speak.

"Probably won't. I'm just looking for some information."

She eyed him through eyes once again reduced to slits to ward off the smoke, looked around, and spied the plate on the car, "Where you from in Arkansas?"

"Mountain View."

"Hey, I've been there. They cook beans on the square in October. Love them beans. They also have the Outhouse Race. Need to get back there." She heard Reginald say thanks as he retreated to his car and left. "Well, if that ain't rude or what, walkin' off like that. Some people ain't got no manners at all." She watched the car leave, puffed on her cigarette, and began coughing. She threw it down after one last drag and disappeared inside the store, blue smoke trailing in her wake as she exhaled.

Curious about what the coughing chimney had said concerning the house where Bottoms lived, Reginald decided to drive past the address before contacting the police department. He found it and immediately saw why it was described as ugly. The house was painted a garish red with peeled patches showing grey wood siding. The shutters were dirty white, hanging at odd angles next to the window frames. The shrubs next to the front wall of the house, badly in need of trimming, covered half the picture window. Untended flower beds were full of weeds and trash. A lonely maple in the back peeked over the house from its seclusion in the backyard, waving in the breeze as if it was beckoning for help. The carport roof sagged, the corner post pushed out at the bottom. Reginald figured that helped the roof to sag. The carport had several black plastic garbage bags piled near a storage unit that held up the far end of the roof. A big brown dog slept peacefully, curled up on one of the bags.

Reginald drove slowly past and when he cleared the corner of the carport, he saw the back end of a blue 1989 Ford Crown Vic sticking out from behind the house. It didn't have a license plate on it. He said to himself, "Well, will you lookee there? What do I see?" He couldn't see if there was damage on the front fender. He went to the end of the block, turned around, gave the car and house another once over, and went onto the police station. Ugly, that's the word the woman used. Horrible fit much better. He saw the tree waving at him again and felt sorry for it.

The police department lived in a one story brick building that looked fairly well kept. The sheriff's office across the street looked the same except for one section having bars on the windows. Two county cars were next to the jail wing, and one patrol car was sitting by the front door of the police building. Both buildings spelled out local government architecture loud and clear, barely functional with no frills. The inside was just as no frills as the outside. The only frill it seemed to have going for it was air conditioning.

An officer at the counter looked up as he entered and asked, "Can I help you with something?" He looked at Reginald intently.

"Matter of fact you can." Reginald fished out his badge and ID for the officer who examined it carefully.

"Mountain View, Arkansas," he said. "Do you happen to know Martin Perkins? Used to be on the Little Rock P.D. Retired a few years ago and lives down that way now. Calico Rock, I think it is. He does special work for a couple of counties now."

"I sure do. He and I worked a stolen car case together a couple of years ago. He's doing some work for us again which is why I am here. How do you know him?"

The officer laughed and said, "He's my wife's uncle. I hate to claim him, but she says I have to, so I do. I'm Steven Bolder. Good to meet you." They shook hands.

"Same here," Reginald said, after they quit laughing at the comment about Martin.

Officer Bolder said, "So you need some information on a case? What do you need?"

"I need some background on Henry Bottoms. He lives on Washington Street." Bolder rolled his eyes and looked at the ceiling, letting out a puff of air from rounded cheeks. "I take it you know him," Reginald replied with a grin. He suspected now that Henry Bottoms wasn't who they were looking for.

"I guess we know nearly everyone in this town. What has Snoopy done now?"

"That's the second time I've heard him called Snoopy," Reginald said, a questioning look on his face.

"Oh, that. He fancies himself a private eye. Has a license and picks up work here and there. He does mostly divorces and piddly stuff. What's he doing down there? Is he in trouble?"

Reginald recounted the events to Bolder and told him that Bottoms was watching people in Mountain View.

"Snoopy does that all the time. We mostly don't pay any attention to his going and coming as long as he stays out of our hair. Sometimes he gets in the way, but he's mostly harmless is our take on him.

"Now, what do you want to know concerning Snoopy?"

"Snoopy's present vehicle is a tan 1995 Ford and is sporting a plate that's supposed to be on a blue 1989 Ford."

"I'll check on the plate and let you know."

"Do you or someone from your department want to go over there with me when I question him?" Reginald asked.

"It isn't necessary. I think he'll co-operate. He likes the attention. Let me know what you find out from Snoopy if anything involves us."

"I'll stop by before I leave town."

The drive over to Henry's place took less than five minutes. A tan 1995 Ford with Missouri plates, AMK 043, sat in the driveway. A man and woman were getting out. The driver looked at Reginald and frowned. The woman, with a bland expression, looked over the top of the car at him. Her stare wasn't the most friendly one Reginald had ever seen. Tired lines of a hard life were etched into her weary looking face. Cigarette smoke streamed from her nostrils. Reginald couldn't help but think she was related to the talking chimney that told him where Bottoms lived.

Stepping from his car Reginald said, "Are you Henry Bottoms?"

The man nodded and said, "I reckon that's me since there ain't no one else around here by that name. Who are you? Do I know you?" He tried to act as if he didn't know Reginald, but the act didn't work. His face betrayed him.

Reginald gave him a cold smile and replied, "Oh, I think you do," and showed Bottoms his badge and told him his name.

"Well, Mountain View, Arkansas. You don't have any say so in Missouri." He turned and walked toward the house. Reginald saw the limp in his right leg. The woman hurried into the carport trailing smoke, flipping the cigarette butt into the yard. The dog got up, looked at Reginald, wagged its tail, turned around, sniffed at the sack, and lay back down.

"Mr. Bottoms, you're right. I don't have much say so in Missouri, but I do have some."

Bottoms stopped and turned to look back over his shoulder. "I don't see how you figure you got any say at all," he said.

"Okay, have it your way," and began to climb into the police car. "I'll go talk to Officer Bolder and either he or one of his buddies will come back with me and they can take you to their headquarters for questioning."

Bottoms turned fully around, looked at Reginald, shrugged his shoulders in defeat, and said, "I reckon that won't be necessary. Come on in the house."

The living room was as drab as the outside. Years of neglect showed everywhere Reginald looked. Dingy wallpaper coming apart at the seams clung desperately to the walls. Dirty window panes gave a grey tinged view of the world. A fairly new looking thirty-six inch TV sat in the corner on a nice looking stand. Reginald remembered seeing a TV dish on the roof. A big yellow cat was sleeping in a big overstuffed chair. He couldn't decide which one looked the most over-stuffed, the chair, or the cat. The woman Reginald presumed to be Mrs. Bottoms wasn't anywhere in sight. The house smelled of stale smoke and stale food. Stale described the whole house.

Henry Bottoms motioned Reginald to sit down. He chose a straight back chair across from the couch where Henry had landed with a thump. The cat looked up at the sound and went back to sleep. Mr. Bottoms said, "Let's get this over with. I know why you're here so let's get on with it. I've got work to do."

Reginald thought that Henry's bluster was fright showing through and he would try to use it to his advantage. He said, "I understand that you have a private detective license. Is that correct?"

"Yes. I've been doing private stuff off and on for thirty years. That's why they call me Snoopy or Snoopy Bottoms around these parts." He paused, waiting for a reply. When Reginald didn't respond, Bottoms continued. "I suppose someone told you that was my nickname?"

"I heard it, yes." Wanting to get off that subject Reginald said, "Is that blue Ford out back yours?"

"It's mine." Bottoms appeared nervous.

"Have you driven it to Mountain View, say in the past three weeks?"

"No, I haven't. It doesn't run. The engine is bad."

Reginald let him stew for a few ticks of the grandfather clock standing in the far corner and said, "Why are the plates on the tan Ford registered to a blue 1989 Ford? I assume it's the one out back." He paused, keeping eye contact until Bottoms looked away. "What did you do, switch plates for some reason?"

"That '89 quit running awhile back. I bought the '95 right before I went … " He glared at Reginald.

"Exactly, right before you went down to Mountain View. Isn't that right?" Bottoms glared again and remained silent. Henry couldn't understand how a man who he was told was dumb could be so smart.

"So why doesn't the registration show the plates registered to the tan Ford?"

"I … I … haven't had time to switch the plates to the tan one. I'll do it tomorrow. I sure don't want to get in trouble for that."

The room was quiet except for the ticking of the big clock. Somewhere in the back, Reginald could hear a radio and the clatter of a sewing machine. Fresh tobacco smoke drifted into the living room. He watched Henry Bottoms fidget and squirm. He hated this part of an interview, but knew it had to be done. He surmised that Snoopy had gotten himself involved in something that wasn't good and it might be dangerous.

"You are the one that called me after you went by the car wash and said it wouldn't do any good to check out the plate? Am I right? You are also the one who came out of the restaurant on Saturday morning when I was going in. Correct?"

Snoopy nodded his head yes and said, "That was me both times. That's how I recognized you today."

"Why did you call me?"

"To tell you the truth, I really don't know. Even at my age, I do dumb stuff. Guess I was trying to be a wise guy. A big shot I guess." A sad look settled in his eyes and his bowed head broadcast his despair.

"Did you ever park and watch Miss Westermann's house?"

"Yeah, a few times, maybe three or four. I don't remember the exact number. Why?"

"Were you there the night you called me?"

"I saw you leave and followed you."

"That's what I figured." Reginald didn't tell Snoopy he didn't see him that night. Score one for Snoopy. He laughed inwardly.

He watched Snoopy squirm and then said, "Not to be rude or disrespectful, I noticed that you limp a little."

"An old war wound from Nam," was Henry's subdued response.

Reginald nodded and then said, "I am sure you know that a lady in our town, Mrs. Matilda Herrington was murdered." Bottoms froze and stopped breathing for a second or two when he heard the name.

His next few breaths were labored as he struggled to begin breathing again. He looked down at his feet.

"Do you know who did it?" Bottoms said, looking sick.

"That's not a question I'll answer. Do you know who did it?" Bottoms didn't reply.

Reginald said again, "I asked if you know who did it?"

Henry's heavy frame shook; he opened his mouth and nothing came out. Finally, he said, "No, I don't. Yes, I heard about it. Yes, I think I know, and no, I don't really know who did it."

"What do you mean you don't know, you think you know, and that you don't really know? You could be facing serious consequences if you don't talk to me and tell me the truth. What do you know? You need to tell me the truth and I won't leave until you do, Mr. Bottoms."

"Do I need a lawyer?" Henry asked nervously.

"You don't unless you have engaged in criminal activity of some kind. Now I want the truth, Mr. Bottoms," Reginald said, emphasizing Henry's last name.

Henry Bottoms looked even more defeated when he heard the increased coldness of the pronunciation of *Mr. Bottoms* in Reginald's voice the second time. He reluctantly said, "A few weeks ago I received a phone call from some man who wanted some work done."

"What kind of work?"

"He wanted some people tailed." Bottoms began to shake.

"Why did he want people followed?"

Henry looked at Reginald and sighed. "He said he wanted you and some others followed so he could make sure you were doing your jobs. A secret investigation by the city was what he told me."

Reginald knew that wasn't true and asked, "Why were you following the woman that works at the bank?"

Bottoms looked at Reginald for a few seconds and said, "He wanted to know where she lived, what time she went to work, when she went home, and where she went after work."

Reginald frowned at Bottoms several seconds before speaking.

The frown made Henry more nervous. "Did he ask you to follow Mrs. Herrington?"

"No, he just wanted you and Miss Westermann followed."

"How did he know her name?"

"He didn't tell me, and I didn't ask."

"So you told him you would do this work without asking any questions?"

"Well … I … I did ask him who he was, but he wouldn't tell me. I needed the job so we settled on the fee, and I began the tail work after the money arrived in the mail."

"How much did he pay you?"

"I got 500 dollars plus expenses for a week's work."

"How did he pay, cash, or check?"

"It was cash each time. It arrived in an envelope in the regular mail with seven 100 dollar bills, wrapped in two sheets of white paper."

"Was there any writing on the paper?"

"No."

"How did he find you?"

"I run ads in magazines and newspapers. I leave my card at various places of business. He probably found me through one of those ways. He called me one evening right before I went to bed."

"And you have never seen him?"

"No, all the contact was on the phone."

"I suppose you gave him a report by phone too?" Reginald watched the trapped man squirm and try to find an answer that would get him out of the jam. In a way, he felt sorry for him, knowing what it meant to be cornered and not having an apparent way out.

Henry Bottoms sighed and said, "I did. He called me Saturday evening at 9:00 p.m., and I gave him as much as I could find out and now I'm finished. I left Mountain View Saturday afternoon. Not going back."

Reginald frowned at Bottoms again and said, "Your private license isn't any good in Arkansas."

"I told the man it isn't good there, and he said all he wanted was for me to drive around and watch. No law against that is there?"

"I don't know of any." Reginald watched the cat awaken, turn around, and curl up the other way. He wished life could be that simple for humans. He wondered how the dog was doing outside on the garbage sack.

Bottoms asked if there was anything else, hoping to end the questioning, but his hope died quickly when Reginald said, "If you have the envelope the money was in and the sheets of paper, I want to see them."

Henry turned his head in the direction of the doorway from where smoke, music on a blaring radio, and the sound of a sewing machine were coming. He hollered, "Bertha, what did you do with that envelope the paper money was in?" The heavy set sad looking woman appeared and handed Henry an envelope that he then handed to Reginald. The surface was smeared and smudged which he knew made any chance of finding good prints doubtful. The return and Henry's address were type written. The letter impressions looked familiar, suggesting that the type was filled with ink and trash. The return was the familiar address in Searcy, Arkansas.

"Where is the paper the money was wrapped in?"

Bottoms yelled at his wife again. "Where's the paper that was around the money?"

A voice came from the back room, "I used it to start a fire in the stove. I didn't know I was supposed to keep it." Bottoms looked even sadder.

"What did you do with the roll of film you shot of everyone?" Reginald asked.

Bottoms jerked his head up and said, "How do you know I took pictures?" He hesitated before answering. "It was that morning at the bank. I ought to have known."

"You ought to have known what?" Reginald asked, though he knew the answer.

"I ought to have known that woman had spotted me when she dangled those keys so I could see them."

"What did you do with the pictures?"

"I sent the roll of film to a post office box in Bloomington, Indiana."

Reginald looked startled for an instant when he heard Bloomington, Indiana. Recovering he said, "Do you remember the name, and box number?"

Bottoms got up and left the room. When he returned, he handed Reginald a piece of paper with the post office box number on it. "This is it," he said.

Reginald looked at it and then after a few more questions he gave Henry instructions to call immediately if the unknown client called again. Henry said he would and gave Reginald permission to look at the blue Ford. It didn't have a smashed right front fender. The tree behind the house still beckoned as he drove away. He stopped at the Ava P.D. to inform them that Snoopy told him about the plates and that the registration would be corrected, He asked them to keep a watch on Henry's place for a while in case the blue 1989 Ford, license plate unknown, payed a visit. He left for Mountain Home to see Sam Hazelton and put the tree out of his mind.

Chapter

SEVENTEEN

D arrell Cumberland was immediately surrounded by news people when he pulled into the high school gym parking lot. The news hounds weren't content to wait for the news release; they wanted it now and not a second later. They shoved, pushed, and yelled. He waded through the seething mass, not giving any answers to the shouted questions. The bleachers were filled with mostly town people. Their talking made Darrell think the place was filled with a swarm of mad bees. He walked to the microphone, hating every moment of what he had to do.

Before he could say one word a voice yelled, "Do you know who the killer is?"

Darrell looked in the direction of the voice and said, "Everyone, please, let me have your attention." The mad bees continued buzzing. "Ladies and gentlemen, please give me your attention. If you don't, I will walk out of here and you can find the information on your own." He quit speaking and the crowd became silent. He began speaking again, choosing his words with extreme caution. "We are working on all the information that we have to date. There are more things that we don't know than what we do know. As you all know, one man was shot and a resident was a victim of a homicide. We have some leads, but they aren't bearing the fruit we had hoped. We are doing all we can to find out who did this and why."

"Have you called in the state police or the FBI?" a voice called out.

"What are you doing to catch the killer?" another voice shouted over the growing din of the buzzing.

"Please folks, let me speak or I will leave." The crowd became silent again. "We have been in consultation with the state police but not the FBI."

Before Darrell could say anything more, someone yelled, "Seems to me you would ask the FBI for help rather than depend on the clowns around here."

Anger flashed across his face and he said, "I won't dignify that uncalled for remark by commenting on it. This is a local crime investigation being conducted in accordance with the state laws." He paused for effect. "The FBI is federal and until there is an indication of a federal violation that would warrant bringing them in, we won't be having them here." The crowd buzzed again.

A reporter near the speaker's stand said, "Do you have any suspects and if so, who are they?"

"As I said, we are checking all the leads and sorting fact from fiction. When we find something concrete, we'll let you know whatever is proper to make public. This is an on going investigation and any release of information, true or false, will make our work much more difficult."

Herman Wheeling stood and said, "Chief, there are people in this town who are scared to turn on their lights at night for fear someone is watching them. What are you going to do about that?" Several people shouted demands that someone investigate how the crime was being handled. Some yelled that they didn't believe anything was being done. One said he was going to write the governor and get some people fired. Another demanded everyone be fired and new officers hired. "Get somebody besides that stupid Gawker. He needs to go back to selling vegetables," an irate man shouted. Several bees buzzed in agreement.

Darrell stood silently for a moment, knowing he would have to cut the meeting off quickly. He said, "I know people are scared, and we are doing all we can to find whoever it is. As for investigating us, that would only compound and cloud the issue if anyone tries it. We have good officers working on this day and night. For your information, Sgt. Gawker is out now running leads."

Chief Cumberland looked out at the worried faces of the residents and visitors sitting in the bleachers and considered what and how much more he could say without giving away anything useful to the culprit. As yet, no one had learned three facts that had been kept from the news releases; that the suspected intruder had a limp in his right leg; that the McGee and Callman bullets matched; and that ice picks at the two crime scenes likely provided another link.

But before he could speak again a loud voice called out, "I heard there was a possible burglary that went bad. That a good amount of money is missing from the victim's house. Is that true?"

Now his problem was answering without telling them anything while at the same time satisfying their curiosity. "We are investigating that angle. There is some indication that could be the case."

The same voice asked, "We heard that there was a strange car in the neighborhood right before she was killed. Is there any truth to that?"

"As I said before, we are checking all leads trying to separate fact from fiction. There isn't much to go on and there isn't anything else to report."

Another voice called out, "Is there any danger to more people in town?"

Darrell didn't want to be an alarmist and neither did he want to leave any hint of suggestion that there wasn't the need to be watchful. He said, "At this time we don't think there is any reason for anything more than being careful and keeping the doors and windows locked. This type criminal generally doesn't pick victims at random, though it can happen when robbery is involved. Thank you for your time. I need to be going."

Several news people called out questions as Darrell made his way out of the building. He ignored them except for wave of his hand and went to his car. As his car left the lot, a man who had been in the gym watched Darrell leave and murmured to himself, "They say they don't have a clue to any of this. I wonder if that is true. Well, time will tell." The limp in his right leg was very apparent, but if it was noticed, he believed there wasn't anyway for anyone to know it might be important to the police.

When Darrell walked into his office, the desk top was littered with telephone messages. One was from Sherry wanting him to call the bank, and another was from Jason Callman who needed to talk to Reginald right away. Darrell called the bank and Sherry said she would be in his office in ten minutes to tell him what she found out about the driver of the blue 1989 Ford. He poured a cup of coffee and sat back down. The whole ordeal at the gym had made him very weary. He wanted to rest his mind and body.

A noise outside drew his attention to the window. He saw a TV truck parked outside and a man with a camera perched on his shoulder walking toward the front door. He grabbed the phone and called the bank. Sherry hadn't left yet. He told her to go home and he would sneak out and meet her there in twenty minutes. He also told her that if she saw any TV snoops hanging around to call him. When he arrived at her house, there weren't any news people to be seen. The garage door was up and he drove inside. The door slid down behind him.

The aroma of coffee filled the house when Darrell entered. He sat down at the kitchen table to a cup of Gevalia Columbia Roast and a big slice of homemade chocolate cake. He took a sip of coffee and a bite of cake and then another sip of coffee. He looked up at Sherry and said, "That bakery downtown sure makes good cake."

She hit him with a dish towel and sat down across the table from him. "You'll think bakery the next time I give you any cake." They laughed and then became serious.

After swallowing another bite of cake, Darrell asked, "What happened to the blue Ford?"

"The driver hit a pickup parked in front of the bank on the east side of the Searcy square. The officer said the driver acted strangely, but he also said most people do after a collision."

"What was he doing when he hit the truck?"

"The officer didn't know, but apparently he was trying to look into front window of the bank according to what two witnesses told him. The officer issued a ticket for reckless driving. Oddly, according to Patrolman Plummer the driver didn't seem to mind being ticketed. He shrugged his shoulders and signed the ticket with no fuss of any kind. He asked where to pay it and the officer told him. I checked and he had paid the fine and costs only a few minutes after getting the ticket."

Darrell remained silent, running through his mind what he had heard and then said, "Something is fishy with that driver. We know that he followed you and then he followed the decoy to Searcy, thinking it was you. He hit a car while possibly checking the bank to see where you went and then quickly paid the ticket. That's interesting, to say the least."

"It is interesting. The plate number is AMA 975, Missouri. The name on the driver's license is Harley Bastin; address 2209 Apt. B, East Pine Street in Poplar Bluff, Missouri. The car is registered to him, too," Sherry related.

"Was the officer able to give a description of the driver?"

"Just a general one is all. He was 5'11," 200 pounds, brown hair, a short beard, green eyes, and according to the license, forty-one years old. All the license info matched the driver. There wasn't anything unusual according to the investigating officer except a slight limp."

"Limp?" Darrell questioned.

"Limp," Sherry said. She was quiet, looking at Darrell. She knew his mind was going a mile a minute trying to process what he just heard.

"Sherry," Darrell said, "I think we have the right suspect in sight now, but who is he? I have the feeling he's hiding something, but what we don't know. There are several things that don't seem to be connected and yet they have to be. It's more than a quirky coincidence."

"I agree Darrell, and yet, none of it makes sense. There is a connection with McGee, Callman, and Matilda. I'll bet on it. But where is it?" Sherry said perplexed by what they knew.

"What is that connection is the question. That's the one we have to answer. We find the answer to it and we solve the case."

The phone rang and Sherry said, "Hello." Silence filled the office. "Okay. Tell him to come over here and to drive the car into the garage." Sherry hung up and said, "That was dispatch. Reginald is on the way into town and coming here." She went out to remove her car from the garage to make space for Reginald's plain wrapper. Ten minutes later Reginald drove his car into Sherry's garage. She pressed the remote and the door closed. No sooner had the garage door closed, than a TV truck went slowly past to the end of the street. It turned around, went slowly toward Main Street, and turned right. Sherry saw it and said, "Close call. That we don't need."

Reginald walked into the kitchen and was surprised by a kiss that made him blush as usual. Darrell walked into the kitchen from the hall. Reginald hoped the Chief didn't see Sherry kiss him.

There was a cup of coffee and a plate with a big slice of cake on it waiting for him. He took a bite of cake and said, "That bakery downtown sure makes ... " and was hit with a dish towel before he could finish what he intended to say. He started laughing at the look on Sherry's face.

"She did the same thing to me. She sure slings a wicked towel," Darrell said.

"You two are just alike. The next time I'll go to the bakery for the cake. Why spend the time making one when you two don't know the difference," Sherry said with mock indignation.

Darrell and Reginald laughed while Sherry poured more coffee in Darrell's cup and filled her own. The phone rang and Sherry answered. "Hello." Pause. "Okay. You can come over. I want to hear what you have to tell us." She hung up and said that Madeline Crompton was coming over to tell them what she saw the other day.

Chapter

EIGHTEEN

T he door bell rang, and Sherry invited Mrs. Crompton into the
house. She stepped into the room and said hello to Reginald and
Darrell. She hesitated and then said, "I don't want you to think I am
nosy, but when I saw Darrell and Reginald drive into your garage
it made me remember something I saw a few days ago. I thought
you should know." Then her face turned scarlet, and she stammered,
"I … I … I don't want you to think I am watching you, Sherry, but I
did tell your mother I would watch out for you. When I hear a car, I
look to see who it is. I hope you don't think badly of me."

Sherry smiled and said, "Think nothing of it. I know you told
Mother that you would watch and besides, when people keep track of
things our job is easier."

Darrell and Reginald nodded in agreement and Mrs. Crompton
began to relax. *Maybe I'm not nosy after all*, she thought.

"Now what did you see?" Sherry said.

"Well, Reginald, you remember what I told you when I saw that
blue Ford parked up the street awhile back?"

Reginald looked off in the distance as the wheels and gears in his
brain began to whir, trying to bring up the event. "Oh, right, now I
remember. The guy looked Sherry's house over and the other time he
left after she came home. Did you see something else?"

"I did. Sherry, do you remember the night you called and asked
me if I had any extra milk? That was the night Reginald was over for
supper."

"I remember that. It was after seven o'clock when Reg arrived. What did you see that evening?"

"Well as you know, I like to sit in my rocking chair next to the front window and watch the birds and squirrels. That evening after you left with the milk and right before Reginald arrived, I noticed that the bird feeder was empty. I went to the cupboard to get the food. I have an extra feeder so I filled it and went out to hang it up. When I turned around to come back into the house, I saw the car up the street. I pretended not to notice it." She stopped talking and looked at Sherry and Reginald.

"Then what happened?" Sherry asked, responding to the cue that Mrs. Crompton wanted her to ask a question.

"When Reginald left, the blue Ford followed. I was going to write down the license number but there wasn't any plate on it."

"There wasn't any the back?" Reginald asked.

"There wasn't any on the back or the front."

All the while Darrell had been listening and making notes. He looked up and asked, "You believe the Ford is the same car you saw before?"

"Oh yes. It has a whole bunch of rust holes on the right side below the doors. It's the same car all right."

"Can you describe the driver?" Reginald asked.

Madeline squinted up her eyes and wrinkled her nose before answering. "Well, I'm not very good on descriptions, but I would say he was near 5'10" or so, 200 pounds or more, and walked with a limp."

"He had a limp?" Sherry said.

"Oh yes. Like his right leg hurt," Madeline said, obviously pleased with herself.

"Do you have any idea of his age?" Reginald asked while making a notation in his notebook.

"Oh, mid-forties I think. That's the best I can do. You didn't ask me these questions before when I told you I saw the blue car and that man walking up to Sherry's house. Why didn't you?"

"Madeline, I can only say that it didn't occur to me at the time and I goofed on it. I should have asked that day, but there are salesmen in town all the time so I didn't think it was too important at the time you told me."

Mrs. Crompton looked at Reginald sternly, "Well, I hope you think it is important now." Disapproval was evident in her tone.

Reginald looked sort of whipped and said, "I do now."

"Good. Now I need to go home and let you folks carry on." She left with a smile on her face.

Reginald said, "I should have ... " and was cut off by Darrell.

"Think nothing of it. We all make mistakes with information. Given that Madeline is the nosy parker of this neighborhood, it won't be the last time she sees something. This time it happened to be important. Remind me and I'll tell you the story of milkman someday. It should have taught her a lesson, but it didn't. Now back to the blue Ford. What did you find out in Mountain Home, Reginald?"

Reginald leafed through his notes and then told them the story about Henry "Snoopy" Bottoms, Snoopy's disabled blue Ford, and the man who hired him.

"You mean he doesn't know the client's identity?" Sherry asked.

"He never saw him. The only thing he received was the money in the mail, all in 100 dollar bills."

"What happened to the pictures he took of everyone?"

"Bottoms sent the undeveloped film to a post office box in Bloomington, Indiana. The caller gave him the name and box number when he first made contact with Bottoms. He sent it the day he took Sherry's picture at the bank which was the last shot on the roll. The box holder's name is J. Daniel Bushman."

Everyone in the room drew in a breath and looked at Reginald. Sherry said, "J. Daniel Bushman rented the post office box and someone using Harley Bastin's name was driving the car in Searcy." The silence made the room sound deadly. "Are they two people or is one going by two different names? We know what Bastin looks like in general from the description given by the officer in Searcy but not Bushman."

Reginald closed his eyes and rolled his head around to loosen the tension. "There's Bloomington, Indiana again. What's the connection?"

Darrell said, "Your friend Callman has property in Bloomington, doesn't he?"

"He does. It's out by the little burg of Stanford west of Bloomington, and he has a post office box at the main post office in town. But Callman was in the hospital. He couldn't have been doing this."

Darrell asked, "Do you know Callman's box number there?"

"No, but I'll ask him when I see him again." He added, "This only makes my headache worse. Who are we looking for and why is he doing what he's doing?"

"Maybe Callman is hiring someone to do this," Sherry said. "What do you think Reg?"

"I don't think so. He's scared and just doesn't seem the type to be doing things like this. He has retirement money but not enough to pay someone given the amount he told me he draws each month. We are definitely missing something."

"I've been considering a trip for you. After you talk to Callman, I think a trip to Indiana in a few days might be worthwhile, especially if he tells you anything. In fact, I think it would be good if Callman went with you. He knows the area and might be able to remember some things while away from the turmoil he's in here," Darrell said.

The Chief left and Sherry kissed Reginald good bye. His face was still red when he turned right onto East Main to go to the police building. He quickly checked out and went home. After a light supper, his bed sure looked inviting.

Chapter

NINETEEN

Morning arrived too quickly when the alarm clock jarred Reginald awake at 6:00 a.m. He showered, shaved, dressed, and was eating a breakfast of toast, bacon, tomato juice, and coffee, when the phone rang. The clock said 6:30 a.m. *Now who is calling at this hour?* he wondered. Dread filled his mind. Fearful of what he might hear, he didn't want to answer it. Finally, he got up and said hello into the mouth piece.

"Am I speaking to the inimitable Sgt. Gawker?" the voice asked. The rasping voice roared through the phone's speaker into the room.

"Yes. Who am I talking to?" He didn't immediately recognize the voice.

"You mean you don't know my voice? You should."

"Why should I recognize it?"

"Because I am the voice of hurt that dispenses pain remedies for people who give me pain. You will really learn that before I am through with you. You are spoiling my plans. All of you in that hick town are making things real difficult. You will pay." The line went dead. Reginald glanced at the caller ID. It displayed a call blocked message.

Reginald's mind went in circles for a moment before he began to put together what he knew and then realized he didn't know much. Then he remembered when he had heard that voice. He hurriedly finished breakfast and arrived at the police department to find his desk top covered with Post-It-Notes. Fortunately, there weren't any new cases to bother him. The first act was to call Jason Callman. The

phone rang in the motel. The voice on the other end said hello and
Reginald said, "Jason, this is Sgt. Gawker."

"Who did you say?"

"Sgt. Gawker."

"Sgt. Gawker? Who are you? Who do you want?" the voice asked,
sounding irritated.

"Uh, uh … Jason," Reginald said hesitantly.

"You have the wrong room. There's no Jason here."

Stunned, Reginald said, "What room are you in?"

"226."

"Thanks," was all Reginald could think to say. He was worried.
Where was Callman and what happened to him? His mind was mud-
dled. He called the motel office. "Do you have an L. Jason Callman
registered there?" He felt the first signs of dread and panic beginning
to form.

After what seemed like an eternity to Reginald, the clerk said,
"Yes, he's in room 221. He said the air conditioner was noisy so we
moved him. Need anything else?"

"Connect me with his room, please." Reginald breathed a sigh of
relief when Callman came on the line. "Jason?"

"Who's calling?"

"Sgt. Gawker. You gave me a fright when you didn't answer the
phone in 226."

"They moved me after I complained. The air conditioner was
noisy. I need to see you."

"I assume you found out some things."

"I think I found out what you wanted to know. Can you come
over?"

"I'll be over this afternoon, if not before. We need to discuss several things concerning this case that involve you." They hung up.

Reginald shuffled through the notes cluttering his desk and called
the local phone office to check the number that had appeared on his
caller ID when the man called to rant at him because Mrs. Sheldon

and Mrs. Hancock were gone. Just as he suspected, the call came from a pay phone near the convenience store on Main Street.

As he shuffled through the mess of papers on his desk, the intercom phone rang. He listened and then punched line one. "Hello, Sgt Gawker."

"This is Sam Hazelton at Mountain Home."

"Good to hear from you, Sam. Were you able to do what we discussed yesterday?"

"We got it done. The techs disabled the automatic information on the Bushman account so that when he calls in and punches his account number, it will tell him there's a problem with the machine and then the recording will ask him to wait while the call is transferred to a live human, me to be exact."

Reginald laughed and said, "Do you suppose I could get my bank to transfer me to a live human?"

"I doubt it. Live ones are hard to find in banks now since robots work more cheaply than people."

Reginald laughed and said, "Now back to Bushman. How will you know it when or if he calls?"

"There is a little light on my desk that will alert me when he punches in the account number and the transfer message triggers. That way when he calls, I won't be caught unaware."

"It's a long shot, and I hope it works. We need to know this guy's identity in the worst way."

"Okay, Reginald. If he calls, I'll get to you immediately."

"Be sure to notify us if he closes the account, too."

"We'll do it."

"Thanks for your help, Sam."

"Glad to be able to help." They hung up.

Immediately the intercom line rang. Reginald punched the intercom button and listened. Then he punched the button for line two and said, "Sgt Gawker."

"This is Robert H. Blandford."

"I am glad you called. I need to talk to you. Where are you now?" Reginald said all business without time for chit chat.

"I'm in Indianapolis, Indiana, right now, but I'll be in Mountain View Saturday evening. Coming down to see how my house is getting along. I'll be at the Blue Bird Inn."

"Okay. When you get into town, call dispatch and whoever is on duty will notify me. I'll get in contact with you."

"Good deal." They hung up.

Next, Reginald called the motel in Clinton and told Callman that he would be over at eleven o'clock. They would have lunch together and talk. He hoped that Callman could provide some answers for all the questions the case kept them asking.

Reginald called Sherry and asked her to find Thomas Dawson to see if he could get the lab to speed up the information they needed on the objects that were found on Mrs. Sheldon's front porch, and to tell her he was going to see Callman. He also asked her if she could make a discreet trip to Poplar Bluff, Missouri, to inquire into the driver of the blue Ford, Harley Bastin. She said she would leave before daybreak tomorrow.

Reginald dialed the state crime lab and asked for the Medical Examiner. He identified himself to the secretary and after he told her what he needed, she put him on hold. After several minutes a male voice said, "Are you Sgt. Gawker of Mountain View?"

"Yes," he said, and before he could say anything else, he was cut off by the voice.

"You want to know if we have done an autopsy on the body that came in on Saturday morning early and what did we find? Correct?"

"Yes, Mrs. Matilda Herrington."

"We don't have a full report, but we do know how she was killed." The line went silent.

"Shoot."

"She was stabbed with an ice pick several times in the right lower back. The shaft went through her right kidney ten times. She bled to death internally. Death came in less than two minutes. She had a large hematoma on the right side of her head and a small cranial fracture. She was most likely unconscious when stabbed. We should know when we finish the autopsy."

Reginald felt sick when he heard the report and took in some deep breaths. He recovered and said, "What was the sticky stuff around her mouth and nose?"

"It came from duct tape that had been pulled off. There was bruising on her arms where someone had grabbed her from behind. She apparently fought the assailant, and he hit her with something that knocked her out."

"Can you tell from the head wound what was used to hit her?"

"From the shape of the indentation it was most likely the butt of a gun." Reginald heard the shuffling of papers. "We couldn't determine the caliber or size of the gun though. But my guess is a small handled one."

Reginald responded immediately, "Could it have been a .22 caliber?"

"Could have been, but small is the best I can do," the man on the phone said mechanically.

Reginald thought for a moment and then replied, "You didn't find any blood on the scalp from the blow?"

"A small amount is all. Even though the scalp was split by the impact of the object, it wasn't a very long laceration; only one centimeter long."

Puzzled, Reginald said, "Since you think it was the butt end of a gun handle and it only made a small laceration, what does that tell you?"

The pathologist was silent for a breath and then said, "I would say the handle grip had a rounded end."

Reginald replied, "That makes sense. Thanks for the preliminary report. It sure helps."

"You are welcome. I'll send the final when it is finished. You should have it by Saturday, no later than Monday."

"You don't suppose that as soon as it is finished you could have it ready to be picked up by a state trooper, do you? I'll call Colonel Cordley and ask him. I'll let you know."

"That is fine with me to send it that way. I know you want it quickly." The line went dead with the click of the hang up.

Reginald called Colonel Cordley to set up the delivery and called the lab to tell them. With that done, he called Sherry to fill her in on the autopsy findings and to tell her he was leaving for Clinton. At least the drive would give him a chance to think over all the stuff he knew in the hope of finding the things he didn't know.

Chapter

TWENTY

Reginald left for Clinton, keeping a watch in the rear view mirror for anyone that might be following him. When he went through Newnata, he was satisfied that no one was tagging along. At Leslie, he turned onto a side street and watched traffic for ten minutes. Nothing suspicious went past unless three pickups with dogs riding in the beds, a log truck, and two kids in souped up cars fit the suspicious category. Reginald went through town, turned left on U.S. 65, and continued to Clinton. The motel sitting high upon a hill gave a good view to the town and the highway. He stopped at room 221 and knocked on the door. A voice inside asked who was knocking. Reginald identified himself and the door opened.

"Boy, I sure am glad to see you. I didn't think you would ever get here. Every car that drove in and the noises outside made me think my minutes on this earth were numbered. How much longer do I have to stay in this place?"

"You're leaving today, and we're going back to Mountain View so you can pack some clothes and personal stuff."

"Why am I going to do that?" Callman asked with traces of fear in his voice.

"I'm going to Indiana, and you're going with me. I need you to show me the way around there. You can tell me on the way back to Mountain View what you've learned."

"I don't know what I can do there, but it's better than staying around here and getting killed."

"I want to look at your cabin out by Stanford and also stop in Petersburg, Indiana."

Callman looked at Reginald oddly and said, "Why stop there?"

"I have a hunch and want to check it out. If I find what I think I will find, then we're a long way down the road to finding the killer, and we may be able to learn the why."

"And you think I can help?" Callman asked.

"I think you and your dead cousin hold some of the keys to unlock this case and you don't realize it."

A puzzled look came across Callman's face. He started to say something and then remained quiet. After a few beats he said, "Do you want to hear what I found out?"

"Go ahead," Reginald said, turning on the tape recorder lying in the seat.

"While I was in the hospital I had time to think about all that has happened. I vaguely remember some guy I met at a convention in Louisville, Kentucky. I can't think of his name off hand, but he owned some kind of an equipment company somewhere in Ohio." Reginald jerked his head toward him and started to speak when Callman continued. "The reason I remember is because I sold a cleaning chemical that he wanted to try at his factory. I told my boss and he made contact with their industrial materials purchaser who set up the deal; and later I began to get nice commission checks for the sales."

Reginald looked at Callman as he ran a few things around in his brain before speaking. "You said Ohio."

"That's right. Now as I recall, it was Cleveland, Ohio."

"The owner' name by any chance wouldn't have been Robert H. Blandford would it?"

Callman remained silent for a few ticks of a clock. "I'm not sure, but I think that's the name. When we get back, I'll look in some old stuff I carry around for some reason. Been aiming to throw it away and now I'm glad I haven't done it."

"Okay, now what else have you remembered?"

"Gosh, it has been so long." Callman let out a puff of air and then said, "I called a friend in Little Rock who worked for a company that bought the chemicals I sold. He was an engineer for a company that made replacement parts for refrigeration equipment. I met him at a party his company had for people they did business with and those who wanted to do business. I made good sales contacts that way. One time I ... "

"Did the friend tell you anything that might be of help?" Reginald asked, interrupting him to steer the conversation back to the subject.

"Let me think." Callman puffed his checks again, let out a gust of air, and said, "There was a guy we both knew. More of an acquaintance is more like it. Remember, I told you a few days ago. His wife was killed in an accident at the refrigeration plant."

"That was Marion Easterly wasn't it? What did he do there?"

"It was. He was in charge of plant maintenance and was responsible for purchasing the products used in the maintenance of various operations at the plant."

"How well did you know him?"

"Oh, not well. I would maybe see him a couple of times per year when I called at the plant. Once an account was set up, the reorders were done by phone, so I didn't need to call on them very often. The calls were more to do with customer relations than anything and to see if they needed other products."

"You told me previously that Mr. Easterly died in an accident somewhere. You said you didn't know. Did your friend know where?" Reginald asked.

"I thought it was Illinois, but he said it was in Indiana." Callman became silent and then continued. "He didn't know where for sure. He said maybe that it was near Bloomington. He didn't know any particulars except that it was some kind of auto accident. The man who called him said he saw it in the paper up there while passing though a few weeks after the accident. He said the caller was vague on details and really didn't say much. He called him because he knew he would want to know since Easterly was his friend."

"Did your friend tell you the name of the caller?"

"He did, but it wasn't anyone I know, and told me it was someone who knew both Easterly and him. He said it was strange that the caller made a collect call. The caller explained that away by saying he wasn't where he could call without doing it that way."

"Did your friend know the date his friend called?"

"It was September 15, 1995. He remembers the month and day because that was his son's first day on the job with the state police that he had his own patrol car. His son dropped by to show him the car after he went off duty."

"When we go to Indiana maybe we can find out the particulars surrounding that accident," Reginald said. Reginald flipped through his mental notes and asked, "Where were you the day the scaffolding collapsed?"

"I was at home, if being somewhere on the road can be called being at home. I don't remember where I was when it happened. Since Easterly is dead why are you wanting to know all this anyway?" Callman asked, puzzled by the questions.

"I have a headache. This case is pounding in my head and I am trying to find out what's causing the pounding. Something isn't right, and I want to know what it is."

They rode in silence the rest of the way to Mountain View. The city limits sign flashed by, and they pulled into the police station. They went inside and entered Reginald's office. Reginald left Callman and went into the radio room and told Mazy Sink to call in a patrolman. When Nance Porter came in, Reginald briefed him on his plan and Porter left. Thirty minutes later Martin Perkins and Darcy Broadway came in through the secluded back door. Reginald told them what he wanted. Officer Porter came in and left with L. Jason Callman in tow.

S herry left for Poplar Bluff, Missouri, at 4:00 a.m., the same morning that Reginald went to Clinton to retrieve Callman. It would be a four to four and half hour drive, maybe more depending on traffic, and she wanted to be there early so she could get back to Mountain View before 4:00 p.m., providing she would have success in finding out information on the blue Ford and could leave by noon. A tense moment occurred on the Walnut Ridge-Hoxie by-pass when she saw a blue 1989 Ford behind her. She slowed a bit and the car passed on by. The car contained an older couple and two small children. Probably the grandkids with the grandparents Sherry thought. She kept looking in the rear view mirror and when she arrived in Pocahontas, she was satisfied that no one was following her. She stopped at McDonald's for an Egg McMuffin, coffee, and orange juice for breakfast.

Arriving in Poplar Bluff at 9:00 a.m., Sherry soon found 2209 Apt. B on East Pine Street after checking in with the Poplar Bluff Police Detective Division. The run down house was a two story that contained four apartments. Apartment B was on the backside, first floor. Trash and old cars littered the back yard. Two dogs looked her over when she knocked on the door. They quickly lost interest and went back to chewing on their bones. Sherry had the fleeting thought that she was glad it wasn't her bones they wanted to chew on.

After several knocks, the door opened. A thin woman with stringy mouse colored hair, tired grey eyes, squinting through the smoke from a cigarette dangling from her lips, looked back at Sherry. A half inch of ash curved down at the end of the cigarette. The dress the woman wore hung on her small frame, giving the appearance of a shapeless empty coat hanging on a hook. A raspy voice sounding of irritation asked through the smoke, "Who are you and what do you want? Do you know what time it is?" The cigarette bobbed in time to the lips. Before Sherry could answer, a hacking cough wracked the small woman as she gasped for her breath. The ashes took a trip to the floor. She scattered them with her shoe.

"I'm Special Investigator, Sgt. Sherry Westermann, Arkansas State Police," she said, showing the woman her identification. "May I come in and talk to you for a few minutes? I need to ask you some questions … "

"Whatchu' want with me? I ain't done nothing in Arkansas or anywhere else. Don't have time what with workin' all the time to make ends meet. But I don't guess you know hard times makin' ends meet what with your fancy job and all. Wish I could afford fancy duds like that."

"Mrs. or Miss …

"I'm just plain Gladys. Gladys Sherman." Gladys eagle eyed Sherry and kept a grasp on the screen door to keep it closed. Realizing that Sherry wasn't going to leave, she pushed it open and said, "Come on in since you're here. Don't know what you're here for, but I guess I may as well find out. Sure is early. Couldn't you have come around later in the day?"

Sherry said, "I'm sorry if I disturbed you, but this is very important."

Sherry went inside and couldn't help but notice that the inside looked like the outside, except there weren't any junk cars in the living room or dirty dogs chewing on bones. Sherry shoved some old magazines aside that covered the cushion of an overstuffed chair and sat down.

Enveloped in a cloud of smoke, Gladys flopped on a couch across the room. She eyed Sherry with suspicion. "Well, get it over with. Don't know what's so all fired important that you would wake up a person this early in the morning. But ask your questions. I need to go back to sleep. The night shift is hard on a body."

"Do you know a Harley Bastin?"

Gladys Sherman stiffened and said, "Why you askin' about Harley Bastin?"

"Do you know him?"

"Well, I did. He's dead now. What's this got to do with Harley?"

"When did he die?"

"A year ago I guess," Gladys said, exhaling blue smoke while making unblinking eye contact with Sherry. With eyes that were red and watery, Gladys continued looking through the cloud of smoke.

"What caused his death?"

"Natural causes if dying from drinkin' is natural causes."

"I'm sorry to hear that," Sherry said, with sympathy sounding in her voice. *That ruins the theory that Bastin is the killer.* She asked, "How did you know him?"

"He was my cousin."

"Can you describe him for me?"

"Well, yeah. He was 5'11" or a bit more. I judged he weighed over 200 pounds. He had brown hair turning grey. I don't remember the color of his eyes."

Same description as the subject in Searcy, she said silently. "What was his age at death?"

"Old." Gladys laughed at her attempt at being funny. "I think he was fifty-nine best I can recollect. I'm young compared to him. I'm only forty-nine and holding."

Sherry ignored Gladys' second attempt at humor and asked, "Did he ever live here?"

"For a short time before he died."

Sherry didn't look up and continued to write in her notebook. "Did he own a blue 1989 four door Ford sedan?"

"He did, and he gave it to me. I sold it right after he died. It was a piece of junk if you ask me. Got enough junk around here without that Ford sitting in the yard adding to the litter."

"How did you sell it? Did you run an ad in the paper?" Sherry continued to write.

"No. I parked it in the yard with a *For Sale* sign on the windshield. It sold it two days later."

"Do you remember the date you sold it?" Sherry looked at her expectantly waiting for an answer that she hoped would shed some light on the case.

"Not the day, but it was in the fall of 1994, October. I remember that because it was the week of the fall parade downtown." Smoke filled the air as Gladys puffed away while thinking. Sherry wanted to go outside the air was so bad. "I remember now. I sold the car the day before the parade, so it had to have been on Friday."

"Are you sure of that? It is important."

"I'm sure. My nephew was in the parade driving his souped up car with a fancy paint job. Musta cost him five grand the way he talked." Gladys hesitated and then said, "Bragged is a better word for it. He throws money around like dogs throwing dirt digging for moles."

Sherry thought for a long moment before speaking again. "Can you describe the buyer?"

"It has been so long. Uh … Let me think." She squinted up her eyes, looked up at the ceiling, looked at Sherry, and then said through the cloud of smoke circling her head, "Yeah, skinny guy. I'd say six feet tall … maybe taller by two or three inches. Not good with height or weight. He was just skinny." Gladys became silent. The whole time she was talking the cigarette dangled from her lips. When the ash again fell off, she slapped the fire out on her dress. She ground out the butt in the ash tray and fired up another Pall Mall. When she inhaled, a wracking cough turned her face red and Sherry thought she was going to quit breathing. She recovered and said, "Those things are going to kill me someday," and laughed. "Now where were we?"

"We were talking about the buyer," Sherry reminded her. "I need his description with as much detail as you can remember. What color was his hair?"

"Grey, sort of mousey looking like mine."

"What was the color of his eyes?"

Gladys screwed up her face and was seized with another horrible hacking cough when she took the cigarette out of her mouth. "I don't know. Didn't see them," she wheezed.

Sherry looked at her startled and said, "Didn't see them?"

"That's what I said. He was wearing sunglasses."

"Oh." Sherry looked at Gladys wondering if any of this was going to be any help at all. "What was the name of the man who bought the car?"

"I can't remember. It was a funny name … uh … let me think … uh … I think it was Bush something."

Sherry looked up quickly from here notebook. "Would that have been Bushman by any chance?"

Gladys looked oddly at Sherry and said, "Yeah, that's it. How did you know? If you knowed why are you bothering me waking me up, and all? A person's body don't do well if it don't get sleep."

Sherry ignored her protesting. "We need to cover all possible leads. Did you put his name on the title?"

"No, I just gave it to him. Harley signed it right before he died and I never did anything with it. I was supposed to put my name on it, but I didn't want the piece of junk. It only added to the litter in the yard."

"You say it was a piece of junk. Why do you say that?"

"It was all rusted out. Rust all along the bottom of the doors."

Sherry smiled and silently said bingo. The word clanged so loudly in her mind she was sure Gladys could hear it.

Then Gladys said, "I sure wish I could find somebody to clean this dump up. Them lousy renters sure … "

"Okay, just a few more questions. Do you have Harley's driver license?"

Gladys stared at Sherry for a couple of seconds and said, "I plumb forgot. All of Harley's stuff was in that car. I put his license and other personal stuff in a bag and put it in the car to store it. I never gave it a thought. It all went with the car when I sold it. Call me stupid."

Gladys whacked the side of her head with her hand and said, "Dumb is me," laughing at her own joke.

"Was there anyone with Bushman when he stopped to look at the car?" Sherry asked.

"No. He was by himself as far as I could see and said that he would be back to get the car. I gave him the keys, he paid me cash, 800 dollars, and left. I was gone when he came back three days later to get it. I went to the store and was gone for over an hour. I didn't see anyone take it."

Sherry thought for several seconds and then said, "I need to know whatever you can tell me about Bushman. Is there anything else I should know that you can think of? Tell me no matter how insignificant you might think it is. Anything at all you can remember might help."

Gladys looked at the ceiling again and at her shoes and started to say no when she began laughing which brought on another hacking cough. She said, "Oh man, I just remembered. It was so funny. Bushman had a chew in his cheek and when he started to spit … this is funny … he lost his upper plate. It landed in the dirt, and he picked it up, wiped it on his jeans, and stuck it back in his mouth. I almost choked. He never let on, and I didn't either. He acted like it was an every day occurrence. It didn't seem to bother him a bit." Then she said as an after thought, coughing from laughter, "Maybe it did happen every day."

Sherry, with a lot of effort, kept a straight face as the scene played out in her mind and then asked, "Is there anything else that you can remember?"

"No, what I've told you is all I remember. I did ask him where he lived and he said Sikeston. That's up the road forty-five miles east of here, still in Missouri."

"You don't remember his first name?"

"No. I did well to remember part of the last one," Gladys said, and began coughing again when she tried to laugh.

Sherry asked a couple more questions, thanked Gladys, and left.

She interviewed three neighbors, one who said they saw a tall skinny guy drive the car away but nothing else. Another said they saw a car follow the blue Ford down the street. No one could describe the other car or the driver. Sherry had hit a dead end, and it was time to return to Mountain View. She grabbed a bite to eat at a greasy spoon outside of town and set her sights on Arkansas. Now they at least had something more to work with and where it might lead was the big question that needed answering. *For good or for bad, we'll let it go where it will. Which way we won't know until it happens*, she thought. She settled in for the drive home in the rain, the windshield wipers with their steady beat fighting the sheets of water falling from the sky.

TWENTY-TWO

The private line rang in Reginald's office. It was Officer Porter. Reginald listened and told Nance to bring Callman back to headquarters. A few minutes later, a white faced Callman came in to see Reginald. He was carrying a sixteen inch mailing tube that had his Mountain View post office box number on it. The return was the false Searcy address. Callman sat down and began to shake. He couldn't talk, and he looked like he might pass out. Reginald took the tube from him after pulling on latex gloves and took off the metal cap. He could see the end of what looked like a handle. He tipped the tube so the contents could slide out onto a blank sheet of paper he had placed on his desk. What he saw sent chills up his spine and made him shiver. It was an ice pick with Callman's name printed with red marker on the handle. Inside was a piece of paper with printing on it in the same shade of red. Big block letters proclaimed the message. *You cheated me out of my life. For that you will die. In, Pain.*

Reginald stood and looked at his desk. He laid the mailing tube aside and nudged the square handled ice pick over. Callman's name was on all four sides. He looked at Callman who now looked even sicker and said, "Should I assume this was in your post office box?" He got a head nod. Then: "Nance, did you go by his motor home?"

"No. Mr. Callman got back into the car and opened the tube. He began to shake as soon as he saw what was inside. We came straight here."

Reginald looked at the tube again and picked it up. Then he saw the Little Rock Post Office cancellation. He picked up the phone and called Chief of Detectives L.P. Wellman. Wellman wasn't in, so he left a message for him to call as soon as he came back to the office. A few minutes later, the phone rang. Reginald informed L.P. of the new development and asked if the postal worker who emptied the mail box the day Officer McGee was killed had been interviewed. Reginald listened and asked questions for more than five minutes. He hung up with a grim look on his face. He said, "I don't know who we are chasing or why, but what I do know, he isn't any dummy. He's diabolical and planning his moves carefully."

"Why do you say that, Sarg?"

"Notice that the tube has stamps on it, not a printed label from a mailing machine. The postal worker who cleaned out the mail box that day said he remembers the tube because he doesn't see packages like that in the drop boxes. He told L.P. that he seldom sees anything but letters." Reginald looked at the tube and then at Nance Porter, hesitated and picked up the phone and dialed the post office. He asked for Sammy Phillips, the Postmaster. Reginald spoke to him a few minutes and then hung. He said, "Sammy will be here in few minutes." He returned the ice pick to the tube and replaced the end cap.

Fifteen minutes later, Sammy Phillips and a postal inspector came in with a small set of postal scales and a chart. Sammy said, "This is William Blackwood, postal inspector out of Little Rock. He wanted to see what you asked me to do." Introductions were made all around and Sammy said, "Tell me again what you want."

"I want the tube with the contents weighed and the postage checked to see if it is more than needed or the right amount." Reginald laid the tube on the scales.

Sammy looked at the readout and checked the chart. He looked up and said, "It's exactly the amount needed to send it. Why did you want me to do this?"

"Sammy, I'm going to tell you as much as I am able. I can't tell you what's in the tube, but I can tell you it involves a case that has the people of the entire town scared out of their wits. You know which one. I want you to watch for mailing tubes like this that may have cancellations from Little Rock, Bloomington, and Indianapolis, Indiana, and anywhere in Illinois and Missouri, particularly between here and Bloomington in those two states."

Sammy looked at the postal inspector and asked, "Can we do that?"

"We can as long as there is reason to believe that it is being used to perpetrate a crime and or make threats through the mails, which is a crime. From the looks of the gentleman sitting there, I would say that whatever is in the tube constitutes a threat to him. If it does, we may be able to help with a federal inquiry," Inspector Blackwood said.

Reginald asked Officer Porter to take Mr. Callman out for some fresh air and to get him something to drink. He looked at the tube and at Sammy and then the Inspector, thinking over what he could say. He exhaled loudly and said, "Okay. I'm going to tell you what's in the tube." He told them what he knew and waited for a reply.

Inspector Blackwood said, "L.P. Wellman called me wanting to interview one of our drop box pick up employees. When I saw that mailing tube, I suspected it was the one that our employee found in the box the day Officer McGee was killed. Wellman told me you were looking for it. So it turned up here. Am I right?"

Reginald said, "You are, but we didn't know until today what he dropped in the mail box. All we knew was that a subject, name and physical identity unknown, dropped a package of some sort in the box. The cancellation is the day that McGee was shot and then Callman was shot while at the square on the 11th. He returned to Mountain View today and found it when he picked up his mail. He also received a letter that was postmarked on April 9. He picked that up on the 11th of April, so the tube had to have been placed in his box after he checked the mail on 11th. Whatever Officer McGee saw was enough to get him killed. But what's the connection to this mailing tube? We don't know, and all we have are pieces that don't fit together very well."

Blackwood looked at Reginald and asked, "Why didn't you tell us he received that letter back in April?"

"I did. I called Sammy and he told me whom to call. I can't remember who I talked to without looking up the case notes."

"That was probably Woodrow Carlisle. He's the one who told me a letter had been received and then said we wouldn't be interested in it since it was probably a prank. And now I remember that he said a note or letter had been sent to a woman who worked in a bank. But he never did anything with it as far as I know. He was ready to retire, and I suspect that he didn't want to get involved in anything new."

"That woman is Sherry Westermann, and she works at the First State Bank here in Mountain View. Whoever this is got mixed up and mailed the envelopes to the wrong banks. If he hadn't done that, we would have never made the made the connection. They discussed the note and the letter some more and then Reginald asked, "Do you want to be involved now?"

"I'll open an information file and see what happens, but officially we'll just watch and let you handle the investigation. Just keep me posted," Blackwood said, "and I'll contAct Indianapolis and Bloomington and inform them to be watching for the mailing tubes, but as for Illinois and Missouri, we can't do that until something shows up from an office in those states. If something comes through from a town, then we can check to see if anyone remembers anything. Doubtful, but we'll try if we learn a mailing location."

Blackwood said he would notify Wellman in Little Rock that an ice pick had been found in the mail. Reginald looked at his watch, wishing that Sherry would return. He was anxious to see her and to find out what she had learned. Officer Porter brought L. Jason Callman back into the office and Reginald told Nance to take him to his motor coach to get his clothes and personal things and then return him to headquarters. They left and Reginald was thankful for the break and time to think. The ringing phone snapped him into consciousness. He realized he had dozed off momentarily. He picked up and said, "Sgt. Gawker." He listened and then said, "Don't touch anything. I'll be there in five minutes."

When Reginald drove up to Callman's motor home, Callman and Nance were standing outside. Callman was white faced, shaking violently, unable to speak. Nance told Reginald to look inside the vehicle. He carefully entered the coach and saw the note laying on the driver's seat. It was pinned to the cushion with an ice pick stuck through the word "you" that had been printed larger than the other letters. *I didn't get the job done the first time. The next time* **YOU** *shall die. Depend on it. In, Pain.*

Reginald started looking around and saw the second note lying on a pair of cheap brown cotton gloves. *I didn't find what I was looking for and there won't be any finger prints as you can see. My plan is going nicely except for some fools who keep getting in the way. I shall deal with them in due time. All shall suffer as I have. You shall feel pain.*

TWENTY-THREE

Reginald stepped outside after finishing bagging and tagging the notes and gloves and other evidence. He told Nance Porter to take Mr. Callman back to headquarters after he collected his things and leave him there. After Callman had his belongings and was back in the police car, Reginald told Nance in a low voice, out of Callman's hearing, "Find Darcy and Martin. Tell them to meet me at Darrell Cumberland's house. I'll be there in an hour, and you stay with Callman until you hear from me again. Whoever is after Callman is going to kill him when he has the opening, and if we let our guard down for even one second, Callman will be dead. None of this makes sense, but until we know why this is taking place, we have to do all we can to protect Callman from the stalker."

Nance left and Reginald went to the sheriff's department to find Sheriff Thomas Dawson before going to Chief Cumberland's house. The sheriff wasn't in so he left a message for him to go to Darrell's house as soon as he received the message. He called Chief Cumberland from the sheriff's office and told him what had transpired since morning. Darrell said he would leave messages for Sherry at the bank, with dispatch, and on her answering machine telling her to go to his house as soon as she could get there.

When Reginald arrived at the chief's house, Darcy and Martin were already there. He asked Darcy, "Did anyone show up at Blandford's house driving a blue '89 Ford?"

"Not that we saw. A couple of cars turned around and went back the way they arrived."

"What did they look like?" Reginald wanted to know.

Martin said, "One was a pickup with two kids in it, and the other was a brown late model Ford. It looked like a '94. Couldn't see who was driving since we were up by the house."

"He did sit down there for a little bit before leaving. We were too far away to see the license plate though," Darcy said.

Reginald looked at Darrell and said, "Chief, we need to get Callman out of town but not in a motel. Do you trust Darcy with your old Plymouth?"

Darrell laughed and said, "Well, as long as he doesn't spin the tires, shift without using the clutch, and careen around corners in that powerhouse, he can use it. Why do you want that car?"

"Martin lives back off the highway between Sylamore and Calico Rock. He said that Callman could stay with him until Callman and I go to Indiana and then he's welcome to stay there for as long as needed after we return. I want Nance to take Callman to Millie's Place on the square and stay out front, pretending he's waiting on him to come back out. Darcy, I want you to take the Plymouth and go around back and pick up Callman and take him to Martin's farm." Reginald called headquarters, talked to dispatch, and told Nance and Callman what they were to do. Darcy went out and left in the powerhouse Plymouth. They heard Darcy squeal its rear tires as he turned it onto the street. They laughed at the sound.

Reginald turned to Martin and said, "I want you to go to the square and park your bike where you can watch Millie's front door. Nance is going to tell dispatch when Callman goes inside and then he will leave with the light bar on as if he has received a call when dispatch calls him three minutes later. I don't know whether this will work or not, but we have to try something to get Callman out of here since I believe the guy is still in town. Martin, after you're satisfied that no one suspicious has entered the store, catch up with Darcy and follow him to your house. You two stay there until you hear from me or Sherry." Martin left with a roar from the pipes of the big Harley chopper.

Silence lay heavy in the living room until Darrell looked at Reginald and said, "Do you have any idea at all what we are up against here?"

"I do some of it, but there are too many pieces missing to see the whole picture. The Little Rock officer was killed by whoever mailed that ice pick to Callman. Why? Whoever it is wants to kill Callman. Why? No answer yet. I think the same perp punctured Blandford's tires and sent the note to Sherry. Why? Don't know. And something tells me that the fire that killed Bud Borders and Carl Alstrom, the owners of that scaffolding company in Little Rock, involves whoever we are looking for. Again why? And there's Matilda Herrington. Why was she killed? And why did he break into Hazel Hancock's house? Then why try to do the same at Mary Sheldon's house? Many questions but no answers, yet." Silence filled the room and then a booming knock rattled the door.

"Come in," Darrell said.

The big frame of Thomas Dawson filled the doorway. "Is everybody peaceable? If you're not, I'm leaving," Dawson said,

"We're peaceable. Get in here," Reginald said.

Wasting no time with chit chat, Thomas asked, "Have you learned anything more?"

"Well, we've learned that we don't know a lot and we hope that Sherry will have something when she returns from Poplar Bluff." Then he filled Thomas in on what they knew and what was being done at the moment.

Thomas sat and looked at the both of them and after a few seconds said, "I don't think that the perp will try anything at Martin's place, but I'll call in one of the deputies who can use the overtime and send him up there to sit tonight. I have some overtime money so I might as well dip into it for this. We have night vision goggles courtesy of the Drug Task Force shared money. We got them last week and this will be a good time to try them out. Roger can sit up there on that ridge and see everything that wiggles down there by Martin's house. Martin has a radio on our frequency so we can be in contact quickly if necessary." Thomas left to arrange for the stake out.

A few minutes after Thomas left, a soft knock sounded on the door. Reginald got up and peeked out. He let Sherry in and not seeing Darrell, she gave him a quick peck on the cheek. He turned red and mumbled something to her. She laughed and then he recovered and said, "Hi Sherry, I sure am glad to see you."

"I'm glad to see you too, Reg."

Darrell came into the room, and they all sat down. As she began to tell them what she had found out, they heard Martin's hog stop in the back yard. He came through the back door and Darrell said, "What's wrong?"

"I went up to the square and had been there a couple of minutes when Nance pulled up and let Callman out. He went into the store just as you arranged and then Nance took off with the lights going. Darcy called me on his radio and told me he had Callman and was headed out of town. I bet Callman really looked funny with that floppy hat and sunglasses Darcy had him wear. Just as I was getting ready to leave, a subject appeared wearing jeans, red plaid short sleeve shirt, and a tan cap. He looked all around and went into the store. It wasn't more than a minute until he was back out looking this way and that way, all over the place. He looked frantic and took off west on Main, walking fast toward the drugstore." Martin paused and Reginald jumped in with a question.

"What did the guy look like?"

"He was ... , oh I would say, your size, maybe a bit taller and slightly heavier and with a short beard."

"Did you notice a limp?"

"Yes. His right leg appeared to bother him. He favored it when he walked away. I pulled out and followed on the bike and saw him go behind the drugstore. I went up the street and turned around, parked, and went into the drugstore. I was watching out the window when he drove out in a brown 1994 Ford. I think it was the same one Darcy and I saw this morning up at Blandford's house. The license number is 53A 1621, Indiana."

Reginald immediately called dispatch and gave Mazy the information. Twenty minutes later, she called back. She told him the plate was stolen four weeks ago from Monroe County, Indiana. He said to her, "And I bet the car is stolen too. Thanks, Mazy." He hung up and told Darrell, Martin, and Sherry what Mazy said. Reginald paused and then said, "Did you see where he went?"

"He turned east on Main and that's when I lost sight of him." Martin left for his house and they turned their attention to Sherry.

Chapter
TWENTY-FOUR

S herry leafed through her notes and said, "Here are my thoughts on this case. One, I think the perp is beginning to feel pressured. Two, his plan is going sour. Three, he failed at killing Callman, and now Callman has given him the slip. Four, he isn't familiar enough with our devious ways to keep tabs on everything we do. I think it's going to make him more dangerous and desperate and that means we have to be extra careful. Martin's sighting, if that was him, tells us he's going to try to carry out his plan, whatever it is. If he had found Callman in the store, he probably would have killed him right there."

"I agree with all of that. Maybe that wasn't such a good idea for getting Callman out of town, but since we don't know his identity or where he's likely to be, and don't know when or where he's watching us, we have to do some things that aren't normal," Reginald said defensively.

"It worked to get Callman out of town and the possible suspect was seen by Martin, so don't worry now," Sherry said.

"You're right." Reginald scuffed his shoe on the floor and then looked up suddenly. "Boy, I almost forgot what I wanted to tell you. I think I know what the perp was searching for in Callman's coach," Reginald said.

Sherry looked up startled and said, "He was in Callman's motor home?"

"Right, but we don't know when. I think he was looking for that letter he sent to Callman. Why I don't know, but nothing was taken.

Nance told me that Callman said he had left the door unlocked the day he was shot, so it wasn't any problem for the perp to enter the coach."

Darrell said, "He may be worried that it can be used as evidence against him. Criminals do strange things when they think they've messed up. They try to cover their tracks and mess up even more and end up making new tracks. As Sherry said, his plans aren't going as well as he expected. What did you learn in Poplar Bluff, Sherry?"

Sherry related all that Gladys Sherman had told her. Darrell got up and called dispatch. He said to Mazy, "Call Sikeston, Missouri, Police Department and ask for Buddy Wellington, a detective there and ask if he's on duty. If he isn't on duty, leave a message for him to call as soon as possible." He also told Mazy that if Wellington called back today to patch him through to the house. They were discussing what they knew and didn't know when the phone rang. Darrell answered and listened for a long moment. He said, "Buddy, good to hear your voice. It's been a long time." Pause. "We need some information if you can give it to us. There are some subjects in your town that we have run across in a homicide investigation and we need answers to some questions if you can give them to us. Here's Sgt. Sherry Westermann, Arkansas State Police, who is helping with our investigation."

Sherry took the phone and exchanged some pleasantries, before asking her questions. She listened and made notes. Then she asked, "What was the date again? I want to make sure it's right." Pause. I got it." She thanked him and gave the phone back to Darrell. He said a few words and hung up.

Both Darrel and Reginald looked at Sherry. The expression on their faces was *well, what did you find out?* She saw the expectant look and said, "I think we struck gold today. The buyer of the blue Ford was J. Daniel Bushman, and now he and his wife Trudy have disappeared. Detective Wellington remembers them because last year they failed to appear in court for their trial on a theft charge he had filed against them. He also has an outstanding warrant for forgery on J. Daniel he obtained in late September. He went out to their house on the north side of town in mid September, right after the skipped court date, and found the door unlocked and no one at home. Most all their clothes were gone, plus their suitcases. Wellington talked to a neighbor that said the blue Ford J. Daniel bought in Poplar Bluff disappeared in late April or early May of 1995. No one has seen any activity at the house or the car since then. The man, his wife, and the car simply vanished from Sikeston. No one knows where they went."

"Do they have relatives?" Reginald asked.

"None as far as the Sikeston Police can determine. They're officially listed as missing persons."

"With a court appearance and the possibility of another arrest warrant hanging over their heads, maybe they lambed out for parts unknown," Darrell added.

"Could be, but what was J. Daniel's car doing in Searcy? It's the one Gladys Sherman told Sherry he bought from her according to the registration. J. Daniel wasn't the driver. It's one of the pieces we have for this mystery and it doesn't fit anywhere. We know the driver had a driver's license with Harley Bastin's name on it and the description of the man fits Bastin, but Bastin is dead. Both Mr. and Mrs. Bushman are missing. None of this makes sense. I have the feeling that if and when they are found it won't be good. Neither do I think that we're going to see that blue Ford in town again. He's switching cars on us faster than a pea being switched in a hide the pea shell game. And don't be surprised if that brown '94 Ford disappears too."

"What makes you say that, Reg?" Sherry asked.

"I think the perp suspects he has been seen, but he doesn't know we don't have a very good description of him. He switches cars to throw us off the track." Reginald grew silent for a few beats and then said, "Sherry, can you run a background on Marion Easterly and find out who his relatives are and where they live? We have to run everything we can think of in our attempts to find a lead."

"Sure, I can do that tomorrow. I'll start first thing tomorrow morning. I'll start with an obituary and go from there. Maybe we're getting somewhere now."

"I sure hope so," Darrell said. "This case is eating us up. At least the news hounds have left town since there hasn't been any excitement for a few days. If anything major happens, they will be back."

"Right and we need to solve this mess before they decide to return. Well, it's after 6:00 p.m., and I am tired. Another long day is coming tomorrow. Reg, will you take me home in my car? Oh, I forgot, you have the police car." Sherry looked defeated.

"Go ahead, Reginald; take her home in her car. I'll drive the police car to work in the morning. Have one of the uniform men pick you up at Sherry's house and take you to the station to get your truck."

"Darrell, you are a sweetie," Sherry said, as she and Reginald went out the door.

TWENTY-FIVE

The next morning Sherry called Reginald at the P.D. and then began checking the family history and background of Marion Easterly. Reginald remained in his office and studied the notes on the case after Sherry called. Nothing popped out and as he started out the door, he received a call on the direct phone line. "Hello, Sgt. Gawker." Pause. "Okay. I'll be here. See you then." Reginald jotted a note to himself that Robert Blandford would be in town Friday morning instead of Saturday morning.

Reginald walked to the dispatch room door and told Mazy Sink he would be in the car and where he was going, but she was not to tell anyone over the radio should they ask. As he was pulling away from headquarters, radio told him to return to dispatch. He entered the room and Mazy handed him the phone. "This is Reginald." Pause. "Where is it?" He paused to listen. "When did that happen?" He paused again. "Last night. Okay. I'll be there in twenty minutes." He handed the phone to Mazy and said, "Tell the Chief I'll be all the way to the end of County 191. Thomas Dawson is out there and wants me to see a car they found. If Sherry calls, tell her where I am."

"10–4, Sarg," Mazy said. "I do that 10–4 real good don't I? I've had a lot of practice."

Reginald laughed as he went out the door to meet Sheriff Dawson and his deputy.

County Road 191 is southwest of Mountain View and all gravel. The county roads that lead to it are rough with houses scattered on both sides here and there along the way. Dogs of all descriptions were seen sleeping in the sun, and a few were sitting on their haunches, watching for whatever mountain dogs watch for during the day. A few chased the police car but gave up after a few feet and watched it disappear in the dust.

When Reginald arrived, the sheriff and the deputy were standing next to a burned out hulk of a car. Reginald got out of his car and walked over to Sheriff Dawson and spoke to Ben Reynolds, the deputy. Reginald said, "A burned out Ford. Bet it's that blue 1989 we're interested in."

"It probably is, but we have to get a VIN number check to make sure," Thomas said. "The plate is gone and whatever else may have been in the car is burnt toast. Didn't Sherry say the doors were rusted out?"

"Right and so did Madeline. She said there were holes below the doors and this one looks like it's the same as she described. What's strange though, if it's the car we're looking for, there isn't any damaged right front fender. What do you make of that, Thomas?"

"I would say that he had it fixed, but where and when is anybody's guess. I'll have a deputy check the body shops."

"Do you have any ideas how it got here?"

"Reginald, that's the sixty-four dollar question, but there may be an answer. Hiram Fowler heard what he supposed was a car with loud mufflers go past at 1:30 a.m., but he didn't think much of it since people go past all the time. Mostly kids looking for a good time or to drink. At 2:00 a.m., he said he heard a noise and thinks it was the same car going out. He was lying awake in bed and that was when he saw the glow from the car burning. He told us this morning."

"What took him so long to call it in?" Reginald asked, slightly irritated, knowing that any delay can give the criminal an advantage.

"He couldn't call. Hiram doesn't have one of those tom fool contraptions as he calls the phone, and since he had to go to town anyway, he decided just to come by my office and report it. But when he went to his pickup, it wouldn't start. He finally made it to town and here we are."

"And he doesn't know anything else?"

"No, that's it," Thomas said.

Reginald looked around and seeing nothing, studied the car before he spoke. "It's likely there were two cars. One was to take whoever was driving that car out of here."

"It would seem that way, but Hiram said he only heard one car. It also looks like it was soaked thoroughly with gasoline the way it burned." They stood in silence and looked at the blackened hulk of the Ford.

"Hey Sheriff, look here," Ben Reynolds called out. Sheriff Dawson and Reginald walked to the front of the car and looked to where Ben was pointing. They saw the faint tracks of dual wheels leading away from the front of the car. "Sheriff, I'd say a tow truck brought it here and whoever it was tried to brush out the tracks and didn't succeed. They missed these and the ones back there where they turned around. He must have been in a real hurry to leave here."

Reginald and the sheriff looked at the scuff marks in the dirt and gravel where someone had scraped their boots back and forth across the tire tread impressions. Sheriff Dawson went to the patrol car and got his camera. He took shots of the scene and then called the dispatcher for a tow truck and told him to include two tires and wheels that would fit the hubs of an '89 Ford Crown Vic.

Two hours later, a procession lead by the sheriff's car, followed by the tow truck pulling the burned out Ford on the tow hook, with Reginald's plain car bringing up the rear, went through town going toward the impound yard. A man with a short beard, dressed in jeans, a red plaid short sleeve shirt, and brown leather boots, leaning against a building, watched the vehicle turn east at the corner of Church and East Main streets. He pushed away from the building and entered a brown 1994 Ford with a stolen Arkansas plate on it that he had taken from a wrecked brown '94. A deep look of anger showed on his face as he pulled out to follow the procession.

When the procession arrived at the impound yard, Reginald's radio crackled. He listened. Then he told Thomas he was going over to Joe Sharp's Service and to come on over if he wasn't back in twenty minutes. Thomas nodded and Reginald left.

When Reginald arrived, Joe Sharp was kicking the tires on his tow truck. Irritation covered his usually serene face. Reginald got out of his car and asked, "What's wrong Joe?"

"Look at my truck," Joe said angrily, pointing at a mashed in left front fender and a broken headlight. "Somebody stole it last night and smashed it up."

"How do you know it was stolen? Maybe someone hit it while parked here on your lot."

Joe looked at Reginald ready to explode, but he gained control of his temper before he spoke. "Reginald, it has been hot wired and over a quarter of a tank of gas is missing. I serviced it yesterday evening before closing up, and it has been driven almost eighty miles since it was serviced, and I didn't drive it except from the rack to where I parked it."

"Was it locked?"

"No, the door lock is broken and I haven't had time to fix it, so getting in wasn't a problem."

Reginald walked over to the truck, a 1979 Ford one ton and looked inside. He inspected the door handle carefully. To open the door, the handle had to be grabbed underneath and pulled up. He looked up at Joe and said, "It looks like the door handle has been polished. Wiped cleaned. Did you do that?"

"No, I opened the other side and slid in when I saw the wires underneath the dash hanging down. That's when I saw the mileage was different."

Reginald walked around the truck to the right side and carefully pulled on the door handle where it wouldn't be possible to obtain fingerprints. He looked inside and saw a nearly spotless interior. He turned to Joe and said, "Did you clean the inside yesterday?"

"Yes and no. I brushed it out and cleaned out the junk, but I did notice it looked like it had been wiped down more than what I did to it."

"Whoever took your truck wiped it to get rid of prints. I also suspect he wore gloves since there are some oily smudges here and there."

Joe looked at Reginald and said, "I keep a pair of gloves under the driver's seat. They're my tow gloves. I put them on before hooking up a vehicle. I wonder if he wore them." Joe looked under the seat, raised and up, and said, "The gloves are gone."

Reginald looked where Joe indicated and as he rose up to back out of the cab, an object caught his eye. He said, "Joe, do you eat candy?"

"I do sometimes. Why?"

"Do you eat Milky Ways?"

"No. Butterfingers when I eat candy. They're the only kind of peanut butter I like. Why do you want to know what kind of candy I eat?"

"There's a Milky Way wrapper under the seat."

"It's not mine," Joe said.

"You're sure that it isn't yours?"

"Yes, I'm sure. I cleaned out the cab last night and took the cups and stuff from under the seat and scrubbed the floor mats."

Reginald started to his car to get a pair of latex gloves and an evidence bag for the candy wrapper when the sheriff pulled onto the lot. He said, "What have you got, Reginald?"

Reginald told him what had transpired and said, "I think we may have something that will help." He walked over to the truck to open the driver's door and looked down. It was a flat toothpick broken in the middle. He stared at it for long seconds and then looked at Thomas and remained silent. He looked around and what he saw sent chills down his spine. "What's wrong, Reginald?" Thomas asked.

"We have a problem. Don't look anywhere except at me. There's a man in the store across the street watching us, and the way he's staring at us, he seems to be very interested in what we're doing. I can't get a good look at him where he's standing. It could be the killer. I'm going over to my car to get the evidence collection kit and call back up." When Reginald headed to his car, the man disappeared from the store. The man left through a side door and joined a group of people strolling along the street. The patrol officers searched the area and didn't find anyone that was acting suspicious. The officers looked right at him and never knew whom they had seen.

Reginald took an evidence bag from the kit, along with a pair of tweezers, and placed the broken toothpick in the bag. Once it was marked with all the information and properly noted on the evidence log sheet, Thomas said, "A broken toothpick was found on the square the night Callman was shot. Do you think that the same perp dropped this one?"

"I'm going to say right now that the same one dropped both. If that was the killer in the store watching us, he left before I picked it up. I didn't want him to see that. I think he is unaware that he's leaving tracks that will eventually lead to him. He's being cagey, but he is making mistakes. And I think he's beginning to show some desperation like Sherry told us," Reginald said.

"I wouldn't be surprised if the brown Ford disappears, especially if he thinks anyone saw him in that car with the Indiana plate the day Martin spotted him," Thomas said.

"That's what bothers me."

"How does that bother you?" Thomas asked.

"The possible suspect has been real careful to keep us from learning his identity. Now he has been seen several times, and if he is the one we saw standing in the store window, and if he's the one that Mandy Gettner saw in the restaurant the evening Matilda Herrington was killed, he is becoming bolder with his behavior and may try to harm those who have seen him. If you're right Thomas, he'll ditch the Ford and then we won't know what he's driving. Something is haywire with our suspect more than ever now. It's as if he's playing games with us."

"I agree, and this whole deal is giving me a bad feeling, Reginald,"

Thomas said with apprehension in his voice. "We don't know who or why and certainly we don't know where he will strike again."

Reginald turned to Joe and said, "Joe, I want you to be extra careful until we apprehend this guy."

"Do you think I'm in danger now?" Joe asked, worry showing in his question.

"I honestly don't know. We are dealing with someone who is very dangerous and very unpredictable, if he's the one who killed Mrs. Herrington." Reginald grew silent and stared at Joe whose face showed the beginning traces of fright.

Thomas looked from Joe to Reginald. "Reginald do you have any ideas that will help us now?"

"Thomas, I have a few, but they are so crazy I can't fit anything together. After Callman and I go to Indiana, we may be able to fit the pieces to the puzzle. Right now all I got is a hunch and a big headache." He stood silently and looked at the ground, deep in thought.

Joe Sharp broke the silence. "What should I do?"

"Do you have a gun and do you know how to use it?" Thomas asked.

"Yes, and I know how to use it, and I have a concealed carry permit too. Why?"

"Keep it with you at all times and if you have to use it, just be sure that it's self defense."

Joe looked at Thomas and said, "I can do that, but I hope it doesn't come to that."

"I hope it doesn't either," Reginald said with doubt creeping through his mind.

Thomas and Reginald left Joe and drove back to the impound lot to take another look at the burned out Ford. They wanted to look at the right front fender and to look in the trunk for anything that might be there that would help them solve the case. The fender showed signs of not matching up well with the mounts. They concluded that the damaged one had been replaced. They had to pry the trunk lid open since the keys weren't in the ignition switch. The lid opened with a groan and filled the noses of Thomas and Reginald with the burned, foul smelling air that spilled out. The first thing they saw was a gasoline can. They carefully moved the can and underneath it was what remained of the keys to the car. Thomas looked at Reginald and said, "He sure didn't want anything left that could identify him."

Reginald looked up at Thomas and said, "This car burning makes me suspicious of that house fire in Mountain Home. Burning is a good way to get rid of evidence, if it is done right. From all indications, I would say that our perp is good at it."

"You have no argument from me after what you told me concerning that fire up there. Do you think he did that one too?"

"I do and have thought so for a long time, but I can't prove my suspicions because the dates don't match."

"What dates?" Thomas wanted to know.

"The date Marion Easterly died and the dates of the deaths of the victims in that house fire. I'm missing something and I don't know what it is."

Thomas Dawson looked at Reginald with a frown plowing deep furrows into his forehead. "I just hope we find out before anything else happens to give us more questions we can't answer. The town's people are getting antsy and wanting answers. A few have called the governor, but he's staying hands off for now rather than order in the state police. Darrell and I both called him and explained that Sherry and two excellent undercover men are here working with us. The governor called Cordley and received assurance that we could handle it. So far so good at this point is all I can say."

"Let's pray it stays good. We don't need what we do know to be spread around and others coming in to stir the pot. I think we are making headway but not very fast."

"Are you leaving for Indiana with Callman on Monday?"

"Yes, and I sure hope we can find some answers." The radio in Reginald's car squawked. He picked up the mike and answered. He looked at Thomas and said, "Robert Blandford is in town, and he wasn't supposed to be here until Friday morning. I need to go to headquarters." The sheriff and Reginald left for their respective offices.

Robert Blandford was waiting in Reginald's office. They shook hands and both sat down. "Did you have a good trip coming back down?" Reginald asked.

"It was fine except for some heavy rain in Kentucky and Missouri. Of course, traffic is always heavy this time of the year. Have you had any success on the case?"

Reginald hesitated before answering as a thought went through his head. "Some but can't say what at the moment. I need to pry into your head to see if there is anything that you can think of that will shed some light on all this."

"I don't know what it could be, but I'll try. I've told you everything I know which isn't much. Ask your questions and maybe I can tell you something that will ring a bell for you," Blandford said agreeably.

"Now," Reginald said as he read his interview notes. "Let's go back to when we first talked. You said that a relative left you that property at Sylamore. Where did he live?"

"I think in a town south of Little Rock. Ah ... Pine ... something."

"Pine Bluff?"

"That's it," Blandford exclaimed. "I never have been able to remember that town's name."

"What was the relationship to you?"

"He was my father's brother's son, my cousin. I was the only relative he liked according to the will. It was strange. I only saw him four or five times that I can remember. Sort of peculiar guy now that I recall him. Like a recluse."

"Was he born in Pine Bluff?"

"No, he was born in Ohio, and his father moved there when Whitlow was five years old. He bought the land here with intentions of building a cabin on it," Blandford said with sadness in his voice.

Reginald waited for several beats before asking, "Was he married?"

"Yes, but his wife died some years back and he never remarried."

"Did he have children?"

"He had one daughter, Mary Beth Blandford Norman. She married a man who owns a trucking company. I think she's twenty-three years younger than I am. I'm sixty-one so she would be close to thirty-eight as near as I can figure."

"Where does she live?" Reginald asked.

"Last I heard she's in Texarkana. She runs a day care there."

"Why didn't her father leave her the property up here? I don't know whether it's important or not. Probably not, but I'm just curious more than anything else," Reginald said.

"She didn't want it," Blandford said. "I found that out from her when we went to settle everything. Her father left her a sizeable amount of money and she was happy that I was the one that got the land. She said her dad talked of me a lot, and truthfully, I don't know why he did or why he liked me."

"Do you ever see her?"

"On occasion when business takes me that way, but I haven't seen her for over two years now. I don't have any reason to go there unless there is a problem with a customer that needs my attention. Seldom happens though." Blandford's face brightened and then he said, "I just remembered. She sent me a letter telling me she was going to be here next week to visit a friend who plays music at the Folk Center. She said she would be there on Friday night since that was the only night the friend was scheduled to play."

"What's the friend's name?"

"I don't know. She didn't say in the letter. I plan on being here next week too, so I'll get to see her and maybe you can meet her."

"I'm going to be gone most of next week, but if she's still here when I get back, I would like to meet her," Reginald said, which he knew pleased Blandford.

Blandford said, "I need to be going, but one more thing before I go. Have you found out who punctured my tires?"

"No. However, I think I know who did it, but I can't say at this time. Thing is I don't know why."

"I don't either, and if it's not connected with the other stuff, I don't have any idea at all. Even if it's connected, I still don't know why." Blandford went to the door and turned back towards Reginald and said, "I'll be at the Blue Bird Inn." Reginald nodded and Blandford left.

After making a phone call, Reginald left for Martin Perkins's place on White River. A moderate to heavy rain made the drive sloppy and slow. He wanted to tell Martin and Darcy what he had found at Sharp's place of business. He also wanted to make plans with Callman for the trip to Indiana next week, and hoped it would help things to make sense so they could solve this most perplexing case. He made a brief stop at the store in Sylamore and then headed for Calico Rock.

The rain had stopped by the time Reginald arrived at the Perkins place. Four dogs of various descriptions greeted him. They were all bark, no bite, and wagging tails. He reached into the car and took candy from the collection he had bought in Sylamore. He gave each dog a piece. They chewed happily on the caramel as Reginald started to the house. Martin Perkins watched with amusement as Reginald gave the dogs the treats and said, laughing, "Man, you have made friends for life. They'll expect a gift each time they see you."

"Some watch dogs you got there, Martin," Reginald teased.

"Well, they watched everything you did. What more do you want? Now where's our candy?" They both laughed and the dogs continued to chew, watching Reginald return to the car, their tails whipping the air.

Reginald reached into the car and got the candy and took it into the house. Darcy and Martin helped themselves. L. Jason Callman was asleep on the couch. Reginald looked at him and then at Martin. "Listen to that man snore. He sounds like a chainsaw with a rough running engine.

"At least he isn't making sawdust," Martin said, laughing.

Chapter

TWENTY-SEVEN

---

he events of the week were hashed and rehashed but nothing new
came of it. The body shops had been checked for a blue Ford with
a damaged fender. None had come in for repair in the county or town
shops. Darcy said that the deputy saw a tan Ford on the river road
going by slowly, but he was too far away to get a description of the
driver. They all doubted it was the suspect since they didn't see how
he would know Martin's identity or where he lived. They decided the
wisest course was to take no chances and consider the possibility that
the man driving the Ford could be the killer.

Callman awakened and looked around. He stretched, yawned,
and said, "I'm not used to doing all this resting. Guess it makes me
tired." He looked around and saw Reginald. "Hey Sgt. Gawker, what
are you doing here?"

"I need to ask you some questions and then make some plans for
the Indiana trip."

"Are we still leaving Monday morning?"

"Yes, bright and early at 5:00 a.m. We should be back Thursday
evening if all goes right up there. If not, it will be Friday. Do you know
a good motel in Bloomington?"

L. Jason Callman looked at the ceiling, the floor, and then at Reginald. "I don't really know, but if we are going to go to the Sheriff's
Department, the Marriott on South College is only a bit over four
blocks south of the Justice Building on the corner of 7th and College

Avenue. As I remember, there are some nice restaurants nearby, so it will be handy."

"That sounds good. I'll make reservations sometime tomorrow."

"What do you think we'll find there?"

"I don't know, but I hope whatever it is will help solve this case. Now I need to ask you questions about your sales trips," Reginald said to Callman.

"Okay, I don't know what else I can tell you, but I'll try to answer the best I know how."

"Did you ever go to Pine Bluff in your line of business?

"I made a few trips there but not very often. I only had three or four accounts there. They weren't big business generators for me. One was fairly decent. Much better than the others though."

"Did you know Whitlow Blandford?"

Callman twisted up his mouth and ran his hand across his face. "No, the name isn't familiar." He looked blank for a few seconds and then spoke. "Is that some relation to the Blandford I did business with in Ohio?"

"It was his cousin who died a few years ago."

"I never knew him or heard of him," Callman said.

"What businesses did you call on in Pine Bluff?"

Callman exhaled loudly and said, "It's been so long. Let me think. Ah, let me think … there was Abe's Industrial Cleaning Company. He cleaned the floors, walls, and windows in factories and warehouses. Not a big customer but phoned in steady orders through the year. Then there were two others that were more the domestic type cleaning companies. They did apartment houses and rentals. The three made calling there on occasion worthwhile. Didn't want to lose the accounts even though they were small," Callman said, reminiscing.

"Is that all?" Reginald asked.

"No, there was one more, a trucking company, but I can't think of the name." He closed his eyes for a few seconds, rolled his head around, and said, "I'm sorry I can't recall the name. If I heard it, I might remember it." He gave Reginald a questioning look. "What good is this anyway?"

"At the moment I don't really know if any of this is any good, but I have to cover all bases. Now back to your accounts. Would the name of the trucking company be Norman Trucking and Transport?"

Callman jerked his head up and said, "That's it. How did you know?"

"I only found out today. Did you know Earnest Norman's wife, Mary Beth Norman?"

"No. I never met her. I didn't even know her name until now that I can remember. Never heard it before you told me that I can recall," Callman said, swiveling his head around on his shoulders again. "But I might have and just not remembered. I met so many people that names didn't stick with me unless they did business with me. Customers I remembered until I retired. Now, I have forgotten most of their names. There's no reason to remember them."

"Do you know what line of work she was in?"

"No. She was never around when I was at the company. I vaguely remember hearing that Norman's wife worked in Little Rock. Beyond that, I don't know. Like I said, I didn't know her name."

"So you never knew what she did in Little Rock or where she worked?"

"That's right."

"Do you know where she is now?"

"I have no idea where she is now or what she's doing. I think the trucking company moved in 1989, two years before I retired, but I don't know where. Mr. Norman closed the account, and I had no further contact with Norman Trucking. I hated to lose the account. They made me good commissions."

"Does Texarkana, Arkansas, ring any bells with you?"

Callman thought for a beat or two and said, "Not that I remember. That was too far southwest for my territory. And I don't think we had anyone down that far when I was on the sales trail. I can't help on that." He hesitated and then added, "Never been there."

All during the questioning of Callman, Darcy, and Martin had been watching out the window. Suddenly they jumped up and ran out the door, heading for the end of the driveway at full gallop with guns drawn. Reginald, peering through the window saw a tan late model Ford going slowly past the drive to Martin's house. When they reached the end of the driveway, the car stopped and the driver, his face as white as a newly laundered sheet, got out.

After a few minutes, the car drove off and the two officers returned to the house. They went inside and Reginald asked them what went on out there. Martin replied, "That was Abner Hanson. He lives down the road a piece and was out looking at his cows. He's the one the deputy saw last night. Abner bought that car two months ago and nobody recognized him. His pickup is in the shop, so he has to drive the car."

"Hope you fellas didn't blow your cover down there," Reginald said, sounding worried.

"Don't worry. Abner is a retired policeman from Fort Smith and knows not to talk. He heard the radio traffic on his scanner the day we came into town, and then after seeing Martin and me walking around on the square one day, he put it all together. He did say our guns shook him a bit. He couldn't figure out what he had done."

"We told him to watch for the tan '94 Ford," Darcy added. "He said he would watch for it when out looking around. An extra pair of eyes won't hurt anything."

Reginald agreed and turned back to Callman to ask some more questions when the phone rang. Martin picked up and said, "Hello. Who's this?" He listened and then slammed the receiver down. Unhappiness was spread all over him. He said, "A telemarketer trying to sell me accident insurance to be paid for on my gasoline card. I get three or four of those calls each week." The phone rang again. "Hello," he said gruffly and then began laughing as he listened. "I thought you were another telemarketer. He's here," and handed the phone to Reginald without telling him who it was.

"Hi, Sherry," Reginald said cheerfully. He listened and then said,

"You and three others are the only ones who know where I am, so I figured it had to be you. If not you, I would have tried more names till I got it right." He listened and then said, "She didn't have any other close relatives?" He listened more. "Easterly either?" A frown appeared on his face as he listened to Sherry. "Then Callman's friend was right on the date of death, June, 10, 1995." He listened, frowning. "He died how?" He listened and frowned again. "He died in a car fire caused by an accident?" Reginald exclaimed incredulously. Then he listened again. "Okay, I'll ask Mr. Callman what he knows about Easterly. I'll be back in town in a little while. Will let you know. Bye." He hung up the phone and looked at the three men in the room.

"From the look on your face this can't be good," Darcy said.

"I'm as lost on this case as I have ever been on an investigation. There isn't anything that fits anywhere and I can't figure out why. All this information and none of it will add up or make sense. All we know is somebody is killing people he doesn't know, and we don't know who he is or why."

"We heard you say that Easterly was killed in an accident and fire. That eliminates him," Darcy said, "or does it?" The way this case is going anything is possible."

"Real hard for a dead man to kill people," Martin said. "But I've heard of crazier things." Nobody laughed or said a word because all of them knew the deadly nature of the case.

They heard a noise and turned to look at L. Jason Callman. He was rocking back and forth and moaning. Darcy went over to the couch, sat down, and put his arm around him. Big tears ran down Callman's face as he shook violently.

Reginald told Martin that he was going, and he would call as soon as he was in headquarters. He walked into his office and called Martin who told him that Callman had calmed down and was asleep. Reginald hung up feeling sorry for Mr. Callman. No man deserved what he was going through.

A shadow appeared on the wall and when Reginald saw it, he

jumped at the same time he heard a voice say, "Hi, Reg. You seem to be extra jumpy today. I didn't know I had that affect on you."

"Sherry, you scared the bee jabbers out of me. I was deep in thought and when I saw your shadow and it, well ... affected me." They both laughed. "What are you doing here?"

"I saw you go by the bank and needed to talk to you. Since we talked on the phone, I got a call from Sam Hazelton at the bank in Mountain Home. He said the checks that came in on the Bushman account totaled 985 dollars. The checks were written for money orders on April 7, 1996. He thinks Bushman might be using the account for money laundering. He apparently keeps close track of the amount of money in it since it is never overdrawn." Wrinkles of a frown made deep creases across her forehead.

"I hope that court order we obtained to monitor that account turns up something else. Whomever we're dealing with, the guy is no dummy. Except for some minor slips, he's doing a good job of hiding his identity."

"That sure makes it much tougher to find him if we're dealing with a perp who knows what he's doing. It makes me think he has had training of some sort."

"What kind of training do you think it might be?" Sherry asked.

"I don't know for sure but some kind of clandestine work like a branch of the military," Reginald said with some alarm showing in his speech.

"You are worried that you're right, aren't you?" Sherry said, sensing Reginald's mood. He nodded his head and they left headquarters wanting to get rid of the headache that they both had from trying to solve the case.

Chapter

TWENTY-EIGHT

When Sherry left the bank to go to see Reginald at police headquarters, she wasn't aware that she was being watched, and that the man watching followed her to the police department. He was dressed much like all the other tourists in town and knew that he had perfect cover for his work. But the idea that his plans were constantly being interrupted made him angrier and angrier. His mind, boiling over with liquid hate, kicked into high gear. *When the time is right, I am going to kill her and that cop boyfriend of hers. They have really messed up my plans, and I am going to teach them a lesson that no one will ever forget. Killing the cop in Little Rock wasn't in my plans and neither was killing the woman who saw me in the restaurant. They just happened to be in the wrong place at the time, and I couldn't take any chances that they might be able to identify me, especially that woman. The cop might not have remembered but ... then again he might have.* "Two down and many to go," he muttered aloud and then laughed. "Have to die sometime, and I'm the one who will provide the sometime for these targets."

The wild thoughts continued as the killer's madness took greater control. *Everything was fine until Lavon Jason Callman didn't die. He didn't go to the postal box and get his mail the day he was shot. He was supposed to get the ice pick that day. He always picked up his mail at 6:00 p.m. I know that because I watched him for several days before I went back to Little Rock. He didn't do it that day and that messed up my plans. My plan was to kill Callman when he came out of the post office, and to do it so silently and so quickly that neither Callman nor anyone else would ever* know who did it. To make it worse, Callman turned that letter and the ice pick over to that jerk of a cop. Those weren't supposed to be found until Callman was dead, when it wouldn't have made any difference. Callman had disappeared, and now my plans are coming apart.

The killer's fantasies roamed through his mind, fueled by his all consuming hatred for Sherry and Reginald. *That pretty little teller, or whatever she does at the bank, doesn't know how much I despise her. She will find out right before I kill her and that boyfriend, the ever nosy Sgt. Reginald P. Gawker. Some people have it all, and others have nothing. I am one of those who have nothing. But, I will get something. I will get revenge on those who have taken my life and caused me this pain. They don't know how much I hate them. This town will never forget me.*

Scalding hatred drove a whirl of disconnected thoughts through the man's twisted mind. *I really don't have it all worked out how I will kill the banker and the cop. There are four others and Callman too that I will kill before I am done. One might be able to throw a real monkey wrench into my plans, so I need to figure out the best thing to do. That nosy old bat tried to fool me by changing her bird feeders. I knew she saw the car and could identify it. That old woman who lived next door to that Matilda woman that I killed has disappeared. The one across the street and that old man are gone, too. They were slipped out of town by that dumb cop before I could take care of them. He's supposed to be stupid. Maybe that Sherry woman is the brains and is telling him what to do. They're together a lot. I bet that's it.*

As his mind began to cool, his thinking became more rational. *Then I had that wreck in Searcy the day they fooled me and I followed the wrong car. They fooled me with the scarf the woman at the Heber Springs Bank wore when she left the building. It wasn't the same color as the one the Sherry woman wore. They made a mistake too, but it cost me and not them as it would have if I had been alert.* "How could I be so stupid as to miss that scarf?" he asked himself aloud.

They wouldn't fool him again, and then he remembered that they fooled him when Callman was with that cop and disappeared when he entered that store. Whoever did that would be paid back, too. And then he considered that those two hippy looking types might be part of his trouble as well. *If they're cops, I'll give them both a real lesson. They will suffer for their foolishness. But they did get arrested in the restaurant for fighting over that waitress, Mandy something or another. They may be just low life thugs looking for trouble and not part of anything. That's it, thugs,* he decided.

He saw Robert H. Blandford sitting in the Home Cookin' Cafe and smiled. *I don't have a plan for that cute little Sherry and that Sgt. Reginald P. Gawker yet, but I have just the plan for Mr. Blandford.* He quit thinking on his plans for Sherry and turned his attention to Blandford. He went in the restaurant and sat down. The waitress came over to his table, and he ordered a piece of pie and a cup of coffee. He noticed that Blandford payed him no attention. He was too busy reading the business section of a newspaper. He knew that Blandford didn't know that the real business was looking right at him. He smiled to himself, ate his pie, and drank his coffee. Now where did the gum chewing waitress go? He would kill her too just because she acted smart the first time he was in the restaurant. Just thinking about it brought forth an evil smile which he quickly wiped away.

Then his mood quickly turned sour when Joe Landers, the owner of the business, came through the swinging door, put a stack of dishes on the shelf, and returned to the kitchen. *What is he doing here?* Now he knew he had another problem to solve. *Well, Mr. Landers, I will just have to include you in the plans for my little party.*

Blandford signaled the waitress for his check and went to the register to pay. Blandford looked at the man briefly and nodded his head in a friendly gesture when he saw the man gazing intently at him as he went out the door. The man paid his bill and followed Blandford, keeping a safe distance behind to avoid detection. He smiled again knowing that he was so good that no one had detected him yet. A killer right in their midst and they didn't know it. But they would know it when he was ready to spring his surprise on the unsuspecting fools. When Blandford entered his car, the man jotted his license number on the palm of his hand. *Now to find out where you are staying is my next order of business. And then …* his thought trailed off and an evil smile appeared.

•

Sherry and Reginald decided that they needed some relief from the case and went into the Home Cookin' Cafe a few minutes after the man and Blandford had left. They took a table near the front windows that gave them an unobstructed view of Main Street. They were busy looking at the menu when the man in the tan Ford passed the restaurant, so they didn't see the car. But he saw them, and his mind began to spin on the plan to kill them.

The man headed for his rental house two miles north of Locust Grove. Locust Grove is a wide spot in the road at the Junction of State Highways 14 and 25, ten miles south of Batesville. The tiny metropolis has a convenience store, an old hardware business, and a dirt race track where Mark Martin, now a NASCAR Cup and Busch driver, began his racing experience. The man drove up the drive and went into the house.

He had rented the house because it sat a quarter mile off the highway behind a grove of trees and fields overgrown with weeds. It couldn't be seen from the road, and no one bothered him—both helped his big plan. The owner, who was in a nursing home, hadn't lived in the house for two years. His daughter was glad to rent it to him for 200 dollars per month. She had told him it was better than the nothing that it had earned for the two years it sat empty. It wasn't much of a house, but for the price what more could he expect. At the least, it had running water, a bath, and heat. Plus the little workshop and the space in the garage were perfect for his hobby. The only problem was he didn't have anyone now to enjoy the hobby with him. His mind drifted to the time of more pleasant memories and then he began to feel the pain again. He went into a rage and screamed until he was hoarse, collapsing into a fetal ball on the floor of the living room.

•

While waiting on their food, Reginald and Sherry discussed the case. Sherry said, "We know a lot and really know nothing. For starters, why is he trying to kill Callman and why were Blandford's tires punctured?"

Reginald remained silent for two ticks and then said, "When we answer those then the other questions will be answered, and hopefully the answers will tell us who. There is a connection, but what we don't know. And there's Officer McGee whose killing is connected, but we don't know how. Why was he killed?"

"The most perplexing question is why he killed Matilda Herrington. That makes no sense at all, but there is a connection of some kind that we can't see," Sherry said with frustration showing.

"Maybe she heard something or saw something that made him think he needed to kill her," Reginald said. Sherry got a far away look and seemed to have floated mentally into space. "Sherry, you okay?" Reginald asked worried. No answer. "Sherry, are you okay?"

"Huh? Oh. I'm okay. What did you just say?"

"I said, 'Sherry, are you okay?'"

"No, that's not what I mean. You said something maybe she saw … "

"Oh yeah, I did. Maybe she heard or saw something. What are you thinking?"

"Reg, what if Matilda Herrington recognized him?"

Reginald looked at Sherry and said excitedly as he leaned across the table, "Sherry, if we weren't in public I would kiss you. You just gave me an aspirin for my headache."

"I gave you an aspirin? Have you gone daffy?"

Reginald began flipping pages in his notebook and said, "We need to question Mandy Gettner again. The thing that has been nagging me is what Mandy said to me when I questioned her. It's what she told me that occurred between Matilda and the strange man in the restaurant the night she was killed."

"What did she say?"

"I asked her if she could remember anything that took place between Mrs. Herrington and the man. Here is her answer exactly as she told me. 'Now I remember. Mrs. Herrington motioned me over and started to say something. That guy turned and looked at her, and when I got to the table, I asked her what she wanted. She said nothing, paid her bill, and left quickly.' Then Mandy said, 'I think he scared Mrs. Herrington.' I asked her why she said that, and she said, 'I don't know. That's just what I thought.' Sherry, I think that Mrs. Herrington thought she recognized him and for some reason changed her mind, perhaps because she wasn't sure, and I also think he believed he knew her from some place. Now if we are correct in our surmising, we can find some more answers."

"Reg, if we can find a connection here more of your headache is going to go away."

"Sherry, when Callman and I go to Indiana, I want you to go to Pine Bluff and find out everything possible related to Norman Trucking and Transport. We need to know what they haul and where they moved. Mary Beth Norman had a job in Little Rock. See if you can find what type of work she did there. She owns a day care in Texarkana now, and that's where the trucking company is located now. You may need to go there to see her and her husband."

"I need to ask for permission from the higher ups. I'll need to call Little Rock for clearance to do this."

"I'll have Darrell call Colonel Cordly tomorrow. And I want you to go to the L.R.P.D. and find out what detail McGee might have been on the day that scaffold fell at the refrigeration plant. I have a hunch I can't explain, and it hinges on Mrs. Herrington and what you said that maybe she recognized him."

Sherry added, "And I'll try to find what the connection there might have been to Mrs. Herrington. Do we know anything that would point to any problems with Mrs. Easterly and the children?"

"No, we don't. Find out as much as you are able. And I'll give you that toothpick found at Sharp's to take to the lab for a DNA comparison with the one found on the square when Callman was shot. I'm hoping that they match each other and also match the blood found on Mrs. Sheldon's porch."

"Reg, when was that Bushman bank account opened?"

Reginald flipped some more pages in his notebook, looked up at Sherry, and said, "July of 1995. That's before Borders and Alstrom were killed and after Easterly died. Could Bushman be our killer?"

"Reg, I don't think so. The description doesn't fit. Gladys Sherman said he was tall and skinny. Who set up that bank account?"

"Sherry, I'm grasping at straws trying to figure this out. I hope the trip to Indiana bears fruit. And with what you might find out, hopefully the door will open, and we can arrest the maniac," Reginald said, trying to sound encouraged.

"I think maniac is a good description. Not politically correct, but good. Based on my studies in abnormal psychology, I think he's criminally insane, and if he is, we have a situation so dangerous that it defies the imagination. It may give dangerous a new definition."

"I agree, and the question is still why in addition to who," Reginald said. "And I need to ask Blandford more questions to learn the type of things his manufacturing business does and how he operates it. I'll try to get some more out of Callman as well while we're driving up there."

Their dinner arrived, and they hungrily dug into the pan fried chicken, mashed potatoes, gravy, green beans, and biscuits. They were too busy eating to talk until the food was half gone. Sherry looked up and said, "Reg, I was starved."

Reginald said between bites, "So was I," and went back to eating, trying to keep his mind off the case. Yet, the gnawing of the things he didn't know were eating holes in his mind and making his headache return. A deep foreboding came over him.

Sherry saw his agony and decided that she couldn't say anything to help him, so she stayed quiet. She began to feel the same as Reginald. Apple pie and ice cream didn't dull the horrible feeling that only grew larger in the both of them.

Chapter

TWENTY-NINE

arly the next morning, Reginald called the Marriott in Bloomington, Indiana, and made reservations for three nights beginning on
Monday. He went over the case with Darrell Cumberland and called
Martin's house and asked Darcy to have Mr. Callman at headquarters
before 5:00 a.m. on Monday morning. Darrell called Colonel Cordley
as Reginald had asked, and when he finished the call, he told Reginald
that Sherry was cleared for the trip. Reginald made sure the evidence
was ready for Sherry on Monday morning. She would meet him a few
minutes before 5:00 a.m., pick up the package, and leave for Little
Rock.

Next, he called Robert Blandford at his motel and asked him if he
would like to have breakfast and talk. Blandford agreed, and Reginald
picked him up. They drove up to Fifty-Six to the Wind Mill Restaurant. They found an isolated booth in the back corner away from the
mainstream of the customers. The waitress brought water and coffee
and handed each of them a menu. They ordered the breakfast special
of eggs, choice of meat, hash browns, biscuits, gravy, and juice, which
was extra.

Reginald took a sip of coffee and a drink of water. He said, "Robert, we have a bit more information, but we still don't know enough to
zero in on a suspect. We're taking a new direction on the investigation
in the hope that some new evidence can be found. I want to go over
everything I have asked you and try some new questions."

Blandford bristled up and said, "Are you trying to suggest that …"

"No, not at all," Reginald said cutting him off. "There are things we don't know and more than likely have overlooked, so I want to start at the beginning and come to the present."

"I'll try to tell you all I can," Blandford said with his emotions once more in check.

"Good. Let's begin." The food arrived, and they talked and ate for over an hour going over the punctured tires, the note, and other items Reginald felt safe in mentioning. Then he asked, "Is manufacturing all you do?"

Blandford reacted with surprise and said, "What do you mean?"

"I mean, do you have any other business besides whatever you manufacture."

"We have a distribution business to distribute our products. It's more efficient and costs less than going through another party for distribution. We sell direct to both the commercial end users and retailers."

"What kind of products do you manufacture and sell?" Reginald asked.

"We manufacture all kinds of industrial and construction items. One of our items is a hydraulic device for leveling portable scaffolds."

"You sell scaffold equipment?" Reginald exclaimed with a question.

"Yes, we do business with scaffold companies. Why are you interested in scaffolds?" Blandford wanted to know.

"Are you aware of that scaffold collapsing in Little Rock a few years ago that killed a woman and her two children?"

"Am I," Blandford said heatedly. "I was in the lawsuit that was filed by the husband of the woman and the father of the children who were killed. Eventually the judge dismissed my company from the suit, when we were able to establish that our product wasn't set up according to the instructions. We sent a man down there to show them how to operate the equipment safely, and they still did it wrong. Their improper setup caused the scaffold to fall. They just plainly ignored the warning on how to use the product."

"After your company was dismissed from the suit, what did you do?"

"My lawyers and I packed up and went back to Ohio, and I never found out what happened to the lawsuit. To tell you the truth, I wasn't interested," Blandford said. "How does this all fit with my tires being punctured and that Callman fellow being shot and the woman killed?"

Reginald was quiet for a few ticks and then said, "I'm not sure, but there is some kind of a link. What it is I don't know or why."

"Is there anything else? I need to get back to meet some friends before noon. They want to see the house. It's going to be finished a week or so from now."

"Just a few more questions and we'll go. Sky High Scaffold furnished the scaffold for the maintenance job. Do you know anything that will help me with that company?"

Blandford thought for two ticks and said, "I don't know much. I did hear they later went out of business since they were the ones who were found liable for the scaffold falling. And the fact that they had to rent more scaffolding from another company put them in a real financial bind is what I heard. They didn't have enough undamaged scaffolding for that job after the collapse and the rental price ate them up. Put the two together and you have going belly up quickly rounding the corner for that company."

"Where did they get the extra equipment?"

"I have no idea. That's all I know." They sat and looked at each other for more ticks of the clock.

"You have been a big help, Robert. I have some more places to look now." They got up and Reginald paid the bill for both of them. They arrived back in Mountain View at 10:30 a.m. Reginald dropped Blandford off at the Blue Bird Inn and went back to headquarters. A note on his desk told him to go to the chief's office.

Reginald went into Darrell's office and said, "You want to see me?"

"Sit down, Reginald. Sherry has been working on the Bushman account statements. She has found something real interesting."

"What is it?" Reginald asked quickly.

"She can tell you better than I can, but the statement shows checks for regular amounts written to the Postal Service for what may have been money orders. The amount of each check was 200 dollars plus the ninety-cent postal fee."

"That's pretty smart. Money orders are hard to trace unless you know where they are purchased or cashed."

"It's real difficult since there's a sixty-day waiting period before information on each order can be released. I've called the Postal Inspector, and he'll be here next week," Chief Cumberland said.

"Sure would be nice to find out where they were bought and where they went or were cashed, but that may be like looking for another needle in a haystack," Reginald said with resignation, "and we don't know where to find the haystack either."

"Reginald, we know more than we did. We'll keep plugging until it is over. In all my years of police work in this town, this is the worst case we have ever had. I know how you're feeling," Darrell said.

Reginald studied the floor and the tips of his shoes for a long interval. The chief watched him and said, "You're thinking of something that none of the rest of us have considered," knowing that Reginald examined every case from all angles. "That right?"

Reginald looked up and said with a half way grin, "You're right. I was thinking that what we know is so obvious we can't see it yet."

"Care to explain that?" Darrell said with a slight laugh.

"No, but there are four facts among others that continue to bother me: One is the murder of Officer McGee. The second one is that house fire in Mountain Home; the third is keeping a vacant lot for an address, and the fourth is Mr. Herrington's murder."

"Do you believe those four are linked?" Darrell asked perplexed.

"Yes I do, but I'm not sure why. First, I'm sure that the murders of

McGee and Herrington weren't part of the original plan—whatever it is that the perp is planning to do. Don't ask me why I think that because I don't know. The two are related, but again I don't know why or how. The house fire was planned, and we don't have an answer to the why of that one either."

"You're sure it was planned?"

"It was planned," Reginald said, "and don't ask me why I think that because I don't know."

The phone rang and after listening, Darrell handed the phone to Reginald. "This is Sgt. Gawker." Pause. "Sure. I'll pick you up at the bank." He handed the phone back to Darrell. "Sherry and I are going to lunch. She wants to discuss that bank account and try to figure out those checks that were written for the money orders. We're going to the Iron Skillet at the Folk Center."

"Good place to eat. If you see John, tell him he sure made the strings on that fiddle smoke with the Orange Blossom Special last weekend. That man sure can fiddle," Darrell said with obvious delight thinking of the music.

"Will do," Reginald said and hurried out the door to meet Sherry. Darrell heard him whistling the tune as he went down the hall.

Chapter

THIRTY

Though the weekend would pass quickly, it was a most welcome interlude to the rigors of the murder case. Relaxation on Saturday and church on Sunday gave all of them much needed rest and relief from the strain they were all showing. A few people at church asked some questions, but the answers were sparse. Some grumbled that they weren't getting told anything, and others said they understood. Reginald and Sherry went to Batesville for Sunday dinner. They didn't realize it when they passed through Locust Grove that they were seen by the man they wanted to find in the worst possible way. He wanted to follow them, but he decided it was too risky. Killing them would have to wait.

Shortly before 5:00 a.m. on Monday morning, Darcy and L. Jason Callman arrived at police headquarters. Callman was taken to the break room down the hall to wait for the time to leave. Darcy poured him a cup of coffee from a freshly made pot. A few minutes later, Sherry walked into Reginald's office yawning. "You sure know how to interrupt a body's sleep. When that phone rang, I wanted to strangle you." Reginald and Darcy laughed. Reginald took the package from the evidence locker and gave it to Sherry.

They discussed the case with Darcy. While Reginald and Sherry were gone, Darcy and Martin were going to try to find where the man was living. They thought it had to be an hour's drive, maybe no more than two, from Mountain View. They had formed that idea from studying the checks that were written for the money orders.

They were for the same amount written on the same date each month, which seemed to indicate they were for rent. Darcy had a hunch the house was in the country. He and Martin would begin the search looking for another needle in a haystack they had yet to identify.

•

When they left the building, neither one of them saw the man standing in the shadows inside the dilapidated vacant house across the street. He sighted through the scope on his rifle but decided it was too risky to shoot Callman. He didn't think he could get the two others without being discovered. And he did want those two also. They had messed up his plan and soon he would mess up their plans for good. He laughed to himself that they didn't know he had been sneaking into the house right under their noses. And the old woman who owned the house was only interested in the rent money, and since he didn't want to pay more rent that she would want in two months, he considered her disposable if her demise became necessary. "Dead people don't need rent money," he said to the walls. With her living in Little Rock, no one would connect him to it. She had told him she had no family, so no one would miss her. Thinking that his landlady didn't have a family began to rekindle the glowing embers of rage that were constantly smoldering in his tormented mind.

Having to stop using that bank account in Mountain Home really put him in a bind. Leaving that dollar in the account kept it active so they wouldn't know he had gotten suspicious. It was a good thing he bought the money orders in 100 dollar amounts since they were easier to cash. The bank account being useless now and the stop payment created more anger. He sent the stop payment for that check made to the hardware store in Petersburg, Indiana, and the bank paid the check anyway. The only reason he wanted the payment stopped was because the clerk acted real smart when he made the purchase. That so called malfunction on the automated account information really bugged him. He was sure that was done in an attempt to find out his identity. He couldn't take any chances on that account being linked to him, so he quit calling. *That cop and Sherry Westermann have caused me all this trouble. I'll fix them,* he thought angrily, as he paced the floor from one room to the next in the small house.

He spent so much time thinking of all the things that had ruined his plan that it had become too light for him to sneak his car from the garage behind the house. He didn't dare allow any nosy neighbor see him leave, not that they would, since the nearest house was a good block away. He would have to stay in the house until night rather than risk the chance of being seen.

And it was obvious that Sgt. Gawker, Callman, and Sherry were going somewhere. He sure would like to know what they were doing. But no matter, with them gone what he had planned would be easier to finish. He continued to watch out the window as the shift changed at 6:00 a.m. He knew that the third shift arrived in headquarters at 5:30 a.m. to do their reports and that the first shift didn't leave the building until 6:10 a.m. That gave him a half hour to do what he needed to do without being seen by a nosy patrolman. Twenty minutes was all he needed to fill and load the boxes. The extra ten would be icing on the cake. Then he would be on the way to Locust Grove without being seen. He smiled in anticipation of his next move.

Chapter
THIRTY-ONE

Rain plagued Reginald and Callman all the way from Pocahontas, Arkansas, to Marion, Illinois. They stopped for lunch there and while eating, the rain stopped and the sun came out. That brightened their spirits until they were near Petersburg, Indiana, when another storm made driving difficult. They found Sprinkle's Hardware Store on the south edge of the town and pulled into the parking lot with an hour to spare before closing time. Reginald left Callman and went into the store. He identified himself and asked the clerk to call the Petersburg Police Department since he didn't have any jurisdiction in Indiana. The clerk was wary though she had seen Reginald's badge and ID, but she made the call after thinking it was okay and asking to see Reginald's badge again. Ten minutes later an officer arrived. After explaining why he was there and showing the officer the cancelled check, the officer called the Chief of Police who gave the okay for Reginald to question the clerk. The officer also filled out a contact report. And it didn't hurt any that the officer's brother was a policeman in Jonesboro, Arkansas.

The clerk, Susie James, at first told Reginald that she didn't remember the man who wrote the check. But when he asked if she remembered anyone buying ice picks she said, "Oh, that guy. Right, Now I remember. We carry two types of ice picks. One type has ads on the square handle. The other is a round handle with no ads. He didn't want those. He wanted the plain square handled ones with no ad.

Donald E. Clem

"How many did he buy?"

"Let me see the amount on the check." She was shown the check and said, "That would have been twelve of them plus tax and shipping."

Reginald was surprised and said, "He had them shipped where?"

The clerk twisted her mouth, tapped the side of her cheek with her finger, and finally said, "Is there a Little Rock, uh … what state are you from?"

Reginald looked at the officer who was shaking his head and having a difficult time to keep from laughing and replied, "Arkansas."

"Oh sure, you said Little Rock, Arkansas." Susie smiled, obviously pleased with herself for having remembered.

"Do you remember the address where they were shipped?" Reginald asked.

"Uh, Mister, uh, Sarg … it is Sarg, right?" Reginald nodded at her. "I do well to remember what day it is, and you want me to remember an address in … uh … oh yeah, Arkansas."

Reginald looked exasperated which wasn't lost on the Petersburg officer. Reginald tried again. "May I presume that he gave you the address on a piece of paper and would you still have it?"

"You can presume all you want, but I don't have it. As soon as the picks came in I put them in a box, addressed it, took it to the post office, and mailed it. I threw the slip of paper away … uh … no, I didn't. He printed the address out real neat, and I taped it to the box," she said, obviously pleased about remembering that piece of information.

Reginald shook his head knowing that this was a dead end, but he had to try for more answers. "Okay, a few more questions, and then we'll leave."

"Hey, I get off in ten minutes so you had better hurry," Susie said sourly.

"Okay, Susie," Reginald said. "Can you describe him?"

"He was six feet tall. Let's see, dark brown hair and a beard. It was a little short one. That's all I can tell you. Now it's time for me to go."

"If you don't mind, I have one more question."

"Well, go ahead, but make it short. It's past time for me to be out of here."

"The check was written on February 1, but it didn't show up at the bank until in April. Why is that?"

Susie looked around, leaned toward Reginald, and said quietly, "Don't tell Charley—he's the owner. I put the check in the wrong bank bag and didn't find it until a couple of weeks ago. That's why. I deposited it without Charley knowing what I did with it."

Reginald studied Susie for a few more ticks and asked, "Do you always take checks written on out of state banks, especially when the writer is a stranger?"

"Do you think I am dumb or something? I called my granddaddy at the First State Bank of Petersburg. He's president of the bank, and I asked him if he could get me the number of the bank, Mountain something or another. He did and called for me. There was enough money in the account to cover the check. I ain't dumb Mister … uh … Sarg. Sheesh, the people you meet now days."

Reginald sighed, trying not to laugh, and said, "Thank you, Susie. You have been a big help."

Reginald and the Petersburg officer left the store. They talked a few minutes and then Reginald got into his car, turned to Callman and said, "Next stop, Bloomington, Indiana." At 6:00 p.m. that evening, they checked into the Marriott on South College. Reginald called the dispatcher and Sherry to tell them they had arrived. He gave them the room and telephone number. They found a nice restaurant, enjoyed the food, and went to bed early. The next two days, maybe three, would be more hectic than they could ever imagine.

Chapter
THIRTY-TWO

ive in the morning seemed to arrive a lot earlier in Indiana than in Arkansas. Reginald and Callman ate breakfast at Ladyman's Cafe on East Kirkwood Avenue. A few minutes before 8:00 a.m., they went to the Justice Building on North College Avenue. Reginald and Callman stood outside and looked at the imposing structure; the headquarters for the County Courts System and associated county government offices, plus the Sheriff's Department. They entered the building and asked to see the sheriff. They were escorted by a deputy who took them to his office. After introductions and a brief statement of why they were there and what they wanted to do, a County Detective, William Short, was assigned to assist them.

The first thing Reginald wanted to find out was the circumstances of the accident that claimed the life of Marion Easterly on June 10, 1995. It took awhile to find the records, but eventually they were produced. Reginald asked for copies and received them. The records showed that Easterly's car, a 1992 Ford Crown Victoria, had failed to negotiate a curve on Breeden Road and had hit a tree with a violent impact. The car burst into flames and incinerated the driver. There wasn't much evidence left. Reginald saw on the report that the investigating deputy had questions but lacked evidence that would indicate it wasn't an accident. The deputy had made a notation that said that since the car was so severely destroyed by fire, he suspected that it had been doused in gasoline or some other flammable liquid. He also indicated that the gasoline tank had ruptured and that could account for the fierceness of the fire. Reginald wanted to speak to the deputy, Phillip Rogers, but he was no longer with the department, having taken a position out of state with another agency. The deputy's case notes said that the air bag either didn't deploy or that it was already popped before the collision. The estimated speed of the car was seventy miles per hour when it slammed into the tree.

Reginald asked for and received the coroner's report and a copy of the autopsy findings. Death was apparently by impact of the car with the tree and then the fire, but the Medical Examiner had noted that the death was suspicious. He had to rule it an accident since there wasn't anything to support the suspicions. The body was so badly burned that the cause of death couldn't be firmly determined. The Medical Examiner did note and underline in the report that the corpse didn't have any upper teeth. The melted remains of an upper plate were found in his mouth. Reginald looked up and said, "Bingo." All of those who heard him utter the word looked at him oddly.

Detective Short said, "You must have found something interesting."

Reginald studied the report for a few ticks and said, "I think maybe I did. The man didn't have any teeth." After satisfying himself he had learned from the reports all he needed for now, he wanted to take a trip to Breeden Road. They left the Justice Building in a county car. The trip took them out West Second Street and Indiana Highway 45 toward Stanford. Callman remarked how the town had grown and how crowded it had become since he had first lived there. They rolled through Stanford and just west of the town they turned left on Breeden Road. Callman's shack was on the right side of the road between the Indian Creek Bridge and Tom Phillips Road. It didn't look like much, the property now overgrown with scrub trees and weeds. Callman said, "Here is my castle," and laughed. "Need to do some serious work here or sell it."

Callman unlocked the door and the three men entered the house. It smelled musty and dirty with the odor of having not been lived in for a long time. Another faint odor that Reginald couldn't identify tickled his nose. He decided it was caused by an old house in the throes of dying. They looked around for a few minutes and then Reginald asked Callman, "When was the last time you were here?"

"I was here both in 1994 and '95. No reason to hang around here full time. An old fellow, Willie Jackson, looks after it. He lives around the next curve from where the car hit the tree. I give him 500 dollars a year, and he takes care of it, such as it is. From the looks of this place, I'm wasting my money and ... " Callman stopped talking and looked at Reginald. "I just remembered. I don't know what it means, but maybe it is something important. When Easterly was here in the fall of 1994, there was an old manual Underwood typewriter on the desk over there. He wanted to buy it, and I told him it wasn't for sale. It's gone now. I guess someone stole it. Maybe he came back and got it," Callman said laughing. "The guy was squirrelly acting. I guess his drinking and losing his family caused it."

"You sure it was on the desk?" Reginald asked, seemingly ignoring Callman's last statement.

Callman moved his head up and down and said, "Yes, I'm sure, and it was here when I was here in early 1995. I know it was here in 1995 because I typed a note on it to see if it worked."

"Okay. It was here in 1994 and in 1995? When in '95?"

"I think it was in middle of January, but I don't keep track of the time like I used to do. I had business in Bloomington and stopped in to check on the house. I hated that trip. Snow was all over the place. Almost didn't make it back to the highway with the coach, the road was so slick."

"And you're completely sure the typewriter was here? This is important."

"Yes, I'm sure. Willie told me he remembered it being on the desk when he fixed a broken window because he tried to make it work."

"When was that?" Reginald asked.

"It had to be before I was here in the middle of January," Callman said.

"I wonder why he didn't report the break-in if that is what it was," Detective Short said.

"Oh, Willie probably figured kids did it and never gave it a thought. Kids play around here all the time, or they did the times I've been here."

"We'll go down and talk to him when we finish here," Reginald said. "I want to see that accident scene anyway. My headache has returned again."

Reginald studied Callman for a few more ticks and said, "I don't suppose you kept the note you typed."

"No, I threw them in the trash box ... " He stopped talking and walked over to a box behind the desk, rummaged around, withdrew a piece of paper, and handed it to Reginald.

Reginald looked at it and said, "I think we may be getting somewhere now. Unless I'm wrong, I think we have found the origin of the typewriter that typed all those notes. Now we have to find the typewriter." He placed the note in a plastic evidence bag, marked it, and smiled as he tucked it into the inner pocket of his jacket. "Maybe my headache is going to get better after all," he said to no one in particular.

They did another quick look around in the four rooms. Before they left, Reginald took pictures of the cabin inside and out. Each of them commented on the dirt that was on the floor. Callman said it wasn't there the last time he was in the house.

Chapter

THIRTY-THREE

Detective William Short stopped the county car near the tree that the Easterly vehicle had slammed in 1995. They sat in the car a few minutes and discussed the accident and then got out and looked at the big maple tree. It still bore the marks of the collision. Reginald examined the tree carefully and then said to the Short, "I read in the report that there were some marks on the tree that didn't correspond with any of the marks made by the car striking it." He handed the copy to Short who read it and then Reginald asked, "What do you make of it? There are some marks still visible on the back side of the tree. Are there any photos in the file?"

"I don't know, Sarg. I can look when we go back to Justice. The deputy who did the investigation always was real thorough and careful. He took pics at the scenes of all fatalities so he probably did this one," Short said.

Reginald examined the marks some more and said, "If I had to guess, I would say that something was strapped around the tree the way the bark is gouged. The questions are why and when was it done. Maybe the marks have nothing to do with the accident, so whatever we say now will be pure speculation."

"I see in the report that Deputy Rogers indicated there were tracks that looked like a vehicle to the left of the tree took off real fast going east toward Graves Road. In his words, 'the asphalt surface was scratched real badly with dual tire tracks back toward the curve in the road.' I wonder what that means, if anything," Short said.

"Rogers' notes indicate that the marks are deeper on the west side of the tree than on the south and the east side," Reginald said. "Well, let's go talk to Mr. Callman's friend down the road. Maybe he can tell us something we don't know."

When the car turned into Willie Jackson's drive, he was working in his garden. He watched the three men get out, and then when he saw L. Jason Callman, he waved and hurried toward them. Willie Jackson was of slight build and five feet ten inches tall. He had white hair sticking out from under a straw hat perched over a creased lined face. His well worn bib overalls were stained with dirt and grease. His hands were gnarled from hard work. Reginald judged him to be close to eighty years old. He stuck out his hand to L. Jason and said, "Good to see you, Lavon. Whut brings you here this time of the year?"

Callman winced when Willie called him by his first name. He said, "Here on business, and I want you to meet my friends." Introductions were made and then Callman said, "They need to ask you questions about the car that hit the tree back up the road."

Willie cocked his head sideways, shuffled his worn leather boots in the dust and said, " Oh man, I've spent the months since it happened tryin' to fergit that mess, and now you want me to put it back in my mind. Never did see anything like it. Don't want to again either."

Detective Short said, "Mr. Jackson, I can't imagine how hard this is for you, and I won't say I know it is because I don't. Sgt. Gawker is investigating a vicious crime committed in his home town and some other matters connected with it. You may have something of importance to tell him, and he won't know what it is until he asks questions."

Willie Jackson looked at the three men, sighed, and said, "All right, if it'll hep. It was the most turrible thing I ever did see in my seventy-nine years." He hesitated and then said, "That ain't quite true. I didn't see much until I was five or so that I can remember," and chuckled to help relieve the tension he felt. "Ask your questions, Sergeant."

"I know a few things from the report, and I want you to see if you

can add anything to it. Now, when did you first know of the crash and
fire?"

"As I tole that depaty, it twas bout 1:30 in the mornin' when I
went outside to tend to a new born calf. It twer mistin' rain, and I
wanted to make sure that its mamma had taken it to the barn stall.
I twas on the way back to the house when I heerd the crash. Kinda
like a big thump more'n a crash." Willie became silent. "Right before
the thump I thought I heerd tires bawlin' on the tarvy. Guess I didn't
though. Just my imagination workin' overtime I reckon."

Reginald wrote "thump" and "tires bawlin'" in his notebook.
"Then what did you do, Mr. Jackson?"

"Call me Willie. That Mr. stuff, it's for old people," he said with a
quick laugh. "I thought no more of it, went in the house and decided
to have a cup of coffee and a piece of toast, so I made coffee and put
bread in the toaster. Then I decided that eggs and bacon would taste
good so I fixed those and while eatin' I saw the fire. I saw it out the
kitchen window." He looked at Reginald and said nothing more.

"How long after you heard the thump did you see the fire?"

"Well, I've been thinkin' bout that. I tole that depaty that it
tweren't but maybe four or five minutes, but now that I've wallered
it around in my mind a mite, I think it was more like ten to twelve
minutes."

"Can you explain that, Mr. Jackson?" Reginald asked pointedly.

"Sure can young feller. When I heerd that thump I was just goin'
in the back door over yonder." He pointed toward the house. "I put the
bread in the toaster and put some coffee in the pot. I use that *Gevalia*
coffee. They send it as often as I want it. I get a box of Columbia in
the mail every four weeks. I drink a lot of coffee." He stopped and
then said, "Where twas I? Yes, while the coffee was makin' I decided
to fix eggs and bacon. Let me think. Bacon takes three minutes in
the mikerwave for two slices and the toast makes while the bacon is
cookin' and the eggs are fryin.' Countin' all this and the time for the
coffee to make, ten to twelve minutes is right. I was eatin' them vittles
when I saw the fire. It was blazin' real high. I called the fire depart-

ment and went up there. Then the depaty showed up. Beat the fire boys there. The fire boys got that fire out in no time after they started pourin' water on it. Them fellars know'd what they was doin.'"

"You are sure of the time you saw the fire?" Detective Short wanted to know.

"Sonny, I'm sure. I been doin' my own eggs and bacon for so long I have it timed bout to the second."

"So you think it was ten to twelve minutes after you heard the thump that you saw the fire."

"That's what I figured out. I will swear to it if'n I have to."

"Why didn't you tell Deputy Rogers what you told us?" Short asked.

"Wall, he never asked bout my early breakfast, and I plumb forgot it and the time in all the excitement."

Reginald thought for a moment and said, "Willie, do you remember seeing a typewriter on the desk in Callman's house?"

Willie looked around, then scratched his neck, and wiped his face with the palm of his hand. "I do. It was there the last time I was up there."

"When was that?" Reginald asked.

"It was right after that big snow in late January this year. I've been up there a time or two since but never payed no never mind bout it bein' there. Lavon pays me to look after the place so I keep my eye on it fer him regular like." Reginald sneaked a look at L. Jason and saw a quick smile and a hang dog look come across his features. Short suppressed a smile and looked the other way.

"Say, who was that feller that got kilt in that wreck?"

Reginald hesitated, but then he decided that it wouldn't hurt for Willie to know the man's name. "We think his name was Marion Easterly."

Willie thought for few ticks and said, "Easterly. Uh … that name is familiar for some reason." He looked at the sky and then at his cows standing along the fence. The cows looked at Willie. One mooed loudly. "Be quiet, Bertha. We don't need your put in." Reginald suppressed a laugh. "Hey, Lavon, was that the strange actin' feller that stopped there right afore your cousin died? That the one whose family was killed?"

Callman winced when he heard his first name before he answered. "That was him."

"Who was the other feller?"

"What other fellow?" Callman asked in surprise.

"There was some feller in the car that never went in the house. He just sat in the car the whole time. I never got a good look at him. Wouldn't recognize him if he walked up right now." Callman's face showed befuddlement when he heard what Willie said.

"Willie, we need to be going, and we thank you for your help," Reginald said. "We may need to talk to you again. It may be tomorrow."

The three men returned to the Justice Building. Reginald went in and thanked the sheriff for his help and the services of Detective Short. He found out where the car was towed and where the body had been taken. He obtained copies of the photos that were shot at the accident scene. He still had a lot to do before leaving for home early Thursday morning.

THIRTY-FOUR

The first thing the next morning, Reginald went to the Post Office to see the Bloomington Post Master, D. Gatewood Farrell. He introduced himself and told the Post Master why he was there. Farrell rummaged around on his desk and found a memo from Inspector William Blackwood in Little Rock. He told them that there weren't any packages or letters with the addresses that Blackwood had given him mailed anywhere in the Bloomington system. Reginald asked for information on the box in the name of J. Daniel Bushman. They were told the box was dropped a few weeks ago when the rent wasn't paid. They thanked D. Gatewood Farrell for his help and left.

Next, they went to the funeral home that took the burned body. The man at the funeral home said they made some phone calls to Little Rock after the sheriff's department had found the next of kin through the vehicle's plate registration. The relative was an aunt who was in a nursing home and wasn't able to talk due to having had a stroke some years before. She was the only relative and since there wasn't anyone to pay the bill, he was buried in Monroe County. The county paid the bill for the pauper burial.

A trip to the Monroe County Library created more questions for Reginald. An article in the Bloomington paper gave an account of the accident, but it made no mention of the identity of the deceased due to the pending notification of the next of kin. Reginald turned to Callman and said, "You said that an unidentified party called your friend and told him that Easterly was killed in the accident. How long after the accident was that phone call?"

Callman thought for an instant and then said, "It must have been three or four weeks later. All I know is that the friend told me that the man told him he saw the Easterly article in the paper."

Reginald searched more of the paper's articles and data bases, and when he finished he frowned and said, "What I found is interesting, but what I didn't find is even more interesting."

"What do you mean?" Callman wanted to know.

"I'll leave it at just being interesting for now."

They left the library and drove to the wrecking yard north of Bloomington where the car had been towed. Reginald hoped it was still there. He and Callman went into the junk yard office. He identified himself and the man at the counter said, "Oh, you're the cop the sheriff's office said would be stopping by. What can I do for you?" Reginald stated his business and the man said, "It's on the last row," and pointed toward the back of the lot.

There wasn't much left of the car. It was a burned out shell with no tires, glass, or interior work. The driver's side seat frame had been removed from the car. The frame of the bucket seat on the right side was in place. The front of the car was bashed in from the collision with the tree. Reginald noticed that all the front parts, the radiator, bumper supports, and grill were mashed back against the engine block. He asked Callman, "What kind of a car was Easterly driving that day he came to see you?"

Callman glanced at the burned out car. He said, "I think it was a white Ford. A big one, but I don't know cars very well. I think it was a Crown something or another. I didn't pay much attention to it. He had been drinking and wasn't doing too well, and I wanted him gone. He only stayed twenty minutes and left."

"What did he do while he was there?"

"He didn't do in particular that I can recall except talk a lot. You know how drunks like to blow off. He said he got a big insurance settlement. He pulled a big wad of money out of his pocket and showed it to me. He talked some more bragging about his money and then left."

"You didn't see the man with him that stayed in the car?"

"I didn't know anyone was with him until Willie mentioned it today. It really surprised me when I heard that," Callman said.

"Do you have any idea who it could have been?"

"I don't. I wasn't really that friendly with Easterly. Only knew him because of selling to his company."

"Was this the visit when he wanted to buy the typewriter?"

"It was. He wasn't here but one time and that had to be it unless he came back and stole it."

Reginald looked at his watch and said, "Let's find a place to eat. Know any good places other than the one we've tried out?"

"Do you like pizza? There's a place on East Kirkwood Avenue that makes the best pizza in the world, the Pizzeria. I haven't been there for a long while."

"It sounds good to me."

They ordered a large sausage, pepperoni, and mushroom pie, and big soft drinks. Reginald looked up from his food and said. "Good doesn't describe this pizza. It's the best I've ever eaten." They left with full stomachs, smiles, and their hunger satisfied.

Since they weren't going to leave until Thursday morning, Reginald decided to drive back to the shack and have another look around. L. Jason asked, "Why do you want to do that?" when Reginald told him they were going back to the house.

"That place bothers me, and I just want to look again to see if I can discover anything useful."

Reginald got out of the car and surveyed the front of the house trying to get a handle on the bugs gnawing at his brain. He said, "L. Jason, did you see anything else that wasn't right when we were here yesterday?"

"That typewriter being gone and that dirt on the floor is all I saw that looks different from the last time I was here. There's nothing else I can think of."

Callman unlocked the door, and they went in. Reginald stood in the middle of the room and moved his eyes around. Callman watched him and said, "Something's really eating at you."

"You're right. That typewriter disappeared after you were here in late January and probably around February 1. Those ice picks were ordered and paid for on February 1. What I can't figure out is if the suspect that ordered the picks also stole the typewriter. If he did, then he might have made the trip to do both. Let's go see your friend Willie again."

When Reginald and Callman drove into the drive, Willie Jackson was sitting on the porch fanning his face with his big straw hat, enjoying the afternoon breeze. They got out of the car and approached the house. Willie said, "Hi fellers. Whut brung youn's out here again? Come up and set a spell. I quit early. It's too hot to work."

They took chairs on the porch. The light breeze made the porch pleasant. The cows watched and mooed.

Callman said, "Sgt. Gawker wants to ask you some more questions if that's all right."

"Don't see why not. Be glad to tell whut I know and don't know." Willie laughed as he said don't know.

Reginald chuckled and said, "We'll start with what you know and then maybe we can figure out what you don't know."

"That's fair enough. Let's go," Willie said with obvious enthusiasm.

"Okay, let's begin this year and work backwards."

"You didn't notice the typewriter being gone when you went up there a couple times after January 1, that right?"

"No, but now that I have had time to think it over, I think it was gone the second time I went to the house. I fixed a window in January that was broken. That was right before Lavon was here and the typewriter was on the desk. Then the second one was broken after Lavon was here. Dern kids come along and throw rocks, and I have to fix the windows they break."

"What window was broken?"

Willie studied the sky and then his shoes and slapped himself in the side of the head. "I shore nuff am not thinkin' so good. That window was on the backside of the house. Do you spose somebody broke out the window and crawled in?"

"When did you fix the window?" Reginald asked.

"Best I can recall it was the middle if February or later. Maybe it was the first week of March the typewriter was gone. I'm sure of it." Willie studied the two men a few seconds and then said, "You don't reckon it twas that Easterly feller that twere here that time? He twas shifty and I didn't like him. He shore nuff seemed to have a shine fer that old typewriter."

Reginald thought for a tick and said, "Do you have time to go up to the house and look around?"

"Wall, I ain't doin' nuthin' else and don't have anything pressin' that I know of. The garden is laid by, and Bessie and Bertha won't need milkin' till five, so I'm free I reckon. Whut are we lookin' fer?"

"I don't know, but maybe we can find something that we've missed."

The three men drove onto the weed filled yard. A rabbit jumped up and ran under the house. Four squirrels were playing in the oak trees, jumping from limb to limb acting like kids playing tag. Reginald studied the house and then swiveled toward the tree that the car hit. "How far is that tree from your house, Willie?"

"It's just a tad under a hunnert yards I reckon. Why?"

"And you heard a thump and after a few minutes you saw a fire?"

"Yup," Willie answered.

"Since you can't see your house from here, can you see this house from yours?"

"Nope, that ridge over yonder in the field this side of my house hides this here one from mine. It would be easy for a sneak thief to break in and steal something."

Not finding anything of value outside that would help the investigation, they went inside the shack. Callman said, "I can't figure out that dirt on the floor. It wasn't here in the spring of 1995." He studied the floor and then said, "Willie, when did you notice it?"

"I don't remember, but it was after that car fire.

"Would it have been in June?" Reginald asked.

Willie studied for a tick and said, "Yep, I think it twas the last week of June I first noticed it. I couldn't figure it out and still can't."

"Is there anything else you remember?"

"Wall now that we're here jawin' there is something. I remember an odor like a dead possum or some such. It lasted a long time and then went away. Figured an animal crawled up under the house and died. Sure did stink somethin' awful."

Reginald studied the floor and moved an old rug aside. He found a loose board and pulled it up and then removed another one. He peered in and said, "I think we just found Trudy Bushman."

Chapter
THIRTY-FIVE

The man woke up with his body drenched with sweat. He stared into the darkness, not sure that the noise he heard was in his nightmare or was in reality, outside of his house. He lay in the black room, his senses alert for any sound. He was ready to respond as his hand found the sawed off shotgun next to his bed. He knew both barrels were loaded with double aught buckshot, and he was ready to send any intruder to wherever he was prepared to go. He had killed five times, missed once, and was determined that the one he missed would die, and that the others for whom he had plans would go to their just reward before he was done. But he would make sure they felt the pain he had endured ever since his loved ones were killed.

He wasn't quite sure about who was fully responsible for their deaths, so he would kill those who had some connection to that scaffold falling. He began to count and decided that he had four more to go, not including that nosy Gawker and his little girlfriend and the old woman who would want more rent if he still needed her house in town. He wasn't sure, but her actions told him she might be an old retired cop or maybe a cop's widow, so he had to be careful until he could deal with her if push came to shove.

And those two women, who were neighbors of the woman he killed, might prove to be troublesome too. They had disappeared which made his anger rise. With people disappearing on him his plans were in shambles. That old man Munsford was gone, too. That nosy cop was responsible for them leaving town. If he had been able to kill all three, then maybe it would have thrown the cops off his track.

The more his thoughts centered on the people he wanted to get even with, the worse his anger became. He remembered that he had missed twice instead of once. Callman moved and so did the other one who disappeared. That was the one that he really wanted. The darkness was suddenly split with screams that drained him of his rage.

After he was able to think again, he set his mind on the reasons for Gawker and that bank woman having left town. He decided that the woman might be on bank business. He knew that her trip could be related to the real estate mortgage work she did, so she probably wasn't a threat right now, but he would keep his guard up just in case that trip was more than it seemed. But it really made no difference since whatever she might find wouldn't matter. He was going to kill her for another reason. He laughed at the anticipation of killing, uh … *Sherry, that's her name.* He laughed again as he recalled the day he was in the bank and Sherry didn't know who he was. He was there the day old Snoopy Bottoms took all the pictures of her. She was so busy trying to fool Bottoms she didn't notice him when he crossed the lobby right in front of her. If everything went right, the pictures would come in handy for what he planned to do next. He was most pleased with himself and emitted a laugh to show his pleasure. His mind was now racing, anticipating the conclusion of his deadly rampage.

"Mr. Bushman, you made me very lucky. Just think, you never knew how you would fit into my plans," the man said loudly. "What a stroke of luck for me to run into J. Daniel at that service station in Sikeston the fall of '94."

He had met him at the Locust Grove race track a couple of years before when Bushman was doing menial work in the pit for a driver from Little Rock. A loser for sure and he helped old Bushy along in the loss column. He needed someone to drive him to Poplar Bluff to look at a car another loser told him was for sale cheap. It was while driving Bushman to Poplar Bluff that he began to make the plan that would pay back all those who caused him to be in pain.

The more pressing situation was Gawker and Callman. He ran several things over in his mind and decided that the only reason they left town was to go to Indiana; he figured he knew why. That line of thinking began to anger him again. He had made a mistake in June of last year when he slammed that car into the tree. He should have killed that old man that was there the day he visited Callman and his cousin. He had a notion to do that in February when he bought ice picks from that dip in ... where ... Petersburg, and borrowed the typewriter from that shack. He laughed at the word borrowed.

If Callman had died, then he and Gawker wouldn't be in Indiana snooping around since Callman wouldn't have been able to link him to that shack. He couldn't believe how easy it was to get the Bushmans to make the trip to meet their end. They must have been into something heavy in Sikeston he reasoned, because they kept mentioning getting a new start somewhere. They got a new start all right, and he was glad to help them along in life. Well, not quite life, he reminded himself. The word was death, and he laughed.

He counted the mistakes he had made. They weren't big ones, but they were enough to make that cop dig even more into things he would be sorry for doing. *When Gawker finds that obnoxious Trudy Bushman, which he will, he has to figure out how to handle it. They will know Bushy didn't die in that car fire and that presents a problem, but yet it might work to my advantage, too.* How, he didn't know, but he knew he was good at altering plans when needed.

The fire in that house in Mountain Home showed his genius. That really paid two of them back for their misdeeds. Those Special Forces lessons he had in the military on how to defuse incendiary devices sure came in handy. He put his defusing knowledge to work and made his own simple device. It was so good they thought it was a gas explosion. It was but not like everyone thought. He was five blocks away when he pushed the button. Poof! He laughed. Well, he just might have to use that again. Maybe he would use it on the old woman who owned the house he was renting in Mountain View. That sure would fool the Little Rock cops. And serve her right for being greedy.

Reginald P. Gawker made him frown with worry. *He isn't as dumb as he lets on. He is Colombo dumb, and that Colombo was one smart cookie. Sgt. Gawker will find out that he isn't as smart as he thinks he is.* "I will out-Colombo Colombo," he said. "Nobody makes a fool of me."

Weary of running all the past through his mind, and since the noise in his head had stopped, he decided to turn on the light. His eyes fell on the small car sitting on the side table next to his bed. He looked at it for a long time and then slowly rolled out of bed and dressed. He picked up the little car, stopped in the trash laden kitchen to put on a pot of coffee, and went out to the garage. As he watched the car scoot around the small track, his mind returned to happier times, and he began to weep uncontrollably.

By the time Willie returned from calling the sheriff's department, the first car had arrived, and the officer had begun stringing the yellow crime scene tape after speaking to Reginald. Since he had no jurisdiction, he had to wait on William Short to arrive; whom the deputy said had been assigned the case. Willie found a stump across the road and sat down to watch. In a few minutes, Detective Short arrived. He went inside and looked into the shallow grave containing the remains of the woman they believed to be Trudy Bushman. He went out to his patrol car and called dispatch and asked for the Indiana State Police Crime Scene techs and the coroner. He was told both would arrive within the hour. Reginald told Short what he believed had happened and how the car had been slammed into the tree and who was in it.

"I'll contact the prosecutor tomorrow and try to get him to get a judge to issue an exhumation order. Since we think the victim in there is Mrs. Bushman, it is more than likely that the victim in that car was Mr. Bushman. Things are not always as they seem," Short said.

"You got that right Detective Short. This case began with a call from someone we can't identify and here we are with another body that makes two more homicides in this county for you to investigate, if the victim in the car was Mr. Bushman."

"Whoever you're after now involves us. You think he's that Easterly subject you're looking for?"

Reginald hesitated for a few seconds and said, "Right, that's what it looks like. At least he's the best we have right now."

"You think it could be someone else?"

"The way this case is going it wouldn't surprise me if it was Frankenstein." Short didn't know whether to laugh or say something. He did neither, and Reginald didn't seem to notice.

They talked a bit more, and then Reginald said, "The '94 Ford that burned makes me even more curious. While you're processing the scene here and interviewing Willie Jackson so you'll know what he told me before we found the victim, I want to take another look at that car. I'll drop Callman off at the hotel, and if you need me, I'll be available there after I look at the car. I need to call Arkansas and advise the chief and the other detective on the case of what we've found."

William Short indicated that was fine and told Reginald that he would be needed to testify for the exhumation if the judge wanted to ask questions, which he probably would. Reginald dropped Callman off at the hotel and drove over to the junk yard. The counter man told him to look all he wanted. He went to the Ford and began a careful examination of what was left of the car. The fire had burned the air bag in the steering wheel, so he couldn't tell if it deployed when the car hit the tree. He was particularly interested in the steering wheel. The one thing that really bothered him and needed explaining was why the steel ring inside the steering wheel grip was deformed and bent toward the dash. He believed it indicated that the air bag wasn't working at the time of the collision or due to some other reason yet to be determined. Deputy Rogers was right to question the accident. Reginald was sure that whoever was behind the wheel was dead before the car hit the tree, and now he knew more than ever how it was done. He took pictures of the items that would back up his belief and then left.

Callman was watching TV in the lobby while he waited for Reginald. Reginald told him that as soon as he made some phone calls that they would go eat and get to bed early. He knew the next day would be a busy one. Reginald went to the room and called Darrell Cumberland. He related what he had discovered and asked if Sherry had found anything. Darrell said she was running leads and didn't have anything concrete to report, but the leads might bear fruit. Darcy and Martin hadn't been able to locate any place that the perp might be living. They had some leads, and due to the sensitive nature of the case, they had to be very careful when asking questions. Darrell also told Reginald that the tan 1995 Ford hadn't been seen either. It was as if it had vanished off the face of the earth. That didn't surprise Reginald at all. He expected it would disappear. The question of *what will happen next* formed in his mind. He didn't have the slightest idea.

THIRTY-SEVEN

Reginald awakened early and called Callman's room to tell him to be ready to leave the hotel at 7:00 a.m. He called dispatch, and Fred Pauly told him that nothing had happened overnight. He collected Callman and left the hotel for breakfast. Reginald took the film to a quick processing store, and the clerk told him he could pick it up in two hours. He left the second roll of the cabin shots in the hotel room. He would have them developed when he returned to Mountain View. They ate breakfast and a bit after 8:00 a.m., they were in the sheriff's office.

An hour later, he and Detective Short went to a courtroom and met a deputy prosecutor. After presenting the facts of the case and with no one present to contest the request, the judge issued an exhumation order for J. Daniel Bushman's body. They went back to the sheriff's office, and Reginald called Mountain View. He told Darrell what he needed, gave him contAct Information on who to contAct In Bloomington. He said they wouldn't be home until Friday and hung up. He turned to Short and said, "My chief is going to contact Sikeston, Missouri, to make inquiry into the disappearance of the Bushmans and request articles of clothing or personal care items that might have Trudy's and J. Daniel's DNA on them. They'll contact you if and when they find out anything. He'll try to find items for Marion Easterly too, but that's a real remote possibility since it has so been so long since he died. I think trying for an exhumation order for Easterly would be futile."

Detective Short said there wasn't much doubt that the identity of the woman found under the shack's floor was Trudy Bushman. A purse found under her body had a driver license and Social Security card in it with her name on them. An autopsy would be conducted, and he said he would send the cause of death to Reginald as soon as he received it. The problem with her homicide was the location of where she was killed. There wasn't any evidence in the shack that suggested she was killed there or anywhere else on the property. Short and Reginald both knew they had some real problems to hurdle with jurisdiction concerning where she and her husband were actually murdered. A successful prosecution of the killer depended on knowing and proving where both victims were killed.

"How do you think the perp got the victim into the house?" Reginald asked Short.

"I suspect he carried her. She wasn't a very big woman so a fairly strong man could have carried her easily."

"Were there any wounds on the body that you could see?"

"None," replied Short. "Why, do you suspect something?"

Reginald told Short the results of the autopsy on Matilda Herrington and said, "I don't want to tell the ME how to do his job, but maybe it would be a good idea to look for ice pick wounds to the kidneys. I have a hunch that is how she was killed, and her killer is the same one we're looking for in Arkansas."

Short eyed Reginald and said, "From what you have told me, I think you're right, but we may never find where she was killed."

Reginald agreed and then said, "I need to pick up the pictures. I'll drop copies of them off for you before I leave town and will write a report and give you a copy of it. I'll explain how I think the car was slammed into that tree and why the steering wheel is bent. Rogers did a good job of investigating, but we know more now than he did when he did the investigation. He questioned it, but he didn't have the facts to back up his suspicions."

Reginald thanked the Sheriff for his help and bid Detective Short good bye. Before he left, he said that he would stop in Sikeston, Missouri, and talk to the detectives there to see if they could add anything to the investigation. He would notify them of anything new.

The photos were picked up, the report was written, and as Reginald was leaving the room to drop the reports off at the sheriff's department, the phone rang. It was Willie Jackson who wanted to see him right away. Reginald told him he would stop by on the way out of town the next morning.

They were up early Friday morning and ate breakfast before leaving Bloomington. Reginald called Sikeston and told a clerk in the detective division he would be there shortly after lunch to near mid afternoon. When he drove into Jackson's driveway, Willie was waiting for him. He excitedly stepped to the car window. He said, "Look what I found," and showed Reginald a rusty pulley.

"Where did you find that, Willie?" Reginald asked with the beginning of a smile.

"I was down there in the field cutting weeds behind the maple tree when I saw this thing. It twere half buried in the dirt and brush along that fence row. It's not mine. I don't know how it got there. I reckoned it might be important and figured I should show it to you."

"Willie, you call Detective Short, give him the pulley, and he'll know what to do when he reads the report I left for him. You made a good find. You've been a big help and this find is one more piece of the puzzle that we are slowly putting together." Reginald took some pictures of the pulley and told Willie to be sure to tell Short where the pulley was found.

Willie returned to the house to call Short. Reginald pointed the car toward Arkansas after taking pictures at the tree where Willie found the pulley. It would be good to get home.

Chapter
THIRTY-EIGHT

I t felt good to get out of the house and begin to put more of his plan in motion. He was elated as he guided the blue 1994 Chevy Blazer down the rock strewn driveway. He steered around the deep ruts and finally reached the highway. He wished that the drive was in better shape, but maybe it was to his advantage that it wasn't, and since he had figured out how to drive in and out without disturbing the landscape, no one would find him easily.

As he began the maneuver to get onto the highway, a motorcycle flashed past going south toward the intersection of 14 with 25. He recognized the rider as one of the two hippies he had seen hanging around in Mountain View. His mind began to reel with wild thoughts. What was the biker doing in Locust Grove? Had he been found out? After calming down, he was relieved that he had seen the bike before pulling out onto the road. *That would have been disastrous if I had been seen by the hippie, especially if he is a cop in disguise.* That possibility made him shake momentarily. He waited until the bike was out of sight and drove onto the highway with his destination being Mountain View. He knew the fools would be watching for a tan '95 Ford that they would never see again. The Blazer was perfect.

The man kept his eye on the rearview mirror just in case the biker turned around and followed him. But since the rider went on by and didn't reappear, he decided that his imagination was playing tricks on him. But he couldn't help the feeling with his nerves being on edge that he would be found out before he could execute his full plan. He knew he always got this way when he was ready to strike again. He knew that the strike was only a few hours away, but he couldn't help being excited and nervous at the same time. He had to scout out the area for the strike to make sure that nothing would tip off what he was going to do when he began to do it. *And just think it's going to happen right under their noses.* His laughter became so uncontrollable that he nearly had to pull over and stop, but finally his laughter subsided and he felt better. He had always heard that laughter was the best medicine. But he had better medicine waiting to be given in big doses, and he knew that his medicine would only be a laughing matter to him. "Dead men can't laugh. Too bad they won't be able to enjoy it," he roared and began laughing insanely again.

Darcy was at the Easy Stop on East Main buying gasoline when the Blazer went past. The man saw Darcy and knew he was the other hippie. Why wasn't he with the biker? He ran possible answers through his mind and decided that the two weren't any danger to him. They were nothing but loud mouthed Cretins; the world was full of them. As long as they didn't bother him, he wouldn't bother them unless … no, that would be stupid for them. "They aren't cops. Have to get that out of my mind," he said to no one.

He checked out the Happy Camper Motor Home Park and received a jolt. Callman's motor coach was gone. Where was it and when did it leave? He checked out all the parks, but he didn't find it. He could feel the anger begin to build and when that happened he needed to hurt someone, but it wasn't time. He calmed down and drove around town looking for Robert Blandford and couldn't find him. "Strike two and I'm not used to striking out," he mumbled, feeling the rage begin to build again. "The ones rewriting the rules will pay. They don't have any idea that I know their identities. Gawker and pretty Sherry will learn how dangerous it is for them to rewrite the rules." He gripped the steering wheel trying to control his anger until his knuckles ached.

•

Hundreds of people were around the square listening to the music being played on the courthouse lawn. The strains of the Orange Blossom Special assaulted his ears as he stepped out the car. How he hated that song now. It was playing the day his family was killed and hearing it only made the rage begin to rise again. If he could, he would deal with the fiddle player and show him how that song hurt him. He turned around and froze, then quickly opened the car door and ducked back inside. He sat with his head down and hid his face as well as he could.

He asked himself how he could be so lucky. His mind danced with the longed for opportunity. *I have been looking for her ever since the event and she's right here in Mountain View. Will I include her in my plan or make a special provision for her?* Thinking about it for several minutes made him decide that a special surprise was what Mary Beth Norman needed. If it hadn't been for her, his family would be alive. He had missed her once before a few months ago. She moved to the right when he squeezed the trigger. He wouldn't miss the next time. He enjoyed the feeling of finally finding another one who had caused him pain, and he was going to relieve a part of it soon. His problem now was figuring out where she was staying and how to apply the pain relief medicine.

He got out of the Blazer and lifted the back door. He rummaged around and then slammed the lid. He was angry with himself; seething rage returned and began building to fever pitch. He had forgotten and left the ice picks at the house. Would he dare do it in a crowd? Would it be safe? He breathed quick and hard until his rage went away. Now thinking straighter, he got in the Blazer and left town. By the time he arrived home, he had the plan worked out for the demise of Mary Beth Norman.

The man had driven east on Main when he left the city. He passed by the Best Burgers parking lot where Darcy's old truck was parked in a spot not easily seen from the street. He didn't see Darcy sitting inside the hamburger palace and never gave him more than a last fleeting thought when he noticed that the old truck had left the Easy Stop. He was too busy working on the plan to kill Mrs. Norman to think of other things.

Darcy, sitting inside where he could watch the street, saw the Blazer go by; and the way the driver acted when he looked over at the lot, Darcy had a hunch that what he saw was not a coincidence. The brake lights flashed quickly and then off. The driver looked back over his shoulder and then went on, nearly running the stop light at the intersection. Darcy picked up his cell phone and called Martin Perkins. When Martin answered Darcy asked, "Where are you now?" Pause. "Okay. You stay in Locust Grove. I'll be there in thirty minutes. Hide the bike and watch for a blue '94 Chevy Blazer. The driver is wearing a green cap." Pause. "Now that is interesting." He hung up and got into the truck. It looked like a wreck, but looks can be deceiving. The 396 cubic inch big block V-8 under the hood shook the fenders when it roared to life. Darcy smiled at the sound and headed east on Highway 14.

For some reason the man in the Blazer decided to watch traffic leaving town. He saw Darcy go by and followed at what he believed was a safe distance. When Darcy saw the Blazer drop in behind him, he called Martin and told him he had a tail and not to worry if he didn't show up as they had planned. He had to shake the Blazer. Darcy turned south on Highway 5 and drove slowly. He saw the Blazer behind him approximately a quarter of a mile back. Five miles out Highway 5 was County Road 31, a gravel road that connected with State 14 four miles to the north. He turned left and made plenty of dust so the tail would know where he went. He took a chance that whoever was following him wouldn't know that the gravel road connected with 14. He also knew he could beat the Blazer to Locust Grove whether its driver went down State 5 or turned around and went back to Highway 14. He really didn't know why he was going to Locust Grove, but a hunch is a hunch, and in all of his years doing police work, more than one hunch had paid off. Maybe this one would, too.

Dust floated in the air from Darcy's truck. When the man arrived at County 31, he debated in his mind whether to follow or not, but he decided that the old truck might belong down that road, if it went that way. Must have though, he reasoned, since he couldn't see it up ahead and the gravel road was filled with dust. He decided the hippie had turned off, so he continued down Highway 5 to its intersection with Highway 25 at Wolf Bayou. He turned left and settled in for the drive to Locust Grove, 14 miles away. But at Concord, he turned right on Highway 87 and went to Pleasant Plains. He made a right on US 167 and drove to Bald Knob.

He checked into a motel there and found a place to eat. He decided that if someone had found his hideout and was watching, they could watch all they wanted. He had altered his scheme and it was so nice to be free when plans had to be changed. He could change plans like a chameleon changed colors and now was the time to change again. "What color would it be this time?" he asked himself. The people in the restaurant turned there heads and looked at him. He smiled and continued eating his deep fried catfish dinner with all the trimmings. Hush puppies, slaw, onions, pickled green tomatoes, and black coffee completed the meal.

Martin Perkins told Darcy on the cell phone where he was secluded. Darcy hid the truck and they settled in to watch the intersection of the two highways, 14, and 25. Four hours later, they gave up. Darcy said to Martin, "Guess my hunch wasn't too good this time. Win some, lose some."

They discussed what Martin had learned from the postal inspector he met in Batesville. They both agreed that the man they were after was living in the area, but where was the question they couldn't answer yet. Discreet inquiries in Locust Grove were negative. They returned to Mountain View, not much smarter but very tired from the mental strain and emotional drain they couldn't avoid.

THIRTY-NINE

Rain hammered the windshield of the car when Reginald turned off the interstate into Sikeston, Missouri. He found the police department and went inside, leaving Callman in the car. After identifying himself, Lt. Carlisle Hanson came out to greet him. He said as they shook hands, "Darrell called me. I got the message that you called and have been expecting you. Sounds like you have a real mess on your hands."

"We do, and I'm afraid it's going to get worse before it gets better. We don't know who we are looking for and that's what makes it tougher."

"So you think you found Trudy Bushman and think that the victim in the car was her husband."

"I don't think there's any doubt that the two vics are the Bushmans. What we don't know is where or why they were killed, and without knowing, prosecution is going to be tough," Reginald said.

"Maybe we'll all get a break," Hanson said.

"We need one. He seems to be two steps ahead all the time. Did you find anything at Bushman's house?" Reginald asked.

"We found items last year after Bushman failed to appear that are really interesting. Seems John Daniel Bushman was into making false IDs. We found the photo equipment, computer, and all that he used. I don't believe he intended to stay gone, and if by chance he did, I think he would have taken his stuff with him. The records we found indicated he was making a fair amount of money with his operation. That being the case, it's strange he would give up a good illegal income. So good in fact, he had paid the rent through next year. That indicates he had settled in and intended to stay in town. The utility companies automatically withdraw the monthly charges, and the bank told us there was ample money in the account to cover the charges for another year. He set those automatic payments up soon after moving into the house."

"What did you do with the Bushman's belongings?" Reginald asked.

"When Detective Wellington went out to the house last year and found them gone, he tried to get a search warrant, but the judge wouldn't issue one since there wasn't enough probable cause to believe that they were there or that they were engaged in criminal conduct beyond the ones known at that time. The judge issued a warrant for failure to appear and that is all he would do. Wellington saw the equipment at that time, but he had no reason to think that it was being used for illegal purposes. He had no choice but to leave the house as he found it. He locked the door and left after talking to the landlord."

"What happened that you were able to seize the computer and related equipment?"

"Detective Wellington had been working three forgery cases and developed information that Bushman had an illegal operation making forged documents. Based on the information, he obtained a search warrant in late September and found all the equipment. Unfortunately, Bushman was smart enough to have destroyed all the data that would have revealed his customers."

"That clears up a question we have had ever since this case began. We knew the perp was using false IDs, and we think that Bushman made them for him. Then he apparently used Bushman's equipment to make himself into Bushman after he killed them both. He might have come back through here and made the ID," Reginald said.

"How do you figure that?" Hanson asked.

"In July of '95, someone named J. Daniel Bushman opened a checking account in Mountain Home, Arkansas. Then drew out all but one dollar of the available amount a month or so ago. Whoever we are looking for used the Bushmans for his own ends and now to find out what those are and why."

"I agree and as usual, the criminal is always ahead of us on what and why," Lt. Hanson said.

Reginald told Hanson the high points of the case's history and said he would send all the reports to him as soon as he could get everything entered on the computer and copies made.

South of Poplar Bluff the rain hit hard again. It rained all the way to Mountain View slowing the traffic, and they didn't arrive until seven forty-five that evening. Reginald made a brief stop at the police department and then he and Callman went back to the car. When they turned North on Highway 9, Callman said it would be good to get in his motor home again. Reginald continued north and drove on past the park, puzzling Callman. "Where are you going? I want to go to my motor home."

"That's where we're going." Callman was even more puzzled until Reginald told him where his motor coach had been taken. After they had left for Indiana, Darcy took the coach to Martin Perkins's place. They didn't want to take any chances that the perp would try something stupid or catch them by surprise.

Callman and Reginald went into Martin's house. They all exchanged greetings and then got down to business. The trip to the Batesville Post Office seemed like a shot in the dark, but it proved to be a bull's eye. Martin told Reginald what he had learned. "Somebody has been cashing 100 dollar money orders at the post office on a regular basis since May 8. The payer on the order is J. Daniel Bushman and the payee is Harley Bastin. All of them were purchased on the same day at different post offices. Blackwood is working on finding the post offices that issued them by checking the serial numbers with all the offices in a seventy-five mile radius of Mountain View. I'm also checking to see if any clerks remember them being cashed."

"How many were cashed?"

"There were two for 100 each and one for eighty-five dollars. The last one was cashed one week ago," Martin answered. "And probably he either cashed the others elsewhere or still has them."

"So he bought money orders that cleaned out his account except for one dollar, cashed them, and in the process he laundered his identity instead of the money. That's pretty slick. Didn't have to worry that someone would remember him wanting to cash a big check and asking questions," Darcy said.

"I goofed though. I asked Sam to notify us if he closed the account. He left that dollar in it and the bookkeeper wasn't the wiser since the account wasn't closed," Reginald said, obviously disgusted for not thinking of that possibility.

"That was slick, too," Darcy said. "He's always one step ahead on most things. Leads me to believe he has been involved in a lot more criminal activity."

"Is there any description for the perp?" Reginald asked.

"A general one," Martin said. "Average build, 5' 9" to six feet tall, 200 pounds or so, reddish brown hair, short beard. Each time he had on a different cap. One clerk said it wasn't the same man. Another said it was."

"Not much to go on, but it's better than nothing which is mostly what we have had for a long time," Reginald replied. "I think he's living real close to us, but where is the mystery." Unspoken agreement was echoed around the room by the nods of the heads of the three others.

Reginald filled them in on the Indiana trip and returned to Mountain View. Before he entered the house, he heard the phone ringing. He hurriedly unlocked the door, rushed across the kitchen, and answered, "Hello." Pause. "It sure is good to hear your voice, Sherry." He paused again. "You're in Texarkana?" He listened intently and then: "I'll call Darcy, Martin, and Darrell. We have a big problem now. How much worse can it get?" He paused for a longer time. "When will you be back?" He paused briefly. "Okay. I'll expect you tomorrow evening." The last pause made Reginald smile. "I love you, too. Drive carefully. Good bye."

Phone calls were made to briefly relay what Sherry had told him. Forty minutes later, Reginald returned to Martin's house to meet Darrell, Thomas, and Darcy in Martin's living room to discuss the new turn of events. The look on their faces was grave and told the whole story after they had heard the facts. The case had taken a turn for the worse. The worst possible event was staring them in the face if they couldn't head it off. Mary Beth Norman was in town and they didn't know where she was or what she looked like. They had every reason to believe she didn't know that the man who tried to kill her a few months back was in the area. If he found her, he would kill her. They were now in a race against time to find her and prevent her death. But knowing she was in town helped them and not him. That was their edge.

FORTY

The man drove around Bald Knob looking for a used car lot. He looked on several lots, but none had what he wanted. Becoming frustrated, he was ready to give up the search when he found the perfect vehicle. He traded the Blazer for a maroon 1996 Dodge Caravan with a long wheelbase. It had dark tinted windows and blackwall tires. He paid the difference in cash and drove away, again congratulating himself on his ability to change his plans at a moment's notice. "Killers don't drive Dodges and that insurance money sure has come in handy, too. Without it, I would be dead in the water instead of driving this killer Dodge," he said, laughing maniacally.

He had things to do, so he hurriedly collected his belongs from the motel and turned the Dodge onto the highway for the trip to Locust Grove. He had to restrain himself to keep from speeding. Though he was in a hurry, the last thing he needed or wanted was a speeding ticket. The Arkansas plate from another vehicle, not the one on the Blazer, was registered to Malcom Brookson, and with an ID that showed him to be that person and the registration from the other vehicle, he shouldn't have any problem if he was stopped. The only problem was the sales slip listing the Blazer as the trade-in. He would deal with that if and when the time came. On Monday he would get it all fixed up legal and proper with the other car listed as the trade-in on the sales slip.

He laughed when he remembered how handy Bushman's ID equipment had been for him. *So fortunate for me that Bushman had two computers with all the equipment. I would bet the cops didn't know that, and now I can be whoever I want to be, just like old times. Keep ahead of those cops and keep them guessing. A true quick change artist and I am the master now. I am in control except for Callman who forced me to change parts of the plan when he didn't die.*

The man's thoughts continued to race through his head. *Whatever was found in Indiana won't make any difference. They will never find me when I leave here. If they find what I have planned for them to find, they will be even more confused. The one thing I hadn't planned on was losing that pulley. Maybe no one will find it. I looked for it in February but didn't have time to search for it carefully with all of the snow on the ground. It snowed that night and covered the tracks I made around the tree where I searched. I covered my tracks around that house when I broke out the window and borrowed the typewriter. Learning about the typewriter was a stroke of fortune and it fit into my plans perfectly. That nosy old man might have been too nosy for the both of us had I spent more time in the house, and that wouldn't have been good for my plan. If someone finds the pulley and the typewriter, they can't trace anything to me.*

He arrived in Locust Grove but didn't immediately turn onto Highway 14. He went on through town and up the mountain and drove several more miles past Locust Grove. He didn't see anything suspicious, so he turned around and slipped into the drive to the house. He had a lot to do and the most pressing one was finding Mary Beth Norman before she left Mountain View. He had seen her on Thursday, and he hoped she would be in town until at least through Saturday night. He didn't have much time, if she was in a motel, to find her and set up his surprise. If she wasn't in a motel, then he would have to try another more public method that would be riskier for him.

Most of his belongings were loaded in the Caravan. What he left behind wouldn't make any difference. He boxed his beloved slot car track with loving care and stowed it in the back of the van. The work caused tears to appear and slide down his cheeks as he remembered the good times he had racing with Nickolette and little Ricky. Oh how he missed them. No one knew the pain he felt daily since their deaths. And their mother he loved dearly; and now she was gone. Their deaths caused by all those who didn't care. Now they would care when it was too late, and then his pain would be gone forever.

•

Friday always brought swelling crowds to Mountain View. People listened to music on the square; some toured the antique shops; others stuffed their faces at a selection of restaurants and food stands. All the people milling around made it easy to hide, and he was good at it. He was Malcom Brookson, residing at West Highway 36, Searcy, Arkansas. He had covered all bases by setting up a legitimate address with a car with a legitimate plate registered to Brookson. Money was no problem, and where he was going when his rampage was over, he wouldn't need money anyway. He locked on the word rampage and it wouldn't be just any old rampage. The words *deadly rampage* flashed through his mind. *Yes*, he decided, *a deadly rampage describes my plan well*. He was pleased with his choice of words to describe the payback those people would receive from him.

Parking places weren't easy to find, but eventually he found one. He mingled with the crowds and visited the shops staying alert for Mary Beth. If he saw her, the problem was finding where she was staying. He hoped it was a motel. Giving up on finding her in the crowd, he began to drive around the town, checking motel parking lots. He didn't find anything that looked like it might be her car. He was ready to give up in frustration when he saw a familiar face at the Blue Bird Inn. It was Robert Blandford. He was exiting a room at the closed end of the horseshoe. His pulse quickened and the excitement began to build. Well, Mary Beth, you will have to wait. Mr. Blandford is a bird in hand, and he will never know what happened to him. He pulled into the parking lot next to the office and parked where those inside couldn't see his van. He watched Blandford enter the office. A couple of minutes later Blandford came out and left in his car.

The man, Malcom Brookson, went inside the office and paid for a one night stay. He had gotten the last vacancy and the room was right next to Blandford. He unpacked what he needed and made sure his tools were in order. He took the equipment from the containers and assembled the pieces. He carefully prepared the two boxes so he would be ready when he found Mary Beth Norman's motel room. The only problem that remained now was to figure out when Blandford would be gone long enough for him to prepare the surprise that he would never know had arrived. "Innocent people might die, but isn't that what they deserve by being so close to the intended victim? Everything has consequences and I am the one who will be dealing them out, and the consequence for Blandford is the medicine this doctor will dispense soon," he hissed loudly. "I will … "

Brookson's diatribe was interrupted by a noise outside. He looked out the window and saw Blandford hurry from his car to the room and slam the door. Then what he saw next chilled him to the marrow of his bones. There was that cop, Sgt. Gawker, pulling in next to Blandford's car. He got out and knocked on the door. Blandford let him in and slammed it shut. Two birds in a room, and he didn't have his revolver. As that thought moved through his mind, a marked patrol car pulled in facing his van. He was glad he had backed in so they couldn't see the plate. He reminded himself not to be stupid as he watched through a slit in the curtains. This wasn't going as planned. *Something has happened that I haven't counted on*, he silently shouted, the sound inside his head so loud he was afraid others could hear it. He could feel the rage beginning to build as he came to the edge, nearly losing control of his behavior.

Somebody was going to pay for interrupting his plans. He wanted to scream and couldn't. He found a towel and stuffed it into his mouth to muffle the sound he was driven to make. The door in the next room opened. Blandford came out with three bags, followed by Reginald with two more bags. They were placed in the trunk, and he got into his car and left, following the patrol car from the lot. He watched that cop, as he called Reginald, enter the motel office, come out, and then leave. His body shuddered with relief. He had had a close call. He gathered up his electro-mechanical friends and stowed them in the van. His rage was at a controllable level now, but one more incident would set off a rampage he couldn't control. He went back to the room to lie on the bed and relax.

He awoke from a short nap and began to make plans again. He could always think much clearer after a nap brought on by emotional trauma. He knew he couldn't dwell on plans that didn't work, so now to make new ones. He decided to attend the night show at the Folk Center and maybe something would get his creative juices flowing again. He had the plans, and if they had gone well, he would have had so many opportunities. Somehow, people he hadn't planned on kept getting in the way. He grabbed his hat and left the room.

Sitting near the window in Best Burgers, the man saw all that passed on Main Street. He watched innocent people conducting their business as he used to do before that scaffold fell. *Why don't people follow the rules the same as I did after I made my get away?* A noise intruded on his day dreaming. Two cars had crashed at the intersection, and he laughed at what he was thinking. *Somebody didn't follow the rules, and when you don't follow the rules, people get hurt or killed.* The anger began to rise, so he quickly got up and left for the Folk Center. When anger began to fill his mind, driving had a calming effect on him.

Cars streaming into the parking lot quickly filled the spaces. He parked near the back of the lot. He was walking to the bus for the trip up the hill when he saw the old Chevy truck. He considered leaving but then thought why should he ruin his evening? *That hippie isn't any problem and besides he won't recognize me the way I'm dressed. I'm dressed differently tonight than on other nights, so even if he has seen me before, it won't make any difference.* The word invisible crossed his mind. *Yes, invisible. That's the word. I'm invisible. I'm so invisible that when they see me they don't see me.* He suppressed the urge to laugh.

Brookson had put on an old droopy, western looking felt hat. The string tie went well with the western and country look that let him fit in with the others dressed the same way that evening. He walked across the lot and was very thankful that his injured knee no lon-

ger made him limp enough that anyone would notice. He banged his
right knee against the door edge getting on the bus. Pain shot through
his leg from the knee to his foot and up to his hip. He made an effort
not to show his pain and tried to hide the pronounced limp. Struggling with the severe pain, he limped to an empty seat near the back
of the bus.

FORTY-ONE

S moke rose in black billowing raging puffs above the trees. The smoke rolled and rose and rolled some more, sending plumes of sparks high into the sky. The house had been burning for several minutes before a customer at the convenience store on Highway 25 in Locust Grove had spotted it. He ran inside and told the clerk, who ran outside to look before calling the fire department. He said to the customer, "That looks like the old Shuman place. The owner is in a nursing home. I wonder if his daughter knows it's burning."

"Go call the fire department, idiot. Now isn't the time to worry about what his daughter knows," the customer yelled at the addled clerk.

The clerk, jarred from his trance caused by watching the smoke billow up over the trees, went back inside, and called for the fire trucks. The nearest department available was the volunteer outfit down the road a mile away. More than ten minutes later, the first truck roared around the corner, turning from 25 onto Highway 14. Several cars with red lights followed. It took over an hour to douse the flames. By the time the fire was out, only a smoldering pile of ashes remained of what was once a house. An Independence County deputy called his department to report on the fire. He was told to stand by and wait for a detective from Mountain View and to mark the area with yellow tape since it was possibly a crime scene.

Ninety minutes later Reginald drove up the driveway to the burned house. He was met by Deputy Lacey Barger and a state policeman,

Sgt. Phillip Hancock. The last fire truck was just leaving, and when it had cleared the drive, they drove up closer to the site and stopped several feet away. The only thing left standing was a garage and an old shed. The siding of the shed and the garage were scorched, but the structures were intact. Officer Hancock looked at Reginald and said, "That was a hot fire. The witnesses said that the smoke was really black and rolling. That might indicate it had some help."

"Who owns this property?" Reginald asked.

"Arnold Shuman," Barger said. "He's in a nursing home and has a daughter, Marjorie Shuman, who lives in Batesville. I don't think anyone lives here now. Never see anyone around."

"Sure is peculiar that the house would burn with no one living in it. We need to look around for anything that might be evidence."

Phillip Hancock said, "I need to get back on patrol. You fellas have jurisdiction so I'll be going. If we can help you in any way later on, give us a holler. We'll do what we can."

"Thanks for your help with traffic," Barger said as Hancock left. "Phil is a good officer. I have known him for ten years. He turned down a promotion to detective because he likes road patrol and his present rank."

"Sometimes I feel like dump patrol would be better than what I do," Reginald said laughing. "There's a lot to be said for the patrol division. Finish your shift and go home. Detectives drag their road kill around with them day and night."

"I was told it might be a crime scene so I strung the tape. What makes you interested in a house fire way out here?" Barger asked. "How does the fire tie in with your interest?"

"We have a murder case in Mountain View and aren't getting much of anywhere on solving it. We think the killer is living around here somewhere so we're looking at everything that might give us help in finding the solution. We've been going to so many places that it feels like an octopus is pointing us in eight directions at once." Barger didn't know whether to comment or stay silent. He chose silent and shook his head trying to keep from laughing. He knew the feeling of eight directions at once from his experience with criminal investigations.

Barger and Reginald began to search the area for whatever they could find that might turn out to be evidence. Reginald took pictures of what was left of the burned house. As he was focusing on a burned area, he lowered the camera for a better look at what he saw. "Lacey, see that?" Reginald said, pointing to a dark object half buried in the smoldering ashes. "That looks like a typewriter. There's one involved in this case." Reginald photographed the object before it was moved.

Lacey Barger found a wide board by the garage, laid it across the hot ashes, and walked out on it to retrieve the typewriter. It was too hot to touch. He retreated and found a pair of heavy gloves in the patrol car trunk. He picked it up and set it on the ground. He said, "If this is the one you are interested in, it won't be used again."

"Lacey, will you call your department and have your people contact the owner's daughter? I need to interview her. I believe she may have information that will prove helpful." Barger went to his car and made the call.

A systematic search in the burned out area didn't reveal anything additional that looked like it might be evidence. Reginald was in the garage looking through the junk, and was ready to leave, when he saw a small object lying near a saw horse leg. He went to his car, took a pair of needle nose pliers from the evidence collection kit, picked the object up by the small pin near its front, and dropped the object into a plastic evidence bag. Deputy Barger was watching and said, "What did you find?" Reginald held the bag so Barger could see it. "That looks like a slot car. My son has a bunch of them."

"That's what it is," Reginald said, "an HO scale race car. I still have one or two in my collection of kid stuff." He stood looking at the yellow toy, mystified by its presence in the garage. "I don't think Mr. Shuman would have played with this. If this place wasn't lived in, how did it get here?"

"I don't know," Barger said, as puzzled by the car as Reginald. "I thought the house had been empty since Mr. Shuman went to the nursing home." The county car's radio squawked and Barger ran over to it. He came back and told Reginald that Marjorie Shuman had been contacted and that she would arrive in an hour or so. They continued to look around the area, made all the more difficult by the briars, tangled brush, and weeds.

They waded through the tangle and broke through into a flat clearing at the back of the property. They both saw the big oak tree at the same time.

"Looks like someone has been using that tree to test a battering ram," Barger exclaimed. "And look at all the ruts and tracks back here. What did all this?"

Reginald took in the scene and then said, "If it's what I think it is, we have found answers to a bunch of questions and a peek into the deep mystery we are wrestling with." Then he saw an object, partially hidden by small trees, sticking up from the bottom of a deep gulley. The mystery was less deep now. Reginald was looking at the pulley on the top end of a tow truck boom sticking out of the brush. He knew now he had answers to a lot more questions. Then he realized that he still had more questions than answers.

Chapter

FORTY-TWO

When the man stepped off the bus in front of the auditorium, his right knee ached badly. He couldn't help limping no matter how hard he tried to walk normally. He decided that since there couldn't possibly be anyone who would know him, he was safe. *It's a real relief to not have to look over my shoulder all the time,* he thought. He bought his admission ticket, went inside, and found a seat in the back row near the center section. He didn't see the hippie so all was going smoothly, and even if he did see that low life, the hippie didn't know him. He could enjoy the evening and the show either way. It was Western Weekend, and he looked western with his string tie and hat. He hated western, but he knew to be invisible he had to go with the crowd, like he did the day he disappeared in the crowd on the sidewalk after that cop saw him watching from that store. People looked at him and never saw him. He liked the word invisible. He was good at it. He smiled and settled into his seat, feeling at ease for the first time in several weeks.

Martin Perkins came out of the concession room when the man took his seat. He saw the man, but since he wasn't any different from the others in the auditorium, he didn't take a second look or give him any thought. Darcy saw him as well and took no special notice either. Both Darcy and Martin hung around the back where the people were milling around greeting friends. They weren't recognized as they walked around observing the throng and that suited them fine. Neither was the man with the limp sitting where he could see the biker and the hippie mingling with the crowd.

The lights dimmed three times quickly and those wandering around hurried for their seats. Martin slid into a seat on the back row across the aisle and to the left of where the man, Malcom Brookson, continued to relax in the center section. Brookson didn't see Martin take his seat. Neither did he see Darcy sit down to Martin's left at the end of the same row. The show began and worldly thoughts were shoved aside by the memories the *old timey music* brought to mind. Jig dancing and story telling delightfully entertained the audience. Those so inclined went to the stage and jig danced to the rhythm of the fiddle tunes John and his group played.

Intermission time arrived. The people left their seats and went to the rest rooms and to the concessions or outside to smoke. Martin and Darcy went to the auditorium office, wading through the teeming masses moving to look at the tapes, CDs, and to greet friends. They asked for an announcement to be made. A couple of minutes after the intermission began, the public address boomed in the auditorium. "If Mary Beth Norman is in the house, please come to the office."

Brookson became alert, startled by the announcement. He rose from his seat so quickly his bad knee collided with a seat in the row in front of him. It hurt so badly he had to sit back down. He felt sick at his stomach. A lady asked him if he was okay. He glared at her and said nothing. Feeling better, he got up and by the time he made it to the rear area, there were so many people he couldn't see whether any-one had gone into the office or not, if he had known where it was to begin with. After asking a lady where to find it, he finally located the room. It was empty.

The rage that he had under control began to surface. He had missed her before months ago, and now here she was nearly in his hand and she had slipped away again. How did anyone know she was here? He rushed to the front doors as best he could, the badly aching knee shooting pains into his leg with each step. He saw the hippie standing outside talking to country looking people. *Did he have something to do with the announcement?* he asked silently. Other silent questions began to flood his mind. *How could he? He's just a hippie bum ... or is he?* He didn't have the answers. Anger began to rise to the surface. His control began to slip away again. He had to get out before he went into a full rage. He slammed out the doors and limped away. He saw that the hippie had disappeared. The bus took him down the hill. He arrived in the parking lot in time to see the old truck's tail lights disappear into the night. Limping to his van, he couldn't help but think that the hippie was somehow involved. Then he saw the biker sitting on his chopper. "Where did he come from? I didn't see him in the auditorium," he mumbled. For the first time, fear crept in to displace his rage. He ducked behind a car to watch.

Martin saw the man duck behind the car, but he didn't make any move that would indicate that he saw him. The lot being dark didn't let him see well enough to get a description. The only thing he saw was a limp or what looked to be a limp. He fired up the bike, made a swooping turn where the man had last been seen, but when he passed the car, the man was gone. Martin drove around and not seeing anything more, he left the lot.

Brookson crawled out from under the SUV where he had hidden. He knew he was close to having been in a situation that would not have been good for him. Those two were beginning to be more than nuisances. Nuisances needed to go, especially the type who continued to get in his way. And those two were getting in his way.

FORTY-THREE

Both Reginald and Deputy Barger were looking at the tow truck resting in the gulley, the front end buried in the mud. Brush had grown up around it and made getting to the cab difficult. They heard tires crunching on gravel. They fought their way out of the gulley and thrashed their way through undergrowth back to the burned house remains. Dark was setting in anyway and whatever they needed to do with the truck would have to wait until tomorrow.

A young woman stepped from the car; Marjorie Shuman introduced herself to both men. She walked over and looked at the blackened hole in the ground where the house had stood that was once her home. She remembered playing in the woods, picking black berries, playing house in the old shed, and looking for snakes. Doing those things made her interested in biology, which she was studying at the local college in Batesville. She planned on going to medical school when she graduated. The memories brought tears to her eyes. She turned to Reginald saying, "Forgive me. It's such a shock. I'm glad mother isn't here now to see this. They both loved this place. At one time, it was real pretty. Daddy took pride in the outside, and mother kept a fine house inside. They worked together to make me a nice home. I'm the only child." She became silent while she dabbed her tears with a tissue. "It is such a shock to see my childhood home gone." Marjorie dabbed at her eyes once more before speaking. "Okay. I'm ready to answer whatever you want to ask."

"Let's get some little things cleared up first. Did your daddy have a typewriter?" Reginald pointed to a box that held a burned typewriter with an evidence tag attached to it.

Marjorie Shuman studied the object and said, "He had one in the corner of the living room," pointing to the general area where it had been found. "Did you find it there?

"It was right there at the end of the board Deputy Barger put on the ashes to get to it."

"That would be right. Daddy used that corner in the living room for an office after mother died. He wrote letters to politicians and newspapers. He always said he had to keep the varmints lined out." She laughed and tears came to her eyes again as memories flooded her mind.

"Did your daddy have any hobbies?"

"What do you mean?"

"Interests that would help him pass the time when he wasn't busy with his other work."

"He has a model train set that the nursing home let him set up in the corner of the rec room. He and his buddies have a lot of fun with it. Everybody enjoys it."

Reginald removed the bag with the slot car in it from his pocket. He showed it to Miss Shuman. "Did your daddy have anything like this?

"What is that?" She looked closer. "That's a little race car. Uh … it's a slot car. I'm sure he didn't. At least he didn't when I was still home."

"You never saw a slot car around here?"

"Not ever. He had trains and things that go with them but not slot cars. Where did you find it?"

"In the garage," Reginald said.

"He wouldn't have had anything in the garage. He had his trains in a spare bedroom. That isn't his."

Reginald put the bag back into his pocket, satisfied that the car didn't belong to her father. Then: "Miss Shuman, who rented the house from you?"

"A guy who said his name was Marion Easterly. I think he lived in Little Rock."

"When did you rent the house to him?"

"Let me think." Marjorie counted on her fingers, then went back to her car, rummaged around, and came back with a small date book. She flipped the pages, found the one she was looking for and said, "It was April 3 of 1995, on Monday. He gave me 200 cash that day, and from then on each month, he sent me cash wrapped in white writing paper. I got 200 per month in 100 dollar bills."

"Do you have any of the paper and the envelopes?" Reginald asked.

"No. As soon as I got the money, I threw them away. Never thought I needed to save them."

"How did he find you to rent the house?" Reginald asked.

"I put a house for rent sign with my phone number on it out by the road in March. Three weeks later, the phone rang. I came up here, and he rented it. He paid me in cash every month like clock work and sent the money to my post office box. I sure hate to lose the rent money."

Deputy Barger motioned to Reginald. He walked over, and the two had a quiet conversation. Barger went to his car and called his department. Reginald went back to Miss Shuman. "Can you describe the man?"

Marjorie Shuman said, "I can't really describe him very well. He was 5'11," reddish brown hair, thirty-five to forty years old, maybe 200 to 225 pounds. That's the best I can do." She grinned and then said, "I could draw a picture of him if I had some paper and colored pencils."

Reginald jerked his head up. "You could do what?"

Miss Shuman tried not to laugh at the Reginald's expression. "I'm an art minor, too. I like portraits, so I study faces. Do you want me to do his face?"

Reginald was stunned by this sudden turn in the investigation and could hardly find his voice to answer. "Sure. When do you want to do it?

"I can drive over to Mountain View."

Reginald thought for few ticks. "No. That isn't a good idea. I'll be here tomorrow and if you want to go home and do the drawing there, then you can leave it at the sheriff's office. If it's possible, perhaps Deputy Barger can bring it over tomorrow as soon as you give it to him," Reginald said, looking hopefully at the deputy.

Barger readily agreed that he could do that. The sheriff told him on the radio that he had been assigned to the case. He also told Reginald that he would stay until his relief arrived. The sheriff didn't want the scene unprotected. The state police would arrive with the crime scene truck and sift the ashes tomorrow. A tow truck would pull the wrecker out of the gulley so they could process it for evidence. If there was anything else on that property, they would find it. They were really interested in that oak tree and what it might tell them. And best of all, they were going to get a look at whom they might be chasing. *A break in a hard case sure would be nice*, Reginald thought.

Chapter

FORTY-FOUR

When Robert Blandford followed the patrol car to Martin Perkins's house, he kept thinking he had awakened in a living nightmare. He had prepared for a nice weekend with his cousin Mary Beth. He had planned to meet her at the Folk Center, and now it was blown apart because some psycho sicko was trying to kill him for reasons best known to only the psychopath. Blandford thought he was safe at the Blue Bird Inn and couldn't see any reason for having to leave. He would have been careful, he had insisted to the police.

The patrol car slowed and turned off the highway. They traveled down a gravel road and then turned into the driveway that led to the house sitting several yards from the road. A medium size motor coach sat next to the log house. A rather rotund man was sitting on the porch swing. Blandford exited his car to talk to Nance Porter, the patrolman. They walked to the porch and Porter said, "L. Jason Callman, meet Robert Blandford. You two will be Martin's house guests until we can make other arrangements. Now I need to leave. Martin said he will be here sometime tonight and to make yourselves at home."

They watched the car go down the drive then Blandford said, "Don't I know you from somewhere? Your name is familiar."

"I sold chemicals to your company for several years. Jaxco Chemical in Ohio was my company," Callman said.

"Now I remember. You had something to do with that trial in Little Rock when that scaffold fell and killed a woman and her two children."

"Only a small part and our company escaped all blame. I sold the chemicals to that refrigeration company, and the lawyer for the plaintiff couldn't convince the judge that the chemicals I sold helped the scaffolding fall," Callman said.

"I guess we can say that somebody doesn't believe it and wants to kill both you and me."

"Kill you?" Callman exclaimed.

"You got it. Somebody is after me, too. I got a note and four punctured tires. That's why I'm here." Callman began to shake with fright again.

•

Before leaving the Folk Center with Mary Beth Norman, Darcy had her leave a note for her friend telling her that she had to leave on business and would call later. Ironically, Mary Beth had checked in at the Blue Bird Inn where Brookson had rented a room. The afternoon desk clerk had neglected to pass on the note to the evening clerk leaving instructions for him to call the police department, if or when she checked in. He had left the same request at all the motels in town. Darcy took Mary Beth to her car; she drove over to the motel, collected her belongings, and then followed Darcy to a Heber Springs motel in order to hide her from the killer.

They left the motel five minutes before the man, Brookson, drove into the lot. He backed into the space in front of his door and entered the room. Since he was so close, he hoped that his very noticeable limp wouldn't be noticed. He loaded his belongings, left the key on the dresser, and drove to the house across the street from the police station, hiding the van in the garage. He laughed that the biker didn't pay him any attention. The biker was just another fool who held no importance to him. *A loser among all the other losers*, his mind told him.

He unloaded several items, and the one that made him laugh loudly was the Underwood typewriter he set on the small desk. They'll figure out that it burned up in the fire and they'll be right. He was pleased that he had found a house that was furnished with a few necessities, even though he believed the old woman who owned the house was ripping him off on the rent. He would deal with her when the time came. But for his purpose, the house and its sparse furnishings were all he needed, and best of all, it sat in an ideal location for carrying out his plan. He unpacked his meager clothes and went to bed.

•

As Martin drove to the Blue Bird Inn after checking all the other motel lots in town to see if he could spot anything suspicious, he passed the maroon van on the street without noticing it. It looked similar to the other vans in town that night. He checked the last lot and then pointed the bike toward Calico Rock. He was tired and wanted to go to bed. It had been a long day with little to show for it. He drove up his drive and saw Blandford's car. *Maybe I need to get a motel license and charge room rent.* He was too tired to laugh at his attempt at being funny.

Chapter
FORTY-FIVE

S herry arrived back in town from Texarkana and tried repeatedly to contact Reginald. She needed to see him before morning to tell him what she had found. "Reginald, where are you?" she said when a car pulled into her driveway. She peeked out and saw him getting out of the car. She opened the door before he could knock and gave him a big kiss. His face turned crimson. "I surely am glad to see you, Reg. I tried to call you four or five times. Where were you?"

Reginald told her all that he had discovered and then asked her what she had learned. She began with the investigation she conducted in the Little Rock. "Marion Easterly worked for the refrigeration company where his wife and children were killed. He filed a lawsuit for wrongful death against the scaffolding company and his company. The insurance companies and Sky High gave him a huge settlement. The scaffold company had to pay in addition to the insurance company payment because their insurance coverage didn't cover the entire damage award. Sky High then went bankrupt later as we know."

"That verifies what we know to date. What else?" Reginald said.

"Easterly began to act strange and quit his job after a few months. He began drinking and left before he was fired. But the kicker in all this is that the woman who was killed was Carl Alstrom's sister. Alstrom was Easterly's brother-in-law. It was a real family tragedy for them."

Reginald looked at her with a dropped jaw. "Carl Alstrom's sister? Does that mean Easterly could have killed Borders and Alstrom?"

"I don't know what it means, but it's possible. I also found where the possible suspect lived in Little Rock. He sold his house, but rented it from the buyer and then one day he disappeared. I was able to track down people who knew him and not one of them has seen him for almost two years."

"The last time anyone can remember seeing him was the fall of '94 when he visited Callman in Indiana. He may have good reason to want to disappear. If he's doing what we think he is doing, that would be reason enough."

"What was the address of his house?"

"It was near the UALR campus, east of University Avenue and south of Asher." Suddenly Reginald jumped up and said, "I'll be right back," as he went out the door. He returned with his briefcase. He quickly found a page in the report given to him by Detective Short. "It says here Easterly's address was a Little Rock post office box. They found that out through the car registration." He remained silent and then said, "We need to find out if Easterly ever had a box and most especially, if he had one around the time of that accident in Indiana. We need to contact Blackwood again."

"What are you leading up to?" Sherry asked.

"I don't know exactly. Portions of the alleged facts in this case aren't right, and I think this is one that has been giving me a headache since this case began."

"I hate to help your headache along, but I have a lot more to make it hammer inside your head," Sherry said seriously. Reginald couldn't find any humor in her words. He wiped his face and sat in silence looking at her.

"After Mr. Easterly disappeared, a man showed up at his former residence with a key. The neighbor went over to see who it was. The man said he was Easterly's friend, and he had come for some things Easterly had given him."

"What was it he wanted to get?"

"This is really strange. It was a slot car track." Sherry saw Regi-

nald's expression change and said, "What's wrong? Did I say something wrong?"

"No. It's just that this case gets weirder all the time. I found a slot
car on the garage floor where that house burned out by Locust Grove.
The owner's daughter says it didn't belong to her father."

"Was there a track there?"

"Not that I saw."

Sherry got up and went to the kitchen to put on the coffee pot.
She opened a pan of ready to bake cinnamon rolls and filled two small
glasses with orange juice. A knock came at the door. Reginald opened
it and stepped back. Darrell Cumberland entered the house. Sherry
saw him when she started into the living room. She turned around
and got out another cup and filled another glass with orange juice. She
came back in the room and said, "Hi, Darrell. I didn't expect you."

"I noticed you hurry back to the kitchen. Did I scare you?" and
laughed.

"No. Cinnamon rolls are baking, and I got out another cup and
poured a glass of orange juice for you."

"I wasn't going to stay very long, but you changed my mind. Reginald, I couldn't get you at home and figured you were here. The Independence County Sheriff called Thomas and asked him to be at the
fire site at 8:00 a.m. The state lab truck will be there before nine. I'll
ride over with you. Do you want to go too, Sherry?"

"Sure I do. I'll drive my own car. I mean the state car," she said
and laughed.

They filled Darrell in on the latest, and then Sherry got up to get
the coffee and rolls. She was serving it when a knock came at the door.
Reginald opened it and there stood Darcy. He entered and said, "Boy,
did I arrive at the right time or what? I have a nose for food."

"And it isn't even doughnuts this time," Sherry said as she went
back to the kitchen to get another cup and more orange juice.

When she came back into the room, Reginald with a dead pan
expression said, "You have made so many trips back and forth to the
kitchen, I can see a path in the carpet now."

"Is that so?" she replied. "In that case, get out your wallets boys. I'm taking up a collection for new carpeting." Everyone laughed.

Darcy was brought up to date quickly. Then Sherry continued, "I dropped off that candy wrapper and the toothpick from Sharp's for examination. They had the report ready on the DNA from the blood found on Sheldon's porch and the DNA from the toothpick found at the Callman scene. They didn't match. The lab tech told me the DNA analysis from the toothpick from Sharp's wouldn't be ready for three to four weeks. I hung up and made a phone call. The tech received a phone call, and he told me when I called back that we would have it by next week. The state police head called in a favor."

"That was a shot in the dark on the toothpick found on the square. It could have been anybody that dropped it. But why were both of them broken in the middle?" Reginald wondered. "I thought we had something."

"I went to Texarkana, and that's why I called Darrell. Sometime in 1995, someone took two shots at Mary Beth through the front window of her house. The Texarkana police haven't solved it yet," Sherry related.

Darcy spoke up. "That's what she told me after we arrived in Heber Springs. What upset her the most was that she didn't get to see her cousin, Robert Blandford. She can't believe that anyone would want to kill her. She thinks it is so much bologna to use her words."

"What kind of work did she do?" Sherry asked.

"She did baby sitting at people's houses for regular customers in Pine Bluff and Little Rock. After her father died and left her a wad of money, she opened the day care in Texarkana when her husband moved their trucking company down there."

Darrell who had been quietly listening said, "Did she tell you who she baby sat for in Little Rock?"

"She was real vague on that and wouldn't say much after I asked her," Darcy said.

Reginald said, "Sherry … " and was cut off.

"I know. Go to Heber Springs and get there early and question Mary Beth Norman before she leaves to come back here. Am I correct?"

"Now you're a mind reader," Reginald joked. "Sure glad you're on our side."

"I'll stop by the Locust Grove site on the way back. Maybe I can get there before y'all are finished. One more thing before you go; I stopped at the lab to see if that candy wrapper turned up any prints. It was negative on prints but they did find saliva traces on the paper. That might tell us something when it's compared to the blood and both toothpicks. Now, it's getting late and we need to get to bed," Sherry said.

They all left looking forward to much needed sleep. Darrell stopped at headquarters on the way home, and when he left, he noticed a dim light shining through a slit in the closed curtains of the house across the street from the police station. *Who lives in that place, and why would anyone want to rent that dump?* he asked himself. He decided some things didn't make any sense.

FORTY-SIX

The next morning Brookson saw Darrell arrive at police headquarters, followed by Sgt. Gawker three minutes later. Brookson's mind began churning. *The ever brilliant Sgt. Reginald P. Gawker has become a real nuisance.* He saw Sherry. Anger filled his thoughts and then his mind raced to the edges of rage. *She is running around, and my loved one is dead. She will be dead. She has to die to make it all fair.*

He remembered that these people didn't work on Saturday. Something was going on, and he wanted to know what it was in the worst way. A bad feeling began to fill his stomach. *What has caused all my plans to go wrong?* His mind settled on Callman. *If that fool had died, then all this would be over. The jerk moved just at the instant I pulled the trigger and nothing vital was hit. I wonder if they found that toothpick I dropped. If they did, I would like to see their faces when the truth hits them between the eyes. Evidence isn't always evidence, and truth isn't always truth, either.* He laughed at his cleverness.

He turned back to the windows and watched all the people that he hated leave the building. He decided to cruise past the Locust Grove house to see if they were there. He would eat breakfast and drive by in two hours. Fear once again began to creep in; not that he was afraid of being caught, but rather that he wouldn't accomplish what he had set out to do.

•

Several police vehicles were at the burned house when Darrell and Reginald arrived. Thomas arrived a few minutes later. A tow truck had pulled the wrecker truck from the gulley. Three state lab techs had arrived sooner than expected and were swarming over the truck like bees over flowers in bloom.

Reginald walked over to the truck, and what he saw made him stop cold in his tracks. He motioned to Darrell and Thomas who walked over to him. They were joined by Harvey Ellington, the Independence County Sheriff, who had just arrived. They greeted each other and looked at what Reginald had found. Reginald asked the techs if the object could be moved. They said it was okay since they had processed it. They hadn't found anything but rust. Reginald picked it up and carried it to the oak tree. He positioned it around the tree and said, "Whoever killed Bushman used this device to guide the car into the tree. There was a pulley on it but it fell off. Willie Jackson found it behind the tree the car slammed into in Indiana."

"Are you sure? How did he do that?" Darrell wanted to know.

"I'm very sure. I think he ran a rope through the pulley and tied it to the car. The other end he hooked to this tow truck and then pulled the car into that tree to make it look like an accident. He set the car on fire which destroyed any evidence that might have been in the car."

"What makes you think that is what he did?" Thomas asked.

"Well, I suspected it earlier. The deputy who worked the Scene In Indiana was suspicious and so was the ME, but there wasn't enough left after the fire for any conclusion other than an accident. The investigating deputy's suspicions and those of the me opened the door for me. The second was Willie Jackson. He said he heard a thump when the car hit the tree. He didn't know it was a car until he saw the fire. What he said he didn't hear made me curious. He said he didn't hear any crash."

"No crash?" Sheriff Ellington said. "What caused the thump?"

"No crash," Reginald replied. "I had an idea what caused it, and now that I see that tree over there, I think I'm right. That tree has had something slammed into it time after time. It was gouged clear though the bark to the meat underneath and now it's healed. The other marks correspond to the harness that held the pulley for the rope. See that mark there," Reginald said pointing to the tree, "on the right side is where the rope rubbed through the bark. The tree in Indiana had the same type mark."

"I'm with you this far," said Darrell, "but what caused the thump?"

"It was the engine block hitting the tree. The front had been smashed so far back that the only thing left to hit the tree was the engine." He pulled the photos from his pocket and showed them to the other officers.

"I believe you're right, Sgt. Gawker," Harvey Ellington said. "Nice piece of investigative work."

Reginald smiled shyly, thanked him, and continued. "I think he killed the Bushmans here and then towed the car behind that wrecker all the way to Indiana. He buried Trudy Bushman under the floor of that shack. He set it up to look like that car hit the tree and then burned."

"You're sure it was J. Daniel Bushman and not Easterly in that car?" Darrell wanted to know.

"I'm sure right now, and I think we'll definitely know that for a fact when we receive the report from the exhumation and the autopsy they are doing. Detective Short will notify me. The other thing is the steering wheel. It's bent, and if the car had hit the tree, the air bag would have prevented the driver's head from hitting the wheel. I think that Bushman was killed, put behind the wheel, and was in there when the car was repeatedly rammed into this tree. It makes me think that the man got extreme pleasure from doing this to Mr. Bushman." Reginald paused, looked at the sky, and puffed air from through his lips. "But why I don't know."

Darrell scraped his shoes in the dirt. He studied Thomas and Harvey. "You fellas have been to the Academy. What do you think about what he said?"

Thomas said, "I can't speak for you, but I think Reginald is right. It makes sense." The other two agreed.

Two techs walked up, and one said, "We went over that truck with a fine tooth comb. With the windows knocked out, the elements did a job on fingerprints and trace evidence. The only things we found were dirt, bugs, woods trash, and this." He handed Darrell a plastic evidence bag with the wrecker registration in it. The name on it was Marion Marvin Easterly with the listed address a post office box in Little Rock. The same address was on the registration for the car in which Easterly supposedly died. Darrell showed it to Reginald. "Well, I'll be," was all Reginald could say.

The lab boys said they would run tests on the registration for fingerprints and let them know. Deputy Barger arrived with the drawing that was shown to all of them; no one knew the man. Sherry arrived and said she had more information gained from Mary Beth. The morning went by fast and everyone had departed the scene by ten o'clock. The last to leave was the tow truck removing the old wrecker. Silence was all that remained. Even the birds were quiet.

FORTY-SEVEN

After the man watched the officers leave police headquarters, he fixed his breakfast and watched the news on the small portable black and white TV. It was the usual hype by talking heads so he switched channels to watch cartoons. They reminded him of Nickolette and little Ricky and the times they watched the shows together. He began to cry. He switched the TV off when he began to feel anger. Now was not the time for the anger or the rage he knew would engulf him if he didn't stop it. He went out to the garage to leave for Locust Grove and found a flat tire. By the time he got it changed, it was well past 10:00 a.m. When he drove past the house, there wasn't anyone there. He wanted to see if they found the wrecker truck, but he didn't dare drive in for fear that he would be seen. He decided to go to Batesville and cash a money order at the post office.

•

Chief Cumberland's office was full. Thomas, Darcy, Martin, Sherry, and Reginald were there for the meeting. Darcy and Martin had slipped in through the secluded back door that was hidden from public view. They were well supplied with chocolate covered cake and yeast doughnuts and coffee. Darrell said, "I guess everyone knows what we're here for."

"Yeah, coffee and doughnuts," Darcy replied to break the thick tension.

"Right, Darcy," Darrell replied gravely without any humor in his voice. "Now that we know why we're here, we can get down to business."

"Sherry, what did you learn from Mary Beth Norman?"

"I may have an answer that explains the mystery of why the perp is trying to kill Blandford, Callman, and Mary Beth, and why he killed Mrs. Herrington. Mary Beth Norman was a day nanny. She kept kids for people who had daytime business activities and for others who had to be away from their homes unexpectedly. The day that Mrs. Easterly and her children were killed, she was supposed to have kept them that afternoon so Marion Easterly and Linda could go shopping when he got off work. He was due to leave early. Mary Beth couldn't keep the kids because a problem developed with the move to Texarkana. So Linda Easterly had the children with her, and you know the rest of the story."

Reginald said, "So you think that Marion Easterly is trying to kill these people to get even?"

"That's what it looks like. One day two years after the trial when she was in Little Rock, Easterly confronted her and went into a tirade. He accused her of all sorts of horrible things and said he would get even. She said he was a drunk and acted deranged. He frightened her. They were in *McCain Mall* and mall security officers had to be called to take him outside."

"Does she still think it's bologna that someone is trying to kill her?" Darcy asked.

"Not now since I told her what was happening. She wants to see the show at the Folk Center tonight, so I told her I would pick her up at the motel in Heber at three o'clock. She can stay the night with me, and I'll take her back to Heber early tomorrow morning so she can leave for Texarkana."

"I'll go with you to Heber to pick her up," Reginald said. Sherry smiled at him and he turned red.

"Sounds like a plan. Let's all go to the Folk Center," Thomas said. "Darrell, you and Mattie join us there. We all need a break from this case. If the perp is there, he won't dare do anything. We'll pounce on him just like Darcy is doing to those doughnuts." Everybody laughed but Darcy.

"I don't think that's funny at all," Darcy said, trying to keep a straight face while reaching for another doughnut and a cup of coffee.

The light on the intercom button flashed, and Darrell picked it up. He pushed line one and said, "Chief Cumberland, how … " interruption by caller. "When did you see him?" Pause. "How long ago did that happen?" Pause. "Where are you now?" Pause. "Miss Shuman, stay in your room until an officer gets there. Under no circumstances should you leave. I'll call the Sheriff and ask for a deputy to pick you up for your protection. Sgt. Gawker and I will be there in less than hour. We'll explain when we get there."

After Sherry, Thomas, Darcy, and Martin discussed a course of action, they scrambled to leave the room. Sherry headed for Heber Springs after calling the motel. Mary Beth Norman was told not to leave under any circumstances.

Malcom Brookson, the invisible man as he liked to think of himself, watched Marjorie Shuman exit her car and enter the post office. She looked familiar, but he couldn't place the face. But he knew that over the years, he had seen people who looked familiar and he didn't know any of them either. She was just another face in the crowd that he would soon forget. *Maybe other people are invisible too.* The thought made him laugh.

•

Miss Shuman glanced at the man when he approached the post office counter; she knew she had seen him somewhere before. Then it hit her. He was the one who had rented her father's house. She started to walk over to him when he finished his business, but for some reason she held back. He left and gave a backward glance as he went through the door. He entered his van and drove away, glancing again toward the post office lobby.

Marjorie Shuman hurried to her car and went back to the dormitory. She called Mountain View and told them who she had seen and what he did. After speaking to the chief, she was thankful she hadn't approached the man. She began shaking with fear as a flood of tears coursed down her cheeks.

When the man realized whom he had just seen in the post office, he frantically began to look for her car. He couldn't remember the make or model. All he could bring to mind was the color and a sticker for a college on the back bumper. *What if she recognizes me? She will call the cops and … I was stupid for coming here*, he roared at himself in his head. He began to beat his fists violently on the steering wheel. He was unable to think straight. His mind was a mess. Disconnected thoughts scrambled for a place to make sense. Slowly he gained control and a clear idea began to form. He smiled wickedly at his brilliance.

He hurriedly left town and parked his van in a parking lot at the top of Ramsey Mountain. The location was perfect. He could see traffic going down into town on US 167 and if she called the cops, they would have to come through the US 167 Highway 25–14 intersection. His wait was rewarded when Reginald and Darrell drove past his vantage spot. She recognized him or the cops wouldn't have appeared, he reasoned. He wanted to follow them, but he knew he didn't dare. Now he had an additional problem to solve if that girl gave him trouble. But he was good at changing plans, so one more change wouldn't be any difficulty at all. Mountain View was the next stop.

Chapter
FORTY-EIGHT

eginald and Darrell arrived in Batesville and entered the post office. The clerk became belligerent when they asked him if he remembered the man who had cashed a money order earlier that morning. He informed them that postal regulations prevented him from releasing any information for sixty days no matter what the reason, and if they didn't leave, he would call the sheriff. Besides, they needed to fill out a form for such a request.

A man came out and introduced himself, "I'm Charley Greenwood, the Postmaster, what's the problem out here?" Darrell told him, and he said, "I'll be right back." He returned and said, "I called Inspector Blackwood, and he said to cooperate in anyway we can to help you." He left and momentarily returned, handing the clerk a pair of tweezers, "Pick the money order up with these. Put it in the plastic bag the officer is holding and let them mark it for evidence. Inspector Blackwood will decide how to handle the item according to postal regulations. Let them see it; and after you have done that I want to see you in my office." Greenwood walked away, and the clerk quickly found the money order and did as he was told.

"Can you describe the man who cashed this?" Reginald asked.

The clerk gave a description and then Reginald showed him the portrait that Miss Shuman had drawn. "That's the man who was in here this morning, but he didn't act any different than anybody else who comes in here," the clerk said, sounding miffed.

"We would like to see Mr. Greenwood again." Greenwood

appeared, and Reginald told him what he wanted. They left with a copy of the money order since the original belonged to the postal system. The names on it were the payee, Harley Bastin, and the payer, J. Daniel Bushman. A few minutes later, they arrived at the sheriff's office. A visibly shaken Marjorie Shuman waited in the interrogation room with the sheriff's wife. Miss Shuman could barely speak when they began their questioning. She told her story and said, "I intended on driving out to the house a couple of weeks ago to see the place again and ask the renter if he liked living there. I'm glad now I didn't go."

"I'm glad you didn't either," Reginald said. Everyone knew what might have happened to her if she had visited her home place. Marjorie realizing it too began shaking again.

•

No one payed any attention when the man drove into his garage. He went into the house and turned on the TV. A chair near the window gave him a good place to view the activities that occurred across the street. His mind was on the events in Batesville that morning. He wanted to know what the cops were doing, but he didn't dare hang around. It wouldn't do any good to deal with that young woman now. It would cause too much trouble. If he could have gotten to her … his anger boiled and seethed just below the surface. He struggled to control his rising anger to keep it from turning to rage.

He fumed under his breath when he saw Sherry drive up and enter headquarters. He said, "I ought to go over there and kill everyone in there and then when the Police Chief and that meddling cop returns, I'll kill them too. Now where is that Mary Beth? She's the guilty one." As he considered what to do about her, whatever reasoning he had left returned; he knew now that he couldn't kill Mary Beth this time and finish what he needed to do to shed his pain. He wanted them to know how much pain he was in and wanted to tell each one as he or she died, that his pain would lessen with each death, and when the last one was dead, he would have no more pain. "Maybe I should be the last one to die," he muttered. "But that wouldn't allow me to enjoy life and part of my enjoyment will be me knowing that all those who brought me pain are dead, except Mary Beth. Someday though, Mary Beth will be in my sights and the plan will be complete."

The man saw Thomas Dawson arrive and enter the building. "What is the sheriff doing there?" he asked the empty room. "I wish I could find out what they're doing. That Callman caused this. I'll deal with him in a special way when the end comes." Brookson went to the back room of the house to get his scoped Remington .222. He picked it up and said, "I might need to use this before I finish." He laughed until he fell in an emotional heap on the floor. When he regained some composure, he hurried to the front window. All the cars were gone except a marked patrol car near the door. He hurled a drinking glass across the room and smashed a coffee cup against the wall. "My plans are gone," he yelled. "Why didn't that Callman die? He had to die. He's the one who has ruined everything. He'll pay for ruining my plans and then he will know what real pain is for once in his dead sorry life. That shot in the back was nothing."

FORTY-NINE

Opening the front door of headquarters to go back on patrol, Nance Porter stopped and listened. He heard a loud voice but couldn't locate it or understand what was being said; and after listening a few seconds, he decided that it was coming from the house across the street. *Why play a TV full blast,* he wondered. He dismissed the loud TV from his mind when he received a radio call. The lights on the roof bar came on, and he was gone.

The plans concerning Mary Beth Norman had been changed. Sheriff Dawson came out of Sherry's house and left. He was followed by Sherry's car with Mary Beth Norman in it, and Reginald followed, bringing up the rear. She was going to be in hiding at his house until time to go to the Folk Center, and then she would stay the night with Thomas and Sarah. They arrived at the Thomas house safely, and Sherry drove her car into the garage. Once inside they were greeted by Sarah Thomas. She showed Mary Beth where she would be sleeping and helped take her bags to the bedroom.

After everyone assembled in the family room, Reginald removed the portrait from his briefcase. "I have a picture here of the man that might be who we're after," he said and handed it to Mary Beth.

She gasped and said, "It can't be. I heard that he's dead ... but this ... uh ... doesn't look right." She sat stunned by the picture she held in her hand.

"Who do you think that it is?" Sherry asked.

"At first glance, Marion Easterly, but now I don't know."

"What do you mean, you don't know?" Reginald asked.

"Let me think. The face is a bit heavier, but … uh … I haven't seen him since that day in the mall two years ago. I remember that Marion Easterly had a small scar on his chin." She put her finger on the right side of her chin. "It's maybe an inch long and curved up on the upper end. I don't know how he got it. It was there when I first started keeping his kids in the mid eighties. But as I remember, it isn't very noticeable now."

"Anything else you can remember?" Reginald asked.

"I can't be sure. The eye color, but … it has been so long. There is something, but I just can't recall. Might be I mixed him up with someone else." She shook her head. "I just can't remember. The hair is the right color and so is the beard. But there is … I just don't know."

"Let's try something else," Sherry said. "Think back to Matilda Herrington's twin sister. I haven't had time to fully tell Reginald and Thomas, so anything you tell me will be new for them too."

"Okay. Where do I begin?" Mary Beth asked no one in particular. "I didn't know Mrs. Herrington. Only saw her a time or two is all. But I did know her sister, Helen Magerson. She worked for a temp employment agency in Little Rock and then for one in Pine Bluff. Sometimes we would hire her to help with the books, especially at tax time. She was good at doing tax forms and several businesses used her expertise."

"Besides your company, do you know who else she worked for?" Reginald asked.

"Not many, but I know she worked on occasion for Sky High Scaffold and the refrigeration company that Easterly worked for."

"Was she working for either one of them when the scaffolding fell?" Reginald asked.

"No. Her husband died before that. She left Little Rock and moved to Pine Bluff. Some years later, a friend told me she married Jackson Finnwicke. I never met him, and I had already lost track of her before the time she remarried."

"Mrs. Herrington's son and daughter didn't know where their

aunt had gotten to either. They were never close with their relatives," Reginald said. "They said their mother seldom mentioned her."

Mary Beth became quiet and tears appeared in her eyes. She dabbed at them and said, "I'm sorry. This is so upsetting."

Thomas who had been listening to the questioning said, "Is it possible the killer thought Matilda was Helen since they looked so much alike?"

"Reg and I have discussed that possibility," Sherry said. "That could explain Matilda being killed since the killer didn't know she wasn't Magerson."

"It makes sense especially if the perp didn't know Magerson had a twin sister. It's a long shot that might help solve this case."

Mrs. Thomas came into the room. "I don't know how y'all are feeling, but I am getting hungry. Why don't we order pizza and salad, and Thomas can go get it."

"That sounds good to me. I'll go along and pay for it," Reginald said.

They left for the food, and when the food order was ready, Thomas pulled out some bills. "Let me pay for part of this Reginald," Thomas said, offering the money to him. Reginald shook his head no and politely pushed the money away.

When they finished eating, not a scrap of food was left in the pizza boxes or in the salad containers. Thomas again tried to pay Reginald for the food. "No, the veggie stand is doing well now, and it's my treat." Sherry smiled at Reginald knowing his tender heart for helping people.

The phone rang in the Dawson living room. Sarah Dawson handed the phone to Thomas. "Sheriff Dawson." He listened. "How are you Mrs. Crompton?" Pause. "She's here, and you stay in the house. Reginald and Sherry will be there shortly." He listened again. "All right, thank you for letting us know." Thomas Dawson's frown when he hung up said the phone call was troubling. "A man left a package on your front step, Sherry. Madeline said he walked with a limp like his right leg hurt."

The trip to Sherry's house took mere minutes. Darrell Cumberland met them and said Madeline had called him to find Sherry but
wouldn't say what it was she wanted. They found the package lying
against the door and after a careful inspection without touching it,
Sherry pulled on the latex gloves she had in her purse before opening
it. Inside was an ice pick with her name on the handle and a picture of
her behind the bank with keys in her hand. A type written note lay on
the bottom of the box. *I left no fingerprints on anything. I wore gloves.
You are going to feel pain so mine will go away. It's not fair that you live
and my loved ones died. Your days are numbered 1–2–3 … Remember the
keys? Right under your nose.*

They didn't see anyone on the street or any strange cars. Reginald
said, "What does he mean 'right under your nose?' The perp is playing
with us now, and he's more dangerous than ever."

FIFTY

Old time fiddle music could be heard when Reginald, Sherry, and Darrell knocked on Madeline Crompton's front door. She opened it; all out of breath and sounding scared, she said, "Come in here. I saw that man, but I don't know who he is. Oh my, I just happened to look out and see him."

"Did he see you?" Sherry asked with apprehension in her voice.

"I don't know. I was looking out the window when he was walking away. I know he left the package. It wasn't there before. I hope everything is all right."

"Everything will be okay, Mrs. Crompton," said Sherry. "Reginald has a picture to show you."

Reginald left to get the picture. When he came back, he gave the drawing to Madeline. "Do you recognize this picture?"

She studied it for several moments and then said, "That is one of the men I saw. This is the second one that was snooping around and the one that left the package."

"What do you mean second one?" Reginald asked.

"Remember that one several weeks ago that I told you about. Well, this is the second one. I thought there was only one, but when I saw the picture, I know now there are two men. What threw me was that both of them limped. This one in the pic didn't have a beard the first time I saw him. Now he does."

"You saw two different men. What did they do?" Darrell asked.

"The first one who was older would park up the street and then walk down to the front of Sherry's house. He would go back, sit in the car, and then leave. The other one, the one in the picture that I thought was the first one, went behind the house a couple of times and then would sit and watch," Madeline said.

"What kind of cars did they drive?" Sherry asked.

"The older man had a tan car. I don't know the make. The second one had the old blue car with lots of rust that I told you came past. I thought he was switching cars, but now I know it was two different men."

"Did you see a car today when he left the package?" Sherry asked.

"No, he walked down the street toward Main and disappeared."

"Mrs. Crompton," said Reginald, "we know who the older man is, and he's harmless. We don't know who the second one is. I think the second man knew that Snoopy had a blue Ford and that is where he got the idea to use one. May I use your phone, Mrs. Crompton?" She nodded her head yes.

Reginald phoned Snoopy from the kitchen. When he returned he said, "Snoopy told me that he probably drove that blue Ford down here one time, maybe two, before the engine blew up. We don't know, and maybe we'll never know how the perp discovered Snoopy's blue Ford, and then again, it could be a coincidence. Whatever happened, we know that Snoopy didn't leave that package today. It was the other man we're after. He's all over the place, and we never see him. It's almost like he's invisible."

"That car is so odd," Sherry said, "especially when Bushman bought the blue Ford, and it stayed registered to Harley Bastin, and with Bushman's ability to forge IDs that wouldn't be any problem. Our killer assumed Bastin's identity and didn't have to change the car registration."

"Mrs. Crompton, I don't want to scare you, but you keep your doors locked and be extremely careful," said Darrell. They left and went back to Sherry's house.

Once inside Sherry said, "That creep had to have been watching me the day Snoopy took those pics. But where was he? I never saw anyone but Snoopy that day that I can remember." A fleeting look of fright crossed her face.

While Sherry was talking, Reginald was studying the note that was in an evidence bag. He said, "I don't think the typewriter he used for this note is the same one that typed the others. The one found in the burned house probably came from that shack in Indiana. Mary Beth told us her father owned a similar Underwood where we found the burned one sitting in the ashes. The perp probably switched machines. The lab can tell us. We need to get the note down there for an examination."

The telephone bell jangling interrupted their talking. Sherry picked up the phone and spoke into it, "Sherry Westermann residence." Pause. "Here, Darrell, this is for you," and handed the phone to the chief.

"This is Chief Cumberland." He listened and motioned for a pencil and paper. "Wait a minute, Mazy," and handed the phone to Reginald.

"This is Reginald." He listened and wrote furiously. "Repeat that." Listened some more. "Make five copies and put the original fax in a folder and lay it on my desk. We needed this. Thanks." He breathed a sigh of relief and said, "The exhumation has been done and the results just came in on the burned body and on Trudy Bushman. It was J. Daniel Bushman in the car. They found his dental records at a Sikeston dentist. He had suffered a broken jaw and the x-rays matched the fracture line in the jaw of the deceased, but they still don't know the cause of death. They looked at the lungs again and didn't find any smoke residue; that's what the first autopsy showed. He could have died when the car hit the tree, but they don't think so and neither do I."

"What killed Trudy Bushman?" Sherry asked.

"She was killed with an ice pick. One pierced the right kidney and the other went through her heart. The ME thinks the kidney was first. She had multiple stab wounds all over her body. The ME said the killer was definitely enraged. The only word that came to his mind while doing the autopsy was rampage." Reginald sat and stared at the floor. He said, "The ME is right. It is a rampage, a deadly rampage conducted by a killer that is going to strike again if we don't find him and stop his carnage."

Sherry and Reginald were too tired from a very trying day to go to the Folk Center that evening. Darrell left to pick up Mattie so they could join Thomas and Sarah for the show.

Hoping that Sunday would bring some relief from the work, Reginald turned to Sherry and said, "I'll pick you up early so we can take Mary Beth to Heber Springs, then we'll come back for Sunday School and church. After church, we can go out for dinner in Searcy just to get away from the town for a few hours. Besides, there's a Super Center there, and I need some stuff. It will be an enjoyable day for a change." Darrell and Reginald left, and Reginald stopped at police headquarters. A few minutes later, he pointed his truck toward his house.

Two hate filled eyes watched Reginald enter and leave the building. "He's going home," the man said to the walls. "Now I could go over there and deal with that pretty little Sherry. I bet she's alone." He continued to think and brood and drifted off to sleep. It was 11:00 p.m. when he awoke.

•

A knock came on Sherry's door after she had been asleep for an hour. The clock glowed 11:10 p.m. in red numbers. Struggling from her bed, she slipped on a robe and went to the front door. With sleep filled eyes, she looked through the security lens and saw Darcy standing there. Opening the door she said, "It's kinda late for you to be out by yourself, isn't it? Does Linda know what you're doing? Who called you? Reg?"

Darcy looked at Sherry with a big grin and said, "My dear cousin, Reggie said that if anything happened to you that he would see to it that I never got any chocolate doughnuts again. So to be sure that nothing will happen to you, the doughnut chomper is here to protect you." They both laughed, and Sherry gave her big cousin a big hug. He turned and went to his truck. The garage door raised, and Darcy put the shaking and rumbling old heap in the garage.

The door had barely closed when Brookson drove the maroon van slowly past Sherry's house. He watched the house carefully for any signs that she was peeking out the windows. The lights were off in the living room when he went past. He turned around at the end of the street. He parked and slipped through the shadows to the back of the house. He saw a light on in what he knew was her bedroom. The blinds were shut and the drapes were closed. That made him angry, but he quickly got it under control by thinking about what he had planned for her later. It would be good. He wanted to laugh but couldn't.

He slipped over to the back door. He decided that the lock wouldn't be easy to open. He would have to use the other plan that would be more risky. Either way she was going to die and he would use her to get the rest before she did. *A pretty woman like her living and having fun with her family and friends while my family is dead isn't right.* He could feel the rage again and had to stop his thoughts. Regaining control, he went back to the van and slowly drove toward Main Street. Darcy thought he heard a noise and looked out the window. He saw nothing.

Hearing a car, Madeline Compton left her bed and peered through a slit in the curtains. She saw a dark colored van go past and turn right onto Main. *Never saw that car before.* She questioned whether she should call Sherry, but she decided not to since that would only wake her up. Probably a lost visitor that turned around at the end of the street, she decided. She could tell her the next morning, and besides, she didn't want Sherry to think she was being nosy.

Sunday was a good day for everyone except Malcom Brookson who teetered again on the edge of losing control. He spent the day biting on a towel to muffle the screams of torment caused by his twisted and tortured mind fueling the insane desire to kill Sherry and all the others.

FIFTY-ONE

onday stared everyone in the face when the sun rose over the mountain range east of town. People went to work, ate breakfast in the many cafes and restaurants, all intent on getting the business of a new week going. Madeline picked up the phone to call Sherry but put that to the back of her mind when her friend arrived to pick her up to go Batesville. She dropped the phone back on the cradle. *That strange van didn't amount to anything anyway,* she decided.

Malcom Brookson, alias Harley Bastin, alias J. Daniel Bushman, or … whomever he wanted to be, watched out the front windows. He didn't know whether he even knew his own identity anymore. *Have I been Harley Bastin? No, I only borrowed his name. And I can't be J. Daniel Bushman because he's dead. I should know; I killed him. Maybe I am Marion Easterly, but that can't be since that man is dead too. The cops are looking for Carl Alstrom so that must be who I am, but for now I am Malcom Brookson. It is so confusing,* he raged silently, *but no more so than when the cops find out I'm not Malcom Brookson.* But, he did know that no matter who he was, in the end, he would snuff out the life of those who had ruined his, and also the life of those who reminded him of things he wanted to forget. He seethed inside and the only relief he could ever have was to kill his tormentors. Then the ultimate end and he would have peace after all these years. He resisted the urge to commence his relief right then and there. He picked up his towel and began to bite it.

He watched all the officers enter and leave police headquarters.

A state policeman went in and came out with a package and left hurriedly. He laughed. He knew he could pick them off one by one the same as he did Officer McGee. He hated that because McGee's kids played with the kids he loved. He began to cry and rolled himself into a ball on the floor. It was late in the day and dark when he once more regained his emotional stability. He was hungry, but he didn't think he dared to go out to eat. Canned food and bologna had grown old, but he had no other choice. He fixed his meager supper and sat down to eat. *Maybe I will go out tomorrow and give myself a treat before the time for the big treat.* The thought made his face and eyes glow wickedly with anticipation.

Tuesday began like Monday for most everyone in the town, but Malcom Brookson had a different idea for the day. He had a new plan and knew what he would do. He would test the cops and see if and how they would react. If they didn't do anything other than their normal activity, then he was ready to carry out his plan. The same state officer arrived and went into the building with a package and didn't leave for quite awhile. When he did, he looked right at the window where Malcom was sitting and watching. Malcom ducked back quickly and watched him drive away. Monday's evil look returned accompanied by evil laughter.

Two cars left headquarters. *Now where are those two going?* he asked himself as he watched Darrell and Reginald leave. He decided to follow them if only he could get out to the street fast enough. He backed the van out of the garage and went to Main Street. He drove east and didn't see their cars until he passed the bank parking lot. He would have bet and won that they were meeting with Sherry. His hate for her was growing. He turned around and pulled into the bank lot. He went inside and went to the check counter. Then he went to a teller. He cashed a check for fifty dollars on the bank account in Searcy held by Malcom Brookson. The teller called the Searcy bank and was told the check was good. Sherry wasn't anywhere to be seen which didn't surprise him. He smiled and limped out to his van.

Sherry had met with Darrell and Reginald in a back office. Reginald said, "The state officer went to Little Rock and brought back good news. The man who lived next door to Easterly said the picture looked like him, but he wasn't one hundred percent sure. It has been several years since he last saw Easterly. The DNA on the toothpick and the candy wrapper would be finished soon. We washed out on Helen Finnwicke. No one knows where she is now or if she's alive. Also, there were seven clear prints on the registration slip for that tow truck. The state is trying to find a match. Neither the FBI nor the state has found anything."

A bank employee stuck her head in the door and said, "Sgt. Gawker has a phone call."

Reginald picked up the phone in the conference room. "Hello, Sgt. Gawker." Pause. "What have you got for us, William?" He listened. "What was the name on the post office box?" Pause. "Okay, got it. Anything on the money order cashed in Batesville on Saturday?" He listened intently. "Nothing but partials and there're not clear. That's too bad. I was hoping those prints would help us." Pause. "Will do and thanks again. We appreciate your help." He hung up and said, "There was a post office box rented at Little Rock by a Marion Marvin Easterly in early 1995. It was dropped when the rent ran out."

Reginald grabbed his briefcase and hurriedly pawed through the folders. He opened the case folder to the page listing the principals in the report. He found Marion Easterly and looked at Sherry, "You said that Easterly's full name is Marvin Marion Easterly, and he goes by Marion, his middle name. You learned that he hates his first name. Either he changed his first name when he bought that Ford or someone is playing more games with names, maybe him."

"Sounds like he's trying to hide," Sherry said, "and he's doing a good job of it." She went silent for two beats and then continued speaking. "But we still don't know if it's him we're after."

"I told the uniform men to keep a watch day and night for anything that might be suspicious or out of place. Nothing is the best word right now for their reports," Darrell said.

"The DNA results for Bushman should be here by Friday. Indiana put a rush on it and maybe we can get the last of the results from Little Rock. There is a gnawing that keeps giving me problems. I can't put my finger on it," Reginald said.

The phone rang and Sherry picked up. "He's here," and handed the phone to Reginald again.

"Sgt. Gawker." He listened. "You say that Officer McGee was the first officer on the scene that day?" Pause to listen. "That is interesting. I think Easterly is the key to this, but I'm not sure what lock the key will fit. Thanks, L.P. We'll be back to you." Reginald hung up and said, "Officer McGee and Easterly were friends. McGee is the one who tried to administer first aid to Linda Easterly and the kids. Easterly is probably the bum McGee saw and that's why he tried to talk to him that day. McGee apparently recognized Easterly, called him over to the car, and then Easterly killed him for reasons we don't know yet. It is likely McGee wouldn't have known about the 1995 homicides, so Easterly had nothing to fear or so it seems. Easterly killed a man who tried to help his family. That's sad. He faked his death and is taking revenge on people who are innocent."

"He killed Mrs. Herrington for the same reason. His twisted mind told him Matilda was Helen Magerson and he was afraid she would recognize him. Now to find Easterly," Darrell said angrily. "This guy exhibits every indication that he's criminally insane and extremely dangerous. Maybe we'll learn what has twisted his mind."

"I think it is more than losing his family," said Sherry. She saw Reginald with a far off expression. "What's wrong, Reg?"

"We're missing a piece to the puzzle." He hesitated. "I'm not sure what it is, but I think I'll recognize it when I see it. Maybe I have already seen it and don't know it."

"What and where?" Sherry asked.

"It's this way. Four facts continue to bother me. One is Officer McGee. Let's assume he was killed because he recognized the suspect, and let's say for now that Easterly is that suspect. Two, Mrs. Herrington was killed because she was thought to be her sister who either Marion Easterly knew or at least he knew who she was. Three, we are assuming that Bud Borders and Carl Alstrom were killed in that Mountain Home fire. Four, we know that Easterly's wife was Carl Alstrom's sister. Then, though not an established fact, there's that possible fourth man. If he exists, who is he?"

"Could Marion Easterly be the fourth man and the killer if our theory is correct?" Sherry asked.

"I don't know and I wish I did." Reginald lapsed into silence. Then: "Why keep a vacant lot for the address on that bank account? Other facts still bother me too, and we don't know at this time where to look for additional answers. We just have to keep turning over the rocks to find the gem that will break the case open. Maybe we'll find Easterly under one of the rocks."

"Reg, have we done a background investigation on Borders and Alstrom?"

"No. Since we assumed they were dead, we didn't do any background on either one, and we should have. Sometimes dead men tell tales that aren't lies. Sherry, can you do that this week?"

"Sure. I've been to Mountain Home already, so I won't need to go back. I can call and find out where they were taken and buried. Maybe they were taken to Little Rock. I'll get on it tomorrow morning early."

They left the bank, and the man in the van smiled when they walked right past him. They never noticed. Like a chameleon, he could change to suit the need. He laughed at their stupidity. They had passed the test of his being invisible to them by being visible. Their eyes saw, but they did not see. He laughed and drove toward the street. "This is a great day," he said to no one.

When he exited the parking lot, he saw Madeline Crompton, whom he knew as that nosy old biddy that lived across the street from pretty Sherry. She and two friends were walking toward the square. When they went into the Home Cookin' Cafe, he smiled.

The time was just perfect to test another part of his plan. He knew he came close to ruining everything when he had the urge to kill her on Saturday night. The whole town would have been crawling with more cops and the news buzzards would have been unrelenting. He hated both for what they did when his loved ones died. Maybe he ought to take a few of the news types along. Them and the stupid questions they asked. *How do you feel?* he mocked silently. They didn't care how he felt. All they wanted was the glory of having their names on sensational news stories, all at his expense. He could show them the price of that expense. He felt the rage coming on and knew he had to stop. *But just maybe this is good practice for putting the plan into effect.* He wanted to laugh but couldn't. He found the perfect parking spot near the front door to the eatery. He settled in to watch the door and then, growing restless, he decided to leave the van and take a walk. "Old nosy will be there when I get back," he mumbled. He left the van carrying a small brown paper bag.

Diners in the cafe looked up when the door opened. A man with a white red tipped cane tapped his way through the door. Thick lenses on the sunglasses hid his eyes. An unusually large fanny pack was strapped around his waist. He leaned on the cane as he made his way with a slow halting gait across the floor. Mandy Gettner came to his aid and helped him find a table since he appeared confused about where to sit. She brought him water and told him she would be back with a menu.

The other diners watched the man finally get seated. Madeline Crompton leaned over to her two friends and said, "He's awfully clumsy for a blind man. Maybe he hasn't been blind very long." The others agreed and snickered. They also noticed that he kept fiddling with a band aid on his left cheek above the beard line.

Mandy brought a menu and started to read the selections to him. He said, "I want a Roast Beef Manhattan with French fries instead of mashed potatoes and put gravy on the French fries, too. Bring a bottle of catsup too."

"I don't know if we can fix it that way."

"Little girl that is what I want and you … " his voice rose and then he caught himself and said, "I'm sorry. I have had a bad couple of days. I'll eat it however you fix it."

Mandy, shaken by his sudden outburst, said with a quivering voice, "I'll ask Joe," and left quickly. Soon his food arrived prepared the way he ordered it.

He asked no one in particular for the time and a nearby diner told him. He said thanks and went back to eating, dribbling gravy on his shirt. The man called Mandy over to the table and asked her a question. She looked at the check lying on the table and replied to him. He finished the food, picked up his check, and tapped his way to the register to pay Joe for his meal. He fumbled with some bills and Joe took what was needed and gave him change. He smiled when he was handed the change. He turned his head toward Mandy and smiled. Shivers ran down her spine when she saw his cold smile.

The ladies in the restaurant watched him tap his way to the door and go out. After the door closed, the blind man and his strange behavior became the topic of conversation for the remaining customers. They decided that people had a right to be strange. Yet, what Madeline saw continued to bother her, but she couldn't figure out what it was.

He tapped his way around the corner of the building. Less than a minute later, he came out and drove away in his van. He began laughing at how easy it was to fool people. The second test was nearly flawless. Dropping gravy on his shirt was the only problem. He fooled them and the fools in the restaurant weren't the wiser. That nosy woman didn't know him from Adam. His mind began talking to him. *I wonder if she saw me last night. Soon she won't be seeing anything ever again.* He drove the van into the garage. He needed time to think before he went out again. He pulled the band aid from his cheek and threw it in the trash can.

Chapter

FIFTY-TWO

A ten-year-old boy sitting in his mother's car across the street in the bank parking lot watched the man drive away and became real excited. When his mother returned and got into the car, Robbie Porter said excitedly, "Mom, Mom, I saw a blind man drive away in a car. Honest, I saw him. He really did."

"Young man, your imagination is running away with you. I am going to speak to your father. All the police talk at home has to cease. Blind man indeed," Nadine Porter, wife of Officer Nance Porter, scoffed.

"But Mom, I saw him. He went around the corner of the restaurant and when he came out, he wasn't blind. Dad said Chief Cumberland told everybody to watch for anything suspicious like. I saw him, Mom. He had a cane and limped."

Nadine shook her head and said, "Okay, you saw it. For your information, young man, people with limps use canes. You sure have a great imagination. Now what time is your swimming lesson Saturday?" she said, a bit disgusted with her son. *Boys and their imaginations sure come up with some peculiar things. A blind man driving a car is a new one.* She laughed at the idea.

Robbie glared at her and said under his breath, "I did too see him. You didn't."

"What did you say, young man?" Nadine asked, more than a bit irritated with Robbie's behavior.

"Nothing," Robbie replied.

When they arrived home, Robbie waited until his mother was in the shower and called police headquarters. "Police department," Mazy Sink, the dispatcher, said.

"I want to talk to my dad."

"Who's your dad?"

"Officer Porter."

"Oh, it's Robbie. Now what do you want with your dad?"

"I want to tell him something. It's important."

"You can tell me, Robbie," Mazy said.

"No. It is police business. I have to tell him."

"Okay," Mazy said, hardly able to keep from laughing. "Where are you, at home?"

"Yes."

"Okay, I'll tell him to drop by your house."

"Tell him to hurry. It's important."

"Gotcha," Mazy said, laughing hysterically after she hung up.

Robbie ran out on the porch to wait on his dad. When Nance arrived, Robbie jumped in the car and excitedly told his dad what he saw. He asked him not to tell his mother. Nance told Robbie that he would watch for the man and then told him to scoot and go play.

Nadine saw Nance drive away and asked, "Robbie, what was your daddy doing here?"

"Uh, he wanted to see me about something."

"You didn't call him so you could tell him what you think you saw, did you?"

"Well … I … uh … wanted to tell him about the great imagination you said I have." His mother could hardly keep her face straight as she hurried back to the house.

Nance Porter drove away from his house laughing, amused by what his son had told him. "That boy sure has an imagination," he said. He went to headquarters to tell Mazy the story of Robbie's sighting. Mazy told Nance what Robbie had said about police business. Before the day was over everyone in the department heard about the conversation that Robbie had with Mazy on the phone. Now, the new buzz words in the department were 'it is police business.'

Late Wednesday evening the direct phone line rang in Reginald's office. It was Sherry. "You'll be back tomorrow evening?" Pause. "Still can't find anything on the location of Helen Finnwicke?" Pause. "No word on Borders and Alstrom?" Pause. "You have a background source located on them now." He listened. "Okay, drive carefully. See you tomorrow." Reginald hung up hoping that the information from Little Rock would help fill in the investigation's blank spots.

•

Early that day Malcom Brookson went to the bank. He went into the building on crutches. He went to the same teller who called the bank in Searcy and who had cashed his check for fifty dollars, the previous day. She made a comment to him telling him that one time she had to use crutches. He said it wasn't enjoyable and left. Several people saw him and didn't pay him any attention. The old floppy felt hat, crutches, and different style sunglasses worked well. Even Joe Landers and the waitress didn't recognize him as the blind man when he went in for coffee. As he sipped the coffee, he tried to find a way to learn where Blandford and Callman had gone. They had vanished along with the Blandford's car and Callman's motor coach. He had to find them or he couldn't complete his plan.

Back home that afternoon he watched Reginald leave headquarters and tried to think of reasons for pretty Sherry not being in the bank. He had hung around the square but didn't see the two hippies or her. That made him nervous, and he didn't like being nervous. People make mistakes when nervous and he didn't know of any he had made. It was the others who were interfering with the method he had created to deal with his problems.

•

Enjoying the comfort of her bed on Wednesday morning, Madeline Crompton lay under the covers in a state between being awake and being sleep. She had to do shopping but didn't want to get going on the day's activities since the bed was so comfortable. Her mind drifted back to the man she saw in the restaurant. What was it that she saw that didn't seem right? She just couldn't get a clear picture of what happened. She was drifting off to sleep again when she bolted upright in bed. She nearly fell she left her bed so fast. She called the police department and asked for Reginald. Fifteen minutes later Reginald was talking to Mrs. Crompton in her living room.

"Tell me what you saw."

"My two friends and I were in the café and a blind man came in. We didn't think too much of it until he almost blew up at Mandy Gettner. He gave my friends and me the shivers, and I'm sure he did Mandy too the way she acted," Mrs. Crompton said.

"What else did you see?"

"Well, the thing that I couldn't figure was when he went to pay his bill. He walked right to the cash register like he could see it."

"Maybe he had been in there before and knew where it was," Reginald said, playing the devil's advocate.

Madeline thought for a few ticks and said, "I never thought of that, but I don't think so. When he left his table, he picked up the check and I thought he looked at it. But I remember now, he must have asked Mandy how much it was when he called her over to the table. I saw her look down at the check so she must have told him the amount. That's the way it looked anyway. Then after paying, I would swear, if I was the swearing type, that he counted his change and smiled after counting it. That's the way it looked to me, and it was strange."

"Did your friends see all this?"

"No, Frieda went to the rest room, and Emily was talking to a friend at another table. I asked them, and they said no. They told me I was imagining things."

Reginald smiled and said, "I think you may have given us a lead."

He took the picture out of his briefcase and handed it to her. "Look at the picture carefully and see if you recognize anything."

Madeline studied the picture for a long minute and said, "I can't be sure. I sure wish I knew. I hate to say it is and hate to say it isn't. The man in the restaurant had a band aid where that little round scar is on his cheek," she said, pointing to the picture.

Reginald studied Madeline's face and watched her expression. "So you think that the guy wasn't blind?" Then what Robbie Porter had told Nance flashed through his mind.

"I have made up my mind. He could see," she said, and the tilt of her head made it plain that she had made up her mind. "I also think now that the picture is the same man. Yes, I will say that. The picture and the man are the same."

"You are sure now, Madeline?" Reginald said ever slowly.

Madeline Crompton swelled up and set her jaw before she spoke. "Reginald P. Gawker, you have known me since you were a little boy. You know when I make up my mind that it won't change. It is the same man," she said with finality.

Reginald smiled and said, "Madeline, I won't argue with you. I'll take your word for it. Though I didn't see the blind man act, I agree with you. It's the same man and he wasn't blind."

"How do you know?"

"Let's just say that big imaginations sometimes help solve crimes."

"You mean mine? Are you saying I'm imagining things?" she asked, showing a hint of indignation.

"Not yours, no," Reginald said replying to both questions, trying to keep from laughing. "It was somebody else."

Madeline looked at Reginald not sure what to think. "Well, whether it's my imagination or not, I sure hope this helps you find him. He gave me the creeps." Reginald patted her hand and left with a feeling that the case would be solved soon.

Chapter

FIFTY-THREE

andy Gettner waved at Reginald when he entered the restaurant. He took a table near the back and when she came over, he asked her to sit down. She said, "Joe don't want us to sit with customers."

"Mandy, I need to ask you some questions concerning the blind man that was in here Tuesday. And then I need to ask Joe the same questions. Did you tell him the amount on his dinner check?"

Mandy's expression said it all. "No, I never thought to tell him. I'm not used to waiting on blind people. He probably was the first one I ever did. Why?"

Reginald ignored the why and asked, "Did he call you over to ask the amount?"

"He called me over to the table, but he wanted to know if we had banana cream pie. I told him no. Joe must have told him how much he owed."

"Next, did you tell him where the cash register was located?"

Mandy screwed up her face and twisted her head and said, "It is so funny that you would ask that question. He went right to it. Like ... you know ... like he could see it."

"Maybe he has been in here before and knew where it was."

"That's not possible. Joe moved that cash register last night after we closed. He wanted it closer to the door. Kids have tried to slip out without paying."

"Maybe a customer went out before him, and he located the register by the sound."

Mandy screwed up her face again. Her eyes scanned the ceiling and rolled side to side. Reginald could almost hear the clicking in her head as she scanned her memory.

"That's not possible. No one left while he was here, and before you ask, Joe didn't open the cash register before creepy went to pay."

Reginald had to work to keep from laughing. "Okay Mandy, anything else?" he asked, knowing there was, but he wanted to know if Mandy would tell him without his asking if she saw what Madeline said she saw.

"Sarg, I'm disappointed with you. You haven't asked me to tell you the best part."

"Okay, what's the best part?" Reginald asked with all innocence.

"He counted his change and smiled at me. That guy is weird." Then her face went white and the shakes took over her body. "Sar … Sar … Sergeant Gawker that's the same guy that was in here the night Matilda Herrington was killed. He was here that night. I know it's the same man. He ain't blind either." Her face was filled with fear. "It's him." The shakes continued to rack her body.

Reginald was shaken too by her possible identification. He recovered and asked, "How can you be sure?"

"It's his voice. It was raspy or like gravel in his throat. Like those who smoke a lot. He made kind of a hissing sound when he talked. It reminded me of a snake." Her shaking increased.

Joe Landers came into the dining room and saw Mandy sitting with Reginald at the table. He opened his mouth to speak when Reginald motioned him over. He came over and said, "What's wrong with Mandy?"

"Joe, we have a problem, and I need for you to allow Mandy to leave and not return to work for a few days. I can't tell you why, but it's for her safety."

Landers' face said he couldn't understand what he had just been told and his expression foretold belligerence. Reginald wanting to defuse the situation quickly said, "Joe, Tuesday there was a blind man in here. Do you remember him?"

"Well sure, but what does that have to do with Mandy not coming to work?"

"Everything Joe," Reginald said, not wanting to say too much. "Did you tell him how much his check was?"

Joe Landers looked at Mandy and said, "Did you tell him? I assumed you did since he told me the amount. His exact words were, 'I owe you 6.21 including tax.' He fumbled with some bills and after I handed him his change, I swear, he counted it. It sure was strange."

"And you didn't ring up a sale before he went to the register?"

"No. It was slow that morning, and he was the first customer after the rush for breakfast. Funny thing, he ordered a Manhattan at ten in the morning. That's lunch time food."

"Now Joe, think. Have you ever seen him before Tuesday?"

"Sarg, I see a lot of people come in here that I have seen before, but him, no. I would have remembered."

"Yeah, Joe would have. He's pretty good at it," Mandy said, not shaking as much now.

"Joe, can I use your phone?" Joe shook his head yes.

Reginald called headquarters and told Mazy he wanted the chief. When Darrell came on the line, Reginald told him what he knew and then hung up after some more words. Twenty minutes later, Sally Hughes, the chief's sister, drove up in back. She came in, and Reginald had a hushed conversation with her. She left through the back door with Mandy who was sobbing quietly, fear etched all over her face.

"Reginald is this about what I think it is? It's Matilda Herrington isn't it?"

Reginald pondered the tablecloth as Joe spoke and then looked up. "It is and that's all I can say. If you see that man again or even think you do, call us immediately. Take no chances. He's extremely dangerous. And don't tell anyone. Your safety could be at stake if you do."

Brooding hate filled eyes watched out the window. Malcom Brookson, Harley Bastin, Marion Easterly, or whoever he was knew that there was a speed up in the investigation. He could tell by the activity taking place with all the cops going in and out of the building. The chief left in hurry and that idiot sergeant came back and went inside quickly. He came out and left faster than he had arrived. Had he been found out? He knew he was doing well, and now he had to think back on what he might have done that could have caused all the commotion. His mind wasn't clear, and he was confused. He needed to relax with his hobby; only it was packed in boxes in the van. There wasn't room for the track in this house.

A car pulled up across the street. It was that pretty Sherry. She went inside and came back out. No, it wasn't Sherry. It was another woman. She was in a hurry, too. Everyone was in a hurry. The whole world was in a hurry except him. *He had time ... or did he?* Such thoughts made him nervous, and he didn't like that. He began to pace the floor in an attempt to stop the anger that he knew would soon turn to rage. He had to save the rage for those whom he hated. He tried to calm himself and couldn't. He slammed his hand into the wall and broke through the sheet rock. He hit the wall again, and again, and again as the violence raged inside him. He only quit when the pain in his knuckles became too great for him to continue the assault on the walls.

Chapter

FIFTY-FOUR

When Reginald stepped onto the porch at the Porter house, Robbie, who eagerly watched him approach, opened the door and said with barely contained excitement, "Hi, Sgt. Gawker, I bet you're here on police business. Daddy said you were coming over to show me a picture. He's in the living room with Mom."

Reginald chuckled and said, "It is police business, Robbie, real police business." They went into the living room and sat down. Robbie squirmed and wiggled around he was so excited with being involved in real police stuff, not just the make believe he and his friends liked to play.

"Robbie, Sgt. Gawker is going to ask you several questions and then show you some pictures. Be as careful as you know how," his father said.

Robbie gave his dad a disdainful look. "I know, Dad. This is real police business just like I told Mrs. Sink on the phone when I called the po … ," His face turned red, and he gave his mother a hangdog look.

"That's okay, Robbie," she said. "I think now maybe you did see a blind man drive away in a car."

"I did, Mom. Honest, I did. I didn't make it up. I saw him. I really did."

"Robbie, tell me what you saw Tuesday," Reginald said.

Robbie described in detail what he saw and then said, "I know what kind of a car it is, too." He hesitated. "Well, it isn't a car. It's a van." Disdain dripped off his words.

"You saw a van? What kind?" Reginald asked.

"I don't know. But it has really dark tinted windows," Robbie said enthusiastically.

The three adults were wide eyed when Robbie mentioned the windows. "Why would you notice the tinted windows, Robbie?" Nance asked.

"Dad, a van is for older people, and older people don't have really dark tinted windows on a van. It's dorky," Robbie stated in a matter of fact manner. Straight faces were difficult to maintain.

"Describe the man for me, Robbie," Reginald said.

Robbie squinted up his eyes and made a face and squirmed with excitement. "He was big. Maybe he was your size. That's all I know. But he wasn't blind. And he had on one of those funny packs."

"Don't you mean fanny pack?" Nadine Porter said.

"Mom, you told me that I couldn't say that word," Robbie said with all seriousness.

Reginald thought that for ten years old Robbie was ahead of his time. He knew that his mother and dad were very intelligent, and he could tell that their intelligence had passed to Robbie. Both Nance and Nadine had graduated from Harding University in Searcy, Arkansas, where they met and fell in love. Reginald thought that Robbie would surely go onto higher education after high school given his already well developed intelligence.

When Reginald opened his briefcase, Robbie wiggled and squirmed again with more excitement. Reginald removed several photos and spread them on the table so Robbie could look at all of them. He looked at the pictures for a long time and said, pointing to the one of the eight photos, "It's that one right there." He pointed at Brookson. "I know it is. He still had that … uh … pack thing around his waist. He had a band aid right here." Robbie pointed to his left cheek to show where he saw the band aid.

"How could you see a band aid that far away?" his dad wanted to know.

"Dad, I had the Terry and the Pirates Spy Glass that Grandpa gave me. I did a close up. I never leave home without it. I can see all kinds of stuff."

"That's true," said his mother. "He takes it everywhere with him."

"One more question, Robbie. What color is the van you saw?" Reginald asked.

"Uh … I think … uh … it's a dark color but not black." Robbie's eyes rolled around; he scuffed his shoes across the carpet and said, "I can't say. I was too busy looking at the dorky tinted windows to see the color." He looked dejected that he couldn't help.

Knowing the seriousness of what Robbie had seen, and that it had the possibility of putting him and his mother in danger, Reginald went over to Nance and said he wanted to see him outside. They went out and decided on a way to protect Robbie. Since Robbie was home schooled, it wouldn't hurt to send him to his grandparents in Jonesboro until the perp was caught. Nadine would go along to play it safe. That settled, they went back inside, and Nance told Nadine what they were going to do. She readily agreed to it.

Nance returned to patrol, and Reginald went for coffee. Nadine packed Robbie's clothes, and he put his favorite toys in a bag. Nadine called her dad who was very pleased to hear that they were coming to visit. He adored his only daughter and loved his grandson immensely.

Nance Porter got out of his car at headquarters and heard the loud voice. He looked at the house and wondered what kind of TV shows the occupant watched and questioned why anyone would play them so loudly. He went inside thinking there sure were peculiar people in the world; really peculiar he decided on second thought.

Reginald returned and entered headquarters. On the way, he watched for vans with tinted windows. Every one he saw had dark tinted windows driven by older people. And most of them were dark colored but weren't black. Maybe Robbie was right about the dorky part.

•

The officers on duty came and went under the watchful eyes of the man across the street. He knew that four police cars were on patrol each shift. He had studied their patrol habits and determined that they patrolled at random. He had to devise a way to keep them busy and out of the way while he carried out his scheme to destroy the vermin that had infected his life and continued to do so. He felt the anger coming on and the usual difficult time he had to keep it from becoming a rage, plagued him once more. The persistent idea that wouldn't go away was that they were close to finding him, and he had to stop it in whatever way he could. But what that was he didn't know. He grabbed his cap and sunglasses and went to the van. He backed from the garage, drove to the side street, and waited to see who might leave. He was going to follow to find out where they were going. All the activity meant they were onto something he had done. What it was he couldn't answer. His planning was perfect. It had to be them.

The man followed Officer Porter when he left headquarters. When Nance drove in the driveway at his house, the van following a half a block behind passed the house slowly. The driver glanced up and saw Robbie on the porch with his back to the street talking to his mother. He also saw the officer carrying bags from the house to a SUV. *Isn't that sweet? That little mommy is going away and probably taking the little boy with her.* The sight of the family being together angered him. He could feel rage deep inside, and he knew it would boil over if he didn't leave now. *It's too bad that I can't do anything with that family.* Tears welled up and ran down his cheeks. He slammed the steering wheel with his palms to release the tension. Suddenly, he saw the stop sign with barely enough time to slam on the brakes to avoid running past it. He stopped with the front wheels a few feet into the intersection. An oncoming car had to swerve to prevent a collision.

Officer George Dugan, who had just finished a report on a minor fender bender, looked up when he heard tires screeching on the pavement and saw the car swerve. The driver of the van made a left turn and sped away. Officer Dugan put the patrol car in drive and accelerated to catch up with the offender. He turned on the red and blue lights, blipped the siren, and the driver immediately pulled over. Officer Dugan approached the side of the vehicle. The man, looking in the side view mirror, watched the officer approach, and thought how easy it would be to send him to wherever he would spend eternity. He didn't dare since he knew how cops worked. The oaf had called in his plate number, so it wouldn't be wise to send him on his journey. He lowered the window and watched the officer in the mirror until he was standing at the rear of the door. He considered slamming the door edge into him, but that notion fled away when he saw that the door would miss the officer when it swung open.

Officer Dugan asked, "May I see your driver's license and registration, please?" Malcom Brookson fumbled for his license and handed it to Dugan. He rummaged around in the glove box and produced the registration. Dugan examined both and as he started to speak, the radio in the patrol car summoned him. He went back and answered the dispatcher. Shortly he returned to the van. Barely able to keep his anger under control, Brookson watched in the side view mirror as Dugan approached the open window again.

"Mr. Brookson, are you aware of the reason I stopped you?" Dugan asked politely.

"Yes sir, I think I know. I had bit of a problem back there at the stop sign."

Dugan saw tears on the man's face and said, "Are you all right? Are you having a problem?"

With anger trying to flare, Brookson swallowed hard a couple of times and rubbed his eyes to push it down. "You won't believe this officer. I had the window down and was putting it up when a bug flew in and struck me in the eye." He saw the nameplate beneath the officer's badge. Thoughts screamed through his mind, creating things he could do to George Dugan, badge number eight.

"How did a bug hit you in the eye? Didn't you have your sunglasses on when I stopped you?" Dugan asked, doubting the man's explanation.

"I did. I put them back on right before you stopped me. My eyes are light sensitive," the man said.

"Why did you take your glasses off if your eyes are light sensitive?"

"My left eye still itches from an eye infection I had a few weeks back. I took the glasses off to rub my eye to stop the itching. I was doing that and didn't see the stop sign until it was almost too late. I'll be more careful from now on."

Dugan watched Brookson before he answered. He had a bad feeling about the driver, but he didn't have any way of determining what wasn't right about the situation. Finally he said, "I called in your plate number before I stopped you, and the dispatcher gave me the same information that's on the license and registration. You live west of Searcy on Highway 36. What are doing in Mountain View today?"

"I come up here and listen to the music and to see the shows. I've been doing it for a number of years." He eyed Dugan intently and then looked away to control the anger he was again feeling.

George Dugan watched Brookson closely as they talked. He did seem to be in distress and had continued to rub his left eye, which turned increasingly red. "Okay. I can understand how you could have been distracted by the bug hitting you in the eye. It happened to me once. You be careful, Mr. Brookson, and enjoy your visit in our town. We don't want you to get hurt." He returned to his patrol car and waited for Brookson to leave. *Strange character*, Dugan thought. *But this town has all kinds of people here in the summer, so I guess he is as normal as all the other visitors we see most of the time.*

Feeling fortunate that he didn't have to do anything to the cop, Malcom went back to the rent house to calm down. That encounter was too close, so maybe he should stay out of the public until it quieted down. He decided he had better find another car in case the van became too well known. He unloaded the van and left for Heber Springs to buy a different car. He might even go to Little Rock and dispose of the old lady who rented him the house. Then his thoughts began to dwell on his landlady. *It would serve the old bat right and then she wouldn't be able to rip off anyone else. There isn't any reason to mistreat people unless they deserve it. She and the ones in my plan deserve it.* "What's it called? Just deserts," he said aloud and laughed.

R ain was falling when Sherry came into town. She saw a maroon van south of town on Highway 9 parked on the berm, and for some reason she noticed the extremely dark window tint. The word dorky flitted through her mind. Why she didn't know, but it struck her funny. When she went past, the man was rummaging around in the back of the vehicle. Before going around the next curve, she looked in the rear view mirror and saw the van pull back on the highway and disappear from view.

The bank was closed, so she let herself in and called police head-quarters after putting away the bank papers she had used to conduct business in Little Rock. Reginald had gone home, so she called his house.

"Hello." Pause. "Boy, I'm glad you're home. How did it go?" He listened. "That's a twist; thirty minutes at your house if you don't mind riding in my '49 Ford pickup, a chariot par excel lance, if I do say so myself." He heard Sherry laugh as she hung up the phone.

Thirty minutes later, Reginald arrived in his chariot and parked in Sherry's driveway. She came out dressed in jeans and a white blouse with a blue collar. Her feet were adorned with shiny brown penny loafers. A large purse with wide straps swung from her right shoulder. She climbed in the truck, and Reginald said, "You sure do look nice."

"Thanks. Wearing my chariot *par excel lance* clothes." She leaned over and kissed him, and his face turned red.

The truck backed out, and when they headed for Main Street,

Madeline Crompton waved at them. They laughed and Sherry said, "I think she sees everything that goes on. It will be all over town that I kissed you." Reginald's face glowed red again and now that she was used to it, she knew it was normal. After several years, she should know that, since it happened often. Most folks didn't consider him a prince, but that was okay with her. He was a prince to her and indeed very charming besides. A very quiet and gentle man whom she knew loved her very much. And her love for him was no less, and she knew he knew that too.

The Wharf on the River wasn't very crowded, so they had some privacy. Small talk filled the time and let them unwind until their orders were taken. Reginald described the Scene In the restaurant for Sherry and the steps taken to hide Mandy Gettner. The food arrived quickly. They ate and bantered back and forth enjoying each other's company without engaging in shoptalk for a change.

Having finished eating catfish with trimmings and while waiting on dessert, Sherry opened her purse and took out a thick file. Reginald tried to read her face as she turned file pages, but he couldn't. She found what she wanted and handed it to Reginald. "Look at this," she said.

After reading for a short time, Reginald looked up and said, "Carl Alstrom was married to Easterly's sister, Julie?" Sherry nodded her head yes. "And Easterly was married to Alstrom's sister, Linda."

"That's right. In 1985, Carl Alstrom's wife Julie and their two children were killed on US 67 north of Jacksonville, Arkansas, when a drunken driver going south crossed the median and hit their car head on when they were going to Cabot for a dental appointment. They think the drunk's car was going over a hundred miles per hour. Witnesses said he passed them and was all over the road before he lost control. Both cars burned, but the coroner said that all were dead before the fire broke out. I saw the pictures and they are horrible."

Sherry handed Reginald a photo. He studied it and said, "This looks like the drawing that Marjorie Shuman did. It's has to be Easterly or I'm going blind."

"You're not going blind," she said and handed him a second photo. He looked at it. She could see the puzzle begin in his brain and spread to his face as his face changed expression.

"Why two pictures of Easterly? I don't get it."

"Look carefully. Compare them," Sherry said. "I was confused too before I figured it out."

Reginald studied both pictures and then exclaimed, "Easterly doesn't have a mole on his left cheek and this other face does. What did he do, have it taken off?"

"Not exactly, that isn't Marion Easterly. Mary Beth said Easterly had a small scar on the right side of his chin. Notice there isn't any scar in that photo. She did say it wasn't very noticeable, but I don't think the scar is important to us right now. It may be later though."

"Huh," Reginald said loud enough for some heads to turn their way. "Wha … wh … who is it then? Does he have a twin?"

"No, but they do look enough alike to be mistaken for each other. Unless I'm wrong, he's our killer," pointing to the photo with the scar.

"Well, who is it then?" Reginald asked, growing impatient.

"Carl Alstrom," Sherry replied softly.

"Carl Alstrom?" Reginald replied, now nearly speechless. He looked at her with a blank face and then said, "He's dead. He burned up in that fire in Mountain Home."

"Reginald, that man in the restaurant that had the band aid on his face was more than likely Carl Alstrom. I think we'll find out he killed Marion Easterly and all this while we have been looking for Easterly and he's dead. He died in that fire."

"You think the killer is Alstrom?" Reginald said bewildered. "Why would he have a band aid on his face?" Then his jaw dropped, and he grabbed the drawing. He said excitedly, "The band aid was to hide the scar where the mole was taken off. Look at the drawing Marjorie did." He pointed to the drawing and then he told Sherry what Robbie said he saw. "It's all beginning to make sense now," he concluded.

He studied the photos and then said, "Where do the Bushmans fit in this mess?"

"I'm not sure, but I think we'll know when it is over. We are supposed to get a phone call from the state police in the morning. They have located a relative who is aware of Alstrom's burial and saw the autopsy photos. I called from Little Rock and talked to the coroner in Mountain Home. He's sending photos of the bodies. Danny Heilburger, a state trooper in that district, will bring them down tomorrow early. He has to go to Little Rock so he'll drop them off on his way through," Sherry said.

"Did you call L.P. Wellman and tell him what we know now?"

"No, I went to see him. He thinks Alstrom is who killed Officer McGee because he probably thought McGee recognized him. But that we'll never know unless Alstrom talks, if we find him, which he more than likely won't when a smart defense attorney tells him to keep his mouth, shut," she said disgustedly. "There are things we may never know."

"Were you able to find information on Bud Borders?"

"Not much. I found some men who knew him and where he lived. The house he lived in is gone. It was torn down after he died. He came into Little Rock in the late '70s, possibly from Dallas, Texas, and went to work for the scaffold company in the early '80s. Later, he became part owner of the company and having no family, he more or less adopted the Alstrom kids and Easterly's for his own. The men I interviewed said he idolized them and was really torn up when they were killed. He had a hard time getting over it, according to them."

Reginald sat with a far off look in his eyes and then spoke. "I'm going to have Darcy work on the Borders angle. We need to know as much as we can find on everyone. There's a lot that doesn't make sense, and it doesn't add up." Growing weary of the subject, Reginald said, "You ready to go or do you want to stay to hear the music?"

They stayed to hear the country music and enjoy the comedy by the men known as the River Rats. Two of them sang while the third told a joke in harmony and in time to the music. It was past 9:00 p.m.

when the show was over. Reginald dropped Sherry off and went to his house to call Darrell Cumberland and Thomas Dawson. They would all meet the next morning in Darrell's office.

Neither one of them saw the maroon van with the man inside watching Sherry's house when they turned off Main Street. "Well, well, well, pretty Sherry is by herself now. I wish it was Saturday night, but I'll just have to wait," he said with eager anticipation. "Forty-eight more hours and my pain will be gone," he yelled.

Chapter

FIFTY-SIX

Brookson watched the street intently and began to think about the day before. It didn't register on him until he was several miles down the road who was in the yellow Mustang that passed by earlier the day he was on the side of the road. He had been looking for his favorite slot car and couldn't find it. He remembered that he hadn't seen it when he carried the boxes into the rent house. He had pulled over to the side of the road to look for it in the back of the van when the Mustang went by. His little car wasn't there. He must have dropped it in the garage the last time he ran it before the fire. He could feel his insides filling with rage and blocking out reason. He did a quick turn around and sped toward Mountain View. He didn't need a different car now and didn't need to go to Little Rock. Good thing the old bat didn't ask for more rent money. She didn't know how close she came to being history. Now he was ready to spring his ending on the fools in that miserable little town. His missing slot car made him angry. He could feel more rage building.

He watched Sherry go into the house and then he left and went home. He passed two police cars, but the officers in them were too busy writing tickets to notice. That had been the problem since the two accidents. His rage rose out of control. "Everybody is always too busy to notice me and my pain. Well, they will notice me now. I will go out in a blaze of glory. I will no longer be invisible," he screamed as he drove into the garage.

•

The note taped to the glass on the police department's front door flapped in the breeze. Reginald saw it as soon as he pulled into the parking lot. It was 5:00 a.m., and shift change wasn't until 6:00 a.m. The note flapped back and forth and up and down. All he could think of was that it might blow away. Then he got a chill from head to toe that wasn't caused by the weather. He hurried inside and got a pair of latex gloves and slipped them on. He carefully removed the note, not aware that smoldering eyes were watching from across the street. The owner of the eyes smiled in anticipation of what he had planned.

Reginald went inside and opened the envelope. It was typed and said, *I wore gloves. Soon you will have the answers. Right under your noses.* There wasn't a signature. Reginald heard footsteps and turned around. Trooper Danny Heilburger stood in the doorway. "Are you Sgt. Gawker? If you are, I have some photos for you from the coroner up at Mountain Home."

"I am," sticking out his hand to the officer. "I'm pleased to meet you. Sure am glad to get these. This is a tough case."

"That's what my father-in-law told me."

"Oh, who's that?" Reginald asked, looking surprised.

"Sam Hazelton, the bank president. Do you know him?" Trooper Heilburger said.

"I do. He's a fine man. He has been a big help in this case. How soon are you going to be back in Mountain Home?"

"I'll be there later tonight. Why?"

"If you would, stop here on your way back. I have some photos I want you to take to him. I'll call your father-in-law and tell him what I want."

"I'll be glad to stop at the bank. I need to go. I have to be in Little Rock by nine for court and hopefully I can leave by noon. Should be back here around four this afternoon at the latest, if all goes well."

"Good. The envelope will be in the dispatch office," Reginald said. Trooper Heilburger gave a friendly salute type wave and left.

Chief Cumberland arrived a bit after 6:00 a.m. and Reginald showed him the note. Sherry showed up at 6:15 a.m. and read the note. Worry was seen on their faces. Reginald had called Martin Perkins and asked that he and Darcy come to the 7:00 a.m. meeting. He also told them, for reasons he couldn't explain, to use the back door again so they wouldn't be seen from Main Street. He explained it to himself by his becoming paranoid over the investigation.

Shift change had taken place under the watchful eyes across the street. He knew the schedule, and 9:55 p.m. tomorrow night would begin his journey to a pain free life forever. And right under their noses. He saw the officer who stopped him yesterday come back and go into the building. *Maybe there are doughnuts in there.* He laughed at his humor.

Not very long after Officer Dugan arrived, Nance Porter returned from patrol and went into the building. Then in a few minutes, the sheriff pulled up and went inside. The man had seen the state police car arrive and leave, and now more state cars arrived and the two officers went inside, one carrying a package. The first one also had a package. What were they doing now? He didn't have any way to find out. Maybe he would begin his plan tonight just in case. No, he had to wait for Saturday.

All the officers assembled in Chief Cumberland's office. Introductions were made all around to the state policemen. Darcy and Perkins knew Harold McInaugh. The lab reports were back on the DNA from both Indiana and Arkansas and on all of the latent fingerprints.

Darrell Cumberland said, "We have a big job now to catch the killer. I have asked the state police for help. I talked to Reginald on the phone last night and he wanted me to get them. We believe we know who he is, but where he is, we don't know yet. What do the lab reports tell us?"

State Trooper Harold McInaugh spoke. "The DNA on the toothpick found on the square when Callman was shot matches the DNA on the toothpick found near the tow truck at Sharp's Service. They don't match the DNA on the Milky Way candy wrapper found in the cab of Sharp's wrecker or the porch blood. Now this next one is really interesting. The candy wrapper DNA matches the blood found on the porch at Mary Sheldon's house."

"The toothpicks don't match the candy wrapper and the porch blood, but the porch blood and the wrapper do match," Sherry said incredulously. "Are you sure the lab didn't make a mistake? We were sure they would match."

"When the lab tech saw that he had a second test run by another tech. It came out the same." He handed the report to Sherry, and she in turn handed it to Reginald. Neither knew what to make of it.

"Go on, Officer McInaugh," Darrell said.

"The lab work came in from Indiana yesterday on the DNA of J. Daniel Bushman. It was J. Daniel who died in that car fire." He looked around and said, "The DNA on both toothpicks matches the DNA of J. Daniel Bushman." Silence engulfed the room. Shock was on all faces. He handed the report to Reginald who couldn't believe what he had just heard. Sherry looked to be in a trance. Darrell opened and closed his mouth and nothing came out. The two state officers didn't know what to say in response to the behavior of their fellow officers, so they remained silent. The same question was on all their minds. How could a dead man's DNA show up in Mountain View months after he died?

Finally, Sherry found enough presence of mind in the mental fog to say, "Like I said, we were sure that the toothpicks, candy wrapper, and blood were from the same man. How did he have toothpicks with Bushman's DNA on them?"

"We may never know," Darrell said, recovering from shock. "But when we go over again what we know, we may find out. Alstrom or whoever it is … " and his voice trailed off. Then: "The killer is diabolical, and that is what worries me."

McInaugh spoke softly to the other state trooper, Hilliard Truesdale. "I have the latent print report on the registration from identification. The lab got a ten card on Bushman from Sikeston, and one of the latent prints on the front of the registration and two on the back belong to J. Daniel Bushman. But we couldn't find a match for the other four. We have no idea who made them. Probably belong to office workers somewhere along the line. It happens quite often."

A knock came on the door and Darrell said, "Come in."

Trooper Freeland McCary came into the room. He introduced himself and handed Darrell an envelope. "Here are the photos y'all wanted and the interview of the relative, but there is a problem. She's blind now and could only say that the description sounded like Carl Alstrom. She said there weren't any other relatives."

Darrell took the photos and said, "Reginald, do you have the photos from the coroner in Mountain Home?" He handed them to Darrell who looked at them for a few minutes and gave them back, along with the others, to Reginald. He and Sherry studied both sets intently.

"Do you see what I think I see?" Sherry asked Reginald. Then she showed them to Darcy and Martin who had been silent the whole time, content to listen.

"Notice the hands on the body identified as Alstrom. There isn't a ring on the right hand. The pictures of him with the kids show a ring on the right ring finger. And the faces in the picture aren't very clear either. Notice the other body doesn't have a ring and according to the reports, none were found in the debris. "

Sherry was reading the report of the interview of the relative. She said, "An aunt said Carl never would be caught without his college ring on. He graduated from the University of Arkansas at Monticello and was so proud of it, according to her. She told the investigator that it was very odd for him not to be wearing his ring. She said he wore it on his left hand, but also said she could be wrong on that. The ring could be the one the teller saw."

"It looks like Carl Alstrom is our man," Darcy said. "He killed Borders and Easterly and then set the fire to make it look like he was killed. Now where is he? But why no ring if he wanted to make it look like he had died in the fire?"

Chapter
FIFTY-SEVEN

The meeting broke up after plans were laid to try to prevent whatever the killer was going to do. The problems were many, and four of them made it most difficult to solve the case. They really didn't know what he looked like; they didn't know what he had planned; they didn't know where he was; and they didn't know when he would strike again. The officers scattered under the watchful eyes of Malcom Brookson.

Right after the meeting, Officer Dugan came into headquarters out of breath. He told Mazy he needed to see either Reginald or the Chief. Darrell was in his office; she buzzed him. She said to Dugan, "Go on in."

Dugan burst into Darrell's office. "What you got George?"

"Well, let's see where to begin. Last night my wife was gone to her mother's and didn't get home until late. I was asleep and didn't get to talk to her. I was gone before she got up so we didn't talk until I went into the bank to cash a check. She was on her break, so I went into the break room. I mentioned the weird acting guy named Malcom Brookson from Searcy that I stopped yesterday. She said the guy had been in the bank twice this week to cash checks. They were written on a Searcy bank."

"You stopped Brookson and he has been in the bank twice?"

"You're right on both counts."

"What kind of car was he driving?"

"A 1996 Dodge Caravan with really dark tinted windows. I

thought it was strange, but when Ellen told me he had been in the bank, I thought it might be important to tell you."

Darrell picked up the phone and called Mazy in dispatch to tell her to summon Reginald to his office. Reginald came in and George gave him the story on Brookson. Reginald said, "So now we have a possible description of the van Robbie saw and a name. The address is on Highway 36 west of Searcy."

Before Reginald could say another word, Darrell was dialing the White County Sheriff's office. He spoke to whoever was on the other end and hung up. "They will call us as soon as they can check out the house. Maybe we have a real break now."

"I knew we were to keep a lookout for dark colored vans with tinted windows, but that description fits ninety percent of the vans in this town in the summer time. Not knowing the make or model makes it impossible," Officer Dugan said, sounding miserable.

Reginald left and came back. He opened his briefcase and showed Dugan a picture. "That's the driver of the van," he exclaimed. "I remember that little round scar on his left cheek. It's the size of the eraser on the end of a pencil. There isn't any beard hair on it."

"Chief, now that we have the photos of Easterly and Alstrom, we need to show them to Sam Hazelton and the tellers up there. I don't have the time to go up to Mountain Home and neither does Sherry. Would it be okay for George to take these pictures up there? Trooper Heilburger was going to stop and pick them up this evening, but I'd like to know sooner what they may say."

"I don't see why not. Give George the photos and he can be on his way." Reginald called Sam Hazelton to tell him photos were coming and what he wanted done. George Dugan smiled all the way to Mountain Home. *It sure is good to do something besides write traffic tickets all day*, he thought.

No one was in the bank lobby when Reginald went through the door. Sherry wasn't in at the time, so he went to see Merton Houston. He showed the pictures to Merton who looked at them carefully. "I don't recognize anyone, but maybe Ellen Dugan will. She was telling me that George stopped some driver yesterday." They showed her the photos of Easterly and Alstrom, along with six other pictures with general similarities.

After studying all the pictures Ellen said, "That one is the man who cashed the check," pointing to Alstrom's picture. "The name on the check was Malcom Brookson. I called the Searcy bank each time to see if the check was good."

"Why did you identify his picture?"

"That little scar on the left cheek. And in this picture with his arm around the child, he has a ring on his right ring finger. The man in here had the same type ring and it was on the right ring finger. It had gold letters on the red stone the best I can remember," Gloria said.

"Is that all you can remember?" Reginald asked.

"That's it. If I think of anything else, I'll tell Mr. Houston or George."

"George might be late getting home tonight. He went to Mountain Home to do some interviews," Reginald told her.

"I know that'll make him very happy," Ellen said with a smile that equaled the one her husband had when he left.

When Sherry returned to the bank, she was told Reginald had been there. She called the department and a few minutes later Reginald appeared in her office. She shut the door to keep the conversation private. She also took the opportunity to kiss Reginald. His face turned red as usual, and she laughed inwardly when she thought about his face turning red if they ever married. She sighed silently and smiled when she realized she had accepted his shyness a long time ago. *Such a fine man and so many think he's an idiot.*

Reginald noticed her silence and said with mild alarm, "Is there anything wrong?"

"No, matter of fact everything is very right," she said and bussed his check. His face glowed red again.

"What is it you want to tell me?" Sherry asked.

"George Dugan stopped a man in a maroon Dodge Caravan yesterday that fits the description of our suspect. It fits Alstrom to a T."

"He stopped a maroon Dodge? I saw a maroon van along the highway yesterday when I came back from Little Rock. A man had the lid up and was poking around in the back. When I checked the rear view mirror, he was pulling back onto the highway. The van had real dark tinted windows. For some reason, dorky came to mind when I saw the glass."

"That's what Robbie said about the van, dorky."

"Robbie said dorky? You're not making sense, Reg."

Reginald slammed the right side of his forehead with an upward sweep of his palm. "I forgot to tell you the deal with Robbie Porter. He made the first identification of our suspect. I was going to tell you last night, and it slipped my mind." He told her the story about Robbie and the police business with Mazy Sink.

Sherry laughed until she had to wipe the tears from her eyes. "Can you believe that, a blind man driving a car? Leave it to a kid to figure it out. Who would have thought it?" And she laughed again. "I wondered where that 'it is police business' came from."

Reginald left the bank to some curious stares from the other bank employees. They thought Sherry wasn't with the state police now and couldn't figure out why Reginald kept coming to the bank. They were aware she spent time at police headquarters, but they thought it was to see Reginald. Some of them complained mildly to Merton, but he told them as long as Sherry did her work he wasn't prying into her private affairs. Ellen Dugan kept quiet since she knew the truth. She knew the officers of the department were close knit with no bickering amongst them as is not the case in many places. They were professionals who took their work seriously. They respected each other and kept quiet on matters concerning Sherry and her police business. She smiled now as she remembered Robbie's line and would kid Mazy about it at the church social tomorrow night.

Trooper Heilburger stopped for the pictures that were already on their way to Mountain Home. Reginald returned to headquarters and sat down in his office. There were a lot more questions that needed answers, and even though they were receiving more information now, the biggest answer was yet to be had. *Where is the suspect hiding?* Reginald's eyes fell on the desk and the note that had been taped to the front door. *What does that mean, right under your noses?* The note appeared to have been typed on a different machine than the one that typed the note to Sherry, according to Barry Feltman, a retired former documents examiner for a police department up north and now the owner of the typewriter and PC shop in town. Marjorie Shuman searched her father's papers, but she hadn't been able to find anything that he had typed. All of it had probably burned with the house.

The red '49 Ford purred from the police parking lot when Reginald left for home. His departure was observed by the angry eyes peering through a slit in the window curtains of the house across the street. "Soon, you won't have a need for that pretty truck, Mr. Smart Cop," he murmured. He began to pace the floor.

Chapter

FIFTY-EIGHT

Saturday morning dawned bright and clear. The streets were teeming with all kinds of cars, trucks, vans, and motorcycles. The sidewalks were clogged with big, little, short, tall, fat, thin, young, and old folks out to get an early start on the day's activities. Music being played by fiddlers, banjo and mandolin pickers, bass, and harmonica players on the courthouse square inspired some of the courageous ones to jig dance on the small stage set up on the south courthouse lawn. To use a teenage term, Mountain View was *rockin'* in country style in an old fashioned, old timey mountain country way, which is what the multitudes came to enjoy.

Traffic was heavy on Main Street, streaming past Brookson's house when he saw Reginald's red truck pull into the lot. He got out; hurrying to the building and quickly went through the door. Brookson knew there were new developments, but that made no difference now because in a few hours all would know and feel with him the grand end to his many years of pain. Maybe he should drop the pretense and admit his identity, but he couldn't, not yet. They would learn it soon enough and he wanted to see their expressions when they heard his name.

An envelope with Reginald's name on it lay on top of the papers littering his desk. He opened it and read George Dugan's report aloud. "*The teller at the Mountain Home Bank picked out the picture of Alstrom and said he had been in there to open the account July of 1995 in the name of J. Daniel Bushman. She never saw him again after that* *day. She remembered that he had a mole on his left cheek and wore a class ring with gold initials **B.A.B.** in the red stone on his right ring finger. She said he was nervous and odd acting. The bookkeeper said that the statements began coming back in the fall of 1995 and thought the first statement returned was for September. Then I checked the date that the deed on the house was transferred, and the land records show the church turned it over to Borders and Alstrom May of 1995 for the sum of one dollar and other consideration. The bank there held a small mortgage on the property."* He looked up and said to no one, "End of report. George sure looked under the stones up there. He might make a good detective if we ever need another one."

"Do you always talk to yourself?" a soft voice asked behind Reginald.

Reginald jumped and swiveled his chair around to see Sherry standing there. "Gosh, you scared me. My mind was in Mountain Home."

"What was it doing up there?" Sherry asked, laughing at Reginald's reaction.

Reginald looked at Sherry for a couple of ticks and then began laughing. "What are you doing here?" he asked after he quit laughing.

"I was up early and decided to see the sights and wonders today. We haven't had a real day off since this case began. I saw all kinds of sights and wonders coming through town, and the square is a madhouse already. Everyone looked to be having fun. What were you thinking about when I came in?"

Reginald handed the report to Sherry. She read it and said, "The report seems to indicate that Alstrom may have killed Bushman for his identification and then killed Marion Easterly for reasons we don't yet fully know. It fits with the conclusion we discussed at dinner the other night when we looked at the photos."

"That all being true, then we know that Marion Easterly was alive when Bushman was killed. The killer took a chance that Mr. Easterly wouldn't find out he was supposed to be dead before he was actually killed," Reginald said, " … unless he faked his own death, which would mean that Alstrom didn't kill Bushman. Then the house burned and we think that it's Alstrom who died, killed by Easterly. But it wasn't, it was Marion Easterly who died in that fire, apparently killed by Alstrom. Now we can't locate Alstrom."

"Sometimes I think we're chasing ghosts in a game of hide and seek. Now you see them and then you don't," Sherry said. "Alstrom might as well be a ghost since we never see him and can't find him."

"We can't find anyone now who knew Alstrom and his aunt is blind and can't identify the picture. Then there's Borders. He came to Little Rock and then became a business partner of Alstrom. He had no family and then he's killed in a suspicious house fire," Reginald said with evident frustration in his voice.

"Is there any reason to believe that Borders is involved in this puzzle?"

"I don't see how. There's nothing to indicate that he's anything but dead. No one has seen him since that fire and his name hasn't cropped up anywhere in this investigation. He didn't lose a family like Alstrom and Easterly did."

"What are we going to do with all the information?" Sherry said, sounding bewildered. "We don't know where Alstrom is hiding and we don't know how all of this fits together. We do know that Marion Easterly's death was faked by someone who killed Bushman, making his death look as if it was Marion's. Then Marion Easterly died in that fire with Borders, which helped eliminate the first theory we had that the killer was Marion. However, if we substitute Alstrom for Easterly, our theory works. But we're back to square one, who faked Marion Easterly's death? Did Alstrom do that or did Easterly fake his own death while playing another deadly game and get caught in his own web? Repeating words we have used many time before, 'none of this makes sense.'"

Mercifully, the phone rang to end the merry-go-round confusion about who died and why. Reginald picked it up. "Sgt. Gawker." He paused to listen and then grabbed a pencil and a note pad. He scribbled furiously and then said, "He hasn't been seen since?" He listened some more. "Thanks for the info. Sure appreciate it." He hung up and looked at Sherry and then dropped his head and shook it.

"What's wrong now, Reg, more bad news?"

"I honestly don't know," he said, and began to tell Sherry what a White County Sheriff's Deputy had found. "A Malcom Brookson rented a house on Highway 36 west of Searcy. The house is empty, and it appears that he never lived there. He picked up the mail a few times in 1995 according to a neighbor, and on one of those occasions, which she thinks may have been in the late spring or early summer of '95, he was driving a wrecker truck. She hasn't seen him since. The deputy asked her to describe the renter and the description fits Alstrom the way she described who she saw."

"He was driving a wrecker truck? Was it before or after the Indiana event?" Sherry asked.

"The best she could remember it was in late June of 1995. So if that's true, that means it was after the Bushmans were killed."

"The deputy found the owner who said Brookson rented the house and paid the rent in cash for six months in early May of 1995. That's before he went to Indiana in June. He was a busy boy with plenty of money," Reginald said.

Darcy came through the door with a box of chocolate doughnuts and three big cups of coffee in a sack, having entered through the back door. He set out the cups, creamer, and sugar packs. "How did you know we were here?" Reginald wanted to know.

"I called dispatch, and Mazy said you and Sherry were in a meeting plotting against the civilized world. Figured I would join in the fun. It might be more interesting than trying to stop the plotting of others. Now let's go to the more important stuff."

"What could be more important on Saturday morning than doughnuts and coffee and plotting against the civilized world?" Reginald asked.

"What I'm going to tell you might be," Darcy said. "I called a pal in Dallas and found out that Borders had lived there for three years, but no one knows anything much that would help. He worked at a small airport for most of the time he was there. Kept to himself and didn't have much of a social life according to the few that knew him, but he did have some seedy friends hanging around at times. My pal said the people Borders hung with mentioned organized crime stuff more than once. Maybe Borders was into something heavy and it got him killed."

"That fits with the suspicions I've had about this case," Reginald said. "A lot of shady characters have … " the phone interrupted Reginald. "Sgt. Gawker." Pause. "He's here." He handed the phone to Darcy.

Darcy listened and then said, "Searcy? Maybe three years before going to Dallas. Thanks. We'll check on it," and hung up. "That was my pal in Dallas who talked to his contact again. He said Borders lived in Searcy and then left all of a sudden. He contacted a detective there who ran the file and couldn't find anything on him. He's clean in Searcy and Dallas. Nothing on him in Little Rock either, according to L.P. Wellman who I called before coming here."

"Sounds like he liked to move around and finally found a place with the scaffold company," Sherry said. "People like that drift around for years before they land."

Darcy was silent for a few moments and then said, "Maybe it would be a good idea if I take the pictures and run down to Searcy today and show them to the owner of that house he rented and to that neighbor as well. Maybe they can make an ID on the picture of Alstrom."

"Good idea," Reginald said, handing the photos to Darcy, "and check with White County as well as with the Searcy Police Department. Maybe you'll find a gold mine down there."

"Either that or more doughnuts," Sherry said laughing. "I understand they have some great pastry shops in that town." Darcy handed her the last doughnut and went down the hall making dire threats to his cousin. He could hear her laughter as the back door banged shut.

Reginald called Little Rock and finished up the loose ends of the case to date. Then he and Sherry called it a day and left to enjoy the rest of the weekend. When they left headquarters, they didn't see angry hate filled eyes watching them from the house across the street.

"Right under their noses, and they are looking for me everywhere. In a few hours it will be over and I will be free," Brookson said in a voice that sounded like a hiss. He then set up his exhibits for the expected and unwilling house guests.

FIFTY-NINE

Darkness fell on the town and the music played on the square until shortly before 9:00 p.m. when a thunderstorm moved in and began to dump buckets of rain on the festivities. Malcom Brookson backed his van out of the garage and drove down Main Street. He parked behind the Home Cookin' Cafe and waited.

Reginald dropped Sherry off at her house having spent the day at the Folk Center and on the square until the rain ended the fun. After they made plans for church the next morning, he left for home. As he passed the Home Cookin' Cafe, he noticed tail lights behind it in the alley. He gave the lights little thought and went on down the street. With what Darcy found out in Searcy, the case looked like it would be solved before the end of next week, providing they could find the killer.

The rain was coming down in a torrent when Brookson drove into his garage. Fifteen minutes later, he left again, and thirty minutes after that he was back inside the house. At 9:50 p.m., he headed out into the rain a third time, and at 10:20 p.m., he hauled Sherry Westermann, bound and squirming into the house where Joe Landers and Madeline Crompton were bound and gagged. He dumped Sherry on the floor beside them. "Now we wait for the fun to begin, ladies and gentleman, but first I have a little show for you. Over here on the table are six ice picks. Each one has a name on it." He paused for effect and noticed the fear on the faces and in the eyes of his captives. He saw them trying to loosen their hands that were tightly bound behind their backs. Sherry could see the madness in his eyes and could hear it in his voice.

"It won't do you any good to struggle to try to loosen the straps. Those are police restraints that I got out of Officer McGee's car the day I had to kill him. So nice of him to leave them on the seat where I could get them with no effort. I knew they would come in handy. I put two on your wrists and one on your ankles as you can see. I hope they aren't too tight." He laughed crazily, and Sherry saw and heard once again the madness and evil he possessed.

He picked up the first ice pick in the neatly laid out row and showed it to Joe Landers. "See your name on the handle in red? Your favorite color if I remember right." Joe kept his head down. "Joe, look at me. I'm talking to you. Answer me!"

"Yes, red," Joe mumbled.

"Joe, I can't hear you." Brookson placed the tip of the ice pick against Joe's throat. "Now answer so all of us can hear you." Brookson increased the pressure against Joe's neck.

Increasing fear flashed across Joe's features. He looked up at Brookson and answered. "Yes, red," he yelled as loudly as he was able.

"Now that's much better. Now they know you like red just as I know it. Sharing information is so nice. The red makes a nice personal touch on the handle doesn't it? There won't be any mistake about the one I'll use when the time comes to send you on your journey." Brookson glared menacingly at his intended victim. The madman's identity slowly dawned on Joe Landers for all the good that it did him.

Next, he showed Madeline Crompton an ice pick with her name printed in black on the handle. "I have to apologize to you for my not knowing your color. It doesn't matter anyway. The reason you're here is because you're nosy, and I don't like nosy people. I couldn't allow you to see me and blow the whistle on me when I bagged the prize sitting right here," touching Sherry on the head.

Turning to a wide-eyed and scared Sherry, who was doing her best to not show her fright, Brookson said, showing her an ice pick with her name on it, "See the colors? You like blue and yellow, so I made yours real personal with blue letters. The yellow didn't look right. As all of you can see, nothing but the best for pretty Sherry. But one thing I don't understand. Why do you have a red and white 1957 Ford Hardtop when your colors are blue and yellow? Before you die, I would like to hear the explanation. And you have a yellow Mustang, too. My, what a rich lady you must be. Such a shame you won't be able to enjoy them much longer."

Sherry watched the madman in disbelief. *He knows I have a red '57 Ford but not the black 1958 Ford retractable top convertible*, she said to herself silently. She wondered what else he knew. The thought was frightening.

His voice began to rise as he walked over to Joe. "You don't know why you are here, but you will find out." He watched Joe and saw him begin to shake. "I want everyone here so all will know the pain I have had for all these years. The other ice picks have names on them and by now pretty Sherry, you have probably figured out the ones they're for. Let's see, there's Robert Blandford's name in green and Sgt. Reginald P. Gawker in uniform blue. The sergeant is very nosy just as is pretty Sherry. I thought I would bring that smart mouth waitress here, but I can't find her. I know she recognized me, and I know one of you slipped her out. Shame on you for hiding her; she is going to miss the party." He smiled at Sherry when he mentioned Mandy and she hoped he didn't see her momentary look of relief.

"The other one I can't find is Mary Beth. She slipped away, and I know who caused it. It was you, pretty Sherry, and that snoopy boyfriend of yours. You are going to pay for that trickery." Brookson paused, breathing heavily before speaking again. "Mary Beth will pay too and then my plan will be complete. Last is Lavon Jason Callman who has been in hiding. He hates his first name so I put it on his ice pick in dark blue. Nice touch, don't you think?" his voice beginning to rise again. "If it hadn't been for Lavon, you wouldn't be here like this. He was supposed to die. He ruined my plans and now all of you will suffer together what I had planned for you to suffer alone as I have suffered all these years." His voice reached a crescendo pitch as he raved and rambled on, becoming louder and louder in his madness. Calming down he said, "Now if you will excuse me, I must make a phone call to start Act II of the show. This is just Act I."

He left in the van to find a pay phone that wouldn't identify his location with a caller ID. When he dialed Reginald's number, it was busy. He tried a second time and the result was the same. *It's not supposed to be this way*, he ranted in his mind. He left the phone booth full of rage and returned to his rent house. He slammed the door open and began to scream at his captives as the door banged shut.

•

Nance Porter had returned to headquarters for a new traffic citation book and was walking to the door when he heard the loud violent talk coming from the house across the street. He said to Fred Wilson, the dispatcher, "Whoever lives across the street is either hard of hearing or he's pure crazy. He sure plays the TV loudly, but it doesn't sound like a TV."

"I haven't heard anything," Fred said, and went back to his book.

Nance remained in headquarters to finish a report, and when he went back out, he heard the screaming again and thought he heard a name he recognized. He dismissed it thinking it was his imagination. *A lot of people are named Joe*, he reminded himself.

•

Snores were softly bouncing off the walls when Reginald's phone rang at 11:10 p.m. He rolled over and squinted at the clock. Groggy with sleep he fumbled with the receiver and said, "Hello, who's this?" He listened. "What? Are you sure?" He listened and then said, "I'll meet you at headquarters in ten minutes. I'll call Sherry. Good bye."

Reginald dialed Sherry's number. He let the phone ring and ring, but she didn't answer. He tried Madeline Crompton, and she didn't answer either. He had a sick feeling in his stomach as he ran to his truck. He slid and skidded around the corners going to headquarters. Darcy was already inside when Reginald, all out of breath, ran into his office. "I can't reach Sherry or Madeline," he said to Darcy as he went to the dispatch office.

"Fred, send a car to Sherry's house and have whoever goes check on both her and Madeline. They didn't answer their phones, and I don't like what I'm thinking." Fred sent Nance Porter and less than fifteen minutes later he called back in with the report. "Tell him to get here as quickly as he knows how. Call Darrell and Thomas too. We have severe problems. And call George Dugan in from patrol."

The eyes across the street watched Reginald arrive, but didn't see Darcy go in the back door. He watched the uniform officer go inside and then watched Darrell and Thomas arrive. He turned to his captives. "We are nearly ready for Act II, Scene II, or is it Scene I? No matter, it's going to be exciting," he said, screaming and berating his captives for helping ruin his life and grand plans.

Nance Porter was getting out of his car when he heard the screaming and ranting coming from the house across the street. He decided the occupant was crazy and went inside shaking his head. He saw Reginald, and Darcy in the room. He said, "Mrs. Crompton's back door is smashed in and Sherry's front door is standing open. There are signs of a struggle in both houses, but no one is there. I looked everywhere." Frantic faces were looking at each other when George Dugan hurried into the room. He was told what had taken place and then he said, "When I drove up I heard screaming and yelling across the street. I would swear I heard a voice say 'pretty Sherry.'"

Reginald snapped around and said, "You heard what?" Dugan repeated the words. Then Reginald began to frantically paw at the case report folder and when he couldn't find what he wanted, he went to the evidence locker. He came back with a plastic bag and another one that was in his pocket. The note to Sherry with the words, '*right under your nose*,' was inside the bag. When he realized their meaning, shock froze his mind; his mouth moved, but his mind wouldn't release what he wanted to say. For Reginald, his inability to speak seemed like an eternity, but in reality, it lasted only a couple of seconds. He yelled as he raced into Darrell's office, "He's in the house across the street, and that's where he has Sherry and Madeline."

Before anyone could react, Fred Wilson hollered from the dispatch room. "Joe Landers's wife just called and said he isn't home yet and isn't at the restaurant."

"Oh, no," Nance Porter groaned. "I heard that guy over there yelling and thought when he said Joe, I was imagining things."

Darrell and Thomas who had arrived only moments earlier heard Reginald yell and what Nance said he heard. Darrell said, anguish in his strained voice, "He probably has Joe, and now we have to figure out what we're going to do to bring this to an end without anyone getting hurt." They hatched a plan and Reginald went outside patting his shirt down and adjusting his right pants leg. The eyes in the house saw Reginald cross the street to the rent house yard and then the eyes disappeared from the window.

SIXTY

In a few seconds, Brookson appeared with Sherry at the window and opened it. He had his face covered with a crude mask. "Sgt. Gawker," he said in a high pitched excited voice, "I have pretty Sherry here and have a nice shiny new ice pick with her name on it. If you don't want to see what I have planned before it's time for Act III, you throw down your gun and come inside. I have some special toys for you to see and they have names on them. One of them even has your name on it." Reginald did as he was told and threw down his gun. He felt naked and alone now.

The door opened and Reginald entered the house, and trying as hard as he could, he couldn't hide his shock when he saw Sherry, Madeline Crompton, and Joe Landers bound with restraints and with duct tape across their mouths. Then he saw the revolver and realized that the business end of the Smith & Wesson .357 was pointed right at him; he saw the ice picks with names on them arranged in a row; and saw a small grey thin plastic box on the table that Brookson picked up and casually dropped into his pocket. The madman's hand was steady and his eyes were as cold as frozen steel. He eyed Reginald with contempt and then smiled. He kept the gun pointed at Reginald.

"You please me so much that you show fear. I appreciate it too since I know what it is. Now you are thinking that you will jump me or try to shoot me with that ankle gun. Take it off and slide it across the floor."

"How do you know I have an ankle gun?" Reginald asked to keep him talking, hoping that the transmitter under his shirt was working and hoped that the perp didn't tumble to it. Brookson ignored the question and watched as Reginald removed the gun from its holster and slid it across the floor.

"Good boy, Reggie," he said. "Now go to the window and tell your chief that I want Blandford and Lavon Jason Callman in here. They are to stand across the street where I can see them." He picked up an ice pick and walked over to Joe. "Now unless you want to watch him die, do as you are told. Then cute little Sherry is next." He smiled coldly at Sherry and then winked. "Such a pretty woman and such a waste that she has to die. But it has to be done." He swung around to face Reginald and then turned back to Sherry and laughed.

Sherry's eyes became wide when he turned back to Reginald again. Now she knew where she had seen him before today. He had been in the bank the day that Snoopy had taken the pictures of her. Brookson had walked across the lobby when she went to her uncle's office that morning to tell him about the incident outside. She had been so absorbed with what happened that she never gave any notice the man in the lobby. Now to her horror, she also remembered that he limped.

"It's up to you, Sgt. Reginald P. Gawker, whether she lives awhile longer or dies now. Do you want to go down in the history of this miserable town as the one who allowed your sweetheart to be killed? Well do you?" He left Joe and reached for the ice pick that had the name Sherry printed on the handle. "Make up your mind. Do as I instructed or Sherry dies."

Reginald, fearful of what Brookson would try to do, went to the window and delivered the message. Forty-five minutes later Callman and Blandford were standing across the street. Both had been outfitted with bullet proof vests. When Brookson saw them he said, "Now tell them to come into the house. When they arrive, we will then have story time. I want everyone to know why all of you are here and what I am going to do to relieve years of pain. Mine will be gone and whatever pain you have now will be no more. The small pain you suffer today from me won't last long. I'm sure you won't remember it." His maniacal laughter sent chills down the spines of the captives. If they had never seen insanity and madness before, they were seeing it now.

Reginald told Chief Cumberland what Brookson wanted. The Chief told Reginald to have Brookson go to the window. When Brookson appeared Darrell said, "We can't allow them to enter the house. That would be endangering the lives of civilians and we can't do it."

"Mr. Sgt. Man, you tell him that they either come in or I am going to begin killing some of the people in here. I think I will begin with cutie pie here," Brookson said menacingly and moved over to Sherry. He had an ice pick in his left hand and stuck the point against her voice box. "Now, what will it be, Mr. Gawker? Now bring them in as I ordered or watch your cutie pie here get this ice pick stuck through her neck. It's up to you."

Reginald looked at Brookson and then Sherry. He could see the fear in her eyes that became worse when Brookson applied light pressure to the ice pick. "You had better not hurt her … if you do … "

"You'll do what, be a hero, Sgt. Gawker, so your friends can watch you die after I kill her? You try anything and I will kill her first. I see that diamond on her finger. The town will be going to a funeral instead of a wedding. Double caskets will be delightful, don't you think? Why you can have a ceremony right there. It will be marriage and death all in one nice neat package." Another maniacal laugh that sent chills through everyone in the room came from deep within Brookson. Reginald and Sherry knew they were witnesses to the worst type of madness imaginable and they hoped they would never see again—unpredictable and suddenly deadly if he added to Brookson's increasing agitation level.

Reginald knew he couldn't do anything that would cause Sherry to be killed or seriously injured. He relented and called out to Chief Cumberland to send Callman and Blandford into the house. They entered with hesitant steps, fear on their faces, and were told to sit down and lean against the wall. They each were given restraints. Callman put the restraints on Blandford's wrists and ankles and Reginald was instructed to restrain Callman the same way. He did as told since Brookson was holding a gun in his right hand and the ice pick with Sherry's name on it in the other. He hoped Darcy and Martin were getting into position.

"You are such a good boy, Reg," Brookson said laughing crazily, "and I bet you do everything pretty Sherry tells you to do. Are we ready for story time? I know all of you are dying to know what and why, but I think you, Reginald, have it figured out or at least some of it." He walked over and ripped the tape from Sherry's mouth. She avoided crying out from the pain when the tape came off. "I want to hear you talk before it's over. I just love your voice, pretty Sherry. It reminds me of ... well, that will come later."

He eyed Reginald who had removed the contents of the plastic bag he had in his pocket and was now holding it in his hand. Brookson didn't see the bag or the object since his attention was on Sherry. Turning to Reginald with a theatrical flair, he said, "Now Sgt. Gawker, you will have the floor after my introduction ... I have already told the three that I killed Officer McGee. I am sure he recognized me and I couldn't take the chance he would talk. He hurt my knee real bad. He tried to open the car door before I shot him. He shouldn't have hurt my knee." He paused and then said, "Now Sgt. Gawker, it's all yours." He took a breath. "My knee is better now."

"Okay, I'll begin with L. Jason ... "

"His first name is Lavon. Call him Lavon," he yelled interrupting Reginald.

Sneaking a look at Callman, who looked near death, Reginald said, "You sent the ice pick to Lavon to scare him and to let him know that he was going to die. Only he didn't and that really messed up your plans. You punctured Robert Blandford's tires to send a message to him, but why you did that I haven't figured out yet. Then you messed up the stop payment and the message to Sherry and I don't think you knew that until just now. In your haste to set up your scheme, you sent the stop payment to the bank here and the note intended for Sherry to Mountain Home. You got suspicious when the bank paid the check and you had to abandon your original plan there and improvise. You had Snoopy up in Missouri do your bird dog work so you would know everyone's habits. Am I right?"

"Keep going. I will tell you when you are wrong," Brookson said with disdain. "I didn't think you were smart enough to figure out how to wake up. I surely must have underestimated you, but it doesn't make any difference now. The ending will be the same no matter what you know. You may continue, Mr. Gawker. I'm all ears."

"At some point you met J. Daniel Bushman and his wife, Trudy. When or how you met them we don't know and maybe we never will know. We do know he was a false ID man who had an extensive shady background. You learned that somehow and used it in your scheme. You knew he couldn't refuse to furnish you with the false IDs. I think it's safe to say that when you conned Bushman into making your false papers, he didn't know you planned to kill him. I think he had the idea you were going to help them get a new start in life. Only it didn't work out that way for them."

Brookson remained quiet with his expression alternating between a sneer and an evil smile. Though he continued to haphazardly wave the gun and ice pick at them, Reginald couldn't find an opening to take advantage of his brief lapses. Reginald knew he had to choose his words very carefully so he wouldn't agitate Brookson anymore than he was already. He noticed that the more he talked and edged closer to all the truth, the more careless Brookson became with keeping control of the situation and the less careful he became handling his weapons.

"How did you kill Mr. Bushman? Was it with an ice pick like *you* used on Mrs. Herrington? You are real handy with them, aren't you? And I would bet that you admire your talent in a sick sort of way."

Brookson fidgeted and leveled the gun at Reginald saying, "You think you have it figured out. I have always admired smart cops who think they know what I am doing. Go ahead tell me all of it, smarty. I might learn more and have to change my plans." Brookson laughed

maniacally once more, pulling the hammer back on the gun. He then eased it back down much to Reginald's relief.

"Sherry and I give you credit for keeping us off balance. Those broken toothpicks that had Bushman's DNA on them really threw us. We found that out in the last twenty-four hours. Your mistakes were the candy wrapper in the tow truck and the broken ice pick. I'll let you figure those out."

Brookson listened and watched with an evil smirk crossing his face. "It was simple to get the toothpicks. Bushy always had one in his mouth when he wasn't chewing. I picked them up when he threw them away and dropped them where you found them. I thought it was brilliant. Old Bushy gets blamed and he wasn't even there." He laughed insanely again.

"You bought that wrecker and killed Bushman to make it look like Easterly wrecked a car you bought in his name. Only you reversed the first and middle names to keep anyone from becoming wise that you weren't M. Marion Easterly. Easterly's first name is Marvin, but he went by Marion since he disliked his first name. We found your post office box in the name of Marion Marvin Easterly where the title was mailed. We also learned of the Bloomington post office box where Snoopy mailed the pictures to J. Daniel Bushman."

Reginald stopped and glanced at Sherry who was listening intently and leaning back against the wall. She had found a nail sticking out from the baseboard and was trying to use it to cut through the restraints. Fortunately, the ones he put on her didn't have the wire in them. The ones he used on the others had the wire. Reginald saw her wiggle her nose and knew she was doing something, but he didn't know what. He wanted to keep Brookson focused on him.

"Go ahead, Sgt. Gawker. Please continue. I'm enjoying this," Brookson said.

"You killed the Bushmans and faked the car hitting the tree. You pulled that off by slamming the Ford into a tree at the Locust Grove house to fool the officers in Indiana into thinking that the tree where the Ford was found did the damage. You very nearly succeeded in that one, but little things tripped you up." Reginald watched Brookson hoping to find an opening to attack him. The gun never wavered. Not seeing an opening, he continued with the story.

"You went up there with Easterly in 1994 and that gave you some ideas. You would have gotten away with it except for Mr. Callman who you thought might remember you. The funny thing is that he didn't remember you until he walked in here a few minutes ago." Reginald saw the perp stiffen and then become nervous. "Isn't that right, Lavon?"

"Yes. I really didn't remember him until I came in here," Callman said, barely able to speak. "I only saw him a couple of times when I called on that plant in Little Rock. He was just another face of the many that I saw on the sales trips."

"You don't know me?" Brookson railed. "How can you say that?"

"Like I said, I never saw you but a couple of times that I can remember when I stopped at that company in Little Rock when the building redo was being done." Brookson's eyes bored holes into Callman.

"Never mind; it doesn't matter anyway," Brookson said. "Continue with the narration of your little saga. I find it quite interesting."

"You used the identities of Harley Bastin, J. Daniel Bushman, Marion Easterly, and probably several others and now you are going by Malcom Brookson. Only that isn't your name is it?" Reginald paused and watched Brookson nervously lick his lips and then spoke before Brookson could answer. "Your full name is Buddy Allen Borders, a cousin of Marion Easterly and the step-brother of Carl Alstrom. I just found that out a few hours ago."

Sherry gasped when she heard the killer's name. She was right. They had been chasing a ghost and now they knew the ghost's identity. Borders glanced fleetingly at her when she gasped and his look interrupted her thoughts. He turned his full attention on Reginald again.

"How did you find out?" the now exposed Borders asked angrily. "I had everything covered. Tell me more."

"I didn't get all of it put together until a few hours ago, but the first tip off was two rings. Alstrom was wearing one of them the day you, Alstrom, and Easterly went to Mountain Home." Reginald paused and watched Borders whose stare was icy cold. Reginald continued. "At first, we thought it was Marion Easterly doing the killing until we heard of his death in Indiana. That threw us too but only for a few weeks. Then you took Alstrom's ring off so we would think that he was the killer if it was ever investigated. I'll give you credit though, you did fool us for a while with that disappearing ring after we learned that Carl wore a ring." Borders smiled coldly at Reginald. During the investigation, we found it was Marion's death someone faked with Bushman, but we didn't find the evidence of that until recently, and when we did, we thought Alstrom had killed Bushman and all the others. Mr. Easterly and Mr. Alstrom were none the wiser that you planned to kill them that day in Mountain Home when you showed up unexpectedly. Everyone thought it was you who died in that fire and it worked for a while. But you messed up in two important areas of your scheme."

"What's that smart guy? Tell all of us since you are so smart and have it all figured out," Borders said, his voice filled with obvious contempt for Reginald.

"You made a mistake by keeping your ring. You couldn't stand the thought of it going through a fire, so you didn't put it on Marion's or Alstrom's hand. If you had put your ring on either one, the photos wouldn't have tripped you up and you might have gotten by with your scheming a bit longer. The ring tripped you again when you went to the bank. The teller saw the initials **B.A.B** in gold on the red stone set in the ring you always wear on your right ring finger, and it's the ring you're wearing now on your right hand. Remember, Carl wore his ring on his left hand. You never noticed that, and we didn't know about it either until we found some old photos. Then after we talked to the teller, the pieces begin to fall into place. The photos and the rings tripped you up, Bud. What I don't know is what you did with Carl Alstrom's ring. You probably threw it away."

Muffled sounds were being made by Madeline Crompton and Joe
Landers. Borders back handed both of them hard across the face with
the back of his right hand and told them to shut up or he would end
the show quickly. Tears appeared in Madeline's eyes and slid down
her cheeks. Borders laughed when he saw her tears. Joe Landers had
blood dripping off his chin from being hit across the mouth. The ring
had lacerated Joe's chin.

Reginald could only watch the horror show and began speaking
again to get Border's attention. "Alstrom's mother died and his father
married your mother after you and your brother moved out and you
started your life of crime. Your brother dropped out of sight and his
whereabouts are unknown. It never made sense why you would turn
up at the scaffold business, but now it does. You want to hear more?"
All eyes were on Reginald and Borders.

"Go ahead, smart guy. It makes no difference now," Borders said
sarcastically.

Reginald studied the man for a few seconds formulating a plan.
"We saw a picture that looked like Alstrom with his arm around his
kids, but the ring was on the wrong hand. As I said, Carl wore his ring
on his left hand and the picture showed a man with a ring on the right
hand." Borders looked at Reginald sullenly, staying alert and keeping
his gun pointed at Reginald.

"I don't know all that took place the day you went to Mountain
Home and killed your cousin and stepbrother," Reginald said, keeping
eye contact with Borders. After a couple of beats, Reginald continued.
"I don't know how you murdered the two of them, but I have a good
idea why you did. Bud, the events before their deaths tell quite a story.
You were involved with a government agency, which one I don't know
and you messed up. Some real big people have been looking for you
since you disappeared and you are still dangerous to them. You went
on the run and went to Dallas and then to Little Rock. Your specialty
for the mob was fires, ice pick jobs, and phony ID papers. There is also
some other deal you were doing. I don't know what it was, but I hope
to find out one of these days. To save your hide you ran, and after you

landed in Little Rock, Alstrom and Easterly learned of your real past a short time later. They were good guys and you had to kill to keep them from talking or so you thought. I think the other reason is that Carl caught you stealing money from the company."

Bud Borders began to talk but made no sense. Finally, he calmed down enough to speak. "I decided I wasn't going back to jail and I claim my rights not to talk about anything you say I did. Prove I killed anyone and set a fire." He grew quiet. Then he said, "This is real good. Go on. I'm all ears."

"I think you convinced Easterly to give you the money he got from the settlement so you could use it in some kind of a scheme. He went to drinking after his family was killed and wasn't thinking straight. He had a wad of money when he went to Indiana in 1994. I think it was you with him that day in Indiana though I can't prove it, but it's the only thing that makes sense."

Borders began to grow more agitated. Reginald saw Sherry out the corner of his left eye. She winked and stared straight ahead. Borders remained quiet. Reginald hoped the officers outside were getting into position since he didn't know how much longer he could stall Borders and keep him from becoming violent.

"You don't have a family and if you do other than a brother who has disappeared, we haven't found them. We learned that you adopted the Easterly and Alstrom families since there was the family connection, and when they were killed, you never got over it and still haven't. Any chance for normalcy disappeared with their deaths." Reginald stopped talking and mulled over whether to say what he was planning. He decided he had to invade Bud's mind. "You began to lose your mind before you went to Little Rock. To put it bluntly, Bud, you are going insane or may be now totally gone mentally. I think it is the latter. In simple layman terms, you are crazy; and in a court of law when you stand trial, you will be judged legally insane." The room grew deathly quiet; all eyes were on Bud Borders.

SIXTY-ONE

A primal scream came from Borders and he began to shake. "You don't know how it is to lose those you love. I thought I had found peace and then they were killed. You're right. I haven't been right since and may not have been right before then. I loved those kids. They were my world and then it got all ruined," he yelled. He then became silent and the cold-eyed stare told Reginald all he needed to know about the mental state of Bud Borders.

"I'm sure you did, Bud, but why do you want to kill us and why did you kill Carl and Marion? I have told you the reasons you had for killing everyone. Tell me where what I said is wrong," Reginald said gently and softly. "Now you tell us why you killed them. We might as well take the whole story with us to our graves." Reginald knew he was taking a big chance with that last statement to Borders and he prayed silently that Borders would open up enough so that all the truth would come pouring out. He also prayed that they would get through this ordeal in one piece. He saw the fright in the eyes of his friends and shuddered at what could happen to them at the hands of this madman.

Bud Borders kept his eyes glued on Reginald. "I'll tell you why," he yelled. "Marion caused that scaffold to fall because he didn't have the legs adjusted right. Carl wouldn't tell him to change it and he wouldn't listen to me. I know you wonder why Joe is here." He went over and ripped the tape off Joe Lander's mouth. "Tell them Joe, why you're here. If it weren't for you, none of this would be happening."

Tears ran down Landers's face, and then he began to speak in a halting manner that showed his fear. "I ran a catering service and the day that the scaffold fell I was parked where Mrs. Easterly would normally park later in the day. My wife worked at the refrigeration company and I knew Linda and the kids. I had no way of knowing she would be there. I regret it to this day that I was parked there, but I didn't know she was going to be there. But Marion didn't cause the scaffold to fall. It was you, Bud. I heard Marion tell you to tighten the leg screws and to set the automatic levelers and you didn't listen. You didn't listen to Carl either when he repeated the instructions. Alcohol does that to people. You were drinking that day just as you had been doing for several days before. You were drunk and shouldn't have been on the site, much less trying to work. Why Carl and Marion let you remain at work that day is a mystery that will never be answered."

"Shut up! You're a liar," he yelled and hit Joe across the face. He picked up the ice pick with Joe's name on it, all the while keeping his gun trained on Reginald. He smiled coldly and said, "Liars get killed and that's what is going to happen to you. It's your fault." He looked ready to kill Joe at any moment.

Thinking fast in an effort to head off an escalation of violence, Reginald said, "Bud, why do you want to kill Blandford and Lavon?"

After glaring at Reginald for what seemed an eternity, Borders said, "I thought Lavon would recognize me and decided to have some fun with him before I killed him. It's that simple. But since he didn't recognize me, I didn't need to kill him, did I? If he had died though, we wouldn't be here like this. So I think I'll kill him anyway. That way he won't cause more trouble for anyone else."

L. Jason Callman fell sideways on the floor and moaned. Borders looked at him with disgust. He walked over and kicked him viciously in the ribs all the while keeping his gun trained on Reginald. Mr. Callman cried out in pain and rolled into a fetal ball.

He then looked at Blandford and said, "I never intended to kill him. What I did was to try to throw everyone off the track. I knew he was the one who sold the scaffolding to Carl and me, so I included him in the plans when I saw him up here a few months ago." He grew quiet and looked at Robert Blandford and said, "Get out of here before I change my mind." He cut the straps on Blandford's ankles with a pair of side cutters. Blandford blinked and struggled to his feet, wobbling with his hands bound behind his back toward the door that Borders was slowly opening. Blandford went through the door and collapsed after he crossed the street. Officers rushed to his aid. The gun never wavered in its pointing at Reginald.

Watching Borders closely Reginald said, "We know why you want to kill Joe, Mrs. Crompton, and Lavon. Why did you want to kill Mary Beth Norman? We know you tried to shoot her, but you missed."

Enraged by what he had heard, Borders said angrily, "She was supposed to keep the kids that day they were killed and she couldn't because she was too busy helping her husband with moving the trucking company. That is reason enough. Now are you happy, Sgt. Gawker?" he said coldly. "Now I know you are just dying to know why I want to kill Sherry." He looked at her and smiled. He picked up the ice pick, waving it at her. He continued to point the gun at Reginald.

Borders began to speak again. "Sherry is so pretty just like Julie, my step sister-in-law, and Linda. It's not right that Sherry can live and enjoy life when they can't. She reminds me of them so much and it is only fair that she die the same way Julie and Linda did." Borders laid the ice pick down and picked up two photos. He showed them to Reginald and then walked over and held them for Sherry to see. "Sherry looks just like them. As soon as I saw pretty Sherry, I knew she had to be the one. She can't be a constant reminder that Julie and Linda are dead. She enjoys life and they can't, ever again."

"Bud, Sherry doesn't look anything like those two women," Reginald said.

Borders wheeled suddenly and backhanded Reginald across the face. "She does and don't call them women. Their names are Julie and Linda. Don't make that mistake again. Do you hear me?" He looked at Reginald more menacingly than ever. Total madness shot from his eyes. His facial features twisted into hideous contortions caused by his uncontrollable rage.

Sherry watched the man descend deeper into the dark pit of mental instability. In all her studies of abnormal psychology and in her work during college with the mentally unstable, she had never seen anyone to compare with the madness of Bud Borders. She suspected that his former sordid life of crime made his condition worse and only served to add to his aberrant and extremely dangerous behavior.

Reginald realized even more so now that he had to try to capture Borders if he could find the opportunity. The backhand had happened so quickly he wasn't prepared to take advantage of any opening the act might have given. One thing was in his favor though. Borders hadn't restrained him with plastic ties when he did the others and he wasn't going to try to figure out the why at this point. He made every effort to keep Borders from noticing the oversight.

Borders seethed with mounting anger. He laid the photos on the table and picked up the ice pick. Madness was embedded deep in his eyes as he waved the ice pick wildly toward Sherry without taking the gun off Reginald. He said, "You haven't asked me to explain poor Helen Magerson. What's the matter, isn't she important to you?"

"Bud," Sherry said ever so softly, "that wasn't Helen Magerson you killed. That was her twin sister Matilda Herrington. Mrs. Magerson's husband died; she remarried and now we can't locate her."

Borders jerked around to answer Sherry and then remembered Reginald. He kept the gun steady as he spoke. "You're lying. She looked at me in the restaurant the day I killed her. She recognized me."

"Whether she did or not we'll never know. You killed a kindly lady who had nothing to do with any of this," Sherry said very softly. "She didn't know you, and if she did, she wasn't going to be of any harm to you."

"That's what you say. She looked at me that day in the restaurant and I know she knew me. I could tell she did. She looked at me the same way that cop McGee in Little Rock looked at me. I know he knew me. You're trying to confuse me by telling me these things. Now shut up! You are all liars." Borders railed on insanely. He waved the ice pick in the air and took a step toward Sherry.

Then a sickening thought went through Sherry's mind as Borders stepped toward her. *Their theory about the killer's motive for the slayings was right; the problem was they hadn't used the right name.* Then she remembered what Reginald told her he had said to Chief Cumberland: '*... what we know is so obvious we can't see it yet.' The answer was there the whole time and Reginald was right; it was so obvious none of us could see it. Borders was the elusive fourth man.* Reginald's voice jarred her into the present.

"Bud!" Reginald said loudly to distract him from going any closer to Sherry.

Borders stopped his outburst and waved the gun at Reginald again, only in a more menacing fashion. "I should shoot you now and get it over with, but if I do, then I wouldn't hear the rest of your fantasy and you wouldn't get to enjoy Act III. Please continue. I think you are going to tell us where I made some more mistakes." Borders's grin was pure evil as he watched Sherry from the corner of his eye. He waved the ice pick in her direction. "It will be such a shame to ruin such a pretty neck, now won't it?" His voice was pure ice.

Chapter
SIXTY-TWO

Reginald never took his eyes away from Borders, watching his every move. Thinking carefully on what to say next, Reginald decided not to mention the drawing done by Marjorie Shuman or what Robbie Porter had seen and began to speak. "That was real smart to rent that house in Searcy for a legitimate address. That also fooled us for a short time after you were stopped, but as you know, we have figured it out. If you are wondering how we learned that Brookson was Borders, you forgot one more thing. You visited Searcy a couple of times after your mother married Carl Alstrom's father. The lady that you rented the house from has a son who just happened to be at her house Saturday morning when she was shown some photos. His mother knew Carl Alstrom and identified the picture as him. The son saw the picture and told the investigator it was you. It is uncanny how much you look like Easterly and Alstrom. I suspect you knew that, and it made it easy for you to be whoever you wanted to be. That is what kept causing all the misidentifications."

"How did he know I wasn't Carl?" Borders asked loudly.

"You lived in Searcy under an alias and played on an opposing softball team for a season. Her son remembered that during a game, you told him that your mother had lived in Searcy for a year and had married a man named Alstrom, whom his mother knew. You didn't know that and wouldn't have known it if I hadn't just told you. That's why she said you were Carl Alstrom since she also had seen Carl on occasion when he visited his dad before he and your mother left Searcy. He also said that you had the mole removed. And you didn't tell him your mother's last name was Borders before she married Alstrom since you were using an alias. He figured it out a long while after you left that town. And since you were Carl's stepbrother that made it easy for you to move into the business with him and later murder Carl, Marion, and the others." Reginald watched the anger begin to boil in Borders and knew more than ever that he needed to keep control of the man by talking until the time was right.

"You called a friend of Easterly's in Little Rock to announce Easterly's death, but it was after the fire in Mountain Home when you killed Alstrom and Easterly. When we at first thought Marion Easterly was the killer, it seemed reasonable that he made the call to throw us off and had possibly faked his own death. Then when we realized he wasn't the killer, we looked at Alstrom and that made sense that he could be the caller and the killer. But before I went to bed tonight, I figured out it couldn't have been them, and the only one left was you. You told Callman's friend that you saw the death story in the Bloomington paper a couple of weeks after the accident. But you couldn't have seen it two weeks after the accident or anytime after that. The only mention in the paper was an article explaining the accident; and it said that the identity of the driver wasn't known and that the coroner was doing an autopsy. I checked the Bloomington daily papers up to the date of the fire in Mountain Home. The driver when tentatively identified as Easterly wasn't reported to anyone except the sheriff's department. It never made the paper."

"Now aren't you the smart one? Now you know why you are going to be killed. I said I don't like nosy people. Do you understand, Sgt. Gawker?" Borders replied angrily. "So I made a mistake, but you made the big one when you got nosy and checked the papers. Sticking your nose in the business of others has signed your death warrant."

"Bud, you might as well know it all. Then we can all die happy after we expose the truth of how brilliant you are." Reginald noticed that Borders was becoming more nervous and he didn't know whether that was good or bad. "We checked the phone records of the person you called in Little Rock to inform him of Easterly's death. You used the name of a person the one you called knew, and made a collect call to him which left a trail. But it was after the house fire in September and you told him Marion died June 10, 1995. That told us that whoever was the killer knew of Easterly's fake death in Indiana. But you didn't make the call until after Easterly was actually dead. You couldn't take the chance that Marion would find out that he was dead when he wasn't. That would have really messed up your plans, not that they aren't messed up now. You staged the whole thing in Indiana with Bushman from Missouri to keep anyone from knowing what you were doing. If you hadn't tried to kill L. Jason … "

"I told you to call him Lavon. Why can't you understand? No one listens to me," Borders screamed.

Sensing the time was right to gain more control of Borders, Reginald pulled the slot car from his pocket and held it out for Borders to see.

"Where did you get that? That's mine," he yelled. "Nickolette and little Ricky gave that to me the Christmas before their daddy killed them. I want it." Tears came to his eyes.

"I found it at the house site in Locust Grove where you dropped it in the dirt when you moved the slot car track that you and the four kids played with in Easterly's house. Unless I miss my guess, the track is in the boxes stacked in the next room. That's the story, every bit of it, and I guess it's time for Act III." Reginald slowly extended the car toward Borders who momentarily forgot to keep his gun on Reginald. When he reached for the car, Reginald yelled, "Now."

Sherry who had gotten her hands loose and had given Reginald a signal, rolled and lunged for Borders's legs. She wrapped her arms around them in a death grip. Reginald grabbed Borders's gun hand and tried to disarm him. Borders, running on excessive adrenalin, succeeded in loosing Reginald's grip and grabbed an ice pick with his left hand and stabbed Reginald in the right arm. A flash of pain went across his face and he let loose, grabbing the ice pick that was now protruding out the other side of his arm. He felt sick and the room began to spin out of control. He sat and stared at the ice pick, trying to keep from passing out.

Borders swung the gun toward Sherry as Darcy Broadway crashed through the front door. Martin Perkins roared into the room to the right of Borders as Darcy yelled at Borders while going for the gun. Borders squeezed the trigger; a deafening gunshot roared through the room. Sherry yelled and let loose of his legs. Darcy knocked the gun loose and when they began to fall, Borders somehow twisted around and kicked Darcy in the shins with heavy soled boots. Borders grabbed at an ice pick on the table to stab Martin who had tripped over a throw rug. He lost the ice pick and bit Martin on the left arm instead. Martin hit him hard in the jaw with his right fist and dislodged Borders from his arm.

Darcy recovering from the kick grabbed the right arm of Borders and twisted it behind his back and snapped a cuff on his right wrist. Borders broke free and tried to get up, swinging his arm with the cuff flying back and forth. All during the fight, Borders screamed vile insults at Darcy and Martin, but whatever he was saying about dirty hippies was lost in his mad effort of trying to get free. Both Martin and Darcy were surprised at his strength and were having trouble getting him subdued enough to cuff the left wrist, when officers Nance Porter and George Dugan, along with two state police officers barged into the room to help them gain control of the man. He fought until he began to wear out enough so he could be handled. Even after being subdued, Borders continued to scream, yell, and kick, in spite of being securely cuffed and shackled.

Borders kept yelling over and over again, "This ain't the way my plan is supposed to end. This ain't Act III. You are supposed to die." He kicked and thrashed with super human strength due to the continuing adrenalin rush. It was all Darcy and Martin and the other officers could do to hold him down. Darrell Cumberland rushed into the house, took one look, and ran out. A siren could be heard in the distance and ten minutes later, a doctor entered the living room.

Borders began yelling at the doctor filling a syringe. Then he looked over at Sherry and said coldly, "You interfered with Act III. Women ain't supposed to do what you did. Julie and Linda wouldn't act the way you do. They were ladies. You're not. I will get you for this. I won't forget." He lapsed into incoherent speech as his rage at Sherry deepened.

His cold words to Sherry sent chills through all of them, and though they knew they had prevented more horror at the hand of Buddy Allen Borders, anger and pity and sorrow were in conflict in the minds of all the officers who heard his ranting and raving. The doctor stuck the needle into Borders' vein and five seconds later, he went to sleep. They loaded him on a stretcher and took him out. It was decided to take Bud Borders to Little Rock to a secure lock up at the state hospital due to not having any facilities at the local jail or the hospital to deal with the insane of the world like Bud Borders. The hospital was alerted and Borders was transported with a state police escort to Little Rock. The doctor said Borders would stay sedated for the trip and wouldn't wake up until he was secure in his room.

The paramedics who had been alerted and standing by, rushed into the room to render aid to the injured. Two of them attended to Reginald who had an ice pick stuck into his arm completely to the handle. The other two went to Sherry who had a bullet wound in her right leg calf. Madeline Crompton, Joe Landers, and L. Jason Callman were freed and taken to ambulances for the ride to Stone County Medical Center for check ups. Reginald and Sherry were taken to Batesville Regional since their injuries were more serious.

Darrell Cumberland stood in the room where the rampage of Bud Borders had finally come to and end. He looked around and walked out, feeling as though the mayhem would remain with him for a long time in spite of his best effort to purge it from his consciousness. He crossed the street to headquarters and entered the building looking for anything that would bring solace to his troubled mind. Deep worry lines creased his face and his agony worsened due to his concern for his wounded officers. "Pain, Mr. Borders. You have caused a lot of it for a lot of people," Darrell said to an empty office. He left his office

and told the dispatcher he was headed for home to change clothes
and then he and Mattie were going to Batesville to be with Reginald
and Sherry.

Chapter

SIXTY-THREE

Martin Perkins was treated for a human bite, given a tetanus shot, and antibiotics to prevent an infection that can occur from being bitten by a human. Darcy wasn't too much worse for wear, but he did have a sore right shin for three weeks where the kick peeled the hide from his leg down to the bone. Sherry was off work for three weeks from the bullet wound and Reginald was on limited duty to help the ice pick wound heal. Additional investigation didn't reveal much more than they already knew. At some point, Buddy Allen Borders had taken a no return trip into insanity. Whether an insanity plea would keep him from the death penalty remained to be seen.

Five weeks after the capture of Borders, Reginald, Sherry, Darcy, Martin, Darrell, Thomas, George Dugan, Nance Porter, and Robbie Porter were in the Home Cookin' Cafe. Reginald and Sherry were enjoying the first meal outside of the hospital rooms and their own cooking. They were guests of Joe Landers who was showing his appreciation for them having saved his life. He said to them, "I had no idea that Bud Borders was anywhere around. I never recognized him the day he came in acting like a blind man. He even fooled Mandy and she's hard to fool. Hey Mandy, you got it ready?"

Mandy Gettner came in carrying a big cake with candles on it and writing that said, "*Thanks Gang. This case is closed.*" Ice cream accompanied the cake to the delight of all.

Reginald said, "I think Robbie cracked the shell on this case when he told his mother he saw a blind man driving a van. Then George stopped Borders, alias Brookson, close to your house, Nance. I suspect he realized someone had seen him before that stop, but I don't know how he would have known it was Robbie. I doubt that we'll ever know the answer to that one, and we sure don't want to ask him."

"Using that slot car was fast thinking, Reg," Sherry said. "How did you think of that?"

"When I went to the evidence locker to get that note he wrote to you after realizing what he meant by the words '*right under your noses*,' I saw that car and slipped it into my pocket. I really don't know why I did it. Apparently, when he raced those cars with the kids he could escape whatever devils were beginning to drive him. The car caused him to momentarily be caught off guard, and when he saw it, he reacted. It gave us the opening and you know the rest of the story."

"I couldn't imagine what you were doing with your hand in your pocket until you showed him the car." Sherry said.

"I was hoping he wouldn't notice until there was an opening to bring it out. He also forgot to tie me up. That one I never will figure out. He was so careful to keep control and then he forgot I wasn't restrained. I saw you wiggling around and knew you were doing something, but I didn't know what, so I tried to keep him busy so he wouldn't notice you. Then when you winked, I was sure you had your hands loose. What did you find back there to cut those restraints?"

"I found a sharp nail sticking out of the woodwork and by moving my wrists back and forth I eventually sawed through the plastic." She showed them the scars and scratches where the nail had cut into her skin. "Then when you yelled, 'Now,' I moved. I thought I had bought the store when he pointed that gun at me and fired. That was way too close and I wouldn't be here now if Darcy hadn't done his Tarzan act."

"When the gun went off I didn't know whether you were shot or not. I heard you yell and that was all I knew until we had him under control. George, I was never so glad to see anyone in my life as I was when you and Nance and the state boys rushed in and piled on. That guy had enough adrenalin pumping to fight a gorilla," Darcy said.

"When he bit me I wanted to knock his head off. My first thought was I would need a rabies shot. I'm not sure what hurt the worst when I hit him, my fist, or his jaw." Martin said enjoying the laughter at his rabies shot remark. "That man set a new standard for crazy."

Darrell said, "While Reginald was in there talking, we couldn't figure out what Borders was going to do. We just listened and waited for anything he might say that would indicate when we should go in. When you yelled, 'Now,' Reginald, you left no doubt that the curtain was going up on Act III."

"I have news for you, Chief. I didn't know what I was going to do either. I just kept talking to him and kept him listening and talking until an opening occurred. I sure am glad you heard the 'now.' I yelled it so loud it hurt my ears. I didn't want to leave anything to chance," Reginald said laughing.

"You didn't, and it left no doubt about when Darcy and Martin were to enter."

"Did you get it all on tape?" Sherry asked.

"We made a tape of all that was said in there. But some smart lawyer may try to argue that Borders should have been advised of his Miranda rights when he began talking," Darrell said.

"A madman in that house threatening to kill folks and Reginald is supposed to stop him and read him his rights so he wouldn't incriminate himself?" Thomas said acidly. "Any lawyer that would try that as a defense is as crazy as Borders. Lawyers should be in our shoes and they might change their attitudes toward the poor maligned criminals. I'm thankful to our God in heaven it is over and that no one else was killed or injured any worse than Martin, Reginald, Sherry, Darcy, and his intended victims." A chorus of amen's resounded all over the room.

"He may not go to trial," Thomas said. "After being taken to Little Rock he was lodged in a psychiatric ward and is now undergoing evaluation to see if he's sane. His lawyer has asked for a change of venue to White County for the preliminary hearing to see if he will stand trial for the murders of Matilda, Easterly, Alstrom, and the kidnappings. I don't think we'll ever know where he killed the Bushmans. It was probably at Locust Grove, but there's no proof."

"I thought once to ask him when we were having that lovely conversation, but I decided it wouldn't help anything, so I didn't," Reginald said. "I had already said enough to make him wild and didn't want to add more fuel to his fire. I decided that Indiana and Independence County can handle that if either one decides to prosecute. I think it will be futile for them, but they will have to deal with it, not us."

"If he could have found Mary Sheldon, Hazel Hancock, and Walter Munsford he would have killed them too. I suppose they would fit his ideas of nosy and we'll never know why he didn't like nosy people. As scrambled as his mind is there will be things we'll never know," Sherry said.

"Speaking of things we'll never know," Darcy said, "I'm glad that deal I set up with Brad Sheldon wasn't needed. I refuse to think about what he would have done had he gotten a phone call from Borders or me. He didn't want to cooperate and that made me very leery of him. We need to be thankful for all those things that didn't happen that could have happened."

"Darce, I know what you mean. I'm thankful too that Borders didn't happen to use that revolver," Reginald said. He really surprised me with that .357. I thought he would have the .22 he used for his other shootings. I wonder what he did with it."

"We'll more than likely never know what happened to it," Sherry said. "He won't talk and as crazy as he is, it wouldn't do much good to try to question him about the gun or anything else. I noticed there were some facts you didn't mention that were mistakes he made."

"I figured the main points he knew were enough and the rest he didn't need to know," Reginald said. "If he hadn't set that Locust Grove house on fire, he might still be on the loose. The little things and the bits and pieces added up. He really out-smarted himself on a few things as do all criminals eventually. Oddly, his insanity worked to our advantage in a twisted sort of way."

"It did, Reg. If you noticed, he implied that he was much smarter than anybody could possibly imagine. His insanity and ego helped blind him to the mistakes he made along the way," Sherry said. "The blind Act In here that day is a good example of it."

"Darcy, what did you find when you and Martin searched the house?" Reginald asked.

"We found a scoped .222 Remington rifle, a sawed off shotgun, and a bunch of rambling notes he had written. None of them made any sense except one. He had written a bizarre note to remind himself to go to Little Rock and kill the lady who rented him the house. The note had Mountain Home printed across the top of the paper, and below the heading were the words printed in big letters, *I will do it in L.R. like I did it there.*

"Why did he want to do that?" Sherry asked. "What did he have against her?"

"I suspect we'll never know why on that one either," Darcy replied. "With his mind, any reason would be good enough for him to kill her."

"Did you ever figure out that little plastic box he dropped into his pocket?" Sherry asked.

"I think so. When it was taken from him during the search before he was hauled away, we had no idea what it was. Then we found one just like it in a box during the search of the house. In another box, we found a small remote control and one other item. I took the three items to the lab for examination," Darcy said, saying no more and looking around the table, a sly grin curling the corners of his mouth.

"Well go on and finish the story, Darcy," Sherry said. "What was the other item?"

"I thought you might figure it out," Darcy replied.

"It's your story. Tell us or you don't ever get doughnuts again," Sherry needled.

"I know a threat when I hear one," Darcy said, acting serious. "Reggie said there was one thing he didn't know, but that mystery is solved."

"What didn't I know and how is the mystery solved?" Reginald asked.

"What happened to Carl Alstrom's ring is what you didn't know. Martin found it in a box in his bedroom. He must have kept it for a souvenir as reminder of his genius."

"That's one more piece of evidence that he committed the crimes," Darrel said. "It's the small things that trip the criminals up most of the time."

"Now Darce, tell us about the remote and the boxes you found," Sherry said, "or we'll definitely revoke your doughnut eating license."

"The little boxes were explosive devices that could be fastened to a gas line and set off with a remote control. Being made of thin plastic, they would melt in the fire. The only metal in them was two thin wires each an inch long. The fire would destroy the evidence."

"He probably used the device at Mountain Home," Reginald said, "and maybe he was going to use another one on his landlady's house, if that is why he wrote Mountain Home on that note."

"I think you're right on both counts. From the way that house went up with no evidence of arson, there isn't any doubt on that one anyway," Sherry said. "We need to call the detective up there and tell him. He'll be glad to close that case."

"He won't be the only one that is glad to close a case. Having the nightmare over is real nice," Reginald said.

"Speaking of nice, the other nice thing, if the thing can be called nice, is that the ending happened late Saturday night and early Sunday morning. The news hounds were a day late and a dollar short and the amazing thing is we kept the lid on it until Monday. By the time they got here, it was over and nothing remained for them to do but go home. As far as locally, the rain helped too since it kept people in their houses," Darrell said.

"Can you imagine what a mess that would have been if the town people and the news hounds had been outside when the capture went down?" Sherry said.

"I don't even want to think in those terms," Darrell said. "That would give me chills and being out in the rain that night gave me enough of those."

Martin Perkins said, "I got to know Robert Blandford and Mr. Callman fairly well while they were at my house. They are decent fellas. I sure hope they get over the trauma they experienced. Callman told me how it got started and he thinks that phone call that morning was so Borders could get a good look at you, Reginald. The man was good at planning, but his plans weren't very good."

"I have given that some thought and Callman is probably right. It was very strange though," Reginald said. "Those plans Borders devised were the most diabolical we have ever had to untangle. I hope we never see anything like that again."

"Mary Beth called me the other day to see how I was doing. She read about it in the paper, and then Mr. Blandford called her. She told me that she was very thankful that we protected her, even though she didn't like it at the time. She said she didn't realize how much danger she was in by being here with Borders in town," Sherry said.

"He made threats against her, and I surely do hope that he never gets out and decides to finish his spree with her," Reginald said.

"Mary Beth said it really shook her when she found out that Borders blamed her for those deaths. But since he was insane, she said she understood some of it," Sherry said.

"We're used to thinking that crime can't come to a small town, but it does. We may have to change our way of thinking," Reginald said. Heads nodded in assent around the table.

Having discussed the events until there wasn't anything left to say, they thanked Joe and left nice tips for him and Mandy. Mandy hugged them all and wiped tears from her eyes. Joe shook their hands and thanked them again for saving his life. They trooped out into the night to go home.

•

Six months later, the police officers went to a court hearing in White

County to determine whether Buddy Allen Borders would stand trial
for three murders and the kidnappings. Borders came into the courtroom in leg irons, his hands cuffed and shackled to a belt. He slung
his head side to side and rolled his eyes in never ceasing movement.
Testimony was given by two psychiatrists, one for the state, and one
hired by his lawyer. Reginald and Sherry took the stand in turn as did
Darcy Broadway, Martin Perkins, George Dugan, and Nance Porter.

After all had testified, the judge retired to his chambers and
returned forty-five minutes later after having a conference with the
prosecutor, the lawyer, and the psychiatrists. The public defense lawyer didn't object to the judge listening in chambers to the tape recording of the conversation between Reginald and Borders the night of
the capture.

When they returned to the courtroom, the judge rendered his ver-
dict. He said, "Buddy Allen Borders, you are hereby committed to the
state hospital for observation to determine if your sanity will return.
During the time of confinement in the hospital, you will remain under
the jurisdiction of this court. If and when you are judged sane, you will
be returned to this court to determine where and when you will stand
trial to answer the charges filed against you for the criminal acts you
have been accused of committing. Court dismissed."

Based on what was heard and seen in court, it remained doubtful that he would ever be tried for his crimes. He would undoubtedly
spend the remainder of his life in the section of the hospital reserved
for the criminally insane. As Borders was led out of the courtroom
under heavy guard, he looked at Reginald and said, "Thank you for
returning my little car. Will they have a slot car track where I'm
going?"

Reginald looked at the prisoner as he shuffled away and couldn't
help but feel somewhat sorry for him. He said softly, "I don't know,
Buddy, but for your sake, I hope they do."